The
Matchmaker
Bride

The
Matchmaker
Bride

NEW YORK TIMES BESTSELLING AUTHOR
GINNY BAIRD

Entangled Publishing, LLC
10940 S Parker Road
Suite 327
Parker, CO 80134
Visit our website at www.entangledpublishing.com.

Amara is an imprint of Entangled Publishing, LLC.

Edited by Heather Howland
Cover design by Bree Archer
Cover art by
mochak/Depositphotos and
Doug Hendricks/Gettyimages
Interior design by Toni Kerr

Print ISBN 978 1-64937-026-6
ebook ISBN 978-1-64937-039-6

Manufactured in the United States of America

First Edition August 2021

For John

With special thanks to my publisher, Liz Pelletier,
for her fantastic support and belief in this book,
and editor, Heather Howland,
for her amazing skill in bringing
out the best in a story.

The Matchmaker Bride is a sweet, small-town romance that is full of humor and heart, but there are themes that might be triggering to some readers. A past divorce and a pretend relationship are discussed in the novel. Readers who may be sensitive to these elements, please take note.

PROLOGUE

This was it. Meredith Galanes's chance to hit it big.

She sucked in a breath, her heart pounding. If she nailed today's television interview, she would be golden. In syndication. *Yes.*

She strode onto the set trying not to let nerves take over. She could do this. Of course she could. She'd appeared on camera a hundred times.

Only this time was different. There were important people watching—people who could make her career. Two network execs were on set and they'd be scrutinizing her every move, trying to see if Meredith had the chops to take things to the next level. Like the host of this program had been unable to do, even though she was a station darling due to her daddy's advertising money.

Meredith's glam squad rushed over for last-minute primping. Joel spritzed her flyaways with hairspray and she shut her eyes, as April clipped a mic to her scoop-neck collar then attached its base to the back of her belt.

"Don't listen to the rumors," April whispered.

"Right." Joel rolled his eyes. "Idle chatter."

Meredith gaped at them. "What rumors?"

April leaned toward her, her purple-streaked hair in a ponytail. "Your syndication deal." A conspiratorial grin tugged at her lips. "The top brass say—"

"That you'll never get it without having a man

yourself," Joel finished.

April grabbed the hairbrush and smacked him with it. "You don't know that."

"I'm just saying." He frowned, smoothing Meredith's curls with his fingers. "We know Meredith is the best, but good luck convincing the network that a single matchmaker has any business telling other people how to run their love lives."

Joel shot a look at the stage and Meredith's pulse spiked when she spied the network "suits" chatting with each other.

Okay, so she hadn't had a date in two years. That had nothing to do with her ability to match people up. Now she just had to hope the network believed that. Hopefully, her love life wouldn't come up in her interview today.

Meredith swallowed hard. "Thanks, guys."

The producer motioned her forward. "Two minutes!"

Meredith took the guest seat and her host, Tanya Gibbs, sat in a tall swivel chair like hers with a high table in between them. They'd each been supplied with large coffee mugs, which, unfortunately, only contained water. While she appreciated less potential for staining her clothes, a shot of caffeine would be a really big help right now. No, make that a double-shot.

She tried to ignore the fact that the execs were here and primed herself for performing.

Deep breaths. Deep breaths.

The execs had already viewed tapings of her show and now wanted to see how she handled interviews, that's all. There would be a lot of those if she got syndicated and was expected to help market her show.

Inhale. Exhale.

A cameraman gave a signal and then they were rolling.

"Meredith Galanes," Tanya said with a pasted-on grin. "Welcome to *Talk Time*!"

The intros went off without a hitch with Tanya summing up Meredith's matchmaking achievements and hinting at bigger things to come. Not that Meredith was able to focus on any of that. Her mind was stuck on those *rumors*. She'd been chasing this syndication deal for months now and had finally believed herself to be on the cusp of securing it. Her appearance here today was supposed to cement things. Assuming she impressed the right people. And assuming Joel's distressingly valid opinion wasn't shared by certain influential others.

She scanned the crew and her gaze landed on the execs. *Nooo.* One of them was taking notes! Or maybe she was texting. That could be good or bad, or have nothing to do with Meredith *at all*.

April waved, trying to capture Meredith's attention. No wait. She was *pointing*. Joel was frantically pointing, too—at Tanya.

"Meredith?" Tanya prodded. "Should I repeat the question?"

Tanya Gibbs looked polished in her pale-peach business suit, blond hair, and spiky designer heels Meredith would die for.

"Um...yeah. Could you?"

"I was asking about *your* love life." All around them, the studio lights gleamed brighter. *No. She wouldn't dare.* "Will that be explored on your show?" She swept one hand through the air. "Boston-area love expert reveals her personal man-catching secrets?" *Oh, yes she did.*

Meredith felt the blood drain from her face. Time to redirect. "That's not how this business works," she said, trying not to squirm in her seat. She adjusted her sunflower-print skirt, draping it over her crossed legs. "It's not so much about the 'catch' as it is the *match.* The *perfect* match. And, perfect matches are hard to come by." She winked at the camera, willing her peripheral vision not to stray to the execs. "That's where I fit in."

"Sounds like the voice of experience. Do tell us about the man you're dating? I'm sure your fans will be interested. All those social media followers, too."

"Ah, actually. Romance is not a top priority for me right now. I've been—"

"No *romance*? What?" Tanya laughed like the idea was absurd, then pretended to share a confidence with the camera. "And here she claims to be *all about* love. An expert. Hmm."

This interview was going downhill fast. Meredith glanced at the shadowy side of the stage, searching for Joel or April or somebody for support, but there were only producers and even more cameras. She didn't dare look back at the suits.

"Well, sure I make time for romance! Of course. But, in my case, I appreciate keeping things a little…private."

"Private?" Tanya challenged, not backing down. "What does that mean?"

Meredith tried not to break a sweat, envisioning cool mountain streams and waterfalls. "All it means is…" She smiled sassily at the camera. "We haven't yet made things public."

Finally. That should work in throwing Tanya off, but nope. She persisted.

"So there *is* a special someone." She tapped her chin. "What's his name?"

Meredith bit her lip. She couldn't—just *couldn't*—admit her disastrous dating history. What would the viewing public think? And those network execs? Joel was right—*Matched Up* would never get that syndication deal then. Tanya would make sure of it with her little humiliation campaign. And she was so close.

Tanya's face fell. "No. Way. You're not matched up at all, are you?" She forced a fake frown. "How sad. 'Matchmaker Meredith' has no match of her own. I wonder…do you tell your clients that you're single? I can't imagine that instills a lot of confidence in your…abilities."

Low blow. Meredith's gut tightened. Tanya was known for skewering her guests, especially her accomplished female ones. You'd think a fellow woman would help a girl up. Not knock her down, then step on her. Especially in front of network people. Tanya acted like she was above getting fired, and maybe she was. Even though *Talk Time* was only local, the show attracted tons of viewers. A few more at the moment than *Matched Up*. But that was mostly on account of Tanya's enormous advertising budget. "Sure I do. I have a match, my *perfect* match."

"Then give us a hint. Occupation. Location. Anything?" Meredith could practically hear the knell of a countdown clock ticking off the seconds in her brain. Her short segment was nearly up.

Ten. Nine. Eight.

Think, think, think. Meredith worked hard to come up with somebody. Anybody. If he was super impressive that would be amazing. Gorgeous would be a plus, too.

Six. Five.

Shockingly, only one gorgeous guy came to mind. One with piercing blue eyes.

And a smirk. How could she forget that part?

Three. Two...

"Well, I guess we have our answer, folks. Thank you for joining us today on—"

"He's a boatbuilder!" Meredith blurted out.

"Fascinating." Tanya leaned forward. "Whereabouts?"

"Blue...Blue Hill," Meredith stammered. *Ooh, this is going to come back to bite me.* She swallowed hard. "Blue Hill, Maine."

CHAPTER ONE

Derrick Albright stood on his deck watching the mid-day sun shimmer across Blue Hill Bay and enjoying the first day of his two-week staycation. His rustic cabin sat on ten awesome acres and he could sail or kayak whenever he wanted. Every once in a while, he still took out the rowboat, or his handmade canoe. The canoe had been a first-run effort when he'd built a similar model for his grandpa. Making that canoe had been his introduction to the boat school. He'd fallen in love with boatbuilding after that, and now it was his career.

Gravel crunched in his drive. Lots of gravel, like a huge party was arriving. Derrick frowned and glanced through the sliding glass door and out the kitchen window on the far wall, spotting several vehicles. There were a bunch of SUVs, a couple of sedans, a big white van...

What's going on?

He walked through his living room, his flip-flops smacking the wood floor. He wore a ratty old pair of shorts and a T-shirt, but was basically decent enough to ward off the intrusion. Unless there was some kind of weird emergency in the area, these people obviously had the wrong address. They sure were insistent. Pounding and pounding on his front door.

He opened it and three different microphones

jutted out below his chin.

"Mr. Albright!" one reporter said. She had on a hot pink suit that was so bright it hurt his eyes. "Is it true that you're engaged?"

"What?" Derrick gripped the doorframe when the crowd of people pressed in.

"Meredith," hot pink woman said. "Meredith Galanes! Your fiancée?"

He frowned. "What—"

Another woman wearing thick red lipstick shoved her mic so close it nearly grazed his cheek. "Is it really a match made in heaven?"

A *what* made in *where*? "Uh…"

A guy in a sportscoat squeezed between his female colleagues. "Can you tell us about your relationship?"

"Mr. Albright, when is the big day?"

Derrick gaped at them all. He hadn't seen Meredith Galanes since his brother's wedding disaster last summer, and he was glad for it.

"Is she here?" sportscoat guy prodded.

If a bunch of cameras shoved in his face wasn't so overwhelming, he might have laughed. Like he'd ever let that woman into his home. This cabin was his respite, and Meredith, with her snippy attitude, sky-high heels, and irritatingly inviting lips, was the *opposite* of calming. "No. Definitely not."

Camera flashes went off.

He tried to close the door but the reporters wouldn't budge.

"Mr. Albright!" red lipstick lady called out. "Are you choosing to live separately until the wedding?"

Annnd…he was done.

"No comment!" Derrick snapped, and he shoved the door shut.

• • •

Meredith took the hands-free call on the second ring. It was her assistant, Beth, in Boston. "Hey! Are you there yet?"

She'd turned off the main highway and was creeping her way along small roads toward Blue Hill. Meredith took the last bite of her sandwich and set down the wrapper. She'd eaten a very late lunch on the road, but was mostly through her five-hour drive. "Not yet. Why?"

"Because, uh. Looks like the press got there first."

"Nooo."

Beth sounded nervous. "It didn't look good."

"What didn't look good?"

"Derrick. He seemed sort of surprised. He didn't really look dressed for company, either. Still was pretty hot though."

She didn't doubt it. Hotness was not Derrick's problem. The man had been hot when he'd stopped on a dime, causing her to ram into his SUV last summer. Then he'd blamed her for her damaged bumper. Seriously? The man was so infuriating. Gorgeous, but still. "You saw footage?"

"Just a short clip."

"Great." Meredith glanced at the Crock-Pot she'd secured in the passenger seat with a seat belt. She'd prepared the meal while she was packing then had transferred it to this carrying container.

Now she kind of wished she'd made two pot roasts, and not just one.

As if an extra pot roast could fix this.

"Don't worry," she said. "I'll smooth things over."

"There's one more thing. Your mom called the station."

"What?"

"Three times."

"Yikes." Meredith checked her phone, noting several missed calls and voices messages. She'd had to turn off notifications after her 8:00 a.m. taping because her phone had been going so nuts.

"She wants to know why nobody told her about this boatbuilder guy. And whether that's why you've been refusing all her Boston area fix-ups."

No. That had been on account of the fact that they were all over fifty. Ick.

"Your dad sounded unhappy, too," Beth informed her. "He was shouting something in the background in Spanish and then she started yelling at him. I think they both forgot I was there for a bit. What does *ay dios mio* and *ay caramba* mean?"

Meredith blew out a breath. "I'll call them. I'm sorry you had to deal with that."

"No problem. I'm just sorry they got so upset."

"Yeah. Me too." Meredith pursed her lips, weighing how she was going to handle that.

The GPS told her to turn again and she checked its screen. "I'd better go," she told Beth. "The roads are really narrow and I need to pay attention."

"Okay then, good luck with everything."

"Yeah thanks!"

"Keep me posted."

• • •

Derrick had just finished making coffee when he heard a car door pop open.

He set his mug down on the counter and scowled. Another reporter? Really?

It had only been a couple hours since the last round had come through, though he'd been smart enough not to answer the door and eventually they left. Instead of fielding questions he had no answers to, he'd been busy googling Meredith, trying to track down her phone number.

As soon as he got rid of whoever the straggler was, he'd give in and call Brent. Maybe his wife, Hope, would be able to get him Meredith's number. He intended to call and demand some answers. What had the infuriating woman said? Or maybe it hadn't been her at all? Maybe one of her unhinged fans had started this rumor. But how did he get roped into it? He yanked open his front door, prepared to do battle with the paparazzi.

Then he froze at the sight of that cobalt blue convertible.

Meredith Galanes stepped out onto his gravel drive and his heart lurched. He'd had to put up with the woman for an entire week during Brent's wedding last summer, and had hoped to never see her again. Yet, here she was, up close and personal, teetering in his direction in towering sandals and a flouncy dress, with her long dark curls bouncing behind her.

She held a large Crock-Pot in her hands, which

she grasped with oven mitts. For an instant, it was hard to believe he was really seeing her and this wasn't some kind of weird dream.

About Meredith? Not a chance.

"I can explain!" she said, traipsing toward his cabin.

This he had to hear. "Can't wait."

She approached his covered stoop, her spindly heels *clack-clack-clacking* against the flagstones hedged by flowering bushes. This was no dream. It was her, all right. In the flesh. And smelling like honeysuckle at the height of summer. Despite himself, he'd never forgotten her perfume, or, well... pretty much anything about her.

"Want to tell me what's going on?"

She stared up at him with big, dark brown eyes and Derrick's heart slammed against his chest.

"It was a simple mistake."

"Simple? Your publicity posse was here not more than an hour ago."

"Ah, um...yeah. About that." She peered over his shoulder and into his empty living room. "Can we talk inside?"

"What are you even *doing* in Blue Hill?" he asked, not budging.

She smiled and shot him a flirty grin. "I came here to surprise you."

Consider him surprised. And more than a little ticked off. What kind of nerve the woman had. "You're not the first one today."

She winced. "I heard."

"And?"

She shoved her Crock-Pot under his nose in a

peace offering. A delectable aroma wafted toward him. For the love of all things edible, it smelled just like a pot roast. A very delicious pot roast. Derrick hadn't enjoyed a homecooked meal in months.

She pressed forward into his cabin and he inched back. "Hungry?"

"No." Derrick's stomach betrayed him with a rumble.

"Uh-huh. I brought this for dinner."

Dinner? What?

"No, no, no…" he said. "You are no way—*no how*—staying—"

But, before he could finish, she used one of her shoes as a lever and kicked the door shut.

• • •

Meredith ogled the gorgeous man in front of her, working hard to remember her plan. Because Derrick Albright was most definitely gorgeous. Maybe even more so than when she'd seen him last. How was that even possible—or fair?

Stick to the plan.

Right.

She'd constructed her plan carefully during the drive from Boston. She just hadn't counted on the paparazzi getting here first. She had no clue how they'd unearthed his name. Maybe there weren't that many boatbuilders in these parts, particularly ones she'd come into contact with, and the Albright wedding last summer had made the society pages. Both she and Derrick had been listed as being in the wedding party. Her as the maid of honor and him as the best man, so there was a paper trail of their connection.

No matter. They could still pull this off. She just needed to get him on board.

The heavy Crock-Pot sagged in her grip. "Er... would you mind if I set this down?"

He spoke with unmasked sarcasm. "Make yourself at home."

Derrick's gaze tracked her, and she nearly tripped on her way to the kitchen. He had his arms folded across his broad chest and his T-shirt tugged against a six-pack, which was as flat as a board. Meredith locked her shaky knees, acting nonplussed. She'd almost forgotten how built the guy was, but she didn't need to dwell on that now.

She set the Crock-Pot on the counter and turned toward him, steeling herself for her next move, but she sank under the weight of his stare.

"What was all that talk about a match made in heaven?" His eyes glinted dangerously and she backed up a step.

"Oh that," she said with a wave. "That was just a little misunderstanding."

"And the engagement part?"

She swallowed hard. "That one was bigger."

"Meredith."

"Okay. All right," she relented. "I was kind of in a spot on this talk show—"

"Talk show?"

"*Talk Time*, yeah. With Tanya Gibbs."

"That's a real show?"

She frowned. "Of course it's a real show. That's where the whole thing started."

"What *thing*?"

"My idea! To…to help you. The thing is Tanya totally got the wrong impression, then everything went off the rails. I guess they looked you up—and hunted you down, those media people, because they falsely believed that you I are together. Which isn't a bad belief if you think about it. Not if it's just for the short term and only pretend."

He was shaking his head before she'd even had a chance to finish. Not a good sign. "Oh, no you don't. I am not pretending anything with you. My family went through enough last time with my brother and your twin friends."

"Hey!" she protested. "That turned out all right!"

Derrick scowled. "It was the getting there that hurt—just about everyone. You know that as well as I do, Mer."

"Don't call me that."

"Why not?"

"Because I don't like it." Didn't help that he'd used it in that snide and superior way.

"Then I intend to." He stepped forward. "A lot."

Meredith bristled, recalling her greater ambitions. "I'm not talking about tricking your family. In fact, I insist they know the truth. I'm just asking you to play along with this in public for a short while."

"*This* meaning the lie that we're engaged?"

"At least pretend that we're serious."

He raked a hand through his hair. "What's in it for you?"

"A syndication contract," she admitted honestly. "Taking my matchmaking show wide."

"It's only local now?"

She nodded. "My station's a network affiliate."

"What does that have to do with me'?"

"Tanya pretty heavily insinuated that my love life is a dumpster fire."

"Is it?"

"That's not the point." Her cheeks burned hot. "The point is the insinuation looks bad for business. Could be seen as a black mark in building my career."

"As a matchmaker." He laughed out loud. *Rudely.* "I see."

She huffed out a breath. "This is serious, Derrick! I've just taped my hundredth episode. I'm on the pinnacle here, maybe of something big. If *Matched Up* goes into syndication, viewers everywhere will see it! It might even get picked up for streaming."

He rubbed a hand over his face. "That does sound big."

"Huge."

"So. How do I fit into this pretty picture?" He crossed his arms in front of him but still looked interested somehow. His eyes were doing that little twinkling thing that said she had his full attention. It also made her a bit nuts because it looked like he was trying to sneak into her head. Well fine. Let him go there.

Welcome Derrick! Now cooperate for once in your life.

"I needed to come up with someone," she added coolly. "I mean, name a person I was involved with so I wouldn't look like a loser in the love department."

"Aww, and you thought of me." She wanted to smack him but she wasn't a violent person so she held her breath instead. One dark eyebrow arched. "Why?"

She huffed, completely irritated, then decided to play nice. She needed his help after all. "I didn't— mention you by name exactly," she said smoothly. "That part got extrapolated by the press."

"You must have given them something to work with."

"I might have mentioned something about a boatbuilder in Maine."

"That's fairly broad."

"Yeah, but Blue Hill's not." She winced. "You're all I could think of in a pinch. Probably due to our, you know, mutual dislike of one another?"

"Sure," he said like she'd lost her mind. And maybe she had. "That makes perfect sense."

"I was desperate," she told him. "If Tanya had her way, I'd lose this syndication deal. She's never wanted me to get it because she failed to get one herself, in spite of her daddy's advertising money."

"Professional jealousy's an ugly beast," he agreed sympathetically. He studied her a moment, seeming to soften. "Look, I'm sorry things are so twisted up, because this sounds like a great opportunity for you—"

"Could be for you, too! That's what I've been trying to say."

The look he gave her was pure skepticism. "Oh yeah? How's that?"

She played her best card, hoping she'd win this

hand. Based on the private conversation she and Derrick had shared last summer, she was willing to hedge her bets.

"I can tell you in one word. Olivia."

CHAPTER TWO

One year earlier…

It had been just after the bouquet toss at the wedding and Derrick had stolen away. Meredith didn't know where he'd gone and she hadn't intended to find him, but she had when she'd climbed down the steep wooden steps to the dock beneath the Albrights' expansive summer estate. Festivities were still taking place on the lawn with guests drinking and chatting, but the wedding couple had already said their good nights.

Meredith held the bridal bouquet, feeling foolish for having caught it in the first place. "Hey you."

Derrick looked up when he heard her coming. He sat on the dock with his knees bent in front of him and gripped a mostly empty bottle of beer. "Meredith."

Okay, so he clearly wasn't happy to see her. "Sorry," she said. "Didn't know you were down here. I can go if you'd prefer?"

"Nah. It's all right." He motioned with his free hand. "There's enough room for two."

Meredith sat down on a step. She and Derrick hadn't gotten off to the best start, what with their little fender bender that he blamed her for when it was absolutely his fault. He'd been difficult to be around all week and the tension between them had been unbearable. But still, when she'd watched him with his family, she'd seen a different guy. Someone who cared for others, maybe just not particularly her. She was a big girl, though, and she could take it. He'd probably make the right woman pretty happy one day. He had potential.

He tilted his beer bottle up toward the cliffs above them. "Had enough of the party?"

"For now." She viewed him in the shadows, thinking he looked drawn and sad. "You?"

"Weddings aren't my thing. Generally." He shrugged. "This one was okay, though."

"Yeah." She sighed and gazed out at the darkened waters. They made her think of her soul at the moment and the guilt she carried over her role in this twisted-up wedding. She inhaled fully, telling herself not to stress any further. This day was done. The rest was up to the wedding couple to sort through and the bride had assured Meredith she would explain everything when the moment was right. Maybe that moment was even happening right now. Meredith let out a breath, allowing her anxiety to finally ease. She'd been carrying it all week long and it had been exhausting.

She glanced around at the scenery, finding it beautiful and calming. The moon was high and casting its glow across the bay. "It's nice out here."

"Can be." He scanned her bouquet. "So, you're the lucky lady?"

Meredith waved her flowers. "Some say."

"Isn't that supposed to mean you'll marry next?"

"Silly superstition."

"Yeah. Well. I wouldn't know. Personally."

"I don't suspect you've been catching any

bouquets," she teased him.

He smiled but still seemed down. "I meant, there wasn't any of that at my wedding."

"No?"

"It was…different."

"I'm sorry, Derrick," she said. "Sorry things didn't work out."

"Yeah. Me, too." After a few moments he met her eyes. "We were kids then. Immature. If we'd gotten together later? Who knows."

Meredith's heart ached for him because it seemed pretty clear to her that Derrick wasn't 100 percent over his ex. "Ever think of trying again?" she asked gently.

"Me and Olivia? Don't think so, but then, you're the matchmaker, so you tell me." He chuckled and finished his beer. "Speaking of, how about you? With your job, I bet you pinned down Mr. Perfect right away. Is he waiting for you back in Boston?"

There he went, poking her about her career again. Meredith heaved a breath. "There's no Mr. Perfect, nor has there ever been. Yet." She fiddled with the bouquet in her hands. "No one like Olivia was for you."

"Shame." He set his jaw. "Or maybe that's better?"

"Hmm. Maybe so. And besides—matchmakers make the worst clients."

The wind picked up, carrying the sound of laughter and tinkling glasses out over the water, and they both sat there a while and just listened.

After a bit, Meredith grew chilly and decided to turn in. Her bridesmaid dress was sleeveless and the night air was getting cool.

"I should probably head back now." She stood with her bouquet.

The air grew heavy between them as the breeze rippled across the waves.

He got to his feet, too, leaving his empty beer bottle on the dock. He looked handsome in the moonlight with dark shadows cutting across his face. He still wore his best man clothes from the wedding, though he'd removed his tuxedo jacket and loosened his tie. He shoved his hands in his pants pockets and studied her.

Her senses tingled, like something was about to happen. Only she didn't know what. She paused near the bottom step, feeling awkward and unsure when he walked toward her.

"Are you, uh, going up?"

He shook his head but his gaze lingered on hers.

"I think I'll stay here another minute," he said.

She nodded and started to go but he stopped her with a question.

"What time are you leaving tomorrow?"

"Early." Her pulse quickened because he was standing so close.

And then, he took a step closer.

He cocked his chin. "So, I guess this is it then?"

"Guess so."

He stared into her eyes in a way that made her heart pound and her face burn hot. And then when he stepped closer and cupped his hand to her cheek, she caught her breath.

"In a funny way," he said. "I'm going to miss you."

"Really?" She thought he hated her.

"Really."

Then ooh…his thumb smoothed over her cheek and he moved closer. Her heart hammered. What was he doing? Her reason tugged with her emotions, and her heart reeled. She detected heat in his gaze. Desire, too. But no, he and she could never—

He dropped his hand. Something glimmered in his eyes, conflict, possibly regret. "Night, Mer." This time when he used her nickname, it didn't sound antagonistic. It was more…sad. "Pleasant dreams," he said and turned away, looking out over the water.

She stood there, clutching her bouquet to her chest, wondering what in the world had just happened. When he didn't say anything else, she took a shaky breath. "Pleasant dreams, Derrick."

Her cheeks steamed as she scurried up the steps and then raced her way across the crowded lawn to the guest cottage, where she packed her bags preparing to leave Blue Hill.

That was the last she'd seen of Derrick Albright until today.

CHAPTER THREE

"What does Olivia have to do with anything?"

Derrick stared at the maddening woman who'd invaded his cabin. She was plenty ballsy bringing up Olivia now. His head still spun from that press assault and the fabricated engagement story, and she dares to mention his ex? He kicked himself for letting down his guard at Brent's wedding. He'd been weak in that moment, feeling sorry for himself instead of being happy for Brent like a good brother would have been, and had said too much. He'd also nearly made a misstep with Meredith. At least she seemed to have put that part behind her.

He knew he had. Way behind him.

Liar.

Meredith's eyebrows arched. "Maybe a whole lot?"

"No."

"Yeah."

"Nuh-uh."

"Uh-huh."

"*Mer*," he said, his tension building.

Electricity crackled between them.

She straightened on her heels with her hands on her hips, displaying her short and curvy figure. He was determined not to notice the way the halter top of her sundress dipped in an enticing V at her chest, or the pretty sparkle in her dark brown eyes.

He was not interested in Meredith. Never had

been. Never would be.

Despite that one slip.

In fact, his emotions toward her ran at the opposite end of the spectrum.

So okay, she'd seemed nice that one time when he'd talked to her about his failed marriage. Caring and compassionate even. That in no way negated the billions of times she'd gotten on his every last nerve in the span of one week.

"You haven't even heard my plan," she said. "My *very excellent* plan."

"Is 'excellent' code word for 'crazy' these days?"

"Funny." She glanced around the living area, her eyes landing on the small two-seater cushioned sofa with a boxy wood frame. "Mind if I sit?" She did before he could answer. "My day was exhausting."

"You're telling me."

"I really wish I'd been here." Amazingly, she giggled. "It had to have been kind of fun being hounded by the paparazzi."

She had to be kidding him. "What?"

"Come on, Derrick. When have you ever had so much excitement in one afternoon?"

His gaze drifted toward his bedroom and she held up a hand. "Wait. Don't answer that."

He took a seat in an armchair beside her. She obviously wasn't going anywhere—yet. He'd make sure she was gone before dinner, though. This was the first day of his two-week break between his spring and summer classes, and he was *not* letting Meredith Galanes ruin it with her cockeyed ideas and nutty proposals. Even if she did bring a pot roast. Maybe he could get her to leave it to make up for her rude interruption—and that media fray.

She stared around the room and into the kitchen that was open from here, divided by his oak dining table with four chairs. She apparently noticed the coffee machine, because she asked, "Coffee?"

Derrick motioned grandly toward the kitchen and Meredith shot him an annoyed look.

"Fine," she said, standing. "I'll make it myself." She walked to the one-cup-at-time brewer, then started hunting around through his cabinets.

"Bottom left drawer," he said, indicating where the coffee pods were kept.

She looked up, her brown curls spilling past her shoulders. He thought her hair looked longer than it had been last summer but he wasn't sure. He hadn't spent much time thinking about her at Brent's wedding before that final night other than to notice the fact that she was generally attractive, and hugely irritating in every possible way.

So irritating that each time she'd tossed out some verbal barb, he hadn't been able to stop himself from sending one back. She'd been so provoking that sparring with her had become a forgone conclusion. Brent had asked him to rein himself in, and he'd tried super hard. But Meredith got under his skin in this inexplicable way. With that sassy attitude of hers, and those really dark eyes. Not to mention her sexy curves.

No. Stop. He was not going there.

He'd probably only been tempted that once because it had been late, and he'd been tired, and had also maybe had one too many beers.

"Want some?" she asked, holding up two small

coffee pods.

He mentally scrubbed all thoughts of her attractiveness from his brain. "Why not?"

While it was true he'd had coffee earlier, he could stand having one more cup. It was the cordial thing to do since she wanted some, and he could be cordial when he wanted to. His Grandmother Margaret would be so proud.

Derrick shook his head. Meredith Galanes back in Blue Hill. His family would be shocked. He never thought he'd see the day. Wait until he told Brent. Or maybe Brent had already been informed of her impending visit? He and Hope were married now, and Hope's sister, Jackie, and Meredith were best friends. So.

"Who else knows about this?" he asked as she prepared the coffee, first his and then hers.

"No one," she said, setting his mug on the counter. "How do you take yours?"

"Black."

"Except for my regular viewers, plus those who watch Tanya." She set her chin in thought. "We have some overlap. And then there's my assistant Beth, and my station manager Jerry. The entire set crew for *Talk Time* of course, and some of them also work for me—"

"Not exactly a secret, is it?" he asked when she handed him his coffee.

"It's not exactly national news, either," she said. "Mostly local to Boston." She shrugged. "And I guess my station's affiliate up here."

"So?"

"So. Maybe we can keep a lid on this press thing

without revealing the truth yet."

"Why would we want to do that?"

"To give you time to win back Olivia!"

"What?" He sighed. "Look, it's been ten years. Who says I even want her?"

Meredith gave him a long look that shot right to his heart. "Are you telling me you don't?"

She was trying to use his late-night post-wedding confessions against him. Fine. Meredith could think what she wanted. That didn't mean she was right. And even if she was, there was no hope for him and Olivia anymore. Was there?

"I know what you're thinking," Meredith said. "That it's impossible. You and Olivia are history, and time's moved on. But it really doesn't, you know? Not when two people are destined for each other. Time has a way of standing still in that case, and waiting for the right moment to come along for those two fated soul mates to be reunited with each other."

He questioned whether she honestly believed that, or if it was just part of her spiel on her matchmaker show. Either way, it sounded like psychobabble to him. Or, more like lovesick babble. Like the sort of story you told people who wanted to believe in happy endings, no matter how long the odds.

"I don't even know where she is anymore."

"I'll find her."

He raised an eyebrow. "What if she's not interested?"

"What if she is?"

Derrick sank back in his chair, weighing this outcome. "Then, I don't know." While it was true he'd vaguely considered the possibility of getting back together with Olivia, he'd never imagined there'd be a real opportunity to pull it off. Now that Meredith had brought it up, though, the idea did sound *mildly* intriguing.

"If she is…" Meredith got her game face on. "You could give things another try."

He leveled her a look, wondering if that's what he wanted. What Olivia would want. "Possibly. No guarantees." But his mind was already wandering through his options. What if Olivia was interested? What if she regretted their breaking up and the harsh way she'd treated him, but had never had the courage to tell him? If given the chance, would she step up to the plate now?

"I mean, of course I won't pursue this if you don't want me to."

He suddenly felt like her big, dark eyes could peer straight through him, right down into his lonely soul. While he'd dated around a bunch over these last ten years, he'd never become serious about anyone. Could it be he'd been subconsciously waiting to reconcile with Olivia?

"Do you?" she pressed. "Want me to pursue it?"

"I'm not sure," he said honestly. The more he thought it over, the more tempted he became. Just to see Olivia one more time. Would they still have their old spark? "What if I do?"

Her eyes glimmered. "Then just say the word. If there's any way on earth, I can make it happen," she said with uncanny confidence. "I'm that good. Give me six weeks and I can do it."

"Six weeks?" He frowned. "That will take most

of the summer."

"Okay, maybe I can do this in four," she conceded. "I need to buy time for my station to negotiate with the network and help secure my syndication deal."

"And where will you be in the meantime?"

She brightened. "Right here in your quaint little cabin with you."

"Pretending to be my girl?"

"We can stay in separate rooms."

"I've only got one."

Her chest reddened first and then her neck until finally her face was in full bloom.

"Are you blushing?"

"No. It's just hot in here. Maybe we should open a window?"

"*Or*...maybe we should drop this whole idea, and you should go back to Boston." He wasn't *that* curious about Olivia.

"Not when I'm this close," she pleaded. She motioned with her thumb and forefinger. "Just a smidgen away from hitting it big. I'm begging you, Derrick, for this one little favor. In return, I can do you a huge one. Once I get the contract, I'm golden. And, with you going back to your ex, everyone will understand why you and I 'broke up.' We can even say that I graciously stepped aside, in light of true love."

He tried to imagine what it would feel like holding Olivia in his arms again, but his mind couldn't quite get there. Not with Meredith standing right in front of him. Though, maybe seeing Olivia again would bring it all back. Now that they were older and had both matured, things could be different.

Better. He and Olivia had shared lots of good times. Not just good times, great ones. In the beginning, before it had all blown apart.

"I don't know, Mer," he said, and this time she didn't flinch at the nickname. "This pretend relationship thing is a big ask." A chance to be reunited with Olivia was one thing, but now she'd coupled it with this other request. Then again, fair was fair. Derrick understood the *tit for tat* and wasn't opposed to Meredith also trying to get something out of the deal. In a way, he'd expect nothing less of the savvy woman.

And, to his surprise, he kind of liked the idea of helping her.

"But it's only short-term," she repeated in an effort to convince him. "And we'll just be pretending for the public, not your family."

"They're not going to like this either way."

"I'm very good at smoothing things over," she said, and he hoped that was true.

She would have to be *extra smooth* to get his family to go along with her strategy. Then again, most of them had actually liked Olivia. A lot.

"How do you plan to approach her?" he asked.

She blinked, bouncing excitedly. "So your answer is yes? You'll do it?"

"My answer's a tentative maybe."

She deflated. "Sorry, Derrick. That's not good enough."

"Okay then, yes," he said, figuring he could always change his mind later, if this got too weird. Why not? He cocked his chin and studied her. "You didn't answer my question."

"About approaching Olivia?" Her eyebrows knitted together. "I'll have to think on it, but don't worry. Just leave it to me. I'll come up with something. Something logical that makes sense."

Sure, right. Like anything was logical or made sense about this proposal. Derrick couldn't believe he was considering this—he must be touched in his head. Or maybe in his bruised and battered heart. "What if she's already involved with someone?"

"What if she's not?" Meredith asked slyly.

Derrick rubbed the side of his neck, pondering the time frame. He was on vacation for this next little bit, but then would be back to instructing at the boat school and didn't need all sorts of additional distractions going on. Not to mention the stress. He definitely wasn't putting up with this scheme for a month. Even a couple of weeks seemed too long, and he didn't want to wreck his whole two-week vacation. Today was Monday so he could spare a week and a half, he guessed. At most. He still wanted a few days of R&R at the end.

"I'll give you ten days," he said, deciding.

"Ten *days*?"

"I thought you were excellent?"

"Oh yes! I am."

"Fine. Then prove it."

"But my contract might not even be—"

"Ten days. Take it or leave it."

He met her gaze and she stared at him, apparently not backing down.

"Starting tomorrow," she finally said.

"Starting *today*."

"Okay," she said. "I'll take it."

CHAPTER FOUR

Derrick hefted Meredith's heavy suitcase out of the trunk of her car. "How long are you planning to stay?" he joked. "Indefinitely?"

She grabbed a rolling carry-on bag and already had a huge canvas tote over one shoulder. "I was hoping for the summer, at least," she said, closing the trunk. "But I'll work with what we've got. Two weeks," she added craftily.

"Ten *days*, Mer." He recalled her arrival at his grandparents' place last year. She'd come loaded down with bags then, and she'd been there less than a week. He waited for her to walk ahead of him and up the cabin's front steps. She jimmied open the door and held it open for him as he lumbered forward with her luggage. "What did you pack in here? Bricks?"

"Shoes, mostly." She set her carry-on down in the kitchen and looked around.

"You won't have much use for extra pairs of heels in Blue Hill."

"We'll see!" she said with a know-it-all grin.

Derrick grumbled to himself, wondering what sorts of fancy soirees she envisioned herself attending. There wasn't a lot going on at his cabin that would call for *wardrobe*. Even if she did imagine herself a television personality, there was no camera crew here.

He thanked his lucky stars for that. He carefully

scanned her big suitcase, hoping it didn't contain video recording equipment. Maybe that was why it was so heavy?

She surveyed two slightly ajar doors adjoining the kitchen. One led to Derrick's room and the other to the cabin's single bath. A third door stood wide open, leading to a small laundry room beside the pantry.

"This couch a sleeper?" she asked, eying the small two-seater.

"Yep, and fairly comfy, too."

"Great," she said, heading for his bedroom. "You take that."

"Oh, no you don't," he said. "I'm not sleeping out here. You are."

She glanced over her shoulder. "But I've got a bad back." She frowned, but it was a fakey-frown.

"Since when?"

"Since my long drive up here."

"You poor thing." For his money—his fakey-frown was way better than hers. "Then absolutely. Be my guest." He motioned toward his bedroom and she smiled and walked past him, carrying her shoulder bag and dragging along her small rolling suitcase.

He crossed his arms in front of him and waited.

She reached the threshold and stopped on a dime. It probably took everything she had to keep her mouth from dropping open. He chuckled to himself, knowing it was a pigsty in there. But hey, it was his pigsty and he hadn't exactly known he'd be entertaining.

She goggled at his unmade bed and the

discarded clothing littering the floor. There might have been a damp towel or two laying around as well. From his vantage point, Derrick saw one of them draped over the back of a director's chair. He couldn't remember if he'd left his dirty dishes in there from when he'd been eating nachos in bed last night and watching the sports channel, but—from the look on her face—he guessed probably so.

"Um…" She turned toward him and her shoulders sagged. "What did you say about that sleeper sofa again?"

He repressed a grin, knowing he'd won this battle. "It will suit you fine. What's more, you'll even get clean linens."

"Well, that's a relief."

"I know it's not the Ritz. Or my grandparents' guest cottage, either," he said, remembering that's where she'd bunked up last summer. He thought a moment. "Hey, there's an idea! You can stay there."

"Derrick." She rolled her eyes. "That would ruin the whole illusion."

"Distance makes the heart grow fonder."

"Ha ha. Good try, but no."

"Maybe we can say you're very proper?"

"I *am* proper. That's why I'm staying on the sofa." She huffed. "Are you changing your mind or something?"

Not yet, but he appreciated leaving himself some wiggle room. "No. Are you?"

"Of course not."

"Okay then." He was embarrassed to admit he enjoyed teasing her, but she was just so easy to rile up. Because she always thought she knew everything, which—obviously—she didn't. It bugged him that she'd assumed he'd agree with her ideas and that she'd be staying for the summer, and had even packed accordingly. After seeing his room she was likely glad for the shorter stay. He was surprised she hadn't asked for a fire hose to wash it down.

Scents from the pot roast lingered in the air, making his stomach rumble. She'd plugged it in and set in on low so it would warm up. He couldn't believe she was really staying for dinner, much less spending the night.

Ten whole nights. Whoa.

He hoped they could handle shacking up together for that long. At Brent's wedding, they'd barely been able to stand being in the same room for more than ten minutes. Okay, maybe they hadn't really fought as much as they'd disagreed about things. Maybe if they remained focused on their objectives, they could avoid any needless bickering.

He checked his phone and saw it was half past five. Since the sun wouldn't set until after eight, he still had plenty of daylight left for an outing. "What time did you want to eat?" he asked, thinking he might put some space between them by taking out his rowboat. That would give her a chance to settle in and allow him time to think things through more thoroughly.

"Does around seven sound good?"

"Seven sounds perfect."

"Maybe I can make us a salad to go with?" She grinned and her dangly seashell earrings clattered. "What have you got in the fridge?"

"Fresh jalapenos and cheese."

"Anything else?"

"There's probably a little milk left and maybe some beer."

She sighed. "How close is the nearest store?"

"It's the co-op in town, far side of my grandparents' place."

"Oh! That's kind of a drive."

"Forty minutes from here."

"What? Seriously?" She peered out the kitchen window and then back at him. "You're telling me you're in the middle of nowhere?"

"Seems like you might have noticed on your way in."

"Yeah, but I came the back way."

Derrick rubbed his chin. "There *is* a lady down the road selling lemonade."

"A lady? Not kids?"

"Why not? It's her business. Besides that, it's hot here."

"Not like it is in Boston," she said.

Derrick tilted his head at the challenge. "It's getting warmer."

She scoffed. "It's only June, Derrick. In Maine."

He tried not to notice that sexy mole by the side of her mouth, but his eyes kept straying to her very kissable lips. The only mouth he needed to contemplate now was Olivia's. Assuming he even *wanted* to win her back. He hadn't decided yet.

She flipped back her hair and seemed to collect herself. If she'd noticed that niggle of attraction in which he'd momentarily lost himself, she'd decided to ignore it. All well and good. Better for them to focus on their deal.

"We need to work on our plan," she said, reiterating his thoughts.

"Great idea," he said. "We can do that at dinner. I was thinking I might go rowing for a bit first. I mean, if that's okay with you?"

"Oh sure, fine," she agreed. "That will give me a minute to touch base with Beth and get her started on her detective work in tracking down Olivia."

Derrick frowned. "You won't contact her yet?" He wanted to be 100 percent onboard with this before moving forward. And now, he was at about, oh, sixty-five.

"Not until you and I have all the details worked out, and you agree." She perused the living area, seeing a router on a shelf below the wide-screen TV, its green light blinking. "Mind if I log onto your internet?"

"Go right ahead." He pointed at the refrigerator, which was covered with colorful fish-shaped magnets holding photos and notes of various kinds, including his shopping list. "Check on the back of the pic of me with William and Brent. Username and password are there."

"Super. Thanks." She settled in at the kitchen table with her laptop and looked up. "A few quick things before I reach out to Beth?"

"Sure."

"Olivia's last name?"

"Collins."

"How long were you married?"

"Less than a year."

If she was shocked, she didn't show it. All businesslike. "Still in college?"

"Part of that time. We eloped to Vegas our senior year."

She raised an eyebrow. "Wow. Bet your family loved that."

"Yeah, well." He shifted on his feet. "Not really."

She bit her bottom lip. "Sorry, shouldn't have—"

"It's all right. Most of my family loved her, Sofia especially."

"Sofia? Really?" Meredith latched onto that. "Interesting."

"Yeah, Olivia interned for her and Sally at their law office, and she and Olivia got to be friends."

"Good information." Meredith was typing rapidly, apparently taking notes. "So she was prelaw at school?"

"No, a commerce major."

"You?"

"French."

Her eyebrows arched. "Seriously?"

"*Oh oui, mon petit Mer*," he said with a joking lilt.

She thought on this a moment. "You're lying, aren't you?"

Derrick chuckled, not minding being called out. "Of course I'm lying. It was Latin. Classics, technically."

"Wow. Impressive. I only speak Spanish because we spoke it around the house when I was growing up."

"Bet you would have been great at classics, too."

"Thanks," she said, but she looked doubtful.

"That it?" he asked.

She seemed to be thinking about something. She

scanned back through her notes. "Law office, hmm. So she and Sally were close, too, then?"

"Uh. Not exactly. There was no love lost there."

"Oh? Why's that?"

"No idea."

"Did Olivia go into law?"

"Last I heard she was studying for the bar, so I'm guessing yes."

"Where did you meet her?"

Derrick grabbed his sunglasses and his hat, hoping this interview was almost over. While he got that it was somewhat necessary, it was strangely uncomfortable sharing all these facts about his ex-wife with Meredith. Although he didn't know why. She was only doing her job. *In getting me back together with Olivia*, he reminded himself. *Weird.*

"Coffee bar at college. I worked there."

"You *worked*?"

"We Albrights pull our own weight." He balked at the assumption he wouldn't. Then again, coming from a wealthy family he'd encountered that bias before.

"Oh, sorry. Didn't mean…"

"That's okay." He met her eyes. "Bet you did, too."

"Scholarship girl, yep." She beamed at him and her well-earned pride was alluring. He'd always admired people who took care of themselves and Meredith was clearly like that, so maybe they could find some common ground while working together. And if they were on common ground, maybe they wouldn't get on each other's nerves—that much.

"What was your major?" he asked her, suddenly curious.

"Communications."

"As in?"

"Media and such."

"Figures."

She smirked. "At least my training was relevant."

"What's that supposed to mean?"

"You use classics in boatbuilding?"

He set his chin. "Actually, I do." The truth was he didn't, but then lots of people held jobs that didn't have to do with their college majors.

"Oh nice," she said. "How so?"

"Ahh…" He thought fast. "There's something very poetic about being out on the water."

"O-kay." Her eyebrows knitted together like she had no idea what he was talking about.

"*The Iliad* and *The Odyssey*?"

She rolled her eyes. "Sounds like Greek to me."

"Ha ha."

He considered her a moment, trying to decide how he felt about her proposal. A little mixed up, he supposed. While he was fine with helping her get the syndication deal, bringing all this stuff back about Olivia made him uncomfortable. And yet, a tiny bit excited, too, at the thought of seeing her again. It had been a long time and she *had* been his first love.

Would she even want to see him again?

Would he have ever considered getting in touch with her had Meredith not barged back into his life?

He glanced out the sliding glass door. His row-boat was moored to the dock beyond his large deck and the view of Blue Hill Bay was stunning from here. A sailboat glided past and then a lobster boat, but the sunlight was already waning. "I'd better get going," he said.

She nodded and he sent her a wave, but she was already glued to her computer screen. Probably creating an "Olivia File" for that assistant of hers.

And why did that make him uneasy?

CHAPTER FIVE

Derrick slid on his sunglasses and headed outdoors, where he snagged a life vest from the back of a deck chair on which it had been drying. As he slipped into it, his cell phone rang. He pulled it from his hip pocket and answered. The call was from Grandmother Margaret.

"Grandmother, Hey!" he said, walking toward his rowboat.

"Why are the grandparents always the last to know?"

His jaw tensed. No way. She'd either seen the story on TV, or one of her Boston friends had told her about it. He turned his back on the cabin, attempting to calm her. "Look. It's not what you think—"

"Let's hope not," her prim voice said. "Engaged without telling the family! And to Meredith Galanes? Not that there's anything wrong with the woman, other than her taste in best friends. She does have a certain energy about her. And anyone can see that she's pretty. But how can you trust her to be honest with you?"

"Grandmother."

"I mean it, Derrick. After what she and the others put us through last summer."

"I thought we'd all made our peace with that?"

"Well, yes." His grandmother *tsked*. "Some of us more than others."

"Are you saying you still hold a grudge?"

"No," she said with an indignant air. "I'm saying I'm *wary*. And, if you were smart—which I know you are—you'd be wary, too."

"I don't have anything to be wary about. Not with Meredith."

"Now that's a very naïve sentiment from a man who's abruptly gotten engaged."

Derrick set his jaw. "I am not engaged, okay?"

"It was on the news!"

"Yeah, well, the media's information was wrong."

He peered back toward the cabin where Meredith sat at his kitchen table working at her laptop. She'd obviously been eager to get on the internet and begin working her matchmaker magic. The real question was: Was he ready for it? "I'll explain everything to you," he said to his grandmother. Better yet, he should make Meredith do it. "I mean, she will. Very soon."

"She? Is Meredith there?"

"Yeah."

"Fantastic," Grandmother Margaret said. "You'll have to bring her to dinner."

"What? When?"

"Tonight. I think it's best we get this settled before the others arrive."

Derrick smacked his forehead. His niece's christening was Sunday. If he'd remembered that all his family was parading into town, he might not have agreed to Meredith's ten-day plan. Getting together with Olivia again—for the first time in ten years—was going to be challenging enough in private. But on display before the whole crew? His head throbbed. Just what had he signed on for? Maybe there was still time to remove his signature from the page.

But was that what he wanted? Canceling this whole deal? No. What he wanted was more time to work things out in this scrambled brain of his, which meant continuing to work with Meredith at least through tonight.

Derrick exhaled. Maybe getting this over with quickly was the right move. He'd let Meredith explain everything to his grandparents in advance of the onslaught of others arriving, and he could observe how they took it. Maybe they'd even endorse the idea.

Could Meredith really make this work? Bringing Olivia back into his life? And what would his family's reception be? What about his own reaction? He didn't know, but it was probably worth a shot to give things a chance. Maybe he and Olivia could finally bury the hatchet. Sofia would like that and a little closure would be good. That would help Meredith out, too.

"It's nothing fancy," Grandmother Margaret said when he didn't answer. "Your grandpa was going to grill out some steaks. We've got plenty of extras in the freezer. I'll just pull out two more and toss a salad together. If she's game, maybe Meredith can help me."

"That sounds great," he said. He was conflicted about Meredith putting him in this position. Then again, he'd put himself here, too. Would seeing Olivia again be worth it? He sure hoped so. Maybe some good would come from all this. Sofia would sure like to see Olivia again, if that's how things worked out.

"Want to come at seven?" Grandmother Margaret asked brightly.

That would scarcely give him time to go boating and grab his shower, on top of driving over there. And he still wanted to get out on the water. "Can we say seven thirty?"

"Delightful! Seven thirty it is. I can't wait to hear your story. Naturally the press was wrong. They so often are."

Except this time, Derrick thought, *they're going to have to keep believing they're right.*

Annnd. He shook his head at the notion. *I am going to help with that.*

• • •

"Okay, great," Meredith said, finishing her call with Beth. "Let me know what you find out." She'd shared what she'd learned about Olivia and had also emailed Beth a copy of her notes. Beth's boyfriend Cody worked for a telecommunications firm and was a whiz at locating people. Meanwhile, Meredith intended to conduct her own research online. She liked that Olivia and Sofia had shared a connection, and was hoping to somehow use that to her advantage.

Olivia Collins had left behind a hard-to-find social media imprint, if she'd left one at all. Maybe she *had* gone into law like Derrick hinted. Sometimes those folks stayed off social media for various reasons, depending on their specialization.

Wait! Her new search turned up a fresh result that included Olivia's middle name: Constance. The link went to an obituary page for…ah. How sad. Olivia's grandmother.

*Leaving behind her son and daughter-in-la*w, et cetera, et cetera. *Three grandchildren, including… and Olivia Constance Collins of Acadia, Maine.*

She checked the date on the obit. Just six months ago. So…

Her chin jerked up as Derrick stepped through the deck doors.

"Howdy," he said, seeming in better spirits. He'd been a little gloomy before but now appeared bright and sunny. That time in his rowboat had done him good. "Have any luck?"

Meredith shot another glance at the computer screen and then back at him. "I think she lives in Acadia."

He jerked a thumb over his shoulder and toward the water. "The National Park? Doubtful. I don't think she could get a manicure or find a hairstylist there."

Meredith's cell rang before she could respond. It was Beth. "That was fast."

"That was easy," Beth reported in her efficient manner. "Cody said her old cell number is just one step removed from the one she had in Bangor."

"One step?"

"She only changed it once when she switched carriers and picked up a new phone. Now she's got a high-tech satellite cell. Probably needs it in her line of work."

"Which is?" Meredith asked, while Derrick watched her, interested.

"Park ranger."

Meredith frowned. A park ranger? Talk about a big jump from working at a law firm, not to mention manicures and hair appointments. Derrick might have a point. "Can you send me everything you've got?"

"No problem." Beth paused. "How are things going?"

"Well enough." She couldn't very well go discussing Derrick now, not when he was standing right in front of her. "Look, um. Gotta run. But thanks tons for your help!"

Derrick removed his hat and then his sunglasses. "You've got the wrong girl. Olivia doesn't do nature." He checked out Meredith's feet under the table. "Her heels might not be as high as yours, but she definitely wears them. Not hiking boots."

Meredith flinched at his assertion. Why did Derrick always have to believe he was right? People changed. Except for—apparently—him. He clearly wasn't thinking logically. "You haven't seen her in a decade."

"Yeah, but still. I know what I know. And I know Olivia."

"Do you?" Meredith challenged. "Really? Maybe she's matured. Grown into her own woman. And, look-it, hey. Maybe into an *even more perfect* woman for you."

Derrick stroked his chin. "That would be something. Seeing Olivia facing down a bear."

"It's Acadia," Meredith quipped. "Maybe she's

more about facing down tourists. Getting them to mind their ecological manners. That kind of thing."

Derrick got a distant look in his eye, and just said, "Huh." After a few seconds of blank-staring, he mused, "Olivia? Back to nature?" Then he chuckled at the absurdity of the idea. "Nope. Don't buy it."

Meredith's email *dinged*, diverting her attention away and she grumbled. She scanned Beth's new message. The attachment, too. "Then maybe this will convince you," she said. Beth's boyfriend had tied phone records into data at the DMV. She turned her computer screen around to face Derrick, showcasing the photo on a Maine driver's license. "This her?" The image was a little grainy but the woman in the photo was recognizable enough with big green eyes and long red hair.

He blanched but only momentarily. "That's Olivia."

"So you admit I was right!"

"I admit you got lucky." He frowned. "What's your plan for reaching out to her?"

"I'm…working on it," she hedged, because she was. He gave her a scrutinizing look like he was second-guessing their deal, and her pulse raced. Maybe now that this was seeming real to him, he was changing his mind. But he couldn't!

Beth had told her that buzz was building at the station. Network execs had amped up their interest in *Matched Up* now that Meredith was making the local media, seeing that as an indication she might achieve a broader reach. Her fake relationship with Derrick couldn't fall apart now. It had barely gotten started.

"You'd better work quickly," he said, "because my grandmother's going to ask what you have in mind when you see her."

"Grandmother Margaret?" She guessed she shouldn't be surprised about interacting with his family. In a way, she'd expected this. Given that they were all so tight.

"Yeah. She invited us to dinner tonight. Seems she saw the news."

What? You've got to be kidding me.

She was in no way prepared to deal with his grandmother. She hadn't even developed her pl... pla...plannn...

Derrick yanked off his damp T-shirt, exposing a smattering of chest hair and extremely taut muscles. Meredith fought to keep her bearings, which was kind of hard to do—considering she'd never seen Derrick bare-chested before. He scrunched up the shirt and mopped it across his brow. "Sorry," he said. "A little sweaty."

"Hot out, huh?"

"I told you it gets hot in Blue Hill." He shot her a triumphant grin that bordered on flirty, and her world turned upside down, her heart *thump-thump-thumping* in some crazy cadence. "Even in June." He flipped open the washing machine and chucked his shirt inside it. "I'm going to grab a shower and freshen up for dinner," he said. "You can go next if you'd like."

"Thanks," she replied, trying to peel her eyes off his rugged frame and broad shoulders. His muscled arms tempted her to touch them to learn if they were really as strong as they looked. But she wasn't going anywhere near the half-naked man she detested. He was arrogant and rude...and totally meant for Olivia. So Olivia was who he was going to get.

Not her.

Definitely not her.

Not even in her dreams.

Okay maybe there, just once. Or maybe two times.

For sure not three times. That would be obsessive.

"Dinner," she said absently. "Yeah." She sat up with a jolt. Wait. No. "Tonight?"

He grinned like the cat who'd swallowed the canary. "They're expecting us at seven thirty. The pot roast will keep, won't it?"

She guessed her meal had lasted this long. What was one more day? Although maybe she should pop it in the fridge. But seeing the Albrights already, yikes. That might mean some serious fancy footwork in dealing with them, especially the judgy grandmother. The grandfather would probably be all right. She sucked in a breath to steady her nerves. Okay, she could do this.

"Oh. Well. Sure. And that will be nice," she said, trying to put a positive spin on it. "Seeing your grandparents again. Will it be just them?"

"For now, yeah. The rest of my family's coming in for Julia's baptism later in the week, except for William and Sofia who arrive tomorrow. Julia's—"

"Sofia and William's new little girl. Yeah, Jackie told me." Her head pounded. Seriously? As if his grandparents weren't complication enough, she'd landed herself in the middle of an Albright family reunion. That was *not* part of her plan.

She racked her brain. How could she make a big family gathering work in her favor?

Given Sofia's former friendship with Olivia, maybe Meredith could finesse a way to get Olivia invited to the christening? That would prove the perfect opportunity for her and Derrick to see each other again and tap into their old feelings for each other. Yes, this could actually be a fortuitous turn of events.

Meredith congratulated herself on her quick thinking, the seeds of this idea taking hold.

"Great," he said. "Then you understand why I said yes to dinner tonight. That will give you a chance to prep the grandparents by explaining everything before the rest of the troops come in." He gripped the doorframe to the laundry room and the motion caused his six-pack to expand into a glistening rock-hard plane.

She stifled a moan. He was probably doing it on purpose. Taunting her with his insanely hot body to get back at her for every mildly unflattering thing she'd ever said to him. And when she was being honest, last summer, she'd said a lot.

Wait. What was that mention of *her prepping*? Meredith gulped. "Me explain?"

"You said yourself that you're really good at smoothing things over." His forehead rose. "Besides that, this whole thing was your idea."

"Yeah, but you agreed to it."

"For now. I guess we'll see how I'm feeling in the morning."

Meredith panicked. Oh no. He was not backing out now. "You'll be feeling like carrying this forward," she said. "You'll see."

"You're certain of that?"

Her dander got up. "Yes, I'm certain."

"Because you have certain goals in mind?"

"I'm not the only one, Mr. Boatbuilder." She bit her lip, but it had just slipped out. What was boatbuilding anyway? It sounded much more like a hobby to her than a serious profession.

His blue eyes flashed. "Says the *TV star*," he said, like it was the dumbest job in the world. The dig stung, unearthing all of his previous insults. It was clear he thought even less of her job than she thought of his, and that spoke volumes.

Olivia could have him and Meredith would deliver—gift wrapped, no charge.

"At least I don't make toy boats," she snapped before she could stop herself.

He scowled at her. "They're not *toys*. They're life-size. And exquisitely crafted."

"Oh really? Is that a fact?"

"Certifiable."

"I'd like to see you prove it."

"That's just it." His eyes twinkled in an infuriating fashion. "I don't need to prove anything to anyone. That's your ongoing issue, it seems."

She lifted her chin. "I'm very happy in my job, and accomplished. I just want to accomplish more."

The corners of his mouth twitched. "You can't fault a lady for her ambition."

Every inch of her skin prickled. "Don't you have a shower to take?" she asked.

"Yeah." He leaned toward her and into the kitchen. "Want to join me?"

"No," she said, knowing he was only trying to razz her. "I'll leave that to Olivia."

"Touché." Then, with a smug smile, he strolled into the hall and entered the bathroom, shutting the knotty pine door.

Meredith waited until she heard the shower water running before bringing her fist to her mouth and muffling her cry. "*Grrrrr…*"

Derrick Albright was going to be the death of her—if she didn't kill him first.

The sooner Olivia arrived on the scene and she got those two ex-lovebirds together again, the better everything would be for everyone.

Including her.

CHAPTER SIX

Meredith opened the passenger door of Derrick's SUV, annoyed with herself for being annoyed with *him* for staying behind the wheel rather than coming around to open the door for her. He'd been sitting there waiting a least ten minutes while she primped that extra little bit necessary when meeting one's adversary's—slash—pretend fiancé's grandparents for the first time since the last big fiasco. Which had *not* been of her making, she reminded herself for the billionth time. And anyhow, this wasn't a date and she was not interested in Derrick.

Nope, not one bit.

He turned to study her as she buckled herself into her seat belt. She'd worn her favorite blue and pink flowery blouse, a long skirt, and pink high-heeled sandals. "You look nice." Did she imagine it, or did his gaze linger on her bare legs?

"Thanks." She flipped back her hair. "You do, too." He looked great in his simple jeans and a polo shirt the color of Blue Hill Bay, but then, he always did. All of the Albrights were gorgeous. It was like a lucky family curse.

He cranked the ignition, and then they were off. Backing out of his gravel drive and onto the main road. "So," he said, with one arm resting across the back of his seat as he navigated, taking peeks in his rearview mirror. "About that plan we were going to discuss at dinner—"

"I'm on it," she said, gaining confidence as she voiced her idea out loud. "I think Olivia should get invited to the christening."

He sent her a sideways glance. "That's kind of last minute. Seeing as how the christening's on Sunday."

"Better late than never."

His brow furrowed. "I don't know, Mer. We'd have to clear things with Sofia and William first, and this is happening awfully fast."

"I *wanted* to give it the whole summer," she reminded him. "You're the one who insisted on ten days. Rethinking that?"

He shook his head. "Nope. Honestly, I'd rather get both things over with," he said, referring to seeing Olivia again as well as to putting up with her as a houseguest she guessed.

"You sure know how to make a girl feel wanted."

"Trust me on this," he said. "When I want a woman, she's very happy about it."

"Ha ha." Meredith lowered her window, feeling a sudden heatwave in the SUV. Derrick had a really high opinion of himself and his manly attributes. That was evidenced by how he'd strutted around in front of her with his shirt off and his not-so-thinly-veiled allusion to all that supposed afternoon action in his bedroom.

But if he was such a catch, where was the woman in his life? She was thinking up a pithy reply when her cell phone rang with an all-too-familiar ringtone. *Ugh. Not now.*

"Hi, Mom," she said, knowing that if she didn't answer, her mom would call several more times until she did. She hadn't played any of her mom's earlier voicemails. In part, because she hadn't had time, but also because she'd been too afraid to. "What's going on?"

She had to hold the phone out from her ear when her mom shouted. "That's what I want to know! Your father is apoplectic over this. Living in sin in Maine?" Meredith cringed when she threw in some Spanish. "Is he even Catholic?"

Meredith angled away from Derrick's curious gaze, holding her cell to her ear on the other side. "Let me call you back later. Okay?"

"No-kay," her mom said stubbornly. "We need to discuss this now. You made the news."

"In Miami?" she asked, dumbfounded.

"In Boston. Your Titi Clarita's ex-stepdaughter Liana saw the story in Gloria Rafael's online gossip column. There was even a video clip! Of a very handsome man standing in the door of his cabin. It looked a little rustic, though. Bare bones. I hope you're not staying there."

Derrick leaned forward as he made a right turn and she shifted farther away from him in her seat as they traversed a low stone bridge. The sun had dipped down in the sky, sending a pretty purple haze across the water.

"Mom," she whispered. "Now's not the time."

Somehow this didn't deter her. "What kind of man is this Derrick Albright?" She could hear her dad complaining in the background, egging her on. "He didn't even ask for your hand."

"That is so last century!" Meredith hissed.

"That is so our culture." She sounded indignant.

"No, not anymore."

"I'd like to see you look your father in the eye and tell him that."

"Look," Meredith said, attempting to placate her. "We're on our way somewhere—"

"You're not staying with him?" Her mom sounded panicked. "Alone?"

"I'm a thirty-year-old woman."

"With apparently very little sense."

Meredith sighed. "I'm hanging up now."

"What's the address?"

"What?" Meredith asked, horrified. "*No*."

"That's Blue Hill, Maine, right?"

"Goodbye, Mom!" she said, ending the call.

She'd never expected her folks to learn about this, but of course they had. And now she was in a bigger mess than ever. But she was great at thinking on her feet. She'd come up with a good story to tell her parents and get back with them in the morning.

Her folks were always blowing things out of proportion, particularly her mom, who inserted herself more deeply into Meredith's personal life than necessary. It wasn't Meredith's fault that her mom hadn't handled *her* affairs to her own satisfaction, but Meredith was constantly paying for Dolores's perceived youthful shortcomings.

"What was that all about?" Derrick asked with wide eyes.

Meredith's face burned hot. "Family."

• • •

They arrived at the Albrights' summer place before sunset, snaking down the familiar blueberry bush-hedged drive. At the end of it, a stately three-story house sat on a lush green lawn overlooking Blue Hill Bay. She'd almost forgotten how spectacular this place was. When she stepped from the SUV, the scenery took her breath away. No wonder this had become the destination-wedding location of choice for Derrick's siblings. The view was far-reaching, all the way to Cadillac Mountain, and the accommodations plush and cozy.

Grandmother Margaret exited the big house, heading toward the drive. The trim, gray-haired woman wore a smart powder blue pants suit that fit her personality to a T.

"Meredith," she said without smiling, and Meredith got the sudden urge to run. She'd been nuts to think she could come here and convince the Albrights to be on her side.

The senior Albrights, especially.

Then, the older woman stunned her by pulling her into a stiff hug. "Good to see you," she said. "Under better circumstances. At least let's hope they're better."

Meredith awkwardly returned the hug. "Mrs. Albright, so great to see you, too."

Margaret arched an eyebrow, gripping Meredith's arms. "Derrick says you have news?"

"Oh, um…yes!" She bit her bottom lip. "It's something very encouraging, actually. About Olivia."

"Olivia?" Margaret asked with surprise.

Just then, Grandpa Chad emerged from around the corner of the house. He'd apparently been in the rose garden because he wore gloves and held garden sheers, along with a clipped bouquet of pretty dark red buds. Meredith couldn't help but smile at his elegantly disheveled appearance in a dress shirt, suit slacks, and a matching vest.

His grin was broad and genuine. "Why, Meredith!"

"Hi there, Mr. Albright," she called as he drew nearer.

"We heard you were in town."

"More like, saw it on the television," Margaret announced. Though she tried to sound disapproving, Meredith caught the hint of good humor in the remark.

Grandmother Margaret's bark was sometimes worse than her bite, and she apparently could be a caring woman. Above all things, she valued her family.

"Grandmother," Derrick interceded. "I already told you that whole thing was a mistake."

"A really big mix-up," Meredith hastily agreed. "Super huge."

"Yes, that's what you said." Margaret eyed her grandson. "We can't wait to hear the explanation."

"I'm sure it's a good one," Chad responded jovially before giving Meredith a nod. "I'm afraid the hugs will have to wait."

She laughed at his outstretched hands. "What pretty roses."

"Some of our finest this year," Margaret told her.

"Where do you want these?" Chad asked his wife.

"They'll make a nice centerpiece for the dining table, don't you think?"

"Splendid idea." He cocked his chin toward the house. "Shall we take this party inside?"

When they began walking, Meredith turned to Margaret. "Please put me to work."

"Oh, I intend to," Margaret said. "You can make the salad."

Chad glanced at Derrick. "You can help with the grilling, if you don't mind."

"Happy to."

They reached the stoop and his grandparents walked inside first, with Meredith and Derrick following. Grandpa Chad beckoned Derrick into the library to show off a new sailing book and Meredith trailed Margaret into the blueberry-themed country kitchen.

She glanced around the bright and airy room. "Should I get to chopping?"

"Not yet." Margaret checked the clock. "I made the twice-baked potatoes earlier and they need to warm up in the oven. The boys will take care of the steaks. Why don't you make up the salad when they start the fire?"

"All right."

"In the meantime…" Margaret pulled two wine-glasses from the rack above the counter and turned to her. "Wine?" She glanced into the dining room which connected with the den. "Or, would you like something stronger from the bar?"

"Wine sounds great."

Margaret handed her a bottle of pinot noir.

"Mind doing the honors?" she asked, producing a corkscrew from a drawer beside the sink. Through the window above it, Meredith spied the edge of the garden path that led to the guesthouse where she had stayed last summer. While there had been lots of stressful things about that week, there'd been good times, as well.

Meredith took the corkscrew from Margaret and opened the wine. "I know you've made things up with Hope," she said, referring to Brent's wife.

"Jackie, too." Margaret nodded. "And their mother sent a very nice fruit basket."

Meredith drew in a deep breath. "I want to apologize, too, for having a part in it."

"That was a strange time," Margaret said. "But there were happy moments, too."

"I was just thinking that."

"Oh?" Grandmother Margaret held out her wineglass for Meredith to fill it.

"Your tea party, for one," Meredith said, recalling the ladies-only sherry-drinking event. "That was loads of fun."

Margaret chuckled. "That boat party, too."

Meredith poured herself some wine, giggling. "And, the sleepover! Wow. What a shocker we got the next morning."

"What a shocker the *boys* got." Margaret's blue eyes twinkled and she chuckled.

Meredith nearly snorted wine through her nose, remembering her manic exodus from the house when Derrick appeared, catching her in her PJs and mud mask. With the men away for the night at Derrick's cabin, the women had planned a bachelorette party for the bride. They hadn't counted on the guys returning at the crack of dawn and discovering the aftermath.

"Sounds like the party's already started in here," Derrick said, entering from the hall.

Chad came up behind him. "I see you've opened the pinot," he said to Margaret.

"Yeah, it's really good," Meredith replied, taking a sip.

"I'll take some of this, too." Chad poured himself a glass.

Everyone headed to the den where Derrick fixed his own drink, a scotch, at the bar.

Margaret gazed out through the French doors facing the bay. "Why don't we have our drinks on the porch? It's a lovely warm evening."

They all filed onto the porch with Derrick holding back the door.

When Meredith hesitated, he motioned for her to go on ahead of him. "After you."

She raised an eyebrow. Seems like he could be a gentleman when he wanted to. "Thanks, Derrick," she said, sashaying past him and out into the pleasant evening.

Grandmother Margaret considered Meredith and then her grandson. "So, when do we get the story?"

"No need to put things off," Chad added. "We can chat over cocktails."

Meredith forced herself to smile. Hopefully Derrick would keep up the gentlemanly thing and take the lead in this. "Yes. Let's."

CHAPTER SEVEN

Derrick watched as Meredith squirmed like a fish on a line. He hated to think that he was getting a kick of out her discomfort, but she'd gotten herself into this mess. He couldn't wait to see how she got herself out. *Great at smoothing things over. Ha.*

"Well, it's all sort of crazy," she said, "to tell you the truth."

Grandpa Chad swirled his wine. "We've had our fair share of 'crazy' this past year."

"Yes," his grandma agreed. "Probably not much would surprise us at this point."

"You don't have a twin sister?" his grandpa asked suddenly and Meredith shook her head.

"No, no. It's nothing like that."

Derrick sipped from his scotch, savoring its peaty goodness and slow-burning warmth. They sat on his grandparents' large covered back porch overlooking the lawn and the bay beneath it. A stone patio housing a firepit was situated between the main house and the rocky cliffs overhanging the water, where the sun sank low on the horizon.

Grandpa Chad's gas grill had been positioned on the patio not far from a set of outdoor chairs. Derrick would fire that up later. For the time being he was enjoying the heat getting generated right here. Meredith was in the hotseat and he was curious about how she would handle it.

"Meredith's an only child," he told his grand-parents.

She stared at him in surprise. "How do you know that?"

Derrick shrugged. "You told me last summer."

"Oh," she said, appearing perplexed.

Actually she hadn't. Brent had. But that was only after Derrick had commented on Meredith acting like a spoiled only child. Brent had retorted that, even if she was an only child, she wasn't spoiled in his opinion. Then he'd ribbed Derrick, intimating that he was the one who'd been coddled, as the youngest Albright boy.

Derrick knew that was a lie. He hadn't been cut any extra slack. In some ways, more had been expected of him in keeping up with his older brothers. Growing up, they'd all had their differences along the way. As time moved on, they'd learned to sort those out.

He noted the lull in the conversation and attempted to fill it. "It's really pretty interesting how everything happened. That onslaught of reporters showing up at my cabin. Meredith can explain." He took a swig of scotch and saw the sky growing darker, and not just because night was rolling in but heavy rain clouds hovered above, portending a coming storm.

Grandpa Chad spoke in encouraging tones. "Go ahead, Meredith. You were saying?"

"Yeah, um." She set down her wine. "So, you both know I'm a matchmaker in Boston?"

"Yes," his grandma said. "It was splashed all over the news."

"Plus, we remember that from last year," Grandpa Chad said more politely.

"Okay. So, what I mean is…" She stared helplessly at Derrick, but this wasn't his wheelhouse. It was hers.

"*Not on your life*," he mouthed when his grandparents weren't looking.

Meredith flipped back her hair, his grandparents' interested gazes still on her. "My matchmaking show. It's been going really well! We've just taped our one hundredth episode."

"That's wonderful," Grandmother Margaret said. "Such a landmark."

"Yes," Grandpa Chad agreed. "Congratulations." He raised his wineglass in a toast, and Meredith used this as an opening.

"Let's not celebrate yet." She smiled mysteriously. "There could be more."

"What do you mean?" Grandmother Margaret asked her.

"*Well*…" Meredith drew out the word. "Things are still up in the air, but I'm hopeful." She gave a small squeal, unable to contain her excitement. "My show might get syndicated."

"That's fabulous!" his grandma said.

"Might." Meredith grimaced. "It all depends."

Grandmother Margaret's eyebrows arched. "On what?"

This was taking a tortuous amount of time and Derrick was getting hungry, so he decided to hurry things along. "On Mer proving her matchmaking abilities." He viewed her playfully. "Personally."

"Mer?" Grandpa Chad asked him.

"It's sort of a little nickname your grandson has for me," she said, her cheeks flushed.

Derrick couldn't help but like having this effect on her. She was so easy to rile up, particularly when she deserved it.

Grandpa Chad surveyed Derrick with a curious air. "How cute."

"Anyhow," Derrick said. "Mer was on this talk show where she was asked about her love life. And since she doesn't have one—"

"Oh no?" Grandmother Margaret's face hung in a frown. "Oh dear."

"That's nothing to be ashamed of," Grandpa Chad interceded.

"It is if you hang out your shingle as a love expert." Derrick chuckled and his grandparents shook their heads.

"Derrick," Grandmother Margaret said.

He slunk down in his chair. "Sorry," he said, not meaning it.

"Anyhow," Meredith continued. "The whole point is that Tanya—"

"Tanya?" Grandmother Margaret asked. "You mean, *Talk Time* Tanya? Oh! I love that show." She read Meredith's expression and changed tack. "I mean—used to."

"Right," Meredith said, seeming to steel her nerves. "That Tanya. Anyway," she continued, "Tanya asked me about the man I was involved with, and since I didn't have anyone, I sort of accidentally blurted out something about a boatbuilder." She swallowed hard. "In Maine."

His grandparents blinked and exchanged glances.

Then Meredith sheepishly added, "Accidents… happen?"

"Why Derrick?" Chad wanted to know.

"Yes," Margaret added. "Why him?"

Her doe-like eyes grew wide. "I panicked. Sheer panicked! It was like my head was all mixed up and I couldn't think straight. I knew, just knew, that if I said I wasn't involved with anybody that would look bad to the network. Not to mention to my clients and my viewers."

"And to her gossip column fans," Derrick said. "She got a mention on Gloria."

"Not Gloria Rafael?" Grandmother Margaret appeared pleased. "Oh my."

Meredith's jaw dropped and she turned to Derrick. "Were you eavesdropping on my conversation with my mom?"

"Your mother's here?" Grandpa Chad inquired, looking confused.

"No," Meredith said, a bit dazed. "In Miami."

Grandmother Margaret remained focused on an earlier piece of information. The one where Meredith had intimated that she and he were involved.

"And so you…lied?" she asked casually. "About Derrick?"

"It was a white lie," Meredith whimpered. "And honestly the first answer I came up with when put on the spot. Besides that, I never mentioned him by name. The press must have done some digging and put a few things together."

His grandparents gaped at him, no doubt astounded that he'd landed in the middle of this.

He shrugged. "What can I say? I have a way with women. I'm apparently impossible to forget."

"Well yes," Grandpa Chad said. "Except for by Olivia. She got over you pretty quick." He lifted a finger. "Did I hear someone mention her earlier?"

"Yes!" Meredith said. "That was me!"

"What does Olivia have to do with any of this?" Grandmother Margaret asked.

Derrick tried to sound blustery, because he knew he'd have to come out with it sooner or later. "Mer, here, thinks I'm not over her."

His grandpa studied him, then asked solemnly, "Aren't you?"

"Well, I…" Now, it was his turn to squirm, and it wasn't nearly as much fun as seeing Meredith do it. "*Thought* I was."

"Now, he's not so sure," Meredith supplied, stepping in. "That's how I plan to help out."

His grandparents seemed stymied, and Derrick couldn't blame them.

This was a lot to follow.

So Meredith took the lead. "I've offered Derrick my professional matchmaking services to help win back Olivia."

"Win back?" Margaret gasped at Derrick. "Is that what you want, grandson?"

He lifted a shoulder. "Maybe?"

Chad rubbed his cheek. "I always did like Olivia." He angled his wineglass toward Margaret. "You said you liked her, too."

"I did like her, Chad, but that was before she behaved so badly."

"We were both young," Derrick said. "And

bullish. Too prideful to admit we were making mistakes."

Margaret laid a hand across her heart. "Oh dear. You do still care for her, don't you?"

"After all these years," Grandpa Chad mused. "Still carrying a torch."

He wasn't sure about *that*, more like a very dim candle of curiosity and an openness to seeing where things would go—if they went anywhere at all—but his grandparents plowed forward before he could correct them.

"Well then, that's very good of you," Grandmother Margaret told Meredith. "To want to help our Derrick."

"Oh, she's not doing it out of the goodness of her heart," he told them.

Meredith shot daggers at him with her eyes before smiling politely at his grandparents. "The whole mix-up thing with the press? We've decided to let it ride."

"Let it ride?" Margaret looked incredulous.

She hesitated and glanced at Derrick. "Not for very long. Just long enough for me not to be made a fool of in public. Once Olivia's here and she and Derrick are back together, I intend to excise myself from the situation and leave Blue Hill."

"And you'll still get your television contract?" Grandmother Margaret asked her.

"I'm hoping so," Meredith said. "Anyway, that's more or less how it happened. I'm so, so sorry for dragging Derrick and your family into it, but hopefully it will all be over soon, and everyone will be happy with the outcome."

Margaret mulled over everything she'd heard. "How long do you and Derrick plan to keep up this charade?"

"Just for two weeks," Meredith ventured.

Derrick shot her a stony look. "Ten *days*. That's what we agreed."

"And Olivia?" Margaret asked. "How will she get included?"

"I was hoping we could invite her to the christening?"

"That will have to be cleared with William and Sofia first," Grandmother Margaret said.

"Yes, definitely," Meredith said.

Grandpa Chad rubbed his chin. "This is going to be the most interesting baptism I've ever attended."

There was a long pause when nobody spoke and there was complicity in their silence. Derrick knew his grandparents weren't opposed to speaking their minds, especially his grandmother. If she was against Meredith's plan for bringing him and Olivia back together, she didn't say so, and she would have.

Maybe he should take the possibility of exploring things with her more seriously.

"Well, all right," his grandmother finally said with a vacant stare. "Who's hungry?"

"Me!" Derrick held up his hand. "Should I go start the fire?"

"Yes, please," Grandpa Chad said.

Meredith got to her feet along with the others. "I'll come help with that salad," she told Grandmother Margaret.

The older woman stared into her eyes. "This

can't be a secret among the others. Everyone in the family has to know the truth."

"Absolutely," Meredith said. "I agree."

"Well, that's something," Grandmother Margaret said.

As they headed for the kitchen, Derrick tried not to notice the enticing sway of her hips or the whiff he caught of her floral shampoo and that honeysuckle perfume. Much better to focus on their mission. If all went well with Meredith's plans, they'd both have something to celebrate soon. She'd secure that syndication deal and he might get to see Olivia again, maybe even get that second chance.

But when he stepped through the cloud of lingering scents Meredith left trailing behind her, all he could think of was the matchmaker from Boston who'd landed on his doorstep this afternoon.

CHAPTER EIGHT

Derrick tossed Meredith a pillow and she caught it. As much as he loved his grandparents, he was glad to be back in his own space and past that uncomfortable conversation on the porch. He'd really expected Meredith to crash and burn, but he had to hand it to her. She'd done amazingly. "One pillow enough, or do you need two?" He'd already pulled out the sleeper sofa and set a stack of sheets and blankets on a chair.

"I'll take another if you've got one."

Thunder rumbled outside. The storm he'd predicted earlier was on its way.

"Sure. Just let me go and grab it."

When he was halfway to the linen closet she said, "I think things went pretty well at your grandparents'. All things considered."

He waited to answer after nabbing the spare pillow off a high shelf and shutting the door. "All things considered," he agreed. "Yeah."

"I guess they really like Olivia."

"Always did."

They'd spent most of dinner reminiscing about Olivia's good points. Her upbeat spirit and the way she'd gotten along with mostly everyone in the family. Notably, nobody mentioned Sally, and Derrick had never understood his sister's problem with his ex. Maybe he'd ask her about it. For their part, Grandmother Margaret and Grandpa Chad told him if trying again with Olivia was what he wanted, they would fully support him. They knew his parents, Parker and Elsa, would, too. Well, his dad for sure at least. When he reflected on it, his mom had always been a little more standoffish with Olivia. Maybe she and Sally shared some secret he didn't know about and he'd finally learn what that was.

Meredith began making the bed, so he set the second pillow aside to help her, stretching the fitted sheet over a corner at the head of the mattress.

"Your grandparents are very sweet," she said, across the way from him. Although she'd met them before, she'd apparently seen a new side to them in light of this Olivia proposition. "It's obvious that they care the world for you. I expected them to act more surprised, or you know"—she shrugged— "protest."

"They're good people who basically want what's right for me. They've always had our backs, mine and my brothers' and sister's, ever since we were little kids. How about your grandparents?" he asked. "Do you see them much?"

"Not as much as I'd like to. My dad's folks passed away a few years ago, and my mom's parents live in Puerto Rico. Mom and Titi Clarita keep threatening to move them to Miami, but they won't have it. They still have a lot of family and friends in San Juan."

"Titi Clarita?"

"Oh, sorry. My mom's sister. In Spanish we sometime say 'titi' instead of 'tía.' It's an endearing way of saying aunt. Kind of like 'auntie' in English, I guess."

"Do you speak to them in Spanish?"

"My parents and aunt? Not usually. To my grandparents, yes."

"I find foreign languages fascinating," he said.

She chuckled. "Like Latin or Greek, you mean?"

He enjoyed the sparkle in her dark brown eyes. "I also speak French."

"I noticed," she said with a grin. Some of the earlier animosity they'd shared had eased. Maybe it was the relief of having a plan and getting over the hurdle of talking to his grandparents.

They finished with the fitted sheet and she shook out the flat one with a snap. It fluttered above the sofa bed before settling down as thunder boomed above them.

"That's a pretty big storm brewing," she told him. "Looks like we got back just in time."

"Yeah."

Outside the darkened windows, lightning crackled across the sky.

He unfolded a blanket and handed the other end to her and they placed it on top of the flat sheet, tucking both under.

"You don't have to help me, you know. I know how to make a bed." Then she added lightly, "Unlike others around here."

He didn't mind the ribbing and was happy to tease her back. "Ah well, I do make my bed," he argued. "Sometimes."

"Oh really? Like when? Once in a blue moon?"

He laughed. "I do it whenever I change the linens."

"Which is when?"

He arched an eyebrow. "Whenever I have a guest over." That ought to get under her skin. She seemed to get prickly at the thought of him being with other women, which made zero sense since she was plotting to get him back together with Olivia.

Her forehead rose. "A female guest, you mean?" She blew out a breath, looking exasperated. "Seriously, Derrick."

Yep. That hit a nerve. But why? "What?" He placed a hand on his chest. "You asked."

"You're right," she said. "Maybe I shouldn't have." She busied herself with the blanket, tugging and smoothing wrinkles and creases that didn't exist.

He sighed. "Look, Mer. I wasn't expecting this."

"No, but you're going to make the most of it, aren't you?"

"I don't know what you mean?"

She put her hands on her hips. "Leaving me out there on my own tonight—with your grandparents."

What? "I was with you."

"Uh, yeah. Physically maybe, but not in spirit."

"That's not true."

"It *is* true." Her eyes widened. "You're still upset with me, aren't you? From all that stuff that happened last summer."

This was an ambush. He didn't know if she was hinting about what had happened with the wedding, or during their moment alone together on the dock. The first one yeah, he was not so thrilled about. The second one, though, wasn't worth thinking about.

His neck burned hot with the lie.

She blinked like she'd just put something together. "Is that what your striptease was all about?"

He gawked at her. "Striptease? Woman, I live
here."

"So you can just take your clothes off whenever
you want to?"

"Pretty much, yeah." He shook his head. "Look.
You had your chance to sleep in the bedroom.
You'd get a whole lot more privacy in there."

"Thanks, but no thanks." She cast a disgusted
glance in that direction. "Besides that, you took
your shirt off out here."

He threw his hands up. "So sue me! I was hot."

She scrutinized him oddly. "You really do believe that about yourself, don't you?"

Ouch. Way to bruise a man's ego. "What? That
I'm hot?" he asked incredulous.

She rolled her eyes.

So what was the big deal? He couldn't help it
that the ladies liked him. Most ladies, anyway.
Except for, apparently, her. "Since when have you
cared what I think?" he asked.

"I don't." She punched a pillow and pushed it
into a pillowcase with all her might. "That's just the
point."

He shoved his pillow into its pillowcase with
extra force, too, wondering about that other thing
she'd said. "In that case, why don't you explain why
you believe I'm upset?" he asked with an agitated
air.

She squared her shoulders. "You were there, too,
Derrick. Don't act like you weren't."

"Okay, fine! If you must know, I wasn't so happy

about what you and your friends did, no." Which was true, but other things about her bothered him, too. Like how she could never let things go until they were full-fledged brawling. Verbally anyway.

"I apologized to your grandmother." She paused a beat. "And earlier to Brent."

"Oh goodie for you." He stared at her and waited. "You haven't said as much to me."

Her jaw dropped. "Is that what you want? An apology?"

They both tossed their pillows onto the sofa bed at the same time and he met her eyes. "Maybe."

"All right. Well then." She licked her lips. "I'm sorry." In a way she sounded sincere but her eyes seemed to be masking something. "Very sorry, I mean it. For what went down with the wedding. Not about anything else, though."

Of course she couldn't resist that caveat. "No?"

"No."

"Nice, Mer," he said in combative tones. "Well, I'm not sorry for anything else, either."

She held his gaze for an electric moment. "Great. That makes two of us."

What did that mean? That she didn't regret their almost-kiss? Or that she didn't regret them stopping it?

Whatever. She could think what she wanted. He never wished for any of that.

What a disaster that would have been. Him and Meredith.

A total disaster. Unless. She was a little more like she'd been that night.

Tender. Sweet. Enticing. His pulse stuttered.

If he'd never seen that glimpse of her, his life would be so much easier.

But he had.

So it wasn't.

She arranged the blanket on the bed, grumbling to herself. "It's been a long day. I think I'm going to turn in soon."

"I hear that," he said. "I'm sure we both need a break—"

Her chin jerked up. "From each other?"

He held up one hand. "You said that, not me."

"No, but you thought it."

"What are you now, the mind police?"

She gritted her teeth. "Why do you always have to be so contrary?"

He laughed. "That's a good one. Coming from the person who's about as contrary as they get." His voice rose to stay above the tenor of the rain outside.

Hers did as well. "Me? Contrary?"

"Yes. You."

"You're the contrary one, *Derrick*."

"You see? There you go again."

Her eyes flashed. "That was a trap!"

"Which you laid yourself and then walked straight into!"

Meredith huffed. "Let's hope you're not this difficult around Olivia," she said. "At this rate, you'll never win her back."

"I'm not trying to win *you* back." He let this sink in. "Or even win you at all."

"Good thing." She flattened him with her stare. "It would be a losing battle."

Winds howled outside, sending the choppy surf sloshing against the dock.

His breath came in ragged fits and starts but he didn't answer at first. *As if* he'd even consider going after her. He'd have to be out of his head.

He scooped up the extra quilt. "Going to need this?"

"Don't think so," she said. "I hear it's warm in Maine."

He paused by the stove. "That's *hot* in Blue Hill."

Heavy rain streaked the cabin's windows, pelting the tin roof.

"Yeah well, you know what they say. If you can't take the heat—"

"You're right," he said coolly. "It's way past my bedtime."

She bent her fingers in a wave. "Nighty-night."

"Sleep tight," he groused before turning away. "Don't let the bedbugs bite." Then he added on purpose. "Literally."

She gasped, goggling at the sofa bed.

"There are bedbugs in there?"

"Only a few."

• • •

Derrick would have paid big bucks to have a snapshot of Meredith's face when he'd mentioned those bedbugs. Naturally, he didn't have them. But if she wanted to worry about the possibility that he did, that was her business. He hoped she wouldn't sleep a wink.

The nerve she had, upending his day from the very beginning. Then, when things had finally begun to settle down between them, she'd gotten him all irritated again. Was it possible for Meredith to *not* irritate him during the course of a twenty-four-hour period?

Probably not.

He sighed.

It was going to be a long ten days.

He shut the door to his room, glad for the quiet. Then the thunder started up again with more wind and heavy rain. How on earth did she have a matchmaker show? She must project a very different persona before the camera and to her clients than she presented to him. A more diplomatic and agreeable one.

He nabbed his laptop off his dresser and carried it to his bed, fluffing a pillow behind his back. The web browser was right where he left it when she'd shown up at his door, pot roast in hand—her webpage. No longer looking for a way to contact her, he focused on the information displayed on the screen. What he found surprised him. She had a super glossy website, probably set up by her television station, or maybe she'd paid to have it done herself.

There were all sorts of stylized photos of her grinning broadly on the set of *Matched Up*, her arms around satisfied clients, meaning the couples she'd brought together. Her set looked really goofy, all pink and red and girly with glittery heart mobiles dangling everywhere.

The pretend living room that served as its centerpiece contained a big white couch holding heart-shaped pillows. The fluffy white rug in front of it looked like it was made from fake animal fur, and the glass coffee table held a stack of books and a few coffee mugs. In the midst of all that, Meredith conducted an interview with a woman he'd seen in another photo paired with a man.

Meredith had told him on their ride home that Beth had spoken to their station manager, and he'd agreed to exert his influence to hold back the press. No sense letting media hounds sniff around if they might blow her engagement cover story. Jerry was apprised of the whole situation and very happy to go along with Meredith's grand plan, since *Matched Up* getting syndicated would benefit him, too.

Derrick scanned Meredith's bio, seeing she'd been doing this for four years, and then clicked on her contact page. There were links to her social media there. He went over and perused her various accounts, gleaning fairly quickly that most of her fans were in Boston.

Wait. Was that a photo of his cabin?

It was. There was also a short video clip, showing him looking disgruntled on his doorstep. Both had been uploaded by @GloriaRafael, who'd tagged @MatchmakerMeredith in her posts. Great, so now he was a celebrity, too. On a micro-scale.

Maybe it was a good thing Meredith wasn't syndicated yet.

Otherwise, he wouldn't be getting a moment's peace.

He closed his laptop and his gut clenched. Meredith was very accomplished at her job and he'd done nothing but pick on her about it. He'd also called her contrary when he'd been acting pretty contrary himself. She obviously wasn't abrasive with everybody, not from the satisfied looks on the faces of the clients on her show. Nor from their glowing reviews and testimonials. He wasn't proud of his behavior, but he could apologize for it.

He carried his laptop to his dresser and set it down, then he saw light streaming in from the kitchen under his bedroom door. Either Meredith was still up or she'd forgotten to turn the kitchen light off. He decided to crack open his door and check.

When he did, he spied Meredith snuggled up under the covers and sleeping soundly already. She really must have been exhausted from her long day. Not to mention all the grief that he'd given her. He frowned, knowing that he could do better.

He stole quietly into the kitchen and switched off the light.

The rain had let up but still lightly pinged against the window. He'd left his bedroom door slightly ajar and dim lamplight glowed from behind it, bathing the cabin's floors and fanning out toward the sofa bed.

Meredith mumbled and rolled onto her side and her long curly hair swept across her pillow. She looked just like a sleeping fairytale princess. His heart warmed and then it gave a funny little twist.

Nope. He was *not* interested in Meredith Galanes.

An image came back to him of them standing face-to-face on his grandparents' dock in the moonlight but then he quickly pushed it away, realizing he needed to put that episode in perspective. A, nothing had happened, and B, that was in the past.

He crept back into his bedroom and quietly shut the door, regaining his focus.

He needed to let all of that go.

Sure right. Like that was so simple.

With Meredith here, it was getting less and less "simple" all the time.

CHAPTER NINE

Meredith rolled over in bed and pulled the pillow over her head.

Knock, knock, knock. Bang, bang!

Seriously? It was barely daylight. Between the thunderstorm and the lumpy mattress, she's scarcely slept a wink. Then there was that little concern about bedbugs. She kept imagining being bitten all night long, miniature phantom fangs feasting on her flesh.

Thanks a lot, Derrick.

Where was he anyway? And why wasn't he answering the door? She was groggy and grumpy and still not completely over his rudeness last night.

She was also annoyed with herself for getting mad at him. Not just about the contrary business but because she hadn't liked thinking about his previous "guests" or whatever he'd called the women he'd had over here. What did it matter to her? He was a grown man, and not her man. Far from it. Good thing, too. He drove her bananas.

The knocking happened again and Meredith pulled the pillow away from her face to listen. What if Jerry's contact couldn't help and it was the paparazzi, back for another try?

Then she heard another noise: the shower streaming in the bathroom, and there was a weird humming sound. No, not humming. Singing! It sounded like an Irish folksong. Or maybe an old sea tune. Yeah, like sailors sing. Begrudgingly, she admitted his voice was pretty good. She tried really hard not to think about what he looked like in the shower. But she'd already seen the top half of him naked. So—

Knock-knock-knock. "Hel-lo!"

Meredith shot up ramrod straight into a sitting position. *No.* Couldn't be.

But she'd know that voice anywhere.

"María Josefina! It's me! Titi Clarita. Are you in there?"

Meredith pressed her palms to her temples, her head spinning. Her aunt was in Blue Hill. But why? She scrambled out of bed dressed in the baggy football jersey she wore as a nightshirt.

She tiptoed to the door and peered through its tiny peephole.

Titi Clarita stood there, birdlike, on the stoop, her pert angular chin tipped up and her big, dark eyes opened wide beneath enormous pasted-on eyelashes. She had short curly dark hair and a petite frame and wore jeans and a paisley top. A gigantic designer suitcase was beside her. She lifted her fist to knock again but Meredith jerked open the door.

"*Titi Clarita,*" she said in hushed tones. "What are you doing here?"

"Nice to see you, too." Her aunt gave her a curt perusal and brushed past her, dragging in her rolling bag by its large strap. She shut the door behind her then wheeled on Meredith.

"Your mom sent me. She wants me to put an end to this disaster at once."

"What disaster?"

"You're living in sin, *mija*. Here." She fished a small paper sack out of her purse that was stamped with the seal of a cathedral. "Take this, and say whatever."

Meredith peeked into the bag, finding a box with a price sticker still on it. "What is it?"

"A rosary." She shook her head. "You really have been away from the church for too long." She shrugged. "Then again, so have I."

The water cut off in the shower and Meredith gaped at her aunt. "You can't stay here. You've got to go!"

"Go? But I've only just arrived." She heard whistling from the bathroom, then another chorus of bawdy belted-out song. "Is that him? He sounds handsome."

"How can someone sound—? Never mind." She took her aunt by the shoulders and gently spun her around. "You need to leave before Derrick comes out here."

Titi Clarita blinked. "That's no kind of welcome."

"You weren't invited."

"Yes, I was. By your mom."

"This isn't anything like it seems. Look," she said, attempting to assuage her aunt's fears. "I'm sleeping out here—see? In the living room."

"There are two pillows," Titi Clarita noted reasonably. "Both appear used."

Meredith sighed. "Please go, and I'll call you. Explain everything, very, very soon."

The door to the bathroom cracked open and a

column of steam escaped from behind it.

"But I'm dead tired," Titi Clarita said. "I caught a late-night flight to Boston and then this morning drove all the way here."

"There are some nice hotels in Bangor. That's not too far away. I'll go online and make you a reservation."

"What? No."

"*Sí, sí.* Pu-leeze," she said, lightly shoving her aunt. "I'll text you with the details if you just g—"

"Good morning," Derrick said, toweling off his head. He had a second towel wrapped around his waist and his sexy chest still glistened with moisture. He did a double take and stared at Titi Clarita and then again at Meredith. "Uh. Who are you?"

"She… She's a reporter!" Meredith said.

"What?" Titi Clarita stared at her aghast. "No, I'm not."

"With a suitcase?" Derrick's eyebrows shot up. "A really big one, too." He scrutinized Meredith and she wanted to sink into the floor. "Wouldn't happen to be a relative of yours?"

Titi Clarita shook herself out of Meredith's grip and strolled right up to him. "I'm her aunt," she said. "Clarita Rincón. Here to help."

"Help?" His forehead creased. "How?"

She swept her hand around the cabin. "With all of this. The mess you and Marijose are making together."

"Marí-josé?"

"Of course, you probably call her María, or maybe María Josefina."

Derrick addressed Meredith and her cheeks

burned hot. "Mer?"

"It's my birth name. I don't use it."

"Which is such a shame," Clarita said. Then as an aside she added for Derrick's benefit, "My niece picked Meredith as her stage name, and her dad's still not over it."

"Anyway!" Meredith said. "My aunt was just leaving."

Derrick interceded. "Now that's not very hospitable, is it?" He smiled at Titi Clarita. "Where did you come from?"

"Miami. This is a busy time of year for Mariah, Meredith's parents. They own a catering company and June stays hopping with weddings." Derrick nodded and she continued. "I myself had a little more time. As it so happens, I'm between husbands."

"Between?" Derrick asked. "How many have there been?"

"Four," Clarita said smoothly at the same time Meredith said, "*Six*."

Clarita *tsked*. "Everyone knows that annulments don't count. And, anyway! I'm here about the two of you, and not me."

"Yeah, well," Derrick said. "I can't wait to hear more about that. In the meantime, let me put on some pants."

"Oh no, don't bother!" Clarita said as he entered his bedroom. "On my account."

Derrick grinned politely before shutting his door. "I'll be right back."

"Titi Clarita," Meredith scolded once Derrick had gone. "Were you actually hitting on him?"

"Of course not." She waved her slight hand. "I'm way over my cougaring stage."

. . .

Derrick tugged on his jeans and a T-shirt and slipped into his boat shoes, considering his new arrival. Word sure had spread fast about his and Meredith's "involvement." All the way down to Miami, first to her parents and now to her aunt. She probably had cousins who knew, too. He peeked out his window, seeing only the one extra car. It looked like a rental. Whew.

The media's presumption that he and Meredith were engaged had led to some interesting situations. Not the least of which was Meredith staying here. Now it seemed her aunt wanted to move in, too. What did he look like? The owner of the Blue Hill B&B?

Having Meredith here by herself wasn't going to be easy. Now things were doubly complicated with her Titi Clarita on the scene. It was hard to imagine Clarita actually staying here—with the three of them constantly bumping into each other. His cabin wasn't that big, and Meredith's gigantic personality was already making it feel crowded.

Derrick needed to come up with an alternate arrangement.

He returned to the kitchen where Meredith and Clarita were having coffee at the table. They stopped talking the moment they saw him.

"Mar—Eh, Meredith was telling me she'll be here nine more days?" the older woman said.

Derrick made himself a coffee using the machine on the counter. "That's our agreed timeline."

"And this is all about your ex, Olivia?"

"In part." He set the coffee to brew. "The other part has to do with your niece's goals."

"Hmm, yes. She told me." Clarita set down her cup to stare at Meredith. "Are you sure this is worth it? The deception? The subterfuge?"

"We're not deceiving anyone — important." Meredith swallowed hard. "And the press can believe what they want to until the second part of the story comes out."

Clarita appeared intrigued. "Second part?"

Derrick grabbed his finished coffee and approached the table. "That's when Olivia and I are supposedly back together, and Meredith gallantly explains to the world how she's stepping back from our 'relationship,'" he said, "out of respect for true love."

"And you expect to get a syndication deal out of this?" she asked Meredith.

Meredith sat up a little straighter. "Yes, I do."

Nobody asked her opinion, but Clarita seemed prepared to offer it anyway. "Well, it seems to me that the two of you are playing with fire."

"Fire?" Derrick and Meredith asked at once. He'd started to pull back a chair so he could sit at the table, but halted halfway.

"*Sí, fuego*," Clarita said. "Too much bending of the truth and someone's going to get burned."

Derrick dragged a hand down his face. "Hey," he said to Meredith. "Maybe she's right."

Meredith gave her aunt the side-eye. "*Titi Clarita*," she whispered. "*You're not helping*."

"Who says I'm not helping? Maybe I am, by stopping things from going any further."

"Ah, Derrick?" Meredith said. "Do you mind if I have a minute or two alone with my aunt?"

He forced a tight smile, glad to be excising himself from their family squabble. "Take all the time that you need," he said, gripping his mug. "I'll just head out to my workshop for a bit."

"What time are we leaving?" Meredith asked him as he prepared to go. Before they'd left his grandparents' house last night, they'd invited him and Meredith to return today for lunch. Sofia and William and their baby were expected late morning, so they would be there, too.

"Twelve fifteen or so." He cast a glance at Clarita. "You're welcome to join us. I'm sure my Grandmother Margaret won't mind. I can give her a call?"

"Oh, wouldn't that be nice?" Clarita asked and Meredith's eyes grew wide.

• • •

When it was just the two of them, Meredith said to her aunt, "Okay. Now that you know the true story, don't you think that you can go?"

"Not until things are resolved, I can't." Clarita wasn't just Meredith's aunt, she was also her godmother, which had made her extra protective of Meredith. But Meredith was a grown-up now. She didn't need Clarita looking after her.

"You remember that boy in high school, eh? Adolfo? You said he was mysteriously secretive. I said he was a member of a gang." She paused for emphasis. "And who was right?"

"You were, but—"

"Then there was that creeper in college."

"You mean my history professor?"

"*Sí*. I told you he wasn't asking you to be his class assistant because he admired your mind."

"Okay. Okay." Meredith heaved a breath. "I managed to get out of that."

"Because you were forewarned and forearmed. When he asked you back to his house to grade tests you said no."

"Ew. Stop."

"And then, when you started in broadcasting, there was that producer—"

"Okay, all right. I get it. But this situation now is like none of those. Derrick Albright's one of the good guys." She shifted in her seat. "I mean, apart from his big mouth and snarky attitude, he's a decent guy. Not anything like those others you mentioned."

"I never said that he was." Clarita looked her in the eye. "Who's to say you're not the one trying to take advantage?"

"Me?"

"Yes, you."

"But, my motives are—"

"Self-serving?"

"Pure. And really about helping Derrick."

"How do you know he even wants to get back together with his ex-wife?"

"He would have kicked me out yesterday if that wasn't true."

Clarita considered this. "Or maybe he is trying to help you?"

Meredith scoffed. "Derrick is not that altruistic. Trust me."

Her aunt shook her head and sighed. "Okay, fine. If you're right and he does want his ex-wife back, you think you can really do it? Reunite the two of them?"

"I've united dozens of couples over the past four years. All of them great and happy matches. It's true I won't know one hundred percent about Derrick and Olivia until I see them together. But, once I do—and believe that destiny is there—I'll find a way to help things along."

"Destiny, hmm." Clarita leaned forward and patted her on the cheek. "That's a sweet, idealistic thing to believe in." Then she surprised Meredith by standing from her chair and heading for the door.

Meredith grinned, a huge burden lifting. "You're leaving?"

"No," she said. "Just getting my bag. I'll want to freshen up before that luncheon." She grinned while Meredith stared at her flummoxed. "I packed just the right clothes!"

"Titi Clarita," Meredith said. "You don't want to stay here. Seriously. There are…" She glanced at the open sofa bed. "Limitations."

"Such as?"

"Only one bed! I mean, Derrick has his back there, but his room is a pigsty. Seriously, you don't want to even peek in there. You could get buried under an avalanche of dirty socks."

"What's wrong with the sofa bed? It looks big enough for two."

"It's uh—lumpy, and there are…bedbugs!"

Clarita's eyebrows twitched. "What?"

"I was scratching all night long."

"Oh!" Her aunt rubbed her upper arms. "Gross."

"Yeah. Exactly."

Clarita grabbed the strap on her rolling suitcase, eying the sofa bed with trepidation. "So, the bathroom's that way?" She looked very eager to get there.

"Uh—do you mind if I grab a shower first?" Meredith asked, because she wanted to make herself more presentable for a private chat with Derrick. Maybe he could help her figure out a polite way to get rid of her aunt. Surely, he didn't want Clarita hanging around and cramping his style. He evidently had trouble tolerating one person in her family. Meredith couldn't picture him eagerly entertaining two. "I'll be really, really fast!"

CHAPTER TEN

While her aunt was taking her turn in the bath-room, Meredith slipped into an animal print top and some white leggings, then hunted for her low-est pair of heels in her suitcase. She found her platform sandals with shimmering gold straps. They were cute enough and would have to do. Plus, they matched her dangly gold leaf earrings, which were more visible with her hair twisted into a topknot. It was a casual look, but probably about right for lunch. The Albrights didn't stand on formality— apart from three-piece-suit Grandpa Chad. And, underneath all that tweed, he was about as relaxed as they come.

She exited the cabin onto the deck to find puffy white clouds hanging high in the blue sky above. Sunshine glistened on the water and Derrick's rowboat tilted lazily in the breeze, bobbing back and forth on the waves. A ramshackle outbuilding stood on a patch of land to the far side of the gravel drive. She hadn't seen it before as she'd parked closer to the cabin and it was tucked behind some bayberry hedges.

The whir of an electric saw caught her ears, punctuating the sound of morning songbirds with its shrill whine. Derrick was apparently in there working on something and she was curious to learn what. Maybe another boat of some sort, although the man appeared to have plenty.

One side of the outbuilding was an open area covered by a slanted tin roof. She counted two kayaks, a canoe, and a small sunfish-style sailboat beneath it. Only the canoe appeared wooden and perhaps handmade. The others seemed to be right out of an outrigger's store and crafted from fiberglass. Meredith stepped off the deck and the saturated ground squished beneath her feet. Ugh. It had rained buckets last night and now the whole lawn was soaked.

She peered toward Derrick's workshop where the saw still buzzed. There was no walkway leading to it or even a simple path. Only a slightly more worn spot in the grass, indicating Derrick's normal trajectory between there and the cabin. Meredith shook out her shoulders and headed that way, her shoes sinking lower in the soggy earth with each new step.

Squish, squish—ew! This was disgusting. And now, nasty cold mud had seeped between her toes. It was too late to turn back now. She might as well get this over with and clean up later. She didn't want to change her pants, though, so she walked extra carefully so as not to cause any mud splatter, her elbows held high at her sides for balance.

"Hi there." Her chin jerked up and she saw Derrick standing on the threshold to his workshop, the door open behind him. He had goggles pushed up on the top of his head and appeared amused. "Just…what *are* you doing?"

"Coming out to talk to you," she said, mildly irritated. Both at his smug look and the mud, which—*noooo*—had just flicked tiny brown spots onto her lower pants legs. "What does it look like?"

He repressed a chuckle, annoying her further. "Um. Taking a mud bath?"

"Ever think of putting in a path?" she asked, getting closer.

"Ever think of not lying on television?"

Meredith twisted up her lips and stepped onto the small stoop outside his workshop door. "I thought we were past that."

"All right." He inched back, allowing her entry to the building. "Come on in."

"My shoes."

This time he laughed out loud, but in a good-hearted way. "This is a workshop, Mer. Not the Taj Mahal," he said, removing his goggles and hanging them on a hook. "A little more mud on the floor won't affect anything."

"What I meant was they're probably ruined."

"Your sandals won't wash?"

"I can try, but they're pretty high end."

"Designer? Hmm." He studied her feet, which were caked in mud. "Maybe you should have worn something more sensible."

"This is the most sensible pair I've got."

"Meaning the flattest?" he asked, studying the platform soles. "Okay," he said. "Noted."

What had he meant by that? Was he judging her?

He shrugged. "So, do you want to come in, or are you just planning to stand there in your ruined shoes?"

"Oh uh, sure." She needed to talk to him about her aunt and about their argument last night, too, but she decided to ease into it. Besides, she was curious to see what he'd been working on out here in his private little workshop.

Meredith dusted off her palms and entered the surprisingly roomy space, discovering it wasn't so little after all. The oblong room contained a couple of windows facing the woods on the far side, and both were cracked open. A workbench stood between them and a pegboard above it held all types of clamps and tools. Titi Clarita's second husband, Raul, had done a little woodworking, so she recognized some of the pieces.

A table saw sat on one side of the workbench and a huge miter saw on a folding stand lorded over the center of the room. A series of wooden planks of various lengths leaned against one wall, and the hull of a canoe balanced on two sawhorses near another.

"Wow," Meredith said. "This is quite a place."

"Thanks. I call it home."

"I thought your cabin was home."

"Nope." He fondly patted his workbench. "That's this place here."

She couldn't help but smile at his relaxed stance. Derrick seemed like a different person out here. Really in his element, surrounded by his projects and sawdust. That was easy to see.

"What are you working on?" she asked, noting several cut pieces of wood leaned up against the miter saw stand.

"This?" He hoisted a rectangular piece into his hands, appearing pleased that she'd asked. "Is the base of a cradle."

"Cradle?"

"It's for Julia."

The thought that he was making something for a baby unexpectedly melted her heart. She never would have imagined this of him. A boat, yeah. A cradle? Never. She examined the piece again, noting the wood's reddish-brown sheen. "Is this mahogany?"

Derrick grinned. "Cherry."

"Nice."

He flipped it over, showing her its underside. "The headboard and footboard will fit in on either end and this is where the slats will go." He indicated the narrow slots with his forefinger and Meredith's insides went gushy. A tough guy like him making a cradle revealed he had a softer side. It also showed he thought of others, and loved his little niece. This was a new element of Derrick she hadn't expected, and it made her wonder what else she'd missed.

He turned the flat piece back over and gently set it down, standing it on one end. "I'm going to have it done in time for the christening."

"How sweet. I didn't even know people used cradles anymore."

"They're not very practical," Derrick said, "since they can only be used the first five or six months. But I'm building this one with nice high sides, and installing a lock on the rockers as a safety feature. Everything will be to code."

"Code?"

"Up to all the modern safety standards." He smiled and she could tell he was thinking about his niece. "Can't take chances with my family."

Meredith didn't know what to say. She was blown away by his kindness and skill. She was also privately embarrassed for how harshly she'd judged him. But she should have known better. Nobody was all one-sided. She'd learned that in her work by helping those multidimensional clients of hers.

"We all used a cradle growing up," he said. "My brothers and sister and me. My dad had one as a baby, too. It's been sort of an Albright tradition, and—so far—we've turned out okay."

It occurred to Meredith that he'd turned out more than okay. Even though he took massive pains to hide it with his blustering and bravado.

"You wanted to see me about something?" he asked, getting back to business.

"Ah, yeah. It's about my aunt."

"Bet that was a surprise."

"You have no idea."

His blue eyes twinkled. "I think I have an inkling."

"Derrick," she pleaded. "You have to help me think up a way to get rid of her."

"She looked like she was intending to stay. Judging by the suitcase."

"Yeah, but she can't stay here. There's barely room for the two of us."

"True." Derrick scratched his chin. "Maybe she can stay with my grandparents?"

"What?"

"In the guest cottage."

"What about the rest of your family? Aren't they coming in?"

"There are four bedrooms on the second floor of

the main house and three additional ones on the third floor."

It was true. His grandparents' summer place was massive. "Oh right. I forgot."

"I'm sure my grandparents wouldn't mind having her stay through the weekend."

"No, but I would."

He chuckled at her consternation. "She might even be a help."

"A help? How?"

"I was figuring Olivia could stay in the guesthouse, too. If your aunt stays there with her, she can help put in a good word for me. Maybe even run intel back here."

The idea was intriguing. Would Clarita go for it? "I don't know. She's supposed to be supervising us."

"There is no 'us.'" His eyes glinted playfully and Meredith's heart pinged. "Remember?"

"Uh, yep." She licked her lips, which felt extra dry. Of course there was no her and Derrick. There never would be. She'd blatantly said as much when she'd mouthed off to him last night. No doubt that suited him fine. Just like it suited her. "I meant from *her* perspective."

"Which has already been cleared up. But if you'd rather your Titi Clarita stay here and bunk on the pull-out with you, I'm cool with that, too."

"No." Meredith shook her head. "Your first idea was better." She thought about how Clarita was into luxury. "My aunt will love those digs. Once she sees them, I'm sure she'd much prefer staying there than here, where there are bedbugs."

"Wait. You told her that?"

"That's what you told me!"

"Mer. I was joking."

"Well, I didn't find it funny, Derrick. Not at all. I was itching all night."

His lips twisted in smile. "I'm sorry I teased you about that, and more importantly about your career ambitions. That was uncalled for and rude, not to mention off the mark. I looked you up last night—"

Her mouth dropped open. "You looked me up?"

"Yeah," he said, unabashed. "That's actually what I was doing when you showed up—trying to find your contact information and demand you get the reporters off my back." He waved that away when she opened her mouth to protest. "But last night, I was curious….and impressed."

Her face warmed at the unexpected compliment. She couldn't believe it. The guy was actually coming around. "Well…thanks, Derrick."

He hung his head and then looked up. "I'm also sorry I called you contrary."

"Which I'm *not*," she teased on purpose.

"There you go!" he said, grinning.

Meredith giggled, then decided to accept his olive branch. "Honestly, I'm sorry, too. Sorry for being so contrary—yes, I admit it, don't look at me like that—and for all those other things I said. I don't want to be at odds with you."

He studied her a moment and it felt like his opinion of her was shifting—for the better. "Thanks for those apologies, and also for apologizing about last summer."

"Even if I didn't apologize for all of it?"

"Hey. Neither did I." He raked a hand through

his hair. "You and I were something, huh? Guess we still are."

She laughed. "Yeah. *So* different."

He grinned. "Night and day."

"Yin and yang!" She bit her lip when she realized this exchange was starting to sound flirty and she was seriously *not* going to flirt with Derrick. That would almost be like hitting on a client. Worse.

He cleared his throat. "In any case," he said. "I don't see why that means that we can't work together." He held out his hand. "Truce?"

She took his hand and shook it. "Truce."

His eyes met hers and their handshake lingered just a second too long.

She had to get back to safe territory. *Think. Think. Think. Bingo! Chaperone!*

"Anyway!" she said, pulling back. "I think the guesthouse is a great solution for my aunt. I tried to suggest to Titi Clarita that she go to Bangor, but she refused."

"What will she tell your folks if she moves over to my grandparents' place?"

"Probably nothing about that."

Derrick laughed. "O-kay. This sounds settled then. I'll give Grandmother Margaret a call and ask her if she minds. But I'm sure she won't."

"Thanks, Derrick. You're a prince."

Okay. *That* sounded like flirting. She had to redirect.

"I mean, I know Olivia will think so when I get the two of you back together!"

He grinned, seeming wistful. "Can't wait to see how you do it."

Yeah. Me, too.

The sooner that was done the sooner Meredith could forget about this crazy-weird attraction she was developing for Derrick. She wasn't sure when it had started. Sometime between their fender bender last summer and last night's mutual bed-making, probably. The cradle-building revelation hadn't helped much, either. But she knew when it had to end.

Right now.

She turned to go and nearly bumped into a narrow cabinet that was about three feet high. It had one long door with two tin plates in it, one placed above the other. Each plate was punched out in a pretty star pattern. "Ooh! What's this?"

"That's a pie safe. I'm making it for Grandmother."

"For her to put pies in?"

He chuckled. "It's what this piece of furniture is called because they were used that way once upon a time, yeah. To keep pies in while they were cooling. These days they're mostly ornamental and used to store other things. My grandma mentioned she's running out of cookbook space in her brownstone in Boston, so…"

"How nice. Is this for her birthday, or—"

He shook his head. "No special occasion."

"Just because?" She stared up at him, a bit worried she looked doe-eyed. She couldn't help it, though. It was hard not to admire him for caring for his niece and grandmother, and working so hard to surprise them.

"Just because." He stepped closer and her heart fluttered.

He was so much more than she'd given him credit for. Talented. Thoughtful. Generous. If she'd known those things about him last summer, maybe she'd have fallen for him herself. Maybe on that dock in the moonlight she might have—

"There doesn't always have to be a reason, Mer," he said, his voice husky. "For doing something nice for someone else." She could smell the scent of his aftershave, all woodsy and masculine. It washed over her like a steamy summer rain, awakening her senses.

"No." She hated the fact that her lower lip quivered.

He searched her eyes. "Haven't you ever had anyone do something special for you?"

"A couple of times," she whispered.

"Only a couple? Hmm. You, Matchmaker Meredith, need to work on that."

"There you are! Oh—" Titi Clarita stood in the open doorway taking them both in. It was only then that Meredith realized she and Derrick stood mere inches from each other, and that her chin angled up toward his.

"Titi Clarita!" she said, stepping back. "What are you doing?"

"Working my way up to a new wardrobe, apparently," she said with a sweep of her hand. She gestured to her navy slacks and black ankle boots that were coated in muck. Her nautical navy-and-white striped top looked pristine, though, and she'd knotted a cranberry-colored cardigan around her shoulders, preppy style.

"Oh Titi Clarita," Meredith said, but she was

laughing. "I'm so sorry that happened to you."

Titi Clarita laughed along with her. "Me, too!"

Meredith scanned her clothes. "What are you wearing?"

"My Blue Hill ensemble." She did a little pirouette. "Do you like?"

"Very nice," Derrick said.

Meredith giggled. "It's awesome."

Clarita frowned. "Was awesome. I guess I'll need to swap out the bottom half for something else." She surveyed Meredith's muddy outfit and then turned to Derrick. "What have you two been up to out here?"

"Come on in," he said in warm tones. "I'll show you around."

"I'd better head back to the cabin," Meredith said, pointing that way. "And clean up."

"See you in a bit," Derrick said.

She glanced at him over her shoulder but he didn't say anything further. He just gave her this barely perceptible smile that said he was no longer as perturbed with her as he'd once been. And, in fact, that he might actually be liking her a little.

Which was big-time dangerous in a major way.

Because, as she made her way back through the mud, Meredith realized that she was starting to like Derrick a little, too.

But liking was okay. Liking was good. Liking helped when you were working together.

She just needed to stay out of kissing range of the hotly desirable guy.

And get him lined up with his intended: Olivia.

ASAP.

She planned to work on that today.

CHAPTER ELEVEN

Curly-haired William wrapped his arms around Derrick, and patted his back. "Bro!" His brown eyes sparkled. "It's been too long."

"You got that part right," Derrick said, hugging him back.

William's pretty, dark-skinned wife Sofia one-arm-hugged Derrick, holding infant Julia against her other shoulder. She wore a tiny diamond stud on the left side of her nose. Her lean frame gave very little indication she'd recently had a baby. Maybe a testament to her going right back to work in her demanding job as a trial attorney, or the fact that she'd been a distance runner for as long as Derrick had known her. She'd only stopped running during her pregnancy, because she and William had experienced difficulties before and had decided to take every precaution.

It was easy to see how those precautions had paid off in one very adorable and healthy baby. The child gurgled, sounding all happy and scented of soap and baby shampoo. She really was a precious nugget with a coppery complexion, chubby cheeks, and huge dark eyes. Derrick could tell from how his big brother looked at her that William worshipped his little girl.

"Meredith!" William said, holding his arms wide. "Great to see you."

"We heard you were here," Sofia said, as

Meredith greeted her and then introduced her aunt.

"Sofia, William, and Julia," Meredith said, smiling down at the child. "This is my aunt Clarita Rincón."

"How nice to meet you," Sofia said.

William extended his hand. "We're glad you could join us. Any friend of Derrick's is a friend of ours."

Sofia grinned at Meredith. "We just didn't realize that you guys had gotten so close."

"Oh no. It's not that!"

William stared at Derrick, confused. "No?"

Derrick sucked in a breath. "Meredith is here on a mission."

"Yes!" Clarita put in brightly. "Like an angel of mercy."

"Well, I don't know about an angel, Titi Clarita." Meredith flushed. "We'll explain everything to you in a bit," she said to Sofia and William.

The couple nodded, then exchanged questioning glances.

"Meanwhile," Meredith said, admiring Julia, "congratulations! She's precious. How old?"

"Four months now," Sofia said.

"Did I hear chatter out here?" Grandmother Margaret asked, striding into the hall. Grandpa Chad was close on her heels and they offered welcomes to everyone, including Clarita who thanked them for their hospitality.

After assuring Clarita they were glad to have her, Margaret reached for the infant.

"Do you mind?" she asked Sofia. "We haven't seen her since she was born."

"Of course," Sofia said happily, passing the babe

into Margaret's arms.

"We have coffee in the kitchen if anyone would like some," Grandpa Chad said. "Or, if anyone's up for a Bloody Mary, I can 'brew' something stronger."

The rest of them laughed.

"I'll take coffee if you've got decaf," Sofia said.

"We have both kinds," Margaret told the group. "Help yourselves."

As they filtered into the kitchen, Derrick waited for the ladies to enter first.

"Such a gentleman," Meredith teased, peering over her shoulder.

"Ha." Derrick grinned, knowing she was ribbing him for how he'd misbehaved last night, and maybe he deserved it. He was better prepared to mind his manners now. He and Meredith had called a truce in light of their greater objectives. She also had a lot more to offer than he'd thought—in the way of helping him with Olivia.

Clarita lowered her voice as she walked on ahead, but he could still make out her words as she whispered to Meredith, "Whatever happened to those Bloody Marys?"

• • •

A short time later, Meredith sat with the group at the large table in the dining room at the back of the house. Tall windows on two sides afforded beautiful views of Blue Hill Bay and the sunny weather.

"That was quite a storm we had last night," Chad said.

"Yeah," Meredith agreed. "It pretty much left

everything soaked."

"Margaret, this Quiche Lorraine is delicious." Titi Clarita took a sip of her Blood Mary, appearing happy and relaxed, and Meredith smiled. Oh yeah, it was going to be easy getting her to stay in the guesthouse—particularly since it was gorgeous, cozy, and bedbug-free. Derrick had already cleared it with his grandparents.

William had been holding Julia who'd drifted off in his arms.

"Why don't you let me take her and lay her down?" Sofia asked him. "You haven't had a chance to touch your food."

"I don't mind," William said, and Meredith felt a tug at her heartstrings. He clearly adored Julia and Sofia did, too. They were both going to be so surprised and pleased by Derrick's gift. She could just feel it.

Then, Meredith began to feel something else. Like a sneaky little question that was forming in her brain, making her wonder about the sort of daddy Derrick would make. Would he be just as loving as his brother? Remembering the expression he'd had on his face when he'd shown her the cradle, Meredith was betting he would. Olivia was lucky to be getting such a great guy. Someone so kind, caring…sexy.

No. Wait. Full stop. Sexy for Olivia, not her.

She recalled Derrick emerging from his shower wearing nothing but a towel and her face felt hot. She took a sip of ice water, hoping he wouldn't keep that up all week. She'd have to be tougher and avert her eyes or something. Focus on her computer and her matchmaking schemes.

And that big-money syndication deal. Yes. That.

"Mind it or not," Sofia said to William. "You've got to keep your strength up, new Daddy." She rose from her chair, gently prying Julia out of William's arms. He passed the baby over with a tender smile and Sofia carried her to a portable crib in the next room.

"When are Brent and Hope getting here?" Derrick asked.

"The day after tomorrow," Margaret said.

"That's when Sally will come, too," Chad added.

"Brent is Derrick's brother," Meredith explained to Clarita. "Hope is his wife."

"Isn't she the one with a twin?" Clarita asked, causing an uncomfortable silence to fall in the room.

"Uh, yeah," Meredith said, shooting dagger-eyes at her aunt, who quietly mouthed *Oh* and took another sip of her drink.

"Sally's our sister," William explained for Clarita's benefit.

"The youngest of the brood," Margaret said. "And still no prospects."

Sofia walked back into the room, then said in knowing tones, "Her day will come."

"Sally and Sofia work together," Chad told Clarita. "They run their own law practice."

"How fabulous," Clarita said. "Where?"

"In Bangor," Sofia answered.

"I'm excited to see her again," Meredith said, because it was true. Sally was so much fun. "Brent and Hope, too. As well as Parker and Elsa," she said, mentioning the Albright kids' parents. "Sofia, when are your folks coming?"

"On Saturday."

"Elsa and Parker arrive then, too," Margaret offered.

William was evidently a lot hungrier than he'd let on because he was really digging into his lunch. "It will be good to see everyone."

"Yes." Margaret smiled around the room. "Such a special occasion."

Sofia turned to Meredith, once she'd settled herself back in at the table. "You were going to explain? About the angel of mercy?"

Meredith puffed up her lungs, gathering her courage. It was now or never, she supposed. She might as well get this part over with. "It's about Derrick, actually," she said, sending him a sheepish glance.

"What? Derrick?" William asked, staring at his brother.

"And his relationship with Olivia."

Sofia dropped her fork and it clattered. She picked it up with delicate fingers, setting it on the side of her plate. "Derrick's Olivia?"

"Derrick's *former* Olivia," Grandmother Margaret corrected.

"Meredith's a professional matchmaker," Derrick said.

"Yeah," William said. "I recall that."

"And very good at her job," Margaret supplied.

Chad held up a finger. "So good, she can work miracles."

Next, Clarita rushed in. "Just like an angel of mercy!"

"Wait a minute." Sofia waved her hand. "What are you guys trying to tell us?"

William put it together. "No. Way." He leaned toward Derrick who sat beside him. "You want her back?"

Derrick pursed his lips. "Yeah." He cleared his throat. "Yeah, I think maybe I do."

"Whoa, bro." William rubbed the side of his neck. "I had no clue you were still hung up on her."

"Truthfully? I hadn't, either. I guess somewhere deep inside I've always wondered whether it just hadn't been the right time." Derrick met William's and Sofia's confused gazes. "Think about it, guys. Olivia and I were perfect for each other."

Sofia's mouth dropped open. "You fought like cats and dogs."

"Yeah, but that was before," Derrick said.

Clarita nodded like she was an expert on the situation. "When they were much younger."

Tension built in the air and Sofia surveyed the room.

"So, what…exactly's going on now?" she asked the group.

"We were thinking it would be nice," Margaret said, taking the lead and Meredith wanted to hug her for it. "If Olivia could come to the christening."

"But, only if it's okay with you!" Meredith said hastily. "Not at all if it would make anyone uncomfortable, or ruin the special occasion."

"Absolutely," Derrick said. "This is your day, and Julia's."

Sofia reflected a moment and stared at the ceiling, moisture glistening in her eyes. She dabbed them with her napkin. "I always felt so bad about what happened with Olivia."

"I never said you had to choose," Derrick said hoarsely.

"I know." Sofia sniffed. "You didn't have to." She shot Derrick a caring look. "We're family, and family comes first."

William squeezed his wife's hand. "This is Julia's christening. We don't have to do anything that takes away from that."

Sofia met Meredith's gaze. "Where is she now? Olivia?"

"Mount Desert Island."

Sofia glanced out the window. "No kidding. So close?"

"She's a park ranger there," Derrick said, his face reddening. "Apparently."

"That's kind of hard to imagine," William said. When the others gawked at him, he said, "What? She was always so *frou-frou*."

"True," Derrick said. "But Mer here is convinced that she's changed. Maybe even in a way that's more compatible with me."

Sofia searched Derrick's eyes. "Is this what you want? What you seriously want? To see Olivia again?"

"Things ended pretty badly." Derrick paused. "If nothing else, it would be good to mend fences."

"Yeah." Sofia sighed. "It would."

"We know it's been a while," Grandpa Chad said, addressing William. "But you and Brent are both happy. Maybe it's time for Derrick to find his happiness, too."

"Yes," Grandmother Margaret agreed. "With the woman he loves."

Meredith glanced at Derrick, but he gave her a weird look, like he was startled somehow. She widened her eyes at him, wondering what was up. She'd been about to send him a signal, or maybe a secretive wink, because things were going so well. William and Sofia had practically agreed to Olivia coming. Meredith didn't believe it would take too much more to convince them.

Derrick stood abruptly from the table. "Excuse me," he said. "I need a minute."

Chad called after him as he walked toward the kitchen. "Derrick!"

William got to his feet. "I'll go."

CHAPTER TWELVE

William came up beside him as Derrick braced himself against the kitchen sink. Was he doing the right thing in chasing after Olivia? So much water had passed under that bridge. What if he was making a mistake? When he'd glanced at Meredith for reassurance, all he'd felt was conflicted. But why? She was doing everything in her power to help him.

"Hey." William placed a hand on his shoulder. "Want to take a walk?"

"Dunno," Derrick said, studying the pile of sudsy dishes in the sink. His grandmother had left stuff there from her prep work. A cutting board, a couple of knives, a glass bowl. A whole lot of bubbles.

"You know," William said, "you can stare into that dishwater all you want, but it's not going to give you any answers. If you'd like, I can get you some tea leaves?"

Derrick heaved a breath. "William."

"Look, bro. I don't know what's gotten into you, but it's clearly something."

"I was just fine until yesterday afternoon."

"Were you, really?"

Derrick shook his head, understanding the answer was no. Olivia's ghost had haunted him for ten long years. It had taken Meredith pointing that out to make him face it. "I mean, on the surface I was fine. I guess there were other things going on underneath. I didn't reconcile with those until after Meredith's media posse showed up."

William's eyebrows shot up. "Something tells me that there's more to this story."

"Yeah."

"Want to tell me about it?"

"Maybe." Derrick wanted to talk to his brother. He really did. The trouble was, he still hadn't sorted certain things in his own head. Like why he'd freaked so badly when his grandparents started talking about him finding love. That's what this whole Olivia thing was supposed to be about, wasn't it? A second chance for him and his ex, best-case scenario?

William nudged his arm. "Come on. The fresh air will do you good."

"I'm not up for a long walk."

"Then let's go check the mail."

"Grandmother already got it. I saw it sitting on the hall table."

"Okay," William said, and Derrick turned to face him. "Then we'll double-check."

"Why are you so stinking nice all the time?"

"I'm not. Remember that time I beat you up when you were in the fourth grade?"

"I'd stolen your girlfriend."

"I broke your front tooth."

Derrick ran his finger along the cap that looked like the real deal. "Good thing Mom knew a great dentist."

"Good thing that I forgave you."

"You? Forgave me?"

William's eyes twinkled. "For stealing Mary Elizabeth."

"Who?" Derrick chortled. "Oh, her."

"We'd better skedaddle," William said, "before we get roped into doing the dishes."

"We shouldn't leave all this for Grandmother."

William grinned cajolingly. "The others will help."

Derrick followed William to the front door as Clarita's voice rose in the dining room. "Oh! Your guesthouse sounds charming. Why, thank you. I'd love to."

"What did you mean when you mentioned the media?" William asked as they walked toward the mailbox. It was breezy out, with sunlight threading through the blueberry bushes hedging the drive.

"They were after Meredith," he said. "Or really, a story about her—and me."

"How did that happen? Last time I checked, you and Meredith Galanes were barely on speaking terms."

"That's true, but times have changed."

"Oh yeah?"

Derrick kicked a pebble with the toe of his boat shoe. "We're in a position to help each other now."

"I get how she's helping you, with Olivia, being a matchmaker and all. But what can you do for her?"

Derrick inhaled sharply, then blew out a breath. He knew William would not take this well. "Pretend to be her fiancé."

"*Oh, no you don't*. No, no, and just no. Derrick," William said sternly. "Didn't you learn anything from last summer?"

"This is not that kind of pretending, all right? This has everything to do with her job and her show getting syndicated."

"Her matchmaker show?"

"Yeah. That one."

"Color me confused."

"Meredith was on some interview program and she got asked about her love life. Since she doesn't have one—"

"She doesn't?" William interrupted.

Derrick scrubbed a hand over his face and shook his head.

"I would have thought— I mean, a woman as hot as she is."

A muscle in his jaw tensed. "Watch it."

"Watch what? I'm just making an observa—" William's lips tipped up in a grin. "Hang on. Are you into her?"

"Mer? Are you out of your mind? No, I'm not *into her*," he said a bit too defensively, in part in an effort to convince himself. Meredith had always rubbed him the wrong way but they had shared that tender moment last summer. And a few other surprising ones this morning in his workshop, too. She'd seemed seriously impressed with his woodworking, and when she'd stared up at him with her big, dark eyes, he'd unnervingly itched to hold her. It was like something in their relationship had shifted—beyond that initial antagonism and into friendship, or perhaps into a more tenuous arena. Which only made things complicated, and Derrick didn't want complicated.

"The problem is," he continued, "her not having a boyfriend looked bad for business, so she asked me to go along with the press's false perception that she and I are an item."

Derrick told William about the paparazzi showing up, then summarized Meredith's arrival and him and her cutting their deal.

"How does the aunt fit in?"

Derrick rolled his eyes. "Mer's very conservative parents worried about her staying alone with me, so they sent Titi Clarita to chaperone."

William belly laughed at this. "But now she's staying here?" He winked. "Nice move."

"Mer and I don't need chaperoning," Derrick grumbled. "We're working together on our plan. That's it."

"Your Olivia plan." William set his chin and thought on this. "Right," he said, like he was finally accepting it. Well good. Derrick needed all the support he could get.

They reached the road and the fluttering ivory pennant with the name ALBRIGHT on it suspended from a post above the mailbox. Derrick checked it as a matter of course and, naturally, it was empty.

William shrugged. "Maybe we'll have better luck tomorrow."

"Suit yourself. I won't be here tomorrow."

"No? Where will you be?"

"Making arrangements with Meredith."

"Ah." William studied him sadly. "I'm sorry, Derrick. I really am. I didn't know about Olivia. Didn't realize you hadn't fully let that go."

"Do you think she'd consider giving us another chance?"

"I guess you'll never know unless you try." William mulled things over as they walked back toward the house. "So, who exactly believes that you and Meredith are engaged?"

"The paparazzi, social media...that kind of thing. This is all part of a show for the public and her network. A very short-term show. That's the deal that Mer and I made. Ten days or bust. Unless she hears something about her syndication deal sooner, and she's thinking she might. After this weekend, we'll probably at least have an inkling about how it's going between Olivia and me."

"So, until then, you're staying together—in very close quarters—at your cabin."

"Don't even think it." Derrick cocked an eyebrow. "She's on the sofa bed."

William held up both hands. "I wasn't thinking a thing!"

"Uh-huh."

His brother chuckled as they approached the house where Sofia stood on the porch, cradling Julia in her arms. The baby gave a little yawn like she was newly awake. "There you guys are!"

"We were checking the mail," William said.

"But didn't...?" Sofia shook her head, and then said, "Never mind." She spoke to Derrick. "Meredith told me about the media mess, her contract. Everything. She also really believes that you and Olivia deserve another shot. And, honestly? I do, too. So, I've made up my mind. I mean, if it's fine with William."

William smiled with his eyes, apparently reading his wife, and she nodded.

"We'd love to invite Olivia to the christening," Sofia said.

Anxiety settled in his gut.

He should be happy, right? Ecstatic.

And he was. He just wasn't feeling it yet.

Probably due to shock. And also the uncertainly.

His excitement would take over once Olivia confirmed.

"But, you know Derrick, she still might not come."

"Yeah, I do. Thanks, Sofia," Derrick said. He patted William's shoulder. "Thanks to you both."

"Oh, don't thank me," Sofia said. Her dark eyes twinkled. "Thank Meredith. She's the one who talked me into it."

CHAPTER THIRTEEN

Derrick hefted Clarita's heavy suitcase into the trunk of her rental car, and glanced at Meredith who sat behind the wheel of her convertible. "Are you sure you're okay going without me?" It was warm and sunny so she had the top down and her oversize sunglasses on.

"Oh yeah, just fine. I remember how to get there. Three stone bridges then a left and a right. Right?" Margaret had told them at lunch that the guesthouse would be unlocked and that Clarita could settle in at any time.

Derrick smiled, probably glad to be left alone for a while. "Correct."

Clarita hopped into her car preparing to back out of the narrow driveway first. Meredith would follow, then ease ahead of her on the road and lead the way. Clarita leaned out her window, talking to Derrick. "Thanks for your help arranging my stay at the guesthouse."

"Thanks for your help in the Olivia department." He winked and Clarita actually tittered.

"It's not that your place isn't great—"

"No worries. I get it. The guest cottage is much better."

Clarita cast a worried glance ahead of her at Meredith's car. "I hope I'm making the right call leaving the two of you alone."

"You have my word as a gentleman. There's

nothing to worry about."

Meredith laid on her horn. "Let's get this show on the road!"

"That's my cue!" Clarita said, inserting her key in the ignition.

"Safe driving," Derrick said. "Enjoy your dinner with my grandparents, and Sofia and William."

"And Julia!" Clarita said brightly.

Derrick smiled. "Can't forget about her."

Meredith began backing up, forcing her aunt to do the same. Clarita gave Derrick a parting wave.

As Meredith drove past Derrick, she said. "Ah, I almost forgot! Can you take the Crock-Pot container out of the fridge and plug in the base? Set it on level two?"

"No problem." He pulled his cell from his pocket and stared at it.

"Derrick?" Meredith asked, unable to read his blank expression.

"It's from William," he said, appearing dazed. "Sofia's already heard back from Olivia."

"And?"

"She said yes. She's coming tomorrow."

Meredith had a weird sinking sensation in her stomach. Which was stupid and completely wrong. She was supposed to be glad about this, and she was. Elated. Yay! Somehow, though, that mental cheer sounded grumpy.

"That's great!" she said, forcing her brightest smile. "Such great news. And tomorrow already? Wow." Her pulse raced because she understood that the tables were turning. She and Derrick would fast forward from planning into action really soon. And that action would be all about getting Olivia to fall back in love with Derrick.

"Yeah," he said, still looking stunned. "How about that?"

· · ·

Meredith was halfway to the Albrights' estate with Clarita following along when her phone rang. "Oh, hi Mom!"

"What's going on with Clarita?" Dolores asked. "She was supposed to call me this morning, but all I got was a text. Something about lunch plans but she never followed up."

"Ah yeah. That's because we got invited to the Albrights."

"Derrick's parents?"

"His grandparents' place. Summer place. Anyway…" Meredith held her breath, recalling her indignance at being babysat. "What in the world possessed you to send Titi Clarita up here?"

"What on earth possessed you to move in with Derrick?"

"I didn't 'move in.' Not in the sense that you're thinking."

"I'd like to speak to Clarita, please. Can you put her on?"

"Can't. She's in the other car."

"Other one? Wait. Where are you going?"

"On…um…a short tour of Blue Hill."

"Well, let's hope it's very brief, because I'd love to hear what she has to say."

"I'll ask her to call you—soon. In the meantime, you honestly don't need to worry."

"It's not me. It's Gustavo I'm concerned about."

"You can tell Dad things are fine. Totally aboveboard. Derrick and I are just…friends." She had a hard time bringing herself to say the word, after their confusing interactions in his workshop. For that fraction of a second they'd felt like more than that. Thank goodness her Titi Clarita had interrupted, because neither she nor Derrick wanted a risky involvement. She was a professional anyway, and he'd essentially hired her to make his match.

"Friends with which kind of benefits?" her mom prodded.

"Zero," Meredith answered. "Look, it's a long story, okay? When Titi Clarita gives you a call, I'll ask her to explain everything. In the meantime, all you need to know is that I'm here in Blue Hill on a mission," she said, using her aunt's words. "A mission of mercy—helping Derrick get back together with his ex-wife, Olivia."

Her mom heaved a sigh. "*Gracias a Dios*, that means there will be no monkey business going on. Not when he's in love with her."

Meredith rolled her eyes. "Exactly. And, hey. I'm not totally unvirtuous, either."

"No! I mean, yes. Yes, I get that. I know your judgment's good, for the most part."

"And it's my judgment that matters, Mom. Whatever I choose to do—or not do—with my own life is completely up to me. We've had this same talk I don't know how many times. I'm thirty years old now and self-supporting."

"I know, I know," her mom said. "It's just that we worry."

"Well, try worrying a little less."

Meredith told her parents what she needed to in order to calm them, then basically did as she pleased. With no serious guy in the picture for the past couple of years that meant not much.

"Did Titi Clarita give you the rosary?"

"Um, yeah. Thanks for that!" she said, trying to remember where she'd put it. Maybe in the bottom of her makeup bag. She should probably get it out and say a prayer or two. With Olivia arriving tomorrow, she needed all the positive energy she could get.

She flipped on her turn signal, spying the familiar Albright family flag by the mailbox. Clarita was right behind her.

"Look, I've gotta run, but I'll ask Titi Clarita to call you."

"Good. That's good. And really good that she's there."

"Uh-huh."

"You can't play things too safe, *mija*. I saw Derrick online and he's very nice-looking. Even if you think you two aren't interested in each other, sometimes hormones take over."

"Mom!"

"Hang on. I'm getting a hot flash. I need a sip of water."

"All right. I'll let you go. Bye!"

• • •

Meredith showed her aunt around the cute guest cottage situated about two hundred yards from the main house and facing the water. It had a big bedroom on the main floor with a tiny kitchen and a sweet living area overlooking a deck with a gazebo and the bay. There was a small den and another bedroom with twin beds downstairs, where Meredith had stayed last summer.

It was hard not to think about all the craziness that had gone on then, but she was glad everything had worked out okay. One thing she never could have predicted was returning to Blue Hill and partnering with Derrick on a project of any kind.

The man had irked her beyond belief at the wedding, but she'd apparently been unable to forget him. Why else had he popped into her brain when Tanya had put her on the spot? Heat flooded her face when she guessed at the answer. It had to do with their intimate moonlight talk. That night after the bouquet toss when he'd almost taken her in his arms, and part of her had wanted him to do just that—so badly.

"This is very nice." Clarita surveyed her surroundings with a smile. "It will certainly do."

"A lot better than the pull-out at the cabin, huh?"

"A lot better for me, yes." She gave Meredith a sly once-over. "What's really going on between you and Derrick?"

"What?" Meredith asked, remaining as guileless as possible.

"There's some kind of tension there," Clarita noted. "Or is a better word for it 'chemistry'?"

"I don't know what you're talking about," she

said, although she most certainly did. There *was* chemistry between her and Derrick, darn it, and it had always been there. Now that they were getting along, it was hard to say whether that made things better or worse.

"I saw the look on your face when I surprised you in the workshop, *mija*. On both of your faces."

"Titi Clarita," Meredith asked firmly. "Where is this going?" As a professional matchmaker, she knew that relationships weren't built on chemistry alone. Couples needed other things to glue them together. Common interests and goals. And right now her and Derrick's interests were aligned and their goals were in sync, but not in ways that brought them romantically together.

She was getting syndicated and he was getting Olivia.

"I just want to make sure you'll be okay with him out there, just the two of you all alone in the middle of the woods."

"While plotting together to get him back with his ex!"

Clarita shrugged and studied the kitchen with its quaint glass-front cupboards and granite countertops. "Would you like a cup of coffee?" she asked, noting the machine.

"Sorry, I can't stay. I'm expecting an email from Beth this afternoon, and I want to be back at the cabin with my computer handy. Oh! I nearly forgot. Mom wants you to call her."

"I'll bet. She's been texting me nonstop."

"What are you going to say?"

"That everything's under control, because it

seems that it is."

"Will you tell her where you're staying?"

Clarita stretched out her manicured hands, which were loaded with rings on nearly every finger. "Probably not. We wouldn't want her and your dad coming up, too."

"No." Meredith's heart pounded. "We definitely don't need that."

"Don't worry about anything, hmm?" Clarita said. Her dark eyes twinkled. "Once I assure your mom that you and Derrick aren't actually involved, things will be fine."

"Great. After that's settled, maybe you won't need to stay?" Meredith said with a hopeful lilt. "You can leave Blue Hill in the morning."

Clarita appeared crushed. "What? And miss the christening?"

"You didn't even know William and Sofia—or Julia—until today."

"Yes, but… I feel like we've bonded already."

"Titi Clarita."

Clarita frowned. "You can't honestly expect me to go? Walk out on a family celebration?"

"They're not your family!"

She eyed Meredith in a curious way. "Maybe not yet."

"What's that supposed to mean?"

"Nothing, maybe nothing." She cocked her chin. "Just that I have a feeling."

"If that feeling has to do with me and Derrick getting together, I can tell you it's wrong." Her stomach churned and her palms felt sweaty. Why? It wasn't like she was lying to her aunt.

Her face burned hot.

Or was she deceiving herself?

"You mean to say you're not attracted to him?"

Meredith recalled that moonlight moment and shoved it aside. Derrick sure had. So she could, too. Extra hard. "Absolutely not. And I can guarantee the feeling is mutual."

"Maybe that's for the best," Clarita said. "With Olivia on her way."

"It's definitely for the best. Derrick and I are like oil and water."

"I'll take your word for it," she said, looking like she didn't.

"You *are* going to help with Olivia, right? Titi Clarita, I can't have you acting on a 'feeling' and completely ruining the plan."

"Of course I'll help. I'll put in a good word for Derrick, and his awesome family. Although, honestly, Olivia probably can figure those things out for herself."

Relief swamped through her. "That would really be so super. Anything you could do or say." Meredith glanced around the room. "Is there anything else you need?"

"No. I can make myself comfortable here. Margaret told me there'd be snacks in the fridge and to help myself to anything. I'm invited to dinner at the main house at seven."

"They're being very kind to include you."

"I know, and I won't take their hospitality for granted. I plan to offer to help if I can."

"Thank you, Titi Clarita," Meredith said. "Also for your help with Mom."

"My big sister is a little uptight, but she means well. You should have seen how quickly she packed her—" Clarita stopped herself. "*Ay*."

A light bulb went off. "*She* was planning to come at first. Not you. Right?"

"I did catch her packing a bag," Clarita admitted. "But I talked her down off that limb."

"How?"

"By saying my schedule's much more flexible—which it is, truthfully. And offering to take charge of the situation if it looked bad." Clarita arched an eyebrow. "But you have to know that I wouldn't have seriously interfered if I'd found you and Derrick together—and happy."

"But, when you showed up, you said—"

"*Hija*, I wasn't born yesterday. But also, not that long ago, either. I'm ten years younger than your mom, but mentally." She tapped her temple. "I'm your age." She proudly swept her hands across her figure. "Physically, too."

Meredith laughed at her aunt's conceit, conceding it was true. Clarita did keep herself in incredible shape, which probably hadn't hurt in attracting so many husbands.

"In any case," Clarita said. "If I hadn't volunteered to come, it would have been your mom standing here in my place."

"Yeah. That could have been bad. Mom's a little pushy."

"But she means well, and loves you very much."

"I know that's true."

"I love you, too." Clarita smiled. "That's why I'm going to do everything in my power to help you land that television contract, including telling your mom I'm keeping an eye on you."

She winked and Meredith hugged her.

"Aww, thank you, Titi Clarita. I love you."

"I love you, too."

CHAPTER FOURTEEN

When Meredith returned to the cabin, she heard Derrick's saw humming in the workshop, so she decided to check her email before disturbing him. The pot roast heating up in the Crock-Pot filled the whole cabin with the yummy aroma of braised beef, potatoes, carrots, and celery cooked in fresh herbs. If Derrick had any red wine on hand that would be nice to go with it. But Meredith didn't want to push her luck in assuming he stocked more than beer.

She switched on an overhead light and settled down at the table, as dusk cloaked the bay outside. The views here were spectacular, even if the accommodations were basic. Meredith was hoping she'd sleep better tonight, now that the bad weather had lifted and she'd cleared things up with Derrick about those imaginary bedbugs.

She logged onto her computer and was pleased to find the expected update from Beth.

Her assistant had dug up more information on Olivia's previous whereabouts. Before moving to Acadia, she'd been involved with a lawyer in Greenville, Maine, in the state's northwestern corner. Meredith supposed that made sense since Olivia had intended to pursue law once herself. Whoa. Not just intended, she'd apparently gone to law school and had graduated. Interestingly, she'd never actually practiced.

Meredith flipped through a few more screen

shots, and then clicked on the various links Beth had sent her. Beth was very good at investigative work. She did an exemplary job running down details of Meredith's prospective couple match-ups. This was useful information to have, since it helped Meredith understand the people she was dealing with. That way, she could better help them appreciate each other.

Beth had obviously been on target about Olivia's current job, as well as her contact information. Sofia had been able to reach her no problem. From all appearances, Olivia had leaped at the chance to attend Julia's christening. She had to know Derrick would be there.

Meredith's gut tightened, but she told herself not to worry. This was good. No, excellent. Precisely what she'd hoped would happen. She didn't know why the thought of Olivia coming made her slightly queasy. Maybe it was just stage nerves, like she got sometimes before going on camera. There was a lot riding on this reunion.

She dashed off a quick thanks to Beth and flipped her computer shut. She should go see Derrick to let him know she'd returned. But first, she'd get things ready for dinner by rustling up some plates and silverware, and maybe even by finding a candle around the place somewhere. Not that she wanted to make dinner seem romantic— Meredith always dined by candlelight. It was a custom she'd grown up with, and it made the evening meal seem special, even when she was eating alone, which she did more often than she liked to think about.

In a strange sort of way, she found herself looking forward to Derrick's company tonight. They had good news to discuss and plans to make regarding him and Olivia. Meredith's cheeks sagged, but she shook off the unsettled feeling. She was good at being a matchmaker. The best. And she was pulling out all the stops to accomplish this one. If things worked out, she'd have her dream job, and pretty much everything she'd ever wanted.

Well, almost everything. The chance to live someplace like this would be nice. She glanced around the cute cabin, thinking it would make a terrific weekend getaway spot. While Derrick's cabin was clearly a bachelor pad with its huge-screen TV and the messy master bedroom, it did have its charms. Meredith imagined it was very cozy here in winter, with a real wood fire burning in the hearth and snow dusting the surrounding trees.

Her apartment in Boston was sleek and upscale but basically outfitted with budget store decor, and it did get a little lonely. Given the demands of her work, Meredith had never considered living outside of the city before. But her taping schedule was flexible and she didn't record her show every day. Although if it went into syndication, she might have to adjust things slightly. Including at her apartment, which she intended to redecorate with top-of-the-line everything.

A tingle of excitement tore through her at the prospect of her deal going through, but then she felt oddly letdown. Like when that big moment arrived, it wouldn't feel nearly as stellar without somebody special to share it with. She guessed she could open a bottle of champagne and call a friend to help her celebrate. Or maybe she would phone her Titi Clarita, or they could do a video chat. She'd put so much energy into making matches for other people, the truth was she hadn't made a lot of time to focus on herself.

Apparently, Olivia had done some soul search-ing and she'd taken her life in a whole different direction. Becoming a park ranger? Wow, that was an about-face. So far afield from practicing law that it had clearly been a bold move. What had inspired the change? She shot a glance out the kitchen win-dow and at the hedge that partially shielded the workshop from here.

Apart from her outdoorsy career, what else did Olivia want? What's more, what did she hope to gain in Blue Hill? Was it a restored friendship with Sofia? Getting back in the Albright family's good graces? Or, in her heart of hearts, had she always hoped this opportunity would come? The chance for her and Derrick to reconnect and start over? Meredith guessed that she and Derrick would dis-cover those answers soon enough.

• • •

Derrick dabbed more fast-drying tung oil on his rag and massaged the railings of the assembled cradle, applying muscle. This would lend the piece's natural wood a glossy sheen and give it a protective coat-ing. The cradle had come together nicely and he was pleased with the result.

He normally wasn't into building baby furniture,

but this case was special. William and Sofia had wanted their daughter for quite some time. After Sofia'd miscarried some years ago, they'd been quiet about their efforts to try again until last summer when they'd shared the news of another pregnancy with the family. Derrick didn't think he'd ever seen William so happy. Sofia, either, for that matter.

They made such great parents and Julia was lucky to have them, just like they'd been gifted with a special treasure in her. Derrick tried to imagine what it would feel like to hold his own baby in his arms. The notion was a tiny bit terrifying but intriguing, too. *Do I have what it takes to be a good dad? The way my dad, Parker, was? And like William is now?*

He'd never put much thought into it until recently. Once he'd started building this cradle, he'd begun wondering how he might have felt if he'd been constructing it for a child of his own.

Naturally, that would mean having a mother in the picture. Namely, a wife. But he'd never totally considered any female in a wifely way. Apart from Olivia. Obviously.

Even then, there had been something far removed about the concept of having kids. They'd basically been kids themselves when they'd run away to get married. Still in school and figuring out their own lives, neither had been ready to have children at the time. In fact, they'd gone to great pains to avoid talking about it. Was it because— subconsciously—both were secretly questioning whether their hasty marriage would last?

He was grateful that he hadn't had kids then. He

hadn't been ready and that would have complicated matters further during his and Olivia's divorce.

He set his rag down on the workbench. If they'd had a family together, would that have changed the outcome of their separation?

Then he shook his head, knowing things were far better the way they were. Now that he and Olivia were more mature, the universe might grant them another chance. For everything. He didn't want to get ahead of himself by imagining their remarriage and them building a life together, and frankly, he wasn't fully ready to mentally go there— but wasn't that what this upcoming weekend was all about?

No, actually, it wasn't.

He pursed his lips, knowing the focus of this weekend's family gathering was supposed to be on William and Sofia and sweet little Julia's christening, not some future imaginary family of his. But, if he did have one…someday…how would he handle things as a dad? Would he really be okay? The Oliva he'd known was brainy. Capable and beautiful, too. There was no doubt she had parenting skills of some kind, but it was somehow hard to visualize them.

Meredith, on the other hand. Now there was someone who was mommy material. He had no doubts about that. She was tough and brassy, but there was a softness underneath. She had a tender fierceness about her. She was protective but caring, like a devoted mama bear. It was easy to intuit she'd make a great mom. No one would mess with her kids. *God help them.* He laughed at the thought.

And they'd grow up with a certain confidence, understanding they'd been supported and loved.

He marveled at the fact that she wasn't seriously involved with someone, or didn't at least have a boyfriend in light of how accomplished she was. She had a fun personality and a sharp mind. And yeah—he chuckled—even her smart mouth, which had a cute way of twitching at the corners when she was annoyed with him. He'd never have figured her for a person lacking in romance. Then again, just look at him.

The door to his workshop cracked opened and Meredith grinned. "Sorry to bother you, but I wanted to let you know that I'm back."

"It's no bother," he said, and in his heart he meant it. Meredith had a warm aura about her, and it radiated throughout the shadowy space like rays of sunshine. He was embarrassed to have been thinking so many favorable thoughts about her. Then he reminded himself she was a matchmaker, and fortunately, not a mind reader.

Her gaze darted to the cradle. "Wow. It's beautiful. Is it done?"

"Just about. I'll need to apply another coat of the finish once this one dries."

She walked over to take a look and he caught a whiff of her perfume, that same honeysuckle one that he'd noticed when she'd arrived. What was wrong with those men in Boston? If he'd been living down there, he certainly wouldn't have let her get away.

Wait. Where did that thought come from?

"You really are very talented," she was saying,

unaware of his shock. "I'm sorry about all that stuff I said last summer. When I made fun of your job." She winced, apology in her eyes, and it occurred to him in this soft light that she was even more beautiful.

Get it together.

"That makes us even." His throat felt tender. "Because I'm sorry about what I said about yours back then, too."

"The pot roast is ready. If you're hungry?" Her dark eyes sparkled and he couldn't help but imagine coming home from work to a woman like her. Meredith Galanes was going to make someone a great wife.

And it won't be you.

He cleared his throat. "Pot roast sounds great, thanks."

He cleaned up while she waited and then switched off some lights.

"You get your aunt settled in okay at the guest cottage?" he asked as they walked back toward his cabin. A full moon was on the rise and darkness cloaked the pines. In many other circumstances, the evening might have seemed romantic.

"Oh yeah. She was pretty impressed."

Derrick quelled all thoughts of romance between him and Meredith. Olivia was arriving tomorrow. He needed to find a way to throw all his energy into thinking about her, and push any nonsensical thoughts about Meredith to the furthest reaches of his mind. "My grandparents are impressive people."

"All of the Albrights are impressive," Meredith said. "From my view."

He glanced at her as he held open the cabin

door, allowing her to enter first.

"Just look at you," she said, sounding flirty, "holding open the door."

His neck warmed but he hoped she wouldn't notice. "This old dog can learn new tricks."

"You're not *that* old."

"No, but I've been around the block a time or two."

"Yeah?" she asked. "Which block is that?"

"The block. You know, the one that folks call life."

"Ooh, that one. Sure." She laughed and he liked how it sounded. "Yeah, I've been around that one, too. More than once."

He stepped into his kitchen, unable to believe his eyes. The whole place was done up so homey, it was hard not to think he was standing in somebody else's house. The cabin was tidy and smelled heavenly with the scent of pot roast in the air, and the table was set for a nice dinner. Meredith had found the blue-and-white checked tablecloth his grandmother had given him years ago and a couple of placemats from the pile he kept in the sideboard. Two places were set with cloth napkins, utensils, and dinner plates and bowls. She'd even managed to produce a candle from his emergency storm stash and plunk it into an empty beer bottle.

"I couldn't find the matches," she said, noting his eyes on the table. "But, given that you've got a fireplace and all, I'm assuming you've got some somewhere."

"I do, indeed." He cast a second glance at the makeshift candle holder and grinned. "Creative centerpiece." It looked like it belonged in a cute little restaurant or something. He was actually kind of touched that she'd gone to the extra trouble.

"It's all I could come up with in a pinch. If you'd had any empty wine bottles, that might have worked better, but since you don't drink wine—"

"I don't?"

"I didn't see any around."

"That's because I keep it in the laundry room."

She giggled. "Who keeps wine in a laundry room?"

He thumbed his chest. "Me. I've got a wine cooler in there, temperature controlled."

"Oh!"

"You probably didn't see it because there are some towels lying on top."

She scrunched up her nose.

"Clean ones," he said. While his bedroom was currently a mess, he wasn't a slob. A man had to have some pride. "I ran the ones through the wash you and your aunt used earlier, but I didn't get a chance to put them away yet."

She stared at him with new eyes, like she appreciated the fact that he did laundry. Which was natural, of course, since he lived here alone. But maybe she was more surprised to learn that he had wine. "You're a very interesting man."

"Thanks. I think." He walked to the high cabinet above the stove and asked her, "Were you hunting for wine for a reason? I mean, would you like some?"

"Um, sure. If you're going to have some, too?"

He opened the cabinet door and took down two wine goblets. "Red?" he asked with a grin. "Or white?"

CHAPTER FIFTEEN

Meredith appreciated Derrick's healthy appetite. He seemed to be really enjoying the food and he told her so several times. He apparently didn't cook much for himself, and only enjoyed homecooked meals when his grandparents were in town and invited him over. For her part, she was enjoying the wine. So much had happened in these past few days it felt good to finally slow down.

While, outwardly, she'd worked hard to maintain her cool, inwardly, the whole scenario in Blue Hill had left her very wound up. First, there was the media fallout to deal with and Derrick's initial reception had been less than gracious. After they'd begun cooperating with each other, he'd started letting down his guard. She'd learned more about him over the past twenty-four hours than she had during the entire wedding week in Maine last summer.

Back then, he'd mostly exhibited snark. Okay, she had seen a tiny glimpse into his spirit on that one moonlit evening, so maybe that should have told her something. There was more to Derrick than she'd at first given him credit for. One thing was sure—she'd never make fun of his profession again. The man was incredibly skilled with his hands, which probably meant he knew how to hold a woman, too. She tried not to dwell on this, telling herself that the only one who should be having those thoughts was Olivia.

She took another sip of wine, deciding to concentrate on one of her reasons for being here, rather than letting her mind take unproductive side trips. "I've got great news," she said. "My assistant turned up more information on Olivia."

Derrick looked up. "Yeah? Like what?"

Meredith filled him in. He appeared a little surprised that Olivia had never practiced law, but seemed to take it in stride that she'd gone to law school. He was relatively nonplussed by the fact that she'd had a serious attorney boyfriend.

"All adds up," he said, sipping from his wine. He'd opened a bottle of hearty cabernet sauvignon, which was delicious. "That's the route she said she'd always wanted to take, and the sort of guy she seemed to want to latch onto."

"Latch onto? What do you mean?"

"Someone educated and accomplished. Someone not like me."

"You're educated and accomplished," she told him.

"You say that now—"

"I already said I was sorry, and I meant it."

The hard edges of his features softened. "Yeah, I know. Apology accepted."

"In any case," she said, turning the conversation back to Olivia, "the attachment didn't last."

He eyed her in the candlelight. "Did your assistant learn why?"

"She's a good data tracker but she can't read crystal balls."

He gave a melancholy laugh. "Yeah, suppose

not." Derrick appeared pensive a moment before speaking. "You know, one of the problems between us was that she thought I lacked ambition."

"You take pride in your work."

"I do. I'm a good instructor, too."

Her lips twitched at the self-congratulatory statement. "If you say so yourself."

"I *do* say so myself." He clinked his wineglass to hers in a toast. "Just like you say you're a great matchmaker yourself."

Meredith laughed. "So, when do your classes resume?"

"A week from this coming Monday."

"So, after I go, you'll have the rest of that time with Olivia?"

"Nobody says she'll be able to take the time off, or that she'll want to stay."

"You have to make her want to stay," Meredith said emphatically. "By romancing her."

He set down his wine. "Sorry. Don't do that."

"What? Romance?"

"You're talking flowers and such? Chocolates?" He shook his head. "No."

"Those things are cliched," Meredith told him. "Sometimes romance isn't in the big gestures. It's in the smaller stuff. Like, the things you notice about her. Things that are special about her and make her different. When you acknowledge those attributes out loud, she'll feel appreciated. Noticed."

"I think I know what you mean." He stared at her and heat rose in her cheeks. She ducked her chin and drank some more wine before returning to her dinner. "Make her believe that I see her, right?"

"Yes! That. Exactly."

His eyebrows knitted together. "What if I don't like what I see?"

"Well then, it's all over. Romantically, that is. You'd just use your reunion as a growth experience for both of you. A chance to put old hurts behind you and part on better terms. Sofia would probably like that, right?"

"I'm guessing yes."

"And maybe, so would you?"

He shrugged. "Sure."

"Derrick, I know this is weird, but the hardest part is going to be that first hello. After not seeing her for so long, it could feel a little awkward. But, don't try to fight it. Just lean into that feeling and say something like—"

"Hey, this is awkward?"

"You got it." Meredith winked. "Once Olivia knows the situation's uncomfortable for you, too, she'll be more at ease."

"Okay. And then what?"

"I can't tell you play-by-play. Some of it's going to depend on your initial reaction to each other. If it's favorable, and you want to pursue things, I'll be there to help with any advice."

"Nothing like having a resident expert on hand." He cocked an eyebrow. "And right under my roof. How do you think Olivia's going to take that?"

"Probably fine, when we explain that we're just friends. We can tell her that's why I'm here for the christening. You and I got close last summer, and I'm a friend of the family."

"Yet no other family friends are invited?"

"Besides her!"

"Seems fishy. Olivia's too bright for that. I'm not sure she'll buy it, especially with your aunt here."

"Okay, then. Maybe something else?" Meredith thought a moment. "How about we say, I showed up in town unexpectedly and surprised you. My aunt and I were together and…going on a road trip!"

He sat back in his chair. "In separate cars?"

"You're right, that won't work." She frowned. Then she got another idea. "Maybe we can say I was up in the area for another reason, and then popped in to see you? Since it was close to the baptism and I know your family, you asked me to stay?"

"All right, but what about your aunt?"

"She, er…was coming to meet me for whatever touristy thing I'd planned to do. I'd raved about Blue Hill from last summer and she wanted to see it. Honestly, I doubt Olivia will think too much about it, one way or another. She'll just be feeling happy about being included herself. You know, on the short list?"

"Short list, right." He sighed. "I should probably have my head examined."

"First things first. Let's take this one step at a time and see how everything goes tomorrow when you see her."

"I don't want to take the focus off of Julia and her christening."

"You won't! This will all be under the table."

They noticed at the same time they'd both finished eating.

"Let me help pick up," she said.

"Nothing doing."

Derrick grinned, and for a nanosecond she wondered what it would be like having dinner with him every night. Then she squashed that thought—pronto.

"You brought the pot roast," he continued, "I can pop things in the dishwasher." He started to blow out the candle and then asked, "Want anything for dessert? I've got ice cream."

"No, thanks." She sent him a hopeful glance. "But I will take just one more glass of wine? I've got a small amount of work to do on the computer, if that's all right."

"Work? Lady, you've been working practically since you got here."

Meredith conceded that she felt exhausted. "That's true."

"So why not take the night off? Things are only bound to get busier starting tomorrow."

With Olivia arriving, she agreed he had a point. "Maybe I could use some downtime."

"You definitely could use some downtime." He grinned. "So could I."

She stared at him surprised, because it sounded like he was suggesting they hang out together. "What did you have in mind?"

"TV? Maybe a movie?"

She yawned, not sure she could last through a whole film after these super busy past few days. She observed the widescreen TV mounted over the fireplace. "How about we stream something?"

"Cool." He started rinsing things to load in the

dishwasher, then paused, drying his hands. "Your wine?"

"I'll get it." She lifted the bottle from where it stood on the table. "Plenty of practice."

His eyebrows arched.

"But not that much." She laughed. "Come on." She poured her wine and set the cork back in the bottle.

"Hey wait!" he said. His eyes sparkled. "Don't forget to pour me some, too."

"Aye, aye captain," she said, joking.

"That will be the day." He rolled his eyes. "When you let me skipper the ship."

• • •

Derrick finished loading the dishwasher and Meredith located the remote on the mantel.

"Go head and sort through some choices," he said.

She laughed. "You and I probably don't watch any of the same shows."

"You're right. Probably not."

She settled in on the sofa with the remote and her wine, feeling happy about relaxing for a while with Derrick. It was hard to imagine the two of them letting down their guard and just being together. It reminded her of their brief time spent last summer on that dock. Things felt strangely comfortable between them, and she was glad to feel her tensions ease.

Most of her life she'd stayed tensed up, chasing after one goal or another. The fact that she

generally achieved them only made her more anx-
ious, not less. Because every mountain she climbed
only reminded her that there was higher peak, just
beyond the next ridge.

She flipped on the TV and a menu popped up
for different streaming services. She clicked one of
her favorites and a banner appeared for recently
viewed shows.

She giggled and glanced back toward the kitch-
en. "You do not watch *Date My Mother*."

His neck reddened. "I might have seen it once or
twice."

"Wait." She goggled at the screen. "*Indian
Matchmaker,* too?" She turned and lobbed a small
sofa pillow at him. "You great big fraud!"

He dodged the pillow, but he was laughing so
hard. "Hey! Watch it!"

"Yeah that! *When* did you watch it?"

His whole face turned crimson. "Okay. Maybe I
saw an episode or two last summer. After." He
shrugged. "You know."

She couldn't believe it. He had to have been
curious about matchmaking after meeting her. "Derrick." She found herself giggling again. "You
watched all of season one!"

He picked up the sofa pillow and his wineglass
and came over to join her. "Hey, maybe I would
have watched *your* show if it had been syndicated
back then."

She blushed, in a strange way believing that was
true.

"So what will it be?" he asked, glancing at the
screen.

"You're letting me pick?"

"You're my guest."

She felt hot all over. "Yeah, but not *that* kind of guest."

He chuckled. "I'm sure your parents were relieved to find that out."

She laughed at his very correct assertion. "Right, hmm." She scrolled through some shows. "Ooh, how about *House Hunters*?"

"Great one. I love the remodels."

She viewed him admiringly. "Do you?"

"I redid my grandparents' kitchen, you know."

"Up here? No, I didn't know that. But I'm not surprised." She sassily set her chin. "You're very good at all that manly handyman stuff."

He laughed. "Manly? Maybe you need to watch some more shows. Women remodel, too."

"Oh yeah, that's true."

"But not you, huh?" His forehead rose.

"Trust me," she said. "You don't want to see me with a hammer. I break things."

"Intentionally?"

She shoved him and he chuckled. "No, you goofball. By accident."

"I'm glad you told me before I asked you to help out in the workshop."

"I like it that the workshop is all yours. Your zone."

His eyes sparkled and he leaned toward her. "What's your zone?"

"Er...other than matchmaking, you mean?"

"Yeah. What do you do for fun?"

"I guess I watch shows like these."

"All right." He sat back against the sofa, looking settled in. "Then let's have 'fun' together."

She playfully rolled her eyes. "That would be a first."

"No, it wouldn't," he said and her heart stilled. Then it started beating faster because of how he gazed at her.

"Shows!" she said, clicking the remote. "Right. How about we start with this one…"

• • •

Two and half hours later, Derrick yelled at the screen. "No! House Three! Pick house Number Three!"

Meredith couldn't believe they'd stayed up this late. They'd only intended to watch one episode, but they'd gotten sucked in. Then, the time had simply melted away.

"It's going to be House Two, and you know it."

"No?" He stared at her incredulous. "Why?"

"Because of the yard, Derrick. It's perfect for kids."

"They don't have any kids."

She rolled her eyes. "You haven't been listening. They keep talking about them."

He crossed his arms stubbornly. "Well, I say go for the view."

"And I say go for the white picket fence."

The couple picked house Number One and they both groaned out loud. "Nooo!"

Meredith gaped at him. "That dingy little place? Why?"

"Closer to the beach?"

"Yeah, but the other had ocean views!"

Derrick shook his head. "Sometimes there's no figuring people."

"No figuring," she agreed. "I thought for sure they'd go with the fence."

"Being a matchmaker and all," he teased. "You're the family living expert."

"Ha! And you're the one who's all about aesthetics in making those beautiful boats of yours."

"Which is why that view would have been awesome." He assumed a smug pose and she laughed.

"I'm not budging from my white picket fence."

"Good woman," he said. "Hold your ground." Then he looked in her eyes and her skin tingled. All this talk about holding and white picket fences made her want to dream.

But no. Her and Derrick?

He switched off the TV and turned to her. "So. You…?"

He seemed to lose his thread. Was he thinking what she was? If they'd made a different choice last summer, then maybe things would be different between them now.

"Tired? Yeah." Meredith swallowed hard. "Uh-huh. You?"

His voice grew rough. "We should probably turn in. I mean," He checked his phone. "It's late."

He gazed into her eyes and Meredith found herself wanting to look away. But she couldn't. His blue eyes were deeply soothing, like lulling ocean waves. And something in her soul ached to dive in and be lost in them. Despite their obvious differences, he helped her feel balanced in a way. Calmed her rocky seas.

"This has been really fun," she said, the words barely more than a whisper. "Thanks for telling me not to work tonight."

His mouth tipped up in a little smile. "Sounds like you work almost all the time."

"It's true, but once I get that syndication deal—"

"Won't you be working twice as hard then?"

"I don't know. Hope not." But she would, and she knew it. He likely did, too, judging by the sadness in his eyes.

"For your sake, I hope not, too."

Her heart hammered because he was so close. Maybe too close.

And when he looked up, met her gaze and held it, she panicked.

"I…should get ready for bed."

He cleared his throat. "Yeah, me too."

"But first. I should probably check in with Beth." He shot her a stern look and she held up her hands. "Sorry. You're right. I'm taking tonight off."

He nodded. "Beth will be there in the morning."

It delighted her that he was looking after her. Then she reminded herself that was just because they'd become friends and nothing more. Derrick was reserving his "more" for Olivia. She and Derrick had missed their moment at Brent's wedding and that time was gone. Or maybe it had never really existed to begin with. Not if Derrick still had what-if thoughts about Olivia.

She gathered her things and went to change and brush her teeth. "Well," she said, pausing in the kitchen. "Night, Derrick."

He stood near the sink, getting the coffee ready to go for the morning. "Goodnight, Mer. Sleep well." He winked and her pulse fluttered. "And no worries about those bedbugs tonight."

"Ha, yeah. Thanks."

When she returned from the bathroom, she saw that he'd pulled out the sofa bed and gotten it all ready for her. Her heart sighed. Derrick really was a very thoughtful guy. Potentially Olivia's very thoughtful guy, she reminded herself pointedly, and not hers. And yet, tonight, for just a little while, she'd been able to imagine a different reality.

She glanced at his closed bedroom door and then crawled under the covers, a heavy blanket of exhaustion draping over her. She would definitely sleep well tonight. She groggily shut her eyes and images from the past few days drifted past, like sailboats carried along by a warm summer breeze. Memories of her moments spent with Derrick, many of them unexpected and sweet. When she dreamed tonight—whether she wanted to or not— she knew she'd be dreaming of him.

CHAPTER SIXTEEN

"Hold. The. Phone. And bring in the smelling salts! Is that her?"

"Titi Clarita! Nobody's uses—" Meredith peered out the guest cottage window to see what her aunt was goggling at and she felt faint herself. There she was: Olivia. Gliding almost seemingly on air across the lawn in a long, flowing sundress that reached down to her narrow ankles. The sheer dress had short, ruffled sleeves made of some gauzy fabric, and it sheathed an inner slip dress with spaghetti straps. She was tall and lithe, with auburn-colored hair cascading down her back beneath a straw sun hat with a pink ribbon around its brim.

In other words, she was a vision of loveliness in a sun-kissed palette of pastels.

Meredith's stomach sank.

She did not look—at all—like a park ranger, or a whole lot like that DMV pic, either.

Olivia reached for Grandmother Margaret with outstretched arms. Grandpa Chad stepped up for his hug next, and their happy chatter tumbled down the hill.

This is worse than I thought! Meredith sucked in a breath. *No. Better. Better for Derrick.* Olivia was a dream come true.

"You didn't say she was gorgeous," Clarita said, standing beside her.

Meredith swallowed hard. "That's because I

didn't know."

"Can you imagine their babies?" Clarita gasped. "Model material, all."

But Meredith didn't care to imagine those babies. She thought of Derrick's cradle, and the love he'd put into it. Someday, he might build one to keep. For a child of his own. Meredith's stomach soured and she clutched it.

Clarita scanned her eyes. "Is something wrong?"

"My stomach's just a little off. Probably nerves."

"But you've made plenty of matches before! Unless"—Clarita folded her arms in front of her—"you're having second thoughts about this whole deal."

"No, I'm not." Meredith squared her shoulders, which she couldn't help but think made her feel like a linebacker in comparison to waif-like Olivia. The woman was completely devoid of hips. "It's just opening day jitters."

"I would have thought you'd have had those when you showed up at Derrick's?"

"That was different. I'd planned out what I was going to say."

"Don't you have a plan now?"

"Yeah, but it's not all down to me. So much depends on Derrick and…her." She opened the refrigerator door, locating a bottle of sparkling water. She poured herself a glass, hoping it would soothe her queasy stomach. "Want some?"

"No, thank you. I hear we're having cocktails at the main house."

Meredith peeked out the window again to see Sofia and William had joined the group. Sofia passed baby Julia to Olivia and Olivia held her naturally, not in the stiff, uncomfortable manner Meredith might have expected from someone so... coiffed. "I wonder where Derrick is?"

"I was just about to ask you," Clarita said.

"Oh wait," Meredith said, standing up on her tiptoes for a better view. "Here he comes!"

• • •

Derrick felt like someone had shoved a big ball of cotton into his mouth and his throat went sandpaper dry. It was really her—Olivia—in all her stunning beauty. She passed Julia back to Sofia and grinned, fine lines forming at the corners of her pretty green eyes. Her features had matured in a manner that suited her. Her skin took on a light golden hue, a testament to time spent working outdoors.

"There you are." Her smile glistened. "Your grandpa said you were hiding in the house."

"Olivia, hey!" He cleared his throat because that came out scratchy. "Long time—"

"No see!" she replied, wrapping her slender arms around him. She tugged him into an embrace, her grasp strong and steady. She was not the willowy flower she'd once been. This Olivia worked out and had the lean strength to prove it.

Derrick caught the others' eyes on them, although they were clearly pretending not to look.

"Refreshments back in the house," Grandmother Margaret declared, heading that way.

"Yes, we'll see you there," Grandpa Chad said.

Sofia held Julia and she and William followed along. "So glad that you're here," Sofia whispered to Olivia when she passed by her.

Derrick pulled out of her embrace, but she clung to the tops of his arms.

"Derrick Albright," she said. "I can hardly believe it's you. It's been years."

"Ten, to be exact."

"That would be ten this August," she corrected. She playfully rolled her eyes. "Not that I'm counting."

"Me, neither." Derrick noted that the others had gone inside. But where was Meredith? She'd left to retrieve her aunt from the guesthouse fifteen minutes ago. He cast a quick glance toward the rose garden and the path that lay beyond it. When he didn't see her, he forced his gaze back on Olivia.

She watched him in a peculiar way, like she was trying to guess what he was thinking.

He stared at her, at a loss for words. Then Meredith's advice came back to him. "Well, this is awkward." He forced a laugh.

Olivia squeezed his biceps harder. "Not as much as it should be, though, right?" She finally let him go with two solid pats on his arms. "You're looking good, Derrick," she said, tilting her chin. "Time's been good to you."

He swallowed hard. "Same."

"Hi there! You must be Olivia!" Meredith emerged from beside a blooming bed of dark red roses with her Titi Clarita beside her.

Olivia beheld her curiously.

She held out her hand and Olivia shook it.

"Meredith Galanes. Nice to meet you. This is my aunt, Clarita Rincón."

Clarita shook hands with Olivia, too, who said, "Great to meet you both."

"Meredith is an old friend of mine," Derrick explained.

"Not that old," Meredith inserted. "Just a year!"

"That's right. I…she…we…" Derrick verbally stumbled. "Met at my brother's wedding last June."

"That would have been Brent's?" Olivia questioned.

Meredith nodded. "That's right. I was the maid of honor."

"The best friend of the bride." Clarita frowned. "Sort of."

Olivia shot Clarita a puzzled look and Derrick stepped in. "Anyway, that's how we met and then Meredith came up this summer to—"

"Enroll in the boat school!" Meredith ad-libbed.

Clarita and Derrick gaped at her.

He scratched his head. "That's right. Of course. The only thing was, Meredith didn't realize it would be closed these two weeks."

"Your pre-summer break?" Olivia surmised.

Derrick nodded. "Yeah."

"And so." Meredith heaved a breath. "He asked me to stay."

"Not stay, stay," Derrick said.

"On the pull-out," Meredith added. "We're honestly just friends."

Olivia appeared as if she was about to get whiplash staring back and forth between the two of them. "I…see." She surveyed Clarita. "So did you come up for the boat school, too?"

"No. Only the *captains*." Meredith elbowed her, then she said, "And! To keep my niece company. Such a shame she got her enrollment date mixed up." Her frown became a grin. "But then, look at this happy outcome! The two of us got asked to the party."

"Oh ah, yes," Olivia said. "I was so happy to get invited, too."

"Meredith is a matchmaker," Clarita proudly informed Olivia.

Olivia perked up. "Is that right? What fun! Do you have a business or a blog or—"

"A television show," Derrick supplied. "In Boston."

"Sweet!" Olivia smiled. "Match up any celebrity couples?"

"Er, not yet," Meredith answered. Derrick guessed that could happen in the future, once she hit it big.

"Maybe we should go in the house?" Clarita said. "I hear they're serving cocktails."

A stiff drink sounded like a good idea to Derrick right about now. Meredith enrolled in boat school? Seriously? Luckily, Olivia didn't seem to think too much about that. All her attention was on him. She glanced at him and her green eyes sparkled.

"Still drinking Old Fashioneds?" Olivia nudged him as they walked along and the back of his neck warmed. She was probably being friendly, not flirty. But then her eyes danced, and he wasn't sure.

"I take my Bourbon straight-up now," he told

her. "On the rocks."

"That sounds like a grown-up drink."

"It is." Derrick paused to hold open the back door from the wraparound porch that led into the den. Olivia entered ahead of him with Clarita, then Meredith following.

"Seems to be going good," Meredith said in hushed tones. "Keep doing what you're doing."

And he would, too. If Derrick could only figure out what that was. He felt like he was just muddling along, fumbling his way through this. Although Olivia did seem pleased to see him. He was sure he'd be just as pleased once the awkwardness wore off. She still seemed like the same Olivia. Only better, or at least he hoped.

Grandpa Chad called Clarita and Meredith into the library, wanting to show them something. Clarita had asked about reading Maritime ghost stories and he'd assembled a collection of tomes from his shelves.

"I found one for you, too," Derrick heard his grandpa say, clearly speaking to Meredith. "*Match Made in Heaven*. It's a volume about historical romances that were all professionally arranged. I thought you might enjoy it."

Their chatter faded as Olivia caught his attention. "Is she always like that?"

"Who?"

"Your friend, Meredith? So…on edge?"

"Well, no." He sank his hands into his pockets. "Maybe just a little nervous about meeting you somehow."

"Me?" Olivia tipped up her chin with the look

of utmost innocence. At one time he'd been entranced by the color of her eyes. He'd even written poetry about them—embarrassingly horrible poetry back in college—though he'd never let Mer know that after going to great lengths to assure her he wasn't a romantic guy. Which he wasn't. Anymore. Olivia still had pretty eyes, though. He wasn't sure if they were *entrancing*, but he'd probably believe that again given time.

"She, um, knows we have a past," he explained.

"It was a marriage, Derrick."

"Yeah, that." His shoulders sagged. "Mer worried it—"

"Mer?" she asked, stopping him.

He laughed. "Yeah. It's just what I call her."

"How charming."

"Not…not really. It's all on friendly terms."

"So you and she have said." Olivia viewed him oddly. "It's okay if you and Meredith are involved. I mean, it would be natural and wouldn't surprise me."

"We aren't."

She lifted an eyebrow.

"Are you involved? With someone?"

Color dusted her cheeks. "What?"

"I mean, I'd like to talk—later," he said awkwardly, because this was awkward. No doubt about it. One hundred percent. "I mean if you would?"

"Oh. Um, sure," she said, looking kind of uncertain about it.

"Who'd like white wine?" Grandmother Margaret asked, stepping from the kitchen. She held two chilled goblets in her hands. "We have other choices in the kitchen. Derrick," she said, "help yourself to something from the bar."

The woman didn't miss a thing. A stiff drink was exactly what he needed. "Thanks, Grandmother." He nodded and headed across the room, while Olivia accepted one of the wineglasses.

"This is such a pretty place," Olivia said, glancing around. "And the view is just as gorgeous as I remember."

Derrick turned a fraction of a second sooner than she suspected, catching Olivia's eyes on him. She pivoted toward the window, pointing to a sailboat on the waves. "So lovely! It never ceases to amaze me."

Grandmother Margaret shot a look at Derrick and then at her. "Yes." She took a sip of wine, joining Olivia near the window. "It's delightful having you back in the house."

"I was really touched when Sofia called."

"She's missed your friendship quite badly," Margaret whispered just as William entered the den.

"Sofia's laying Julia down upstairs," he said. "She's just finished with her bath."

"Did you leave the bedroom window open so we can keep an ear out from the porch?" Margaret asked him.

"Yeah, but I also have this." He patted the walkie-talkie type contraption strapped to his belt that Derrick recognized as a baby monitor.

He studied Derrick's drink and the wineglasses in the women's hands. "I think I'll pour myself a glass of red and grab some sparkling water for Sofia."

Margaret turned to Olivia. "How about we head on outside and you can tell everyone what you've been up to?" She glanced around the room. "Derrick, can you help Meredith and Clarita to some drinks and let them know where we are? There are more glasses in the kitchen."

• • •

Grandpa Chad stacked another book on the load in Clarita's arms. They sagged under the weight.

"I'm sure that's probably enough," Meredith said, holding her one little book.

"Ah yes!" Clarita agreed. "Plenty of spooky stories to keep me up at night, thanks."

Chad ducked behind the doorway and out of view from the den. "So how do you think it's going?" he asked quietly. "Between my grandson and Olivia?"

"Well, uh." Meredith licked her lips. "She's only just gotten here."

"And looks very lovely," Clarita put in.

"She always was a looker, that Olivia," Grandpa Chad said. "She had a kindness about her, too."

"Oh, really?" Meredith knew she should feel pleased and not disappointed by this, but she wasn't. Not completely.

"Heart of gold." Chad motioned Meredith and Clarita closer. "Used to foster rescue kittens. Adult cats, too. Puppies and dogs. I believe rabbits, at one point, she told us."

"Rabbits?"

Grandpa Chad nodded. "Olivia's like a regular…

who's-it? The woman who talked to the animals?"

"Doolittle?" Clarita asked. "No, he was a doctor, a man."

"Not Doolittle." Chad shook his head. "The one who lived in the woods with all the dwarves?"

"Snow White?" Meredith asked weakly. *What? Now I'm competing with Disney Princesses?* No. Not competing! Where was her head?

"Oh! Well, that's…awesome," Meredith said, regrouping. "And great information to have. Thanks so much for sharing it, Chad."

The older man nodded. "There was not one thing wrong with that girl besides her age and immaturity. Derrick had those problems, too. Now that they're past them…" He smiled. "There could be a happier ending in store."

"Could be!" Meredith agreed.

"He's a very eligible bachelor, your grandson," Clarita said. "It's amazing he wasn't snatched up earlier."

Chad confided behind the back of his hand. "Oh, there've been plenty of single ladies trying, believe me. But the lad's heart wasn't in it. Now we all know why."

Derrick appeared in the doorway to the library. "Grandmother Margaret wanted me to find you and let you know we've moved onto the porch. Can I get you ladies a drink?"

"I'd love a glass of wine," Meredith said. "Red, please."

"I'll take the same." Clarita nodded, her arms heavy with books. Grandpa Chad relieved her of them.

"Here, dear, let me take these for you and set them on a side table in the den. That way you'll remember to take them to the carriage house later." Clarita thanked him, tittering on about which book she'd read first, and followed Chad out of the library.

Then it was just Derrick and Meredith. "Wow," she said, beaming up at him with the most pleasant smile she could muster. "Olivia seems great."

"Yeah." He shifted on his feet. "Are you all right?"

"Me? Mmm-hmm, yeah. Why?"

"You just seem…not sure."

"I'm fine," she said. "Really, really good! You?"

He rubbed his cheek. "I'm good, too."

"And happy?"

He stared down into her eyes, then he blinked. "Happy? Yeah, of course. This is…great. Thanks for arranging it."

She nudged him playfully. "It's only going to get greater."

He touched her arm and her pulse fluttered. "Mer," he whispered. "About Olivia…" He leaned closer and she stared up into his dreamy blue eyes.

"Huh?"

"She keeps looking at me. Like…differently. I'm not sure what she's thinking. Is she interested, or? Maybe just trying to figure me out?"

"You mean you can't tell?" she teased. "Considering all your experience with women?"

"Yeah, but I haven't experienced this one in a decade."

She lightly shoved his arm. "Derrick, it's still so

early," she said in low tones. "So hard to say."

"What?" He grinned. "Come on, Mer."

She rolled her eyes at the nickname but truthfully it was growing on her. He wasn't nearly as awful as she used to think. He actually had a few positive personality traits.

"We're a team here," he said. "I value your opinion."

She arched her eyebrows at him. That was a first.

He chuckled at her reaction. "You're a matchmaker, right? Maybe you have a feeling?"

She had a feeling all right and she wasn't liking it at all. The feeling that Olivia was beyond-belief-perfect and that no single guy on earth could resist falling for her, especially a guy who'd spent the past decade pining for her. "I think…yeah. Things are going well. But, Derrick," she whispered. "Let's give this a little more time, okay?"

"Oh, right. Sure." He glanced toward the den and the bar. "I'd better go and grab that wine for you and your aunt. See you on the porch?"

"Yeah. Good."

• • •

"Olivia!" Sofia said once they'd all made it outside. "I want to hear all about you. I can't believe you're a park ranger now. That's exciting."

"Yeah, it is," Olivia said. "And perfect for me. I get to spend lots of time outdoors."

Meredith could just see her now, talking to deer, black bears, and rabbits.

"That's a far cry from where you started, dear,"

Margaret said. "With law and at Sofia and Sally's practice."

"That's true." Olivia gazed out at the horizon before answering. "But, let's say life had other plans." She turned to William and Sofia. "What about you guys? Did you ever buy that cute bungalow you wanted?"

"We did," William replied.

Sofia smiled beside him, sipping from her bubbly water. "Bought and renovated. It looks really super. We'd love for you to visit sometime."

Olivia's eyes glistened and Meredith could tell she was touched. "I'd like that. I'd like that a lot. Thanks, guys."

"Derrick's been busy," Grandpa Chad hastened to add. "He was promoted to lead instructor at the boat school, and then just last fall became its director."

"How fab," Olivia said.

"He's very talented," Meredith added. She glanced at Derrick whose forehead rose, like he wondered what she was doing. "He's working on a couple of amazing projects right now."

"At the boat school?" William asked him.

"No," Derrick said. "Home projects." He shot Meredith a silencing look, but she hadn't intended to blab anything. She was just talking him up in front of Olivia, which was part of her job. Although sort of a stinky one at the moment. Derrick didn't need any talking up. If he did, then Olivia probably didn't deserve him. Still, she wanted to help.

"They're top-secret," she reported, as if she was in the know. Because she actually was. For whatever reason, she found it gratifying that she knew something that Olivia didn't. She certainly couldn't talk to animals. When she'd commanded her ex-Uncle Raul's bulldog to sit, he'd only stared at her.

Olivia giggled like she was remembering something. "Ooh, Derrick was always really great at keeping secrets." She stared at him. "Like about our crazy elopement."

"That *was* crazy," he said with an uncomfortable chuckle.

Meredith begrudgingly continued her role in helping things along. That's what professionals did. Some days your heart was in your work more than others, but dedicated matchmakers soldiered on.

"Bet those were good times," she said sunnily to Olivia and Derrick. "Back in the day."

Olivia looked wistful a moment. "Yeah."

Derrick shook his head. "When we weren't fighting and tearing each other's hair out."

"You were such a stubborn guy," Olivia said, teasing. "I was always butting heads with you."

He rolled his eyes. "You're the one who inspired the headbutting as far as I recall."

"Not so. That was you."

Meredith watched with a keen eye. There was still tension between them. Maybe some low-lying heat, too.

Good. This was good.

So why did Meredith feel so terrible inside. What on earth was wrong with her?

"Yeah." He exhaled, apparently mulling over the happy memories. About fighting, apparently. "I guess we were a pair."

Olivia let out a peal of laughter that resonated toward the waves, and Meredith's knee started bouncing. *Oh nooo...* Even her laugh was pitch perfect. Musical. Like it'd come off a soundtrack somewhere.

"Oh, Derrick." The woman giggled in a ridiculously beautiful way. It sounded like champagne bubbles of joy floating up toward the ceiling. "Those definitely were the days." She cheerily studied the rest of them, then gratefully changed the subject. "When does Sally get here?"

"Tomorrow," Margaret said. "Just in time for the baby shower."

Sofia stuttered with surprise. "Baby what?"

"It's just a little fun time that Sally has planned for you," Grandmother Margaret said.

"A hen party sounds fine," Grandpa Chad said. He nodded at his grandsons. "Maybe you boys and I can go out on my boat."

"Not so fast, darling." Margaret leaned toward him. "The men are invited, too."

William sank down in his chair. "Oh boy."

Clarita appeared caught in the middle. "Don't mind me. I'll be sure to stay out of your way in the guesthouse."

"Nonsense," Margaret said. "You and Meredith must be there. Brent and Hope are arriving at four."

Derrick appeared pumped to learn his brother and his wife would get there a day early. "That's awesome. I can't wait to see them."

"Yeah," Meredith said. "Me, too." While she'd kept up a ton with Jackie, who lived in Boston, she hadn't seen Hope since last year.

"I always loved Brent," Olivia said. "So stable. And shrewd. Nobody could ever pull anything off on him!" She stared at the pale faces around her and everyone who had frozen in place. "What is it? What did I say?"

Next, she misjudged her mistake. "Oh no. I'm sorry. I didn't mean it to sound like I was playing favorites. Naturally, William," she said, addressing him, "I've always had the greatest respect for you. *Loved* Sally, too. So much sass! And well…" She glanced helplessly at Chad and Margaret. "Pretty much all of you."

Meredith sighed. "The Albrights are pretty easy to love," she said mistakenly out loud. Her face burned hot and she avoided Derrick's gaze as Titi Clarita gave her the side-eye.

"Thanks, Meredith," Margaret said warmly, accepting the compliment like the gracious hostess she was. She tried soothing Olivia next. "And it's no problem, sweetheart. About Brent. We know what you meant."

"Oh, um…good." Olivia drained her wine, appearing very intent on her toenail polish, which was expertly applied.

Where had she found a salon out in the wilderness?

• • •

Dinnertime was pleasant enough, but it mainly centered on Olivia. How did she like her job as a ranger?

Loved it. It was such a "natural" fit. Ha-ha-ha!

Meredith had wanted to hold her head at the laughter.

Fortunately, she'd restrained herself.

What made her go in that direction?

She'd always been a fan of the outdoors. That answer had caused Derrick to wince a little, but he'd covered it quickly.

"Can I get anyone more coffee?" he asked, standing to refill his cup.

"I'll take some, thank you," Clarita said.

Meredith decided she'd better not. She was already jittery enough. Olivia sat next to Derrick and Grandpa Chad was to her left. Meredith was on Derrick's other side near Grandmother Margaret and Sofia. William and Clarita were across the way.

Meredith picked up her fork to savor her last bite of strawberry cheesecake. Grandmother Margaret was a baking fiend in the kitchen. It was no wonder that Grandpa Chad stayed a little thick around the middle. Margaret managed to stay slim, though. Maybe because she never stayed seated for long. "Julia seems to be sleeping like a lamb."

"Shh," Sofia smiled softly. "Don't jinx it."

The next instant, a sputtering cry broke out on William's monitor. He'd laid it on the sideboard and reached for it behind him. "No truer words."

Margaret shook her head. "Oh dear."

"Babies that age never sleep for long. At least our Parker didn't," Chad volunteered.

"I'm sorry that he and Mom will miss the fun and games tomorrow," Derrick said. "Your folks, too, Sofia."

"My folks can probably do without the fun and games this time," Sofia said.

"This time?" Clarita questioned.

"There were quite a few party games leading up to our wedding." Sofia giggled like she hadn't minded. "Sort of like the ones we played on the boat?"

Meredith chuckled at the memory of the rowdy bachelorette party. "Oh."

"My folks were a little thrown off guard." Sofia pulled a face. "They're very serious."

"But terrific people," Grandpa Chad said, finishing his dessert.

Julia's whimper became a whine and Sofia turned to William. He'd already stood up. "I'll get her." He exchanged a knowing look with his wife and rolled his eyes toward Olivia. "You probably want to stay and visit for a while."

Sofia nodded her thanks, addressing Olivia. "I was thinking you and I could take a walk after dinner? Before it gets too dark out."

"That would be great," Olivia said.

Derrick shot a questioning look at Meredith and she kicked him under the table. Olivia getting in good again with the family would work well for everyone. Besides that, it wasn't like he was needing to work too hard to recapture Olivia's interest. The woman's interest in the youngest Albright brother was written all over her face.

CHAPTER SEVENTEEN

Once the kitchen was tidied up—and after Meredith promised to check in the next morning—Clarita retreated to the guesthouse with her big pile of books. Derrick's grandparents were clearly tired and Sofia and Olivia had not yet returned from their walk. Since William was still occupied upstairs with the baby, Derrick suggested to Meredith that they should return to his cabin and she'd readily agreed.

Derrick had no clue what she'd been concocting in that matchmaking mind of hers, but he was eager to find out. "So," he said on their drive home. "I think things went okay, don't you?"

Meredith stared out her window. The sun dipped low in the sky edging toward sunset, but it wouldn't be down for an hour. "Yeah. I mean, Olivia seems perfect."

He frowned. That was an odd choice of words. "Nobody's perfect, come on."

"Derrick," Meredith said seriously. "She didn't have a hair out of place."

"Maybe that's because I'm no longer pulling on it," he joked.

"Were you really that bad?" She glanced at him. "The two of you constantly at each other's throats?"

"Not constantly. We did have our happy moments, Sweet Pea and I."

She pulled a face. "Sweet Pea? That's what you called her?"

"Well, I definitely didn't call her Mer."

"Funny." She scowled and slumped back in her seat. "I actually kind of wish you didn't call me that, either."

Wait. "Why not?"

"It sounds like a horse."

He chuckled at her indignation. "Neigh, neigh."

She harrumphed. "It's no wonder you and Olivia fought. You bring out the worst in people."

Why was she being so cranky? She should be elated, right? Her plan was working. Olivia was here. For better or worse. He hoped for the better, but he wasn't sure.

"Not always," he answered. "I've been told—as an instructor—I bring out the best."

"I meant personally."

He grinned, attempting to encourage her. "Personally, I seem to be bringing out the best in you. Just look! Today went super."

"Super. Yeah."

She mumbled something under her breath. Maybe she was grumpy from thinking so hard about Olivia? If he was honest, obsessing about Olivia made him a little testy, too. He let out a breath, ready to let all that frustration go.

There was one thing he could do to cheer her up.

At least, he *hoped* it'd cheer her up.

She didn't say much else until he pulled into his driveway. Maybe this wasn't a good idea. Or maybe it was a great idea. There was only one way to find out.

"You know." He cleared his throat, feeling slightly geeky about what he was about to do. But no. This was good. He should go on ahead. "I made something for you. Or, I'm making it still. It's almost done."

Her big, dark eyes went wide. "You what?"

"A gift, Mer," he rasped. "I was going to give it to you later, but I figure." He shrugged. "Why wait?"

She gaped at him. "Why?"

"Just because."

She studied him curiously, but he could tell he'd piqued her interest. Good.

"Oh. Wow." A smile tugged at her lips. "That was nice of you."

He grinned. "Want to see it?"

This time her grin was huge. *There's the money note.* "Sure."

They reached his workshop and he flipped on the light. Then he led her over to the workbench and the project that was laid sideways but facing them. "This, Matchmaker Lady, is for you and all those shoes of yours."

She goggled at the short cabinet with an open front and multiple small compartments sectioned off, and tears sprang to her eyes. "*Der-rick.*" She cupped her hands to her mouth. "You didn't!"

He gestured to the rack he'd built out of quality white ash. He still needed to stain it. "It'll hold twenty-four pairs. So." His forehead rose. "That should get you through, I don't know, a week?"

She laughed and playfully swatted his chest. Then she studied it again, running her hand along its top. "It's amazing." Emotion flickered in her eyes. "I love it. Really I do."

Warmth spread through his chest. "I'm glad."

She reached out and hugged him tightly. "Thank you."

His heart soared as he held her close. Having her in his arms felt like heaven, almost like she fit there, and for a moment he didn't want to let her go.

"You're welcome," he said hoarsely when they pulled apart. "Don't forget to take it with you when you go."

"I won't." She smiled. "I'll use it every day and think of you."

"In a positive way?" he joked. "Now that would be something."

She laughed and more warmth flooded his soul. Turned out he liked making her happy—who'd have thought? And that realization made him want to do it again. He liked the thought of spending more time with her, just the two of them. Having fun, like they'd done while binge-watching all those house-hunting shows.

As they walked back to the cabin, he scanned the sky over the cove. "The sun's almost down," he said. "Maybe we should fix some tea or something and sit on the deck?"

"That sounds ideal," she said.

A short time later, they both sat outside with their mugs, watching as the gorgeous horizon faded from orangey-purple to charcoal gray and then black.

Derrick had looked forward to more downtime

alone with Meredith, but then she had to go back to that plan of hers by bringing Olivia up. "You were right, you know. Things with you and Olivia went super today."

He frowned and sipped his tea. "Your match-making skills are stellar. I'll give you that. Plus, they appear to be working."

"That's only because Olivia never lost interest in you."

"You think?"

"Derrick." Her dark eyes glimmered, but she looked a little sad again. "I'd lay money on it. I saw how she looked at you. She's still interested. This isn't going to be nearly as difficult as I thought."

"Less work for everybody, I guess." Though he wasn't so sure he should be thinking of wooing his ex-wife as "work." Did he want to woo her, really? That seemed like biting off a whole lot more than he could chew right now. Spending time together was probably the right move. See if anything was there. Maybe also to mend fences like he'd thought about before. If something grew between them, great. If not, at least he'd never wonder *what-if*.

He stole a peek at Meredith. Shockingly, he was enjoying spending time with her. Also, weirdly, getting kind of used to having her around. He admired her pretty profile, appreciating her smarts and strength. Her warmth and determination, too.

That warmth seemed to be missing tonight, though. Other than when he'd showed her his gift, she seemed distracted, her thoughts on something else.

He sat back in his chair and studied her. "Hey,"

he asked gently. "Is everything all right?"

"Yeah. Sorry."

"Care to tell me what's on your mind?"

Meredith shook her head and seemed to change her mind. "I'm sure it's nothing. The important thing is that Olivia's here, so let's focus on that," she said, looking up. "She's repairing things with Sofia, and by extension William and your family. You're up next."

"You're forgetting about Sally and my parents."

"Hate to say so, but they're secondary. Besides, your parents aren't coming until Saturday."

"We can't count on Sally not to run interference," he said. "She never liked Olivia much, and I can't promise she'll be any better now."

"That's why you need to meet with Olivia first," Meredith said. "Solidify things between you before Sally arrives and is able to cast fresh doubts."

"I'd planned to talk to her tonight before Sofia jumped in."

"Maybe it's better if you two go off on your own."

"Off? Like where?"

She groaned. "Gee, I don't know. You know Blue Hill better than I do. You keep saying that it's hot here"—she shot him a pointed look—"why not go out for ice cream? Or have you forgotten how to date entirely?"

"Hey," he protested. "I know how to date. I'm just making sure I don't mess up your grand plan, whatever it is. It's *your* syndication deal on the line."

"Sorry," she groused. "You're right. I shouldn't have snapped at you."

"Okay, then." He eyed her. "Ice cream is a great

idea," he said. "Even better, there's a farm stand on the far side of town that sells homemade blueberry frozen yogurt. All organic. Olivia totally digs that sort of thing." He paused. "At least she did."

She looked past the deck and up at the darkened sky, and wrapped a lock of her dark hair around a finger. "Why don't you give her a call and ask her?"

"What? Right this second?"

"She and Sofia are bound to be back by now."

"All right." He pulled his cell from his hip pocket and dialed Olivia's number. Meredith had shared it with him earlier.

Olivia answered on the second ring. "Derrick? Oh hey!" She sounded pleased that he was calling and clearly still had his number on her list. "What a fun dinner that was with your grandparents."

"Uh, yeah. It was great." He hesitated, his stomach churning. "Did you have a nice walk with Sofia?"

"Very nice. We cleared up a lot of things, which was good."

"I'm glad. She and William seem really happy that you could make it."

Meredith made a fast-forward motion with her hands.

"Yeah, I'm happy that I made it, too," Olivia said happily. "It's been so great seeing you again."

These were the words he and Meredith had hoped he'd hear and yet they didn't hit the way he'd anticipated. "Yeah, um…about that. It's been great seeing you, too, but I'm still thinking we need to talk."

"Agreed."

"So, I was thinking about a little outing tomorrow?" Olivia waited and so did Meredith, who had her eyebrows raised. "How does going for frozen yogurt sound?"

"Perfect." Her smile practically sparkled through the phone. "Especially if it's blueberry."

She had to know it would be, so this made him chuckle. "Yeah."

"Sounds great! What time?"

"How about if I pick you up after lunch? Say around two?"

"I'll look forward to it then," she said, ending the call.

Derrick stared at Meredith dumbfounded. "I'm actually going on a date with my ex-wife. Until this moment, I don't think I ever really believed it'd happen."

"You doubted me?" she asked, but her smile looked forced.

"So. Um. What should we talk about? Any topics I should avoid?"

"Derrick." She rolled her eyes. "You're the ladies' man."

"Sure, and you're the matchmaker."

"Yeah, I am." She picked up her tea and sighed. "And a pretty great one it seems."

• • •

Meredith tossed and turned on the lumpy sofa bed. It was ridiculous she was having trouble sleeping. She should have drifted right off into dreamland, fully accomplished in her mission. Getting Derrick and Olivia together had been a piece of cake. *Wedding* cake.

She recalled that happy grin on his face when he'd showed her that shoe rack and her heart ached. It was the sweetest thing anyone had ever done for her. But then she got in her head about it because, sure, he'd made it for her, but he was probably dreaming up things to build Olivia. Like what? A manicure supply cabinet with a gazillion drawers. Why did the woman have such great nails? Probably because she had great everything.

She groaned, pulling her pillow over her face. What on earth was wrong with her and why was she so grumpy? This was exactly what Meredith wanted, and Derrick had kept his end of the bargain so far. Her phone buzzed on the side table.

She sat up and switched on the light, grabbing her phone.

You and Derrick?
When were you going to tell me?

Uh-oh. That was from her friend Jackie. She must have caught wind of "the Matchmaker and the Boatbuilder" media story somehow. There'd been so much going on here, Meredith had completely forgotten to warn her. She'd tried calling Jackie during her drive up, but Jackie nearly never answered her personal calls. Then, afterwards Meredith had been so thrown into the thick of things, she'd mostly forgotten about the outside world beyond Blue Hill.

She dashed off a quick text.

In Maine at Derrick's. Not what you think.
Getting him back together with Olivia.
Engagement story's made up, but please don't
blab until I clear things up myself. Let's grab lunch
soon and I'll explain everything! Love you!

She texted right back.

Wait? What? Olivia? She's in Blue Hill, too?

Meredith and Jackie had once been really close,
but they'd had a falling out after some of Jackie's
shenanigans last summer. Once things calmed
down, they'd restored their friendship, but things
hadn't exactly been the same. They'd been working
on it, though, and still kept up casually by grabbing
drinks once in a while. Sometimes lunch or a movie.
Meredith typed in her reply.

Yeah. She's staying at the guest cottage.

And, you're at Derrick's cabin…with him?

Meredith didn't miss the nosy innuendo.

Everyone's here for Julia's christening.

Oh yeah. Hope said she was going to that. Wait.

How did you wind up there?

Meredith startled when she heard a rumbling
sound coming from the bedroom. The door was
slightly ajar but it was dark inside. The rumbling
sound happened again and she realized it was
Derrick snoring. At least she wouldn't have to live
with that. Olivia would.

Look, she answered Jackie, gotta run. Let's meet up when I get home!

All right.

There was a break then another text followed by a shamrock emoji.

Good luck!

Meredith was about to put away her cell when Jackie texted a final time.

Love you!

This message was followed by a heart emoji. Jackie had become really sentimental in her texts ever since her basic breakdown last summer. The hard edges of her personality had also softened a bit. She'd even connected with a nice guy, and they'd been going out for a few months. Meredith hoped things would work out for her this time. Despite her insecurities, Jackie did have her good side and was a decent person underneath. Twelve months of counseling and meditative yoga had helped a lot with that.

Meredith set aside her phone and climbed from the sofa bed, suddenly famished. Though the dinner at the Albrights had been delicious, she hadn't eaten as much as she normally did, because she'd strangely lost her appetite. It was probably sitting across from perfect Olivia that had done it. The woman had an amazing figure even though she ate like a horse. A horse with good table manners, but still.

Meredith shook off her annoyance at being

called "Mare" by Derrick. Sometimes she didn't mind it, but tonight it had rubbed her the wrong way. Especially after hearing how he'd called Olivia "Sweet Pea." Seriously? Gah. Maybe she should start teasing him back by calling him "Dare" to see how he liked it?

Her stomach rumbled. What she wouldn't give for some nice chocolates. Melt-in-your mouth silky designer chocolates. Oh yeah. She could eat an entire box. Her gut contracted painfully and she realized this wasn't helping one bit.

But chocolate would. If she could find it.

Derrick didn't strike her as the baking sort, but maybe he kept chocolate chips around? Or a hidden stash of candy bars? Maybe he even had something left over from last Halloween, stored in his freezer?

Now she was getting desperate. No way did Derrick get trick-or-treaters living way out here. She rummaged through the pantry and checked some cabinets, but was disappointed to find nothing more exciting than canned soups, oatmeal, and grits. He had an unopened bag of chips, but Meredith was in the mood for sweet—not savory.

Then she yanked open the freezer compartment.

Score! Two whole pints of double-chocolate-chunk ice cream!

She popped the lid off of one and then the other, noting that both containers were still covered by a protective plastic covering. Neither had been opened.

Meredith bit her lip, considering her options. Then her stomach contracted again.

Okay. This is fine. I mean, didn't Derrick just offer me ice cream for dessert?

That was yesterday, but surely he wouldn't mind her having a tiny scoop now.

She set one pint container on the counter and took a bowl out of the cabinet. After locating an ice cream scoop, she served herself one nice round ball.

Ooh, that looks so good with walnuts in it and everything. Chewy caramel chunks, too.

Her mouth watered and she served herself another scoop.

Who was she kidding?

She went with two more, so she had a total of four.

Happily satisfied, she carried her bowl back to the sofa bed and snuggled down under the covers, her back propped against a pillow.

One bite of ice cream and… *Ahhh, this is heaven.*

She glanced at the book that Chad had given her and thought about reading. Then she decided she wasn't up for a bunch of *happily-ever-afters* tonight. No, thanks. She'd much rather enjoy this chocolatey frozen treat, while trying not to think about Derrick's date with Olivia. Of course it was for yogurt, and of course it was blueberry. So healthy. Olivia probably couldn't even spell chocolate. Oh yeah, she went to law school. So never mind, she probably could. Maybe even in Latin. That would give her and Derrick one more thing in common.

Meredith scarfed down her ice cream, realizing that four scoops weren't nearly enough. They'd been smallish scoops anyway. So one more helping would make up for their subpar size.

She grumbled and got out of bed, carrying her empty bowl back into the kitchen.

Part of her brain set out a warning signal: *Wait! Stop! Stress eating!*

But other parts of her honestly didn't care. Like her mouth and her stomach.

She yanked open the freezer door, noting that the open pint on the counter was pretty much empty. What a rip-off these tiny cartons were! Barely even a one-person serving. Her gaze lingered on the second pint, just sitting there waiting. Tempting her with its deliciousness.

She couldn't possibly eat all of Derrick's ice cream. Not that he'd likely even notice. Not once he was in his happy love bubble after his stellar afternoon outing with model-like Olivia.

She opened the second pint container, peeling back its plastic covering, and it looked just as good as the first one had. All pristine across the top, like a glistening chocolate pond just waiting for her to dive in, and so she did. And then she did again with the big ice cream scooper. Oh who cares?

Things between Derrick and Olivia will be sewn up soon enough.

She scooped again.

Then they'll be in love.

Just one more scoop. No, two.

Possibly even getting married.

And making those beautiful babies together.

She paused in her ice cream scooping and sighed.

While I'll go home to my empty apartment in Boston and eat raw slice-and-bake cookie dough out of the freezer.

She reached the bottom of the container and — scrape, scrape, scrape — scraped it clean.

CHAPTER EIGHTEEN

Meredith woke up feeling totally grossed out from her sugar coma. How much ice cream had she eaten?

Oh yeah.

She pulled the covers over her head.

All of it.

"Good morning," Derrick said from the kitchen and sounding awake. Unlike her. Ugh. "Coffee?"

Meredith lowered the blankets and rubbed her eyes. "Coffee sounds good, thanks."

"How'd you sleep?" he asked. Naturally, he was in a good mood. He was taking Olivia out for ice cream. No. Scratch that. Frozen blueberry yogurt. Only low-fat and healthy would do. Which had totally been her idea. Yay. She should be so proud of herself.

Only she wasn't.

Meredith propped herself up on her elbows. "Okay, and you?"

"Slept like a baby." Sunlight flooded the kitchen behind him as he carried over a coffee mug and set it down on the table beside her. She nodded in thanks.

"Yeah, so I heard."

His forehead rose, then fell. "Oh no, was I snoring?"

She pinched her thumb and forefinger together. "Just a smidge."

He winced. "Sorry. Olivia used to say I snored

like a bear."

"Huh."

He shook his head. "That's how she got her nickname for me: Cuddly Bear."

Ick. A big tough guy like him called Cuddly Bear? No. She couldn't see it. Imagining Olivia saying it was even worse. *Cuddly Bear, coo-coo-coo.* Baby talk. Ick. Ick. Ick.

"And she was Sweet Pea, how *cute*." Meredith hated that her tone dripped with sarcasm. Why should she care?

Derrick seemed to be wondering that, too. He set his hands on his hips. "Is something wrong?"

Meredith sipped from her coffee, which was nice and strong. Good. She needed a swift kick this morning. Like, in the brain. *Did I really eat all that ice cream? Whyyyy????*

"Nope, not really," she answered him. "I was just thinking of nicknames, and the one you call me."

"Oh yeah?" He sat down beside her in a chair as she propped herself up in the sofa bed.

"Yeah. And I've decided I should call you one, too."

"Have at it," he said, not looking the least bit afraid.

She took a sip of coffee. "What do you think of Der?"

"Der?" he asked. "As in, you *dare* me not to call you Mer again?"

"That's right."

His eyes danced. "Fine by me."

Wait? Fine?

"Sounds kind of *daring*. Rugged. Dangerous." He set his elbows on his knees and stared at her, holding his chin in his hands.

"You are so not…" She caught a whiff of his cologne and lost her bearings. He'd dressed in jeans and a maroon polo shirt, and his hair was still damp from his shower. Olivia probably couldn't wait to get her hands on that hair and run her fingers through it. "Da…dangerous," she finished, recalling where she was.

His lips twitched. "At least we've established that part." He stood and glanced at the door. "I'm going to go and work on the cradle for a bit. It's nearly done."

"That's great." Her voice was kind of a growl. So she took another sip of coffee, hoping he hadn't noticed. Wasn't his fault that his world was all glowingly perfect right now. She could take a lot of the credit for that.

And she would, if it didn't make her sick to her stomach.

Like all that ice cream. She'd probably never eat that flavor again.

Derrick strolled into the kitchen and took the lid off the standing trash can. "I'll take out the trash when I go."

Meredith's breath seized in her lungs. Her empty ice cream containers were in there, even though she'd tried to bury them below some other stuff. "No! Wait!"

He stared at her puzzled. "Wait? What?"

"I'll do it!" She tossed back her covers and stomped into the kitchen wearing her baggy sleep jersey. It came down to her thighs so pretty much covered everything it needed to. Although, she'd have to be careful bending forward to cinch the ties on the waste bag. She wasn't exactly wearing her best underwear.

Derrick rubbed his chin. "You can't possibly go out there like that."

"Why not? We're in the middle of nowhere." She peered out the window. "Has the press come back?"

"No." He chuckled. "It's just that you're barefoot and all. Not even dressed, and it's chilly out."

"I feel it's important for me to do my part," she told him. "You can't do everything."

He stepped in front of her. "And neither can you, dressed in your nightie."

"It's a football jersey, Derrick. Not lingerie."

"From the New England Patriots," Derrick went on. "Did you date that guy?"

"The player?" Yes, but she barely thought of it as Jack's old jersey anymore. He'd given it to her so long ago. "Would it be shocking if I had?"

"No," he said, but his ears reddened. "Not at all. Your personal life is personal."

"Exactly. Glad we're on the same page." She squared her shoulders and approached the trash bin.

"I'll get that," he said, turning away.

"No, me!"

She darted around him nearly knocking him over and yanked the bag out of the container, cinching its ties. He goggled at the bag and her face burned hot.

"Hang on." His eyebrows knitted together. "Are those ice cream cartons in there?"

Meredith stared in horror at the bulging outlines of two containers, clearly visible through the thin plastic of the opaque bag.

"Oh wow! You're right." She gazed at him big-eyed. "I guess they are." She hoisted up the bag and scuttled toward the door. "I'll just—"

He took two long strides and suddenly they were face-to-face with him blocking her escape. His fingers clenched around the top of the bag and her heart hammered. He grinned. "Please," he said with mock formality. "Allow me."

Meredith held her breath, looking up at him, and he stared right down at her. Knowing she'd eaten every ounce of that yummy ice cream all by herself. He leaned closer and she felt the heat of his breath on her lips. Which made her all light-headed and caused her pulse to pound in a wicked rhythm.

"I'm sorry you didn't get enough to eat last night."

"I, um…" She licked her lips. "Did."

"Eventually, it seems," he said in a cocksure way. Then he took that traitorous trash bag and walked out the door.

She wanted to sink into the floor and die of humiliation, but she didn't have time. Her cell rang first. She expected Clarita but it was Beth.

"Good news!" Beth said. "I just spoke with Jerry and he says the network execs he's talked to are very impressed with your numbers. Viewership from your last show broke a record!

Even higher than when you were on *Talk Time* with Tanya."

"Wow." Meredith sat at the kitchen table. "That's better than I hoped."

"This whole Derrick thing is majorly working for you," Beth said. "Other stations have started calling about syndication. From out of state! And of course *Maine* is right at the top of the list." She squealed and Meredith couldn't help but squeal along with her.

"Everyone says you must know what you're doing. Even if you and he are private and don't want to talk about it."

"Thanks for shutting down the press."

"Helps to have friends in high places." Meaning, Jerry's second cousin once removed, who worked for the local area county commissioner's Office of Media Affairs. While Jerry's cousin couldn't exactly prohibit news coverage of a resident's story, he could discourage inflaming a tale he had on good authority would be debunked soon.

"Yeah, appreciate it!" Meredith noticed her coffee mug was empty and stood to refill it. "And anyway, it looks like that small bit of attention is paying big benefits."

"There's going to be a huge outpouring of sympathy for you when Derrick Albright breaks your heart."

Meredith's chest clenched uncomfortably. "Yeah. Maine sure as heck won't be interested then."

"Meh. We'll be fine without them. Everyone will be so impressed when you step aside for true love,"

Beth went on. "Genius move. I'm in awe of your talent. Really I am."

"Who wouldn't support the gorgeous pair?" Meredith said out loud. But deep down in her soul she grumbled. *Cuddly Bear and Sweet Pea are so ideally suited for each other. Derrick will probably even build a brand new cradle for each and every one of their exceedingly beautiful babies. Ugh.* It was too much, imagining their perfect family, so she stopped.

Meredith lifted her coffee mug in a toast with an imaginary friend, recalling her reasons for being here. "Here's to a sweet, sweet syndication deal!"

"Or something even better," Beth said. "Jerry scheduled a Friday morning meeting with some people from QuikPix."

"What?" Meredith grinned. "The streaming service? You're kidding me?"

"No. Totally serious. Think about it, Meredith! This could be even better than syndication. Viewers could binge watch *Matched Up.*"

"Maybe I'll get both?" Meredith said with a hopeful edge.

"That would be a-ma-zing," Beth sang.

Meredith's head swam with the possibilities, all of which involved dollar signs. Derrick could keep his cozy little cabin in the woods and populate it with all the red-headed Olivia offspring he wanted. Meredith had bigger things in mind. Large, expensive, glamorous things.

Like a standalone house with a swimming pool out on the Cape somewhere. She wouldn't be lonely. She'd make lots of celebrity friends, maybe even marry a movie star. One bright enough to outshine Derrick and Olivia's couple-y supernova.

"I'm so proud of you, Meredith," Beth said. "You're really going places."

"Wherever I go," she told her, "you're coming with me."

At least then she'd have one true friend to ask to dinner.

. . .

"Thanks for coming to pick me up," Olivia said. "That was really sweet." She batted her big green eyes and Derrick waited to be swept away by them. Then he waited a moment longer. He finally gave up and started his ignition. He was probably just out of practice.

"I'd nearly forgotten how beautiful Blue Hill is," Olivia commented as they drove along.

"You've got some great vistas over at Acadia."

"Yeah, that's true." She wore jeans and a tube-top with a light jacket over it, and her hair was in a ponytail today. "Derrick," she said bluntly as they passed through town. "Is it true what Sofia said?"

"I don't know." He tried to sound noncommittal, though he knew precisely what she was getting at. "What did she say?"

Olivia watched him quietly until he shot her a sideways glance. "That you wanted to see me again."

He cleared his throat. "Yes."

She kept her gaze on him while he tried not to

look at her, instead focusing on the winding road. "Why?"

He shrugged. "I guess I wanted to see if anything was still there."

"Between the two of us?" She stared out the window. "I see." An uncomfortable moment passed before she added, "I'm glad that Sofia called, and so happy for her and William about the baby."

"Yeah. Their family's really sweet."

"And Derrick," she said softly. "I'm happy about seeing you again, too."

They got to the farm stand and Derrick got them a couple of frozen yogurts in paper cups. They ate with small wooden paddle-style spoons at a picnic table by the water.

They made small talk for a bit, chatting about college days and what had become of their former friends, none of whom they'd kept up with except for casually on social media. It was cool catching up with Olivia. He'd expected things to be super awkward, but they really weren't too bad. After having broken the ice in front of his family yesterday, today felt more like visiting with an old friend.

At last, Derrick braved it. "Olivia, about how things ended…"

She rolled her eyes. "With a big fight."

"We both shouted a lot, yeah. For my part, I'm sorry."

"I'm sorry, too." She frowned. "I'm especially sorry about what I said about you not going anywhere. You've clearly made a life for yourself here."

He appreciated her comment and her apology.

"Your career path sure changed. What happened to practicing law?"

"Hard to practice without passing the bar."

Her face colored and Derrick felt a wave of emotion. Sympathy maybe, or something more. Without thinking about it, he reached out and took her hand. And it felt like…well, Olivia's hand. Cool and a little bony.

"Not everyone passes the first time."

"I took it four times." She ducked her chin and then looked up at him, appearing helplessly lost. "I didn't know what else to do. I'd spent my whole life prepping to be a lawyer, even interning with your sister and Sofia. And then the whole thing fell apart." She winced. "Please don't tell them. Not yet."

"I won't." He squeezed her hand. "So, what led to Acadia?"

"I always liked being outdoors—"

"Liar," he teased and she laughed, withdrawing her hand. She rubbed it with her other one a moment before continuing.

"You're right. I didn't. Not in a camping sort of way. But then I met Paul and he was into it."

"Paul?"

"My ex-boyfriend."

"The lawyer?"

"No, that was David. Paul came after Jason."

"Oh," Derrick said, losing track. "He wasn't a football player, was he?" Derrick wasn't sure how many of those he could take in one day. So Meredith had dated a big beefcake guy? *Good for her. That was probably her type,* he thought sourly.

Derrick had been more of a baseball player and crew member himself, but had never been good enough to turn pro.

She blinked at the apparent non sequitur. "No, a park ranger."

"Ah. I can see the connection."

Olivia fell silent a moment. "You know, now's probably not the *best* time to discuss old boyfriends."

Derrick chuckled. "Except for one of them, maybe?" he said, indicating himself.

Olivia smiled, "I guess I can make an exception. So, what have you been up to?"

"Boatbuilding."

She laughed. "Of course. I remember that canoe you built for your grandpa. Has he still got it?"

"He does."

"Does he take it out?"

"I sure hope not," Derrick said, and she laughed harder.

"You're right," Olivia said. "He's probably a little past that."

"They keep it around, though," Derrick told her. "And people use it from time to time. People in the family, I mean, when they're up here."

"That's good it hasn't gone to waste."

He looked into her eyes, and this time he felt something. A distant fondness maybe. Like gently rolling waves tugging him out to sea along with all those old memories. It wasn't exactly the tumultuous ocean scene he saw very presently in Meredith's dark gaze. Meredith's eyes were like a Dark 'n' Stormy cocktail—full of heat and mystery.

A mystery that part of him ached to unravel. But who was he kidding? Meredith wasn't interested in him. Just this morning, she'd practically shoved him out the door and straight into Olivia's arms.

He sighed. "Olivia, Olivia."

"Derrick Albright," she said, her eyes sparkling.

He set his elbows on the picnic table and placed his chin in his hands, considering her. She was still as pretty as she ever was. Possibly even more beautiful. And she did seem like she'd matured. "Where do we go from here?"

"Don't know," she answered. "Where would you like to go?"

She locked on his gaze and his heart thudded in a dull ache. Like underneath the comforting familiarity, something was off. The thought of going places with Olivia didn't fill him with joy. No, the emotions he was experiencing felt more like dread. Maybe because this was all so new and he was still getting used to the idea?

Or maybe there was a bigger problem. One with gorgeous brown eyes, a suitcase full of not-at-all sensible shoes, and a whole lot of opinions.

"I'm not sure," he said after a bit.

She pursed her lips. "Me neither."

They sat there a moment and finished their frozen yogurt. Derrick was unsure of what to say next. He guessed he could drive her back to the guesthouse but that didn't seem right. They still hadn't discussed the future. Then again, Meredith had warned him to take his time, to not rush things. Maybe she was right and they needed to take things slow. They had a plan—one that required him to end up with Olivia so he and Meredith could break off their fake liaison.

Olivia stood and cleaned up their trash, carrying it to an outdoor waste bin. "Thanks for the yogurt. It was great."

"You're welcome."

She glanced toward his SUV. "Should we—?

"How 'bout we go for a drive?"

CHAPTER NINETEEN

Meredith and Clarita sat in the cute café overlooking the bay. They'd come here after visiting the in-town bookshop, where they'd purchased copies of the classic children's stories *The Runaway Bunny* and *Goodnight Moon* for little Julia. Since neither of them was sure whether people would be bringing presents to the baby shower, they'd decided to err on the side of caution, and the store had been kind enough to giftwrap the books.

Clarita observed the cache of boats moored in the small marina, as gulls darted in and out of the waves. "It's so beautiful here."

"Yeah, I know," Meredith answered. "It's no wonder Blue Hill has become the prime location for Albright family weddings."

"What do you mean?"

"William and Sofia were married here. Then Brent and Jackie planned to next…"

"Right," Clarita said. She rolled her eyes at the memory of that fiasco. Meredith had told her all about it. "What about Derrick?"

"What about him?"

"Do you think he and Olivia will have their wedding here as well? Assuming they marry again?"

Meredith's stomach soured. That's *exactly* what she wanted to think about—another Blue Hill wedding. With Derrick and Olivia who were probably planning it all out on their lovey-dovey frozen yogurt date. Or maybe they were discussing honeymoons and the really awesome one they'd had in Vegas.

No, she was definitely not going to think about Derrick and Olivia's wedding.

"Probably." Meredith lifted a shoulder, feigning indifference. "Unless her family has better plans."

Clarita sighed. "Hard to imagine anything much better than this."

"Yeah."

"Hey." Clarita got an excited gleam in her eye. "Maybe you'll get invited to the wedding?"

Meredith groaned inwardly. So much for not thinking about it. "Oooh, wouldn't *that* be nice."

Clarita touched her arm. "*Hija*?"

"I'm sorry, Titi Clarita." Geez, what was wrong with her? She'd been snippy with everyone lately. "I'm just not big on society weddings."

"Since when? I thought you loved them?"

"Since last summer, I guess."

Clarita gave her a sage look but said nothing.

"So, how did things go with Olivia sharing the guesthouse last night?" she asked.

"We didn't interact much," Clarita said. "She was polite and fixed herself some herbal tea before retreating downstairs to read magazines."

"What kind of magazines?"

"They had birds and butterflies on them. I think someone from the family left them in the guesthouse."

"Oh." A quiet night reading magazines about butterflies fit the growing picture of Perfect Olivia.

Nobody was that together all of the time, and Meredith felt like a hot mess in comparison. "Was she at least a wreck when she woke up? Big bags under her eyes, ratty hair, and—"

"Actually," Clarita said. "She appeared in the kitchen looking like one of those *au natural* actresses out of the movies."

Darn it. "None of them are *au natural*. They use makeup. Every last one."

"I don't think she had any on at the time," Clarita reported. "Some women are blessed like that. Their coloring and features give them that fresh-faced look regardless."

They stared at each other wide-eyed.

"Not us," they said together and giggled.

"She was in a pretty great mood, though," Clarita said. "Something about going out for frozen yogurt with Derrick."

"Yeah, I think Derrick was looking forward to it, too. He seems eager to put their rocky past behind them. Olivia's clearly into him, though. She's probably hoping he'll come around. And maybe he will. That kind of perfection is hard to pass up."

Meredith frowned and Clarita leaned toward her. "You don't look so happy about this interest of Olivia's in Derrick."

"Of course I'm happy." She bared her teeth in a fake smile. "See."

"What's going on with you?" Clarita lowered her voice to a whisper. "Oh no. Are you jealous?"

"Jealous, me?" Meredith whispered back. "Don't be ridiculous. That's never happened before."

"What? Falling for a client?"

Meredith shook her head. "I don't do that. It's not professional." Besides that, what was the point? Derrick had had his chance to put his moves on her last summer, but he hadn't. He'd been stepping back ever since she got here this year, too. Except when she'd seen that look in his eyes when he'd given her that gift. Okay, and a few other times. Like after they'd been watching TV together, and when he'd showed her Julia's cradle. Even this morning when they'd fought about that trash bag, she thought she'd felt something. Then again, her imagination had always been really good.

"He made me a shoe rack," she told her aunt. "Can you believe it?"

"A what?" Clarita chuckled. "How sweet. What for?"

She shrugged. Honestly, she wasn't sure why he'd thought to make her a gift. It was such a thoughtful gesture, and really sweet when it came down to it—and "sweet" wasn't a word she'd have used to describe Derrick. At least not before. "As a thank-you I suppose for all my help."

Clarita smiled mysteriously. "And you think he doesn't know you."

"Oh, he does know me." And feeling seen like that, even if it was because she had a shoe addiction, was unexpected and…nice.

"Just not in the way you'd like?"

"Titi Clarita."

Clarita's eyebrows perked up. "He is pretty dishy."

"Sure, but he's Olivia's main course and not mine."

"But you want him to be?"

"No!" Heads swiveled their way and Meredith lowered her voice again. "Titi Clarita, that's not how it is with me and Derrick. He and I are helping each other out. That's all there is to it." She decided to change the subject since the topic at hand was making her testy. "I almost forgot to tell you. I got the best news from Beth." Meredith's spirits brightened at the thought of reaching this goal. So, okay, she didn't have love, but she was going to have money. *Yay!* "Our general manager's meeting with a streaming service exec tomorrow."

"Streaming? That sounds promising."

"Could get that *and* the syndication deal. And the plus side?" She grinned broadly, and this time her smile was genuine. "No commercials."

"Ooh, I like that idea."

"I think my audience will, too. Just think! They could binge-watch the first four seasons of *Matched Up*. Fingers crossed."

Clarita crossed her own. "Fingers crossed."

• • •

When Meredith and her aunt returned to the Albrights, Sally was standing in the drive beside her car, chatting with her grandparents. The effusive blonde with long, wavy hair and big, dark eyes bounded toward Meredith for a hug. "I heard you were here, and on a mission."

Meredith laughed uncomfortably because of what Derrick had said regarding Sally and Olivia not getting along. She grimaced. "You okay with that?"

Sally heaved a sigh. "What's good for my big brother is great with me. As long as Olivia's changed."

Grandmother Margaret scowled, but Sally's gaze was on Clarita. "Oh, hi! I'm sorry—"

"This is Meredith's aunt," Grandpa Chad supplied. "Clarita Rincón."

The women nodded their hellos as Sofia and William emerged from the house.

Sally hugged them. "So, where's the precious bundle?"

"Upstairs." Sofia smiled. "Sleeping, thank goodness."

William picked up Sally's bag. "I'll take this upstairs for you."

"Such a gentleman," Sally teased. "Or maybe you just don't want me waking up the baby."

"I always knew you were smart," William said, then darted away laughing when Sally made to chase him.

"All the Albright men are so gentlemanly," Clarita said with a sigh.

Grandmother Margaret nodded. "They'd better be." It came out stern, but made everyone laugh.

"So, where are the lovebirds?" Sally asked as they all walked toward the house.

"Wait," Meredith said. "They're not back yet?"

Grandpa Chad shook his head. "Saw the two of them leaving when I was out working in the garden."

William checked his watch and smirked. "And that was two hours ago."

Meredith's heart sank. *But this is good*, she tried

to tell herself. *Fab.*

"So, I know the parental units can't join us until tomorrow," Sally said. Her expression turned impish. "In the meantime, I've planned some fun and games." She glanced around at the group now, standing in the hall. "Grandmother and Grandpa, will you all play?"

Grandpa tugged at his snug vest. "That all depends—"

"Of course we will," Grandmother Margaret said, giving him an elbow. "We wouldn't want to be spoilsports."

• • •

Derrick and Olivia sat in his SUV at a pullover on a high cliff. The waters of Blue Hill Bay roiled and splashed below them. Neither one had said much since the frozen yogurt stand and the silence was starting to get uncomfortable.

"This feels pretty crazy," he said. "Being here together again."

"Well, we're not *together* together." She rolled her eyes and he chuckled.

"Hey, you know what I meant."

She relaxed in her seat. "Yeah."

"Do you…" He proceeded cautiously. "Think much about the old days?"

"I have." She met his gaze and her eyes glimmered sadly. "I mean, I do. But that was a long time ago, Derrick."

"It was," he answered, thinking it was seeming further and further away instead of closer. Which only had to mean he wasn't trying hard enough. Meredith had gone to all this trouble to get Olivia here. It would be like letting her down to not at least make an effort with his ex. Besides, he really wanted Meredith to get that syndication deal and her calling off her supposed relationship with him because of Olivia could build so much viewer sympathy. When he spoke, his throat felt scratchy and dry.

"I've thought about you a lot these last ten years."

"Yeah, I've thought about you, too."

"Did you ever wonder? What things might have been like if we'd kept at it?"

Her lips crept up in a smile. "Tearing each other's hair out you mean?"

"Ha!" He shook his head. "Yeah."

"Yeah, sure." She cocked her chin. "I wondered."

"Do you still wonder now?"

"A little bit."

"You're not seeing anyone?"

"No. And you?"

For some unbelievable reason he thought of Meredith. His gut churned and his heart gave a painful twist. Then he snapped himself out of it. She didn't want him and she'd never want a life in Blue Hill. And he definitely wasn't moving to Boston to become the sidekick to some big television star. "No. No one," he said and his heart sank.

"What's Meredith to you, really?" she asked, like she'd sneakily invaded his mind.

"Mer—edith and I are just friends."

"Just friends? Hmm."

"Yeah," he said, only this time when he said it, it felt like a lie.

Olivia's eyebrows arched. "Are you sure *she* knows that?"

"Yes." But the problem was he wasn't sure *he* did. "You ready to go back?"

She studied him, then gave a wistful smile. "Sure."

CHAPTER TWENTY

William lowered the green party balloon he'd inflated and knotted the end. "How many more of these do you want blown up?"

Sally finished a yellow one and dropped it in the laundry basket in front of where she sat on the porch swing. She glanced at Meredith, Clarita, and the others, who were helping out, too. Grandpa Chad and Margaret had also completed a couple of balloons. Sofia participated as their cheerleader, holding Julia on her lap. The baby wore a cute onesie, leggings, and a tiny knit cap. Even in June, it was on the cool side for a little one.

Hope and Brent were due to arrive any minute, but Derrick and Olivia still weren't back yet, which concerned Meredith more than it should. That had to mean they were enjoying each other's company. Maybe they'd even gone back to his cabin for a little privacy.

And wasn't that just awesome.

"We'll need a total of ten," Sally said. "No. Let's go for an even dozen to have a few spares."

"I think this is fun," Clarita said. "I haven't been to a baby shower in forever."

"It's a first for Julia, too," Sofia joked and everyone laughed. It was late afternoon and they sat around on cushioned wicker furniture, sipping bubbly pink champagne. Even the guys indulged because Sally said it was mandatory. Since she was nursing, Sofia stuck to the non-alcoholic sparkling cider Sally had brought along. That also was pink in honor of Julia, and the back porch had been decorated with streamers and a big sign proclaiming: It's a Girl!

Grandmother Margaret had ordered tea cakes, savory treats, and petits fours from a local bakery and set out bowls of salted nuts.

"These goodies are so delicious," Meredith said, sinking her teeth into a tiny-tiered square of layered chocolate.

Chad polished off a mini ham biscuit. "Going to ruin our appetites."

"We'll have a late dinner." Grandmother Margaret turned to Sally. "What are we going to do with all these balloons?"

Sally just grinned. "You'll see, Grandmother."

Sally glanced at Clarita and Meredith. "You ladies want to help with a special project?" When they both nodded, she grinned. "I expect you both have experience putting on diapers?"

Meredith exchanged glances with her aunt and Sofia held Julia a bit tighter.

"Um, sure." Meredith said on behalf of the two of them. "Why?"

Sally giggled and moved aside the balloon basket. She got to her feet, encouraging the rest of them to keep up the good work. Then she motioned to Meredith and Clarita. "Come with me."

Once they were in the kitchen, Sally hoisted a canvas bag out of a chair at the kitchen table. The table stood by a bay window overlooking the front lawn and beside a white brick hearth. A painting of some garden gloves and a basket of blueberries hung above the mantle.

"Here we are," Sally said, taking five naked baby dolls out of her bag and laying them on the table. Next, she dug into the bag for some disposable diapers and—wait. A big jar of chunky peanut butter? "And here you go!" She handed the peanut butter to Meredith and the diapers to Clarita. "Let me just go and grab two spatulas."

Meredith started putting things together. "Oh no. You're not planning to—"

Sally laughed. "Oh yes, I am. We're going to have a contest to see who can clean and re-diaper their baby the quickest. We'll divide up in teams."

Meredith hooted, trying to imagine Derrick's face when he removed the diaper and found nasty-looking peanut butter inside.

"New babies are messy." Sally pulled a face. "If you get my drift."

Clarita cackled. "All right. I'm in. Just tell me what you want me to do."

Sally handed Meredith and Clarita spatulas. "Load those baby bottoms up!"

• • •

A short time later, the women carried the five diapered dolls onto the porch and set them on a wicker rocker. "Oh how sweet," Margaret said. "Dolls!"

Grandpa Chad shook his head. "Sailing might have been better."

William chuckled. "Come on, Grandpa. Get in the spirit."

A car door slammed shut around the front of the house and then another.

"Derrick and Olivia?" Sally questioned. But the couple that rounded the corner was Brent and Hope.

Derrick's middle brother was dark-haired and dark-eyed and slightly shorter than William. His fair-skinned, brunette wife was Jackie's identical twin. Only Hope's layered brown hair was a little longer.

"We thought we heard voices out here!" Brent said, as they drew nearer.

"Hi everyone!" Hope held out her arms as the senior Albrights and William went to greet them.

"Greetings!" Sally called over to them. "You're just in time."

Meredith watched as Grandpa Chad, Margaret, and William took turns hugging Hope and Brent. She'd half expected things to be awkward between Hope and the family after what had happened last time in Blue Hill, but everyone appeared relaxed enough. Meredith had heard they'd all seen each other over the winter holidays and then again at Easter, so that buffering time had probably helped.

"Meredith!" Hope grinned broadly, approaching the porch. "I heard you were here!"

The women exchanged hugs and Meredith was instantly reminded of all the things she liked about Hope. Her sunny nature and optimism were paramount among them.

"It's nice seeing you both again," Meredith said.

"Where's Derrick?" Brent asked, noting his absence.

"And Olivia?" asked Hope. "We heard she's here, too."

"I texted Derrick a couple of minutes ago," William offered. "They're on their way."

Meredith's stomach knotted.

Get ready to see the happy couple…

• • •

Derrick pulled into the driveway at his grandparents' house. "Looks like Brent and Hope are here," he said, noting the extra SUV in the drive.

"I'm excited to meet Hope," Olivia said. "And see Brent again."

"Yeah," Derrick said. "They'll be happy to see you, too." While he wasn't entirely sure that would be the case with Brent, he'd said it anyway.

Of all his family members, Derrick had shared most of his post-Olivia angst with Brent. Brent had gotten him back last summer by bemoaning his issues with Hope. Yet, things were working out for the two of them. Maybe things would work out for him and Olivia, too.

When Olivia climbed from the SUV, she said, "I'm going to dash down to the guesthouse for a sec if you don't mind, and grab my gift."

Derrick swallowed hard. "We're doing gifts today? I thought that would be on Sunday? The day of the christening?"

"Well, this is a shower gift. I picked it up yesterday afternoon after I heard there was going to be one. It's really more for the mom than the baby."

"Right. I see," Derrick said. It hadn't occurred to

him to pick up a present for this event. Even if it had, he'd have been at a loss over what to buy. Hopefully, he'd make up for his misstep today with the gift of the cradle. Maybe he should even bring it by tomorrow.

Derrick entered the house but it was empty, with happy chatter spilling in through the open windows. He found everyone on the back porch drinking sparkling pink libations from champagne flutes. To his dismay, Sally handed him a glass the moment he set foot on the porch and filled it to the brim.

"Welcome, brother," she said in a teasing way. "We were worried you'd gotten lost."

"Where's Olivia?" Meredith asked, trying to look over his shoulder into the room behind him.

Had Olivia been right about her?

"She ran down to the guesthouse to grab something," he said before Hope popped out of her chair.

"Derrick," she said, hugging him. "Great to see you!"

Brent stood and clapped him soundly across the back. "How ya doing, man?"

"Good," Derrick said. "Really good." He sipped from his pink champagne, which was...awful. A little too sweet and a lot too fizzy. He'd stomach it, though, for the cause. He noticed the brimming basket of inflated party balloons, the streamers and banners, and five bare-chested baby dolls in diapers on a chair. "Wow, Sally," he said. "You outdid yourself."

She smiled at Meredith and then at the others. "Oh, I've had some help."

Olivia reappeared with a prettily wrapped package. "Hi, everyone! Is there someplace I should set this?"

"On the coffee table in the den," Margaret said. "Along with the others."

"You guys didn't have to do gifts." Sofia ducked her chin. "This is all really sweet."

"It's about to get sweeter," Sally said. "Olivia, hi!" She pasted on a bright smile and Derrick could tell she was doing her best to be polite. "Can I pour you some bubbly?"

"Sure," Olivia said. "I'll take some."

A few bottles of bubbly later, the group was all champagned up and ready for their first game, according to Sally. Derrick cast a glance at Meredith. She seemed to be enjoying the party. Her Titi Clarita, too. For his part, he was doing okay, with Olivia sticking very close by his side. The group kept them from needing to pass the time with idle chitchat.

He felt conflicted about the conversation they'd had. He'd always wondered what it'd be like to see her again, but the reality hadn't stacked up to his fantasy. Once again, he reminded himself of Meredith's advice—don't rush it. He and Olivia had rushed into marriage the first time, so they really did need to take things slow. They were older, wiser, and as Olivia's new career made it clear, they were different people. Getting to know her again would take time. Maybe he'd finally get there, especially once Meredith left Blue Hill. He found her presence…distracting.

She caught his eyes on her, blushed, and quickly

turned away, chatting with Sally. Sally and Meredith really seemed to be getting along. Maybe this go round Sally and Olivia would, too.

Sofia smiled down at the baby who'd drifted off to sleep in her arms. "I'll just watch."

"Oh, no you won't," Sally said. "Let's put her down for her nap in the porta-crib in the den. If she wakes up, I'll get her."

"But—"

"Come on," Sally coaxed. "Even moms deserve some fun."

"Yeah," Olivia concurred, chiming in like she was already a part of the family.

William nodded, shooting a gaze at the baby dolls. "I'm not doing any of this alone."

"I'm not doing any of it at all," Grandpa Chad said.

Grandmother Margaret's light eyes twinkled. "Oh yes you are, *Great-Grandpa*."

· · ·

"Okay!" Sally called minutes later, taking charge. "Let the games begin!"

Derrick went along with everything because the other guys did, too, and hey, who was he to grumble at William and Sofia's baby shower? The first game was a contest between "the boys" and "the girls" about pinning random baby things on a clothesline. The girls had squeaked out a narrow victory—in large part thanks to Meredith, by hanging up a higher number of items first. She'd been plodding along in her super tall shoes in the beginning, but then her competitive nature had won out and she'd kicked them off. He'd laughed so hard at her determination, which had actually paid off since her team won.

Then the boys took the lead in the relay race with people placing balloons under their shirts to look like fake baby bellies. That one had been pretty hilarious to watch. All the while Olivia had sent him happy, secretive glances, like she was enjoying being part of the fun and around his family again. He couldn't help but wonder if it was all an act, though, because when she didn't think he was looking at her, Olivia seemed to mostly be yawning or wearing a frown.

Meredith, on the other hand, was so engaged in the party it was hard to stop paying attention to her instead of Olivia. She got into the games in a very intense way. Highly competitive. Not at all like him. Okay. Maybe he'd been slightly competitive, too. He'd beat all the men across the finish line during the fake-baby-belly race, hadn't he? That was after seeing Meredith secure that clothesline win for the ladies by nearly trampling over the others in her barefooted haste.

"This game will come as second nature to some of you," Sally said, prepping them for their final challenge. She gestured to the baby dolls. "It has to do with changing diapers."

Brent chuckled uncomfortably, but Grandpa Chad and William seemed cool with it.

Derrick wasn't sure how he felt about changing baby doll diapers. What if he did something wrong and tainted Olivia's view of his daddy potential? Or

Meredith's? He shook his head, wondering why Meredith's opinion of him even mattered in the baby department. It wasn't like he and she were going to go making babies together.

Okay. He really didn't need to let his mind go there.

He glanced at Olivia, reminding himself that she was the woman he should be thinking of as mommy material, but somehow didn't feel that vibe. He'd believed before it was because they'd been younger and not ready. Now he wasn't sure what it was. He still didn't feel ready with her. In the future, maybe he'd come around… Assuming they started over and got remarried. But Olivia being a mom? Hmm. He tried to picture it in his head, but drew a great big blank. It was like imagining a cartoon dialogue bubble with nothing written inside it.

"We're going to have five teams," Sally said. "Everyone will draw a playing card and you'll find the person you're matched with. There are two Aces, two Kings, two Queens, two Jacks, and two Tens." She indicated the small pile of presorted playing cards on a side table. They'd been anchored by a bowl of nuts against the wind. "Sofia?" she asked, "Will you deal?"

"Sure!"

Grandmother Margaret got paired with Olivia.

Grandpa Chad with Hope.

William with Clarita.

Brent with Sofia.

And *Ten of Hearts with Ten of Clubs*, Derrick with Meredith.

Well, fine. If they were both out to win this, they

might as well be working together.

Sally reached for a tote bag resting on the porch swing. "Grandmother, do you mind passing these out?" Next, she addressed William. "And could you grab those beach towels from the sofa in the den? Each team will need one of those, too."

"What?" Sofia asked blankly.

"Things could get messy."

"She's really thought these imaginary messes out," William joked, returning in short order with the towels.

Sally grinned slyly. "Maybe my imagination's better than yours."

Margaret peeked into her bag. "Travel packs of baby wipes and fresh diapers," she reported all around.

"Each team gets one set of supplies and a baby," Sally said. "You'll each have sixty seconds to change your baby and leave its little bottom squeaky clean."

"That hardly sounds like a contest." Grandpa Chad winked at Hope. "I could probably do that job with my eyes closed."

"I'm sure that you could," Margaret said, handing him a diaper and some wipes. "But, let's see if you can beat this old pro with 'em open," she said, clearly speaking of herself.

"I'm so glad you're on my team." Olivia sighed. "I was never into babysitting."

William glanced at Clarita. "I've got us covered, unless you—"

"Oh, I've changed plenty of diapers," she chimed in. "Including Meredith's."

Meredith reddened. "Thanks, Titi Clarita."

"It's nothing to be embarrassed about," Sofia

said. "We were all changed sometime." She smiled at Brent, who appeared a bit pale. "Don't worry. We'll do fine."

"Sure," he said, "as long as you do it."

Meredith peered up at Derrick and giggled. He didn't know why. The game wasn't that funny. In fact, it sounded really straight-forward. All you had to do was process things quickly.

Sally walked around the porch, presenting each pair with a baby doll.

Olivia wrinkled her nose. "Does anybody else smell peanut butter?"

Meredith pursed her lips together and Derrick's forehead shot up. "What's going on?"

"No consulting in advance," Sally said. "Except for on one topic. Each pair will need to decide who changes the baby and who'll clean up afterward."

"Clean up, ha!" William waved his hand. "If this were a real infant," he said, holding his baby doll, "then maybe I'd be worried about it."

"Funny," Grandmother Margaret said. "I smell peanuts, too."

"No time to waste!" Sally warned. "Who's changing?"

Olivia vehemently shook her head.

"I will," Margaret said.

Hope deferred to the older gentleman. "Grandpa Chad, would you like to—?"

"No, dear. You go ahead. I'll do the dirty work after." He chuckled.

William shrugged at Clarita.

"Why don't you?" she said. "I'm probably out of practice."

"Sofia's taking the bullet for us," Brent said.

Sofia grinned playfully. "Oh no, I wouldn't dare. It's probably good for you to learn how to. Seeing as how you're newlyweds and all."

"Wait? What? No."

"Come on, Brent," Derrick teased. "Be a man."

Hope chuckled at this.

"I think you should both be men," Meredith said, announcing her challenge. She addressed Sally, without giving him a choice. "Derrick will change for us!"

He cocked his chin at her and there was a defiant twinkle in her eyes. Those pretty Dark 'n' Stormy eyes. *No. Stop. Get your head back in the game, dude.*

Sally readied her stopwatch and glanced at the others.

Margaret began to lay down her doll but Sally interceded.

"Not yet, Grandmother! I haven't started timing."

"Oh," the older woman said. "Sorry!" Derrick chuckled to himself, thinking a competitive nature ran in his family.

He assessed the situation, surmising he and Meredith would have more room to work in the yard. "Let's go down to the patio," he told her. "No one will get in our way there."

"Good idea." She checked her shoes and asked Sally, "Will there be running this time?"

"No running," Sally said. "Just changing. Pick the spot where you want to work and then when I blow the whistle, you'll all get started."

They reached the patio and Derrick whispered, "When it begins, you lay down the towel and hand me the wipes. I'll remove the diaper and swab the deck."

"Aye, aye, Captain!" Her eyes danced. "You sure you know what you're doing?"

"It was your idea I do it," he contested. "Besides…" He shot her a confident grin. "How hard can it be?"

"Just don't hurt the baby."

"Funny."

"I mean it. Olivia might be judging you."

He peeked up at the porch to find Olivia peering his way. He gave her a small wave, then set his eyes back on Meredith. "We're going to win this."

"O-kay."

"On your mark," Sally said. "Get set." She blew her whistle. "Go! Sixty seconds!"

Meredith spread out their towel and Derrick threw down the doll. Hard.

"Derrick, whoa."

"Sorry." He patted the thing on the head. "Didn't mean that."

"It would be wailing by now. Probably brain damaged."

"You're not helping." He pried at the tiny strips of tape, but they didn't budge.

"Get your fingernails underneath."

"Fingernails?" He gawked at her. "What fingernails?"

"Maybe I should do it. Move over!"

"Ah-ah!" Sally called. "No changing places! Too late!"

"Fine." Derrick tucked his fingers under the rim of the paper diaper and yanked hard. *Rip!* That did it! One side was free. *But—yuck. Nasty. What's that cool, slimy stuff?*

He pulled his hand back in horror holding it up in the sun. Brown goo trickled down his fingers and his stomach roiled. "What the…?"

Meredith cackled with laughter and hoots and hollers broke out on the porch.

Olivia groaned like she was about to hurl. "Oh gross!"

"It's only peanut butter," Margaret said sternly. "Now, hurry up and hand me those wipes."

Hope was busily cleaning up her baby and handing soiled wipes to Chad who accepted them, stone-faced, while Brent sat back on his haunches and stared.

"Come on, Brent!" Sofia urged. "Don't give up!"

"Fifteen seconds!" Sally called.

"What?" Derrick sent Meredith a panicked look. "Already?" He held out his hand like a doctor awaiting a scalpel. "Wipes!"

She tore a couple free from their dispenser handing them to him. "Wipes!"

Derrick removed the rest of the diaper and grimaced. *Only peanut butter*, he told himself. Right. He'd probably never eat peanut butter and jelly again.

"Ten!" Sally announced.

"Nothing like pressure," Derrick groused. He picked up the naked doll and held it upside down clamping its bulbous head between his knees. He quickly swabbed its front and bottom then scissored its legs apart, one of them forward and the other one back.

"Derrick!" Meredith said aghast. "What are you—?"

"Not now. I'm busy." He held a wipe at both ends and buffed back and forth—and back and forth—until the plastic shone clean. Then he laid down the baby, as Meredith watched wide-eyed.

"Diaper!" He reached up and she was ready.

In a flash, he had the darn thing on, and had sealed the straps.

"Done!" He yelped just as Sally's whistle blew.

Derrick stared up at Meredith, sweat beading his brow. "How'd we do?" he asked, panting.

Meredith surveyed the others and gaped at him, amazed. "I think we won."

"And the winners are," Sally said with a flair, "Derrick and Meredith!"

He leaped to his feet and raised the baby doll high above his head, dancing around like a fool. "Ye-es! Yes! Woo-hoo!" Who knew it could feel so great diapering a baby?

Until…wait.

Something that felt like bird poo plopped down and hit him on the head. Ick. He reached into his hair, discovering it was more of that sticky peanut butter.

He wiped down his head.

Meredith grinned and dabbed at his temple, further cleaning him up.

"I think you missed a spot." She giggled but he wasn't mad. His heart had never been so light. He was energized, like he and Meredith had just pulled off the world's greatest feat.

From the look on her stunningly beautiful face, she felt the same way.

"Great job, Daddy."

"We make a pretty great team, huh?"

Heat flickered in her eyes. Warm heat. Like the glow from a low-burning flame.

She blushed. "Yeah."

His heart thudded and his neck grew hot.

And, suddenly, it was just the two of them.

The rest of the world melted away.

CHAPTER TWENTY-ONE

"Nice work, you two!" Olivia walked toward them, clapping loudly. She adjusted her sun hat, teasing Derrick. "Who knew this was one of your talents?"

He rubbed the side of his neck, avoiding Meredith's gaze. She'd been looking at him in a way he wasn't sure of, but now the spell was broken.

Derrick smiled politely at Olivia. "A man has to have some secrets."

Olivia laughed and Meredith addressed the two of them, her face flushed. "I think I'll go and ask Sally if there's anything I can do to help."

"She seems to have things pretty much under control," Derrick said.

Meredith had already collected her stash of dirty wipes and rolled everything, including the baby doll, up in the beach towel. "Pretty much, yeah. But something tells me this one needs a bath." She patted the baby doll's bottom through the towel and Derrick chuckled.

"Probably so," he said.

Meredith departed and he turned to Olivia, who was wearing a frown. "Talk about a nasty game. That peanut butter—yuck."

"But it was only peanut butter," he said. "Try to imagine the real thing."

Olivia made a grossed-out face. "No, thanks."

"Come on, Olivia," he said as they started walking back to the house. "Surely you've changed a baby?"

"Uh, no. Why? Have you?"

Derrick cleared his throat. "Not exactly. But that doesn't mean that I wouldn't."

Her eyebrows arched. "I'd love to see you try."

Derrick didn't exactly care for the way she said that. He knew she'd been kidding, but still. It wasn't like her pre-parenting skills were any better than his. She'd admitted herself she'd never babysat. At least he'd done a little of that. Sally was four years younger and he'd sometimes looked after her when his parents were out and his older brothers had other plans. She'd been way out of diapers by that time, though, so it was true he'd never changed any. That didn't mean he couldn't figure things out with a real child if he had to.

They reached the porch and William stuck his head out the back door, holding Julia.

"Julia needs changing," he said. "I'm going to just take her upstairs and—"

"I'll do it!" Derrick said, stepping forward. The rest of the group swapped curious glances, but Meredith wasn't around. She was in the kitchen helping Sally and Grandmother Margaret with something.

His brother didn't totally trust him because he followed him all the way up to the guest room where he and Sofia were staying. There was a diaper bag on the bed and a bath towel had been stretched out beside it. A stack of diapers and a container of wipes sat on the dresser.

William still held Julia. "You really want to do this, huh?"

"Sure, why not? I've just warmed up."

"Uh."

Derrick laughed at William's nervous expression. "Don't worry. I'll be gentle."

"You don't even know what to do."

"I have a general idea."

"Not based on the way you were manhandling that doll. How about I show you?"

That actually sounded better to Derrick than him doing it himself, but then he wouldn't have risen to Olivia's challenge. "How about you direct me?" he said, holding out his arms.

William tentatively handed him Julia and the precious baby cooed. Derrick chuckled in spite of himself. "Hey, I think she likes me." As amazing as it seemed, he'd never held a baby before, apart from Sally when she was born and he was still a kid. Weirdly, he'd been afraid to as an adult man. He'd had opportunities before with Julia, but had never jumped right in.

"Relax," William's brown eyes twinkled. "You won't break her."

Derrick held her closer, jostling Julia gently in his arms and she made another sweet baby sound. "You like this, huh?" he whispered softly. "You like your Uncle Derrick?"

She made a little gurgling noise, but it came from the bottom end. And then there was that rank stench. Definitely not peanut butter. "Maybe we need to get on with it?" he said, staring pleadingly at William.

William chortled, holding his sides. "If a picture's worth a million bucks it would be of your face."

Derrick set his jaw, telling himself he could do

this. He could do just about anything when he put his mind to it.

"Support her head when you lay her down," William said.

Derrick nodded and held his breath. Then he tenderly removed the diaper and got to work.

• • •

Meredith carried two of the newly cleaned up baby dolls through the hall and toward the den. Sally was a few steps ahead of her. The two of them had bathed the dolls in dish soap and warm water before drying them off and giving them fresh diapers. While they did that, Grandmother Margaret had tended to her dinner preparations. She'd ordered a huge lasagna from a caterer's and now had it warming in the oven. Since she knew she'd be busy with the baby shower this afternoon, she'd thought to plan ahead.

Sally walked into the den as Meredith heard footsteps on the stairs. She peered up the staircase and suddenly couldn't believe her eyes. William and Derrick were coming toward her, but it wasn't William holding Julia. It was Derrick.

"Well, hello," she said with unmasked surprise. "What's going on?"

Derrick held Julia protectively against his strong shoulder. "Just doing a little diaper duty."

Her eyebrows shot up. "Diapering? You?"

He chuckled at her reaction and so did William.

"No worries," William said. "He was very gentle. A lot gentler than"—he paused to laugh some more—"he was outdoors."

"That's a relief!" she replied, chuckling.

They reached the bottom of the stairs and Meredith scanned Julia from top to bottom. The infant appeared contented, even a little drowsy, sagging against Derrick in a relaxed way. Her heart melted at the scene, because it was so easy to picture Derrick adoring a child of his own. He was going to make a really great daddy someday. She felt a tug at her heartstrings, when she realized that any babies he'd be making wouldn't be with her.

She glanced down at the plastic baby dolls she held, getting a grip on reality and the moment at hand. "I'd better get the twins back outside," she said lightly. "Sally says they're needed on the porch."

"Oh boy," William said. "Not more changing games?"

"Don't think so." Meredith laughed. "Just as decorations at this point."

William went into the den and Derrick paused in the hall with Meredith, while holding his sweet baby bundle.

"You seem to be doing very well with her," she said about Julia.

"I was only getting warmed up outside." He winked, and her face felt flushed as she thought again about what a great dad he would make.

Julia gave a soft coo and he chuckled, patting her back. "Hey, little nugget. You having a good baby shower?"

Meredith grinned up at him. "I think she's having the best."

"How about you?" he asked. "Having fun?"

"Yeah." Heat swept her cheeks. "You?"

"Loved the diapering game."

"Did not."

His voice got husky. "Loved working with you."

He stared down and into her eyes in such an honest, telling way, she couldn't help but wonder... no, hope...that maybe more was going on. Was he starting to like her? Really like her, like she was beginning to fall for him? When they'd been outside in the yard, there'd been that moment after the games. But no. That would be terrible. She couldn't ruin things for Derrick and Olivia.

"There you are!" Sofia said, discovering them in the hall. "I was just looking for Julia." Her gaze fell on Derrick and she shot him an admiring look. "Well, well, well. What's this?"

Derrick and Meredith followed Sofia back into the den, where William laid his hand on Derrick's free shoulder. "Announcement, everyone! My little brother just changed a baby. A real one this time, and he did a great job."

Olivia entered the den from outdoors and her mouth fell open. Surprised by Derrick's baby-tending skills, perhaps? Surprised and probably pleased. Of course she would be. What a happy snapshot of the future Derrick made, holding his tiny niece. Meredith's heart thudded in a dull ache when a stunning realization hit her. She was starting to wish that would be her future, and not Olivia's.

• • •

Derrick sat next to Olivia again at dinner, but his gaze kept wandering across the table to Meredith. He'd never seen her laughing as much as she had this afternoon, and he'd liked it. She'd been spontaneous and carefree, diving in with both feet and getting soaking wet. Olivia had participated, too, but every other second, it seemed, she was complaining. Which was fine. Boisterous group games weren't everyone's scene. It was the Albrights' family's scene, though.

Olivia should know that. While she hadn't been around them in years, Derrick's family basically hadn't changed. Then again, Olivia had never totally fit in, not even back then. But that was pretty minor in the scale of things. What mattered was that she'd fit in with *him*. She'd been his first love. He'd never fallen harder. Until… He shifted in his chair recalling the look in Meredith's eyes when she'd seen him in the hall holding Julia.

It had been a short moment but had somehow felt special between them. Intimate. He was proud of the job he'd done in taking care of Julia. He could tell Meredith admired him for it, and her admiration had warmed his heart.

Meredith laughed at some joke William made, and her eyes sparkled in the candlelight. He'd always known she was attractive, but he'd never fully given her credit for how beautiful she was with her long dark hair and that bold, beautiful smile of hers. Then again, Olivia was really great-looking, too, and she was the one he was supposed to be making an effort with.

She leaned toward him and whispered, "I love

being around your family. They're so much fun."

Did she mean that? "Yeah, but a little rowdy sometimes."

"A lot rowdy," she said, her tone bordering on disapproval and Derrick winced. "Not that I mind it!" she self-corrected. "I think they're—great."

After the meal, Derrick and Sally offered to carry the dirty dishes into the kitchen. Once it was just the two of them there, Sally said, "Interesting seeing you and Olivia back together."

"We're not 'back together' yet."

"She's here. That must mean something."

"Mostly, it means she came for Julia's christening."

Sally set her stack of dishes by the sink and began rinsing them off. Derrick opened the dishwasher and started loading it as she handed him things. "Grandmother says Meredith's *mission* is two-fold. Is it true that her show might get syndicated?"

"Yeah, that's what she's hoping."

"Well good for her!" Sally smiled and continued working. "I like Meredith. She's fun."

"I've always liked Mer… Meredith, too," he said, his throat going raspy.

"Liar," Sally said, but she was laughing. "I was here last summer."

"Yeah, and so was I." His mind drifted back to that moment on the dock and the urge he'd had to kiss her. He'd had that same urge today after the baby game, but the timing had been so wrong and they'd been surrounded by all the others.

"How about Olivia?" he asked Sally, wanting to

get to the bottom of this.

"How about her?"

"Come on, you know what I mean. Do you like her? Do you think she's fun?"

"Um." Sally pursed her lips. "Olivia and I have never totally seen eye to eye."

"Yeah, and why is that?"

"I've never told anyone in the family this, but of course Sofia knows. When Olivia interned at our office, her work was very slipshod, Derrick. Sofia took her under her wing...cut her a lot more slack than I did. I actually don't think her heart was in it. Going into the law."

"That can't be all there is."

Sally blew out a breath. "Okay. I'll spill." She met his eyes, looking so much like their mom, but years younger. "I never thought she was right for you."

"What? Why not?"

"I mean, physical attraction's fine. I get that she's very pretty."

"But—?"

"She doesn't appreciate you, Derrick, and all your talents. Never has. Olivia is all about herself."

He found that hard to believe. "Wait. Does Mom think that, too?"

Sally's eyebrows arched but she didn't betray whatever she and their mom had talked about.

"Well, maybe things have changed," he said a bit too defensively.

"Hmm." Sally shrugged, but she'd planted a seed of doubt in his heart. "Maybe."

• • •

They had dessert and gifts in the den after dinner. Grandmother Margaret had ordered a sweet "It's a Girl" baby shower cake from the same bakery where she'd picked up the other goodies, and everyone had a slice. Derrick tried not to think about Sally's comments in the kitchen but they niggled at him just the same.

"You all right there, bro?" Brent asked quietly, leaning toward him where they sat on one of the sofas.

"Yeah, fine. Why?"

"Not sure. You just seem a little quiet."

"It's a baby shower, Brent."

"Gotcha." His brother chuckled. "It's left me pretty speechless, too."

Olivia was in a club chair on Derrick's other side, fawning over each new unwrapped present, while Meredith eyed her skeptically from across the room. Sally wasn't the only one who didn't cotton to Olivia. He had a sneaking suspicion that Meredith didn't like her much, either. Yet, he didn't know why. It wasn't like Meredith and Olivia had a history together the way Sally and Olivia did. The only thing Olivia and Meredith had in common was him.

Meredith caught Derrick looking at her and she smiled. It wasn't a fake smile, either, but a genuine one like she was having a really great time. Olivia pasted on a sunny face but it was hard to know what was going on underneath. Her veneer wasn't tougher than Meredith's, because—there was no denying it—Meredith was tough. It was more like it was harder to see who Olivia really was on the inside. With Meredith, her personality bubbled up to the surface like an erupting volcano, whether she wanted it to or not.

He remembered Meredith's advice to him about making Olivia believe he really noticed things about her. He'd not been doing such a great job with that and he needed to work harder. He'd do well to focus on the goal of them getting to know each other again, seeing if there's something still there, instead of letting ridiculous notions pop into his head about kissing Meredith. Even though they were getting along better, Meredith didn't *like* him in a romantic sense. She was putting up with him in interest of her television deal.

He needed to keep that front and center in his mind. Meredith was here for one reason and one reason only—her career. Helping him with his love life was a convenient way to further that goal. Would she be at this baby shower if she hadn't lied to save face about her lack of relationship? No. If she'd actually been thinking about him, she'd have reached out without needing his services as a fake fiancé.

The idea that Olivia had floated about Meredith having an interest in him was flat-out wrong. Olivia didn't know Meredith like he did. Amazingly, he was getting to know her pretty well. He knew that she was smart and funny, and that she had a great sense of humor. She was certainly a lot of fun to be around. More fun than he might have imagined last summer, when neither of them had been able to resist taking pot-shots at the other.

His mouth twitched when he realized he'd actually enjoyed some of that bantering, too. If hindsight were foresight, he might have followed through on that attraction by taking her in his arms on the dock in the moonlight. But their relationship probably wouldn't have gone anywhere then, just like it wasn't going anywhere now. If "Matchmaker Meredith" had a million matches to choose from, it was very unlikely she'd pick him.

He frowned. Once she hit it big, and she became more of a known celebrity than she was already, she was going to have more options than ever.

CHAPTER TWENTY-TWO

The evening wound down, with folks breaking off to say goodnight. All the presents had been unwrapped and their dessert plates were empty. Sally gave Julia a cute baby outfit, and his grandparents, her first U.S. Savings Bond, which was honestly so them. Meredith and her aunt had picked out some classic baby books, and Olivia had thoughtfully purchased an assortment of "spa day" items for Sofia, so the new mom could pamper herself. Derrick told Sofia and William that he'd bring his present by tomorrow.

Everyone thanked Sally for the party and Grandmother Margaret for the great meal, before parting with hugs and goodbyes. Meredith waited in his SUV while he said good night to Olivia near the path to the guesthouse.

"What a great day," she said, grinning up at him. Olivia removed her hat and auburn hair spilled past her shoulders. "Really memorable, all of it."

Derrick nodded. "I know Sofia appreciates you being here. William, too."

"Julia's adorable."

"Yeah, she is." He tried to drum up his enthusiasm for "romancing her." It was all about the little things he needed to pay attention to. He studied her green eyes, hunting for something flattering to say, but commenting on their color seemed lame.

"You've changed your eyebrows," he said, noticing

the finely arched lines.

Her hand shot up covering them. "My what?"

"Your eyebrows. Are they different?"

She flushed self-consciously. "I've been going to a different salon for threading."

"Threading? What's that?"

Her color deepened. "Never mind."

"In any case. I just wanted to say…you look very nice." He cleared his throat. "Even better than before."

"Oh well, thanks." She viewed him curiously. "You look great, too."

"But it's not all about looks, is it?" Sally had been wrong about that. Dead wrong. There was a lot more to him and Olivia than physical attraction. Wasn't there? And where was that physical attraction anyway? As beautiful as she was, he wasn't feeling it.

"What? No. Of course not."

"What matters most is who we are inside."

"Yes."

"And that is?"

She eyed him suspiciously. "Is this a trick question?"

"No, I…" Derrick pursed his lips. "I just wanted to point out what matters." And maybe find something new to grab hold of, because so far, things had felt just like they had ten years ago when they'd separated. Only minus the heated animosity.

"Derrick," she said seriously. "It's what's inside of us that first drew us together. Our passion! Our spark!"

He shifted on his feet, knowing those things

were great. But they weren't exactly standalones.

"We've always had that." She reached up and placed a hand on his cheek. "Can't you still feel it?"

Uh no. The fact was he didn't. Not exactly.

But he would need to soon—if they were going to have a shot at reconnecting.

She tilted up her chin and he got what she was hoping for.

She was angling for a kiss.

His throat tightened. No. This was wrong.

He abruptly stepped back and her hand dropped to her side.

"I'm sorry, Olivia." He swallowed hard. "I think we'd better call it a night."

She looked crestfallen and he felt like a heel for hurting her. "Going already?"

"Meredith's waiting. I need to drive her home."

"Funny how she's staying at the cabin," Olivia said.

"I already explained that. We're friends."

He understood that he needed to tell her about the fake fiancé story before she stumbled across it herself, but now didn't seem like the right time. Not with Meredith sitting in his SUV. He wanted time to calmly talk to Olivia, hopefully without any of that shouting that used to transpire between them.

"You and I need to talk," he started and then realized how ominous that sounded. "I mean, there are some things I need to tell you."

"But not now?" she said, looking disappointed.

"It might take longer than a minute."

"And a minute's all you've got, isn't it?"

"At the moment, yeah."

"Okay fine." She sighed, sounding resigned. "I guess I'll see you tomorrow."

"Tomorrow. Yeah." He backed away. "See ya."

As soon as she headed toward the carriage house, Derrick climbed into his SUV and slammed shut the door.

"Everything okay?"

He glanced at Meredith as she sat in the shadows. He was so jumbled up in his head, talking was the last thing he wanted to do. "Yeah. Sure."

"Things went pretty well today with Olivia, huh?"

He made a three-point turn in the drive. *Not really.* "Yep."

From his sideview he saw her adjusting her seatbelt. "The frozen yogurt must have been good."

"It was."

"You were out a long time."

"There was a lot to catch up on."

"And did you? Catch up?"

"She's just like I remembered." He shouldn't be disappointed in that, but he was. They hadn't worked before for a reason, and he'd really hoped there'd have been some growth on both of their parts. He'd been counting on it, actually.

They said nothing for a while as his headlights painted white trails against the darkened road. After a pause, he said, "I'm going to tell her. About the whole fake engagement thing. The paparazzi mix-up. All of it."

"Yeah." She sighed. "It's probably time."

"Maybe I should have told her tonight, but I

didn't want all the drama. Not after such a nice day."

"Who said that there'd be drama?"

He shrugged. "It's Olivia."

"Well, if you really want a future with her, then you'll have to accept that, because in my experience, drama doesn't go away," Meredith said. "So, tomorrow, let her know why I'm really here. That will help clear the air between the two of you, so you can move forward. Olivia's probably worried about our relationship. She doesn't understand what's going on between us. Once she does, things will get better." She paused. "Hopefully."

"Sally said something to me in the kitchen." He didn't know why he was telling Meredith this but he felt like he ought to. After all, she was his matchmaker and on his side. "Something about Olivia."

"She still doesn't like her, does she?"

"I don't believe she *dislikes* Olivia. It's more like she doesn't think she's the right person for me."

"Why's that?"

"She said Olivia doesn't appreciate me." He laughed like that was absurd, but deep inside he wondered whether Sally was right. What did Olivia say they had in common? Passion? Spark? Had that really been all there was?

"Um. I'm not sure what you want me to say?"

"I want you to convince me that I'm doing the right thing."

She was silent a moment. "I'm afraid I can't do that."

He glanced at her. "What do you mean?"

"Only you can convince you, Derrick. That's

what real love's about. You either feel it in here"—
she thumped her chest—"or you don't. It's really
that simple."

Nothing about his current situation seemed
simple. Least of all, with Olivia. He'd believed
there was a chance they could reignite their old
flame, and based on today's events, he stood a
chance. But ever since Meredith had come to Blue
Hill, his life had turned on a dime. It felt wrong
pursuing Olivia when all he could think about was
a brassy matchmaker from Boston. And yet it was
on account of Meredith that Olivia was here, and
them getting back together would benefit Meredith
just as much as it'd benefit him.

This is so messed up.

"Maybe it's too soon for love," he said, thinking
that might be it. It felt like he was trying to force his
feelings.

"Maybe so."

"Is that how it was for you?" he asked. "With
Mr. Football?"

She appeared startled a moment before answering. "Oh! You mean Jack?"

"Yeah, the guy with the jersey. Did you feel it
in"—he patted his chest—"here?"

She glanced away and when she turned back,
her eyes were moist. "Yeah, I did."

"Oh wow, Mer. I'm sorry. I didn't mean to—"

"The real problem was"—she drew in a shaky
breath—"he didn't return my feelings."

Derrick kicked himself for broaching this topic
now. He should have guessed that mentioning her ex
might upset her. He pulled over to the side of the

road and put his SUV in park. This conversation demanded his full attention and his compassion, and he was prepared to deliver both.

She sniffed. "You don't have to pull over."

"It's okay," he said. "We have time." They were on a darkened stretch of road with a stone bridge up ahead and the low-rolling waves of Blue Hill Bay sloshing below them. The tide had turned and was ebbing out to sea, receding with a steady rhythm.

He viewed her tenderly. "I'm sorry. I shouldn't have pried." He wanted to hold her. But he couldn't. They didn't have that kind of relationship. A lump welled in his throat when he found himself wishing they did.

She took a tissue from her purse and dabbed her eyes. "It's okay, really."

"So," he pressed gently. "If this guy was such a dirtbag, why still wear his jersey?"

"He wasn't a dirtbag at first." She sighed. "Not really at the end, either. He just wasn't into me in that way."

"In which way?"

She avoided his gaze. "The long-term way."

Derrick swallowed hard. She was talking marriage. "I see."

"And the jersey?" she said. "It was a gift in the beginning, when things were good. You know— hopeful." She lifted a shoulder. "I guess I wear the jersey because of that more than anything else. It's less about Jack and more about how he made me feel at the start. Special."

His voice was husky when he said, "You *are* special, Mer."

She smiled sadly and he wished he could take those painful memories away. "Thanks, Der."

"How long ago did you break up?"

"It's been more than two years."

"So there was no one last summer?"

She turned to him in the pale light. The moon was high on the water, casting shadows across her face. "You mean, did I have a boyfriend then?"

He was dying to know. "Did you?"

"No." She blushed. "If I'd had one, I never would have—"

She stopped and bit her lip. Was she recalling the same moment he was? That moment on the dock. She ran a hand through her hair and seemed to collect herself. "What I mean is, I wouldn't have been nearly as flirty with you."

He was bowled over by her remark. "Wait. You were being flirty?"

Her eyebrows arched at him. "Weren't you?"

His neck burned hot. She was right. Only he'd never admitted that to himself. "I…" He hesitated and shook his head. "I guess I didn't look at it that way at the time."

"Didn't you?"

He turned to her and that low-burning flame flickered in her eyes. His heart thudded as he accepted this new truth. Maybe she was right. Maybe that's what all that tension and heat had been about at Brent's wedding. They'd been flirting with each other, while desperately fighting their mutual attraction, although neither one had fully recognized that at the time.

"Mer," he said hoarsely. "I'm sorry. Sorry if I

messed things up back then."

She laughed sadly. "Both of us messed them up in that case."

He imagined the two of them on that dock but with a different outcome. Him taking her in his arms and pouring everything he'd been feeling into a kiss. Maybe things wouldn't have ended badly. Maybe they could have stood a chance, but not now.

Not with Olivia here and this new plan of action in force.

She was probably thinking the same thing. "What's important is we've moved past that."

"Yeah. Good thing, huh?" he said, shooting her a wistful look.

"Good thing for Olivia." She smiled wanly. "That's who you were thinking about that night, not me, remember?"

Actually, no. After seeing Brent's happiness, he'd been wallowing in a bit of self-pity about his own failed marriage, but once Meredith had come down the steps carrying that bouquet of hers his thoughts had taken a different course. He'd begun thinking of her in a new way. A romantically interested way. Maybe he'd been drifting toward Meredith that whole wedding week without consciously knowing it.

Meredith inhaled deeply, then brightened. "And hey, look! Things are going great now, and you're definitely on track for winning Olivia back."

He frowned. "Yeah."

She studied him. "Once you get through the hurdle of your confession tomorrow," she said, "things will improve. You'll see. The guilt of not being honest is probably holding you back, and she'll feel that."

"You're probably right." His shoulders sagged at this hollow victory. There was a chance he and Olivia could be a couple by Julia's christening day. That was what he'd thought he'd wanted, and what he'd allowed himself to consider as a possibility since Meredith showed up with a pot roast and a plan. But what if he'd been wrong? "Ready to head home now?"

Home. It sounded so right saying that to Meredith. Not that her home was going to be with him anytime soon, or anytime at all.

Still, his mind took a little side trip, wondering what that would be like.

Maybe cozy. Maybe warm. Maybe they'd laugh and watch silly shows and sunsets together. He might even have to build her tons more shoe racks.

"Sure."

He eased them back onto the shadowy road, then made an effort to lighten the mood. "Man," he said. "I am baby diapered out."

She grinned at that. "You were terrific."

"Thanks," he said, as they drove along.

"I mean it, Derrick." She giggled. "One of a kind with that baby buffing action."

"I've had a lot of experience with buffing," he said, attempting to return her banter, but somehow it didn't seem as lighthearted as before, because now his heart felt heavy.

He needed to buck up and look at the bright side. By this time on Wednesday, there was a good chance that both he and Meredith would have achieved their goals. It was nice to have someone pulling for him and to be able to pull for her in return.

Had he and Olivia ever been supportive of each other?

That's not the bright side.

Her lip twisted wryly. "Let's hope you don't use that on your real kids someday."

"Don't worry," he said. "I won't." Her skeptical expression was enough to break through his mental turmoil and jar a laugh out of him. "Hey, I did a very careful job with Julia and she came out *just fine*."

"Mmm-hmm." She grinned. "The party was fun. I had a really great time with your family."

"They loved having you around," he said and he meant it.

"How do you know?"

"I could tell." After a beat, he added, "Plus, Sally said so."

"Aww. I love Sally. She's her own woman."

"Yeah, she sure is."

"She's not seeing anyone?"

"She'd never tell any of us if she was. She's endured far too much ribbing from the family, and more than enough intrusiveness from Grandmother."

"Well, I hope she finds the right one," Meredith said. An idea seemed to occur to her. "If not, maybe I can help her?"

"Oh, no you don't." He chuckled. "One match-making venture with the Albrights is probably plenty."

She smiled and sank back in her seat. "You're probably right about that."

CHAPTER TWENTY-THREE

Meredith texted Beth the next morning as soon as she made her coffee, and Beth said to check her email. Derrick wasn't around, so she figured he'd gone out to his workshop to spruce up that cradle. He was giving it to William and Sofia today.

She and Derrick hadn't talked a whole lot after returning from his grandparents' last night. They'd said their good nights pretty quickly and retreated to watch television in their respective rooms. As she flipped past *House Hunters*, she'd given a wistful sigh. That had been a fun night. Knowing it wouldn't happen again…hurt.

It was hard to think about their conversation without feeling sad about it. When he'd said that thing about maybe having messed things up between them last summer, her heart had thumped so hard. Still, she'd given him the opportunity to say his heart wasn't in it in trying to win back Olivia, but he hadn't.

So it was full-steam ahead with that reconciliation plan. Meredith knew it was her duty to support them. Derrick in particular. She's the one who'd suggested he try to reconcile with Olivia in the first place. If she'd never arrived in Blue Hill with her proposal, she doubted Derrick would have tried to reconnect with Olivia on his own. In fact, the more she watched what was happening between him and Olivia unfold, and especially Derrick's body language and what he'd chosen to share since the moment Olivia arrived, she suspected reconnecting with her hadn't actually *ever* been in his plans.

At least she'd received encouraging news from Beth. Her email revealed that Jerry's meeting with the streaming exec had happened. No word yet on how things had gone, but Beth had sounded hopeful. There was still no decision on the syndication deal, either. Though Beth had been encouraging regarding that, too, assuring her that the buzz around the studio was good.

Rumors were spreading that *Matched Up* was destined for bigger things, a larger promotional budget, too. Word was advertisements on billboards and city buses. Boston's hometown girl was making good, even if she hailed from Miami.

"Good morning," Derrick said, walking in the door. He had his coffee tumbler with him and was dressed in a T-shirt and jeans.

"Oh, hey!" She shut her laptop and picked up her coffee. "You were up early."

"Out in my workshop," he said. "Finishing things up."

He set his tumbler down on the counter, his eyes sparkling. "Want to see?"

Meredith glanced down at her football jersey. "Sure! Let me put on some—"

Derrick motioned her back into her seat. "Wait right here."

He stepped outside and returned with the cradle, its wood taking on a maroon hue. Meredith slid aside her laptop as he set the cradle down beside the coffee table in the living area. The mattress

portion of it stood about waist-high and the spaces
between the smooth slats on either side were narrow. The headboard and footboard were exquisitely
tapered and its supporting legs and rockers looked
sturdy.

"What do you think?"

It was gorgeous with a mattress pad tucked inside, along with a sealed package of fitted sheets to
match. They were decorated with cute cartoon
ducks, resembling the toys little kids play with in
bathtubs.

"Oh, Derrick." She glanced up for permission to
touch it. He nodded and she stroked her fingers
along the buttery smooth surface of one of its rails.
"It's beautiful. But the mattress? Where did you get
it?"

"Custom ordered from a shop that makes them."

Meredith giggled at the ducky pattern, trying to
imagine him picking that out. "The ducks are so
sweet!"

He grinned proudly. "Yeah, I thought so, too."

Meredith gripped one of its sides and attempted
to rock it, but it wouldn't budge.

"Wait," he said. "Let me release the lock." He
tugged at a lever underneath then said, "Now, give
it a try."

She did and it gently swayed from side to side.
"Aww." Meredith bit her lip, overcome with emotion. "It's awesome."

"You think they'll like it?"

"Are you kidding me?" She playfully pushed his
arm. "They'll love it."

"There's one little thing. I haven't figured out

how to wrap it." His eyes met hers and she flushed. "Will you help me?"

"I'd love to."

He headed to his room. Meredith took the opportunity to quickly dress in jeans and a blue short-sleeved top.

She sure hoped Sally was wrong about Olivia not appreciating his talents. Because Derrick Albright was one amazing guy.

• • •

Derrick hauled a huge roll of extra-wide, heavy-duty wrapping paper out of his bedroom. It was light pink with white storks on it carrying baby bundles. Some were swaddled in pink and others in blue.

"Okay, now that is cute," Meredith said about the wrapping paper. "Where did you get it?"

"From a favorite artist who sells it on Etsy."

He was an artist himself, so it shouldn't surprise her that he'd have thought to check Etsy, but it did. Had Olivia ever appreciated his thoughtfulness? Did she even know?

She surveyed his handsome features, loving this side of Derrick. The side that did thoughtful things for others and went to the trouble to order baby-themed wrapping paper for a cradle he'd built.

"I'm afraid we'll need to use packing tape," he said, producing a couple of clear rolls from the built-in desk's drawer in the kitchen. "The heavy-duty stuff."

Derrick approached her with the wrapping

supplies and stared down at her feet. "Um. I'm not so sure those shoes are the greatest for working."

Meredith laughed. "We're wrapping a gift, Der, not running a marathon."

"Yeah. I saw how well you did racing around in your heels yesterday."

"That is so not fair. I wasn't expecting those kind of games."

"Neither was I," he said, laughing at the memory. He walked to the front door and lifted an oblong package off a bookshelf by the door. He used the top of the bookshelf like an entrance table, keeping his keys there, but the shelves were loaded with paperbacks.

"What do you like to read?" she asked, seeing that many of the books looked worn and dog-eared.

"Detective stuff mostly. Police procedurals."

"Whodunits?"

"Yeah, but not the cozy kind. Something more grisly."

Meredith grimaced. "I preferred the lighter stuff."

"Such as?"

"Podcasts."

"Oh yeah?"

"Who has time to read, Der?" She shrugged and he laughed. "Except for maybe scripts."

"I would have pegged you for glamor-type magazines, maybe the online ones. With all those fancy clothes and high-heeled shoes."

She chuckled at this. "Okay, I might peek at those occasionally—for inspiration."

He cocked his chin. "Or maybe one of those glossy news magazines you see at the grocery store.

You know, the ones that profile celebrities." His blue eyes twinkled. "Hey. Maybe you'll be in one someday?"

She couldn't help but be thrilled by the idea. Her face on the cover of some widely circulated periodical. As long as the coverage was flattering. "Wouldn't that be amazing?"

He cocked his chin, studying her, and her heart skipped a beat. "Yeah, it would. For you. For me, though? Not my thing."

She laughed. "Publicity you mean?"

"Anything like that. Staying out of the limelight. That's what works for me. The thought of going on a TV show in front of a camera?" He shuddered. "Fills me with dread." He walked over and handed her the package. "Here. This is for you."

"Me? But, wait. I didn't order anything."

"I know." His blue eyes twinkled. "Because I ordered it for you."

Her face heated beneath his stare. "Aww, Derrick. Thank you. You shouldn't have." But she was secretly happy that he had. Meredith loved being surprised by gifts, and that didn't happen often. "Should I open it now?"

He chuckled at her excited look. "I think you'd better."

She unwrapped the outer packaging, unveiling a shoebox. Interesting. What did Derrick know about women's shoes?

A pair of navy blue slip-on-style, flat-soled sneakers were tucked inside. They were simple but attractive and looked functional, too. She looked up at Derrick and grinned. "Shoes?"

"With rubber soles."

It was a quirky but thoughtful gift. "How sweet! But…when am I supposed to wear them?"

"What's wrong with now?"

Nothing, she supposed. She slipped into them, showing them off on her feet.

"They suit you."

She peered at them. "They seem very Blue Hill."

"They *are* very Blue Hill."

She grinned, thinking of the baby shower. "I probably could have used these yesterday."

"And the day that you trudged out to my work-shop through all that mud."

"Yeah." Her skin grew hot. "But how did you know my size?"

He glanced at the pile of shoes in the corner beside her large suitcase. "Easy detective work." He shrugged. "And anyway, someone might want to take you out on a boat someday. You definitely can't go boating in those heels you wear."

Her heart pounded. Against her better instincts, she wanted that someone to be him. Meredith warned herself not to jump to conclusions. Like the ones that painted visions of them on a romantic journey in that rowboat he kept moored outside. "That would be nice."

He held her gaze, seemingly lost in a daydream of his own. "Yeah," he said. "It would."

"Maybe we can go out sometime?" she blurted before she could stop herself. "In one of your boats before I leave?"

A slow grin spread across his face. "You've got yourself a deal."

Meredith's heart sighed, then she told herself not to make too much of his offer. He was probably just being nice. She tried hard not to let disappointment get the better of her as Derrick examined the cradle.

"Okay," he said, rubbing his hands together. "Let's get this baby wrapped. I told William we'd bring my gift by after lunch. I mean, if you'd like to come along, too, that would be great."

She envisioned Sofia's and William's happy faces. "I wouldn't miss it for the world."

"Awesome." He broke the seal on the wrapping paper and removed it from its cellophane covering. Next he handed an end of it to her while holding the roll. "Hmm. Where to start?"

"Well, we…" She moved to the far side of the cradle holding her end of the wrapping paper and more of it unraveled. Then she tried lowering it down over the cradle's side. "Um."

"It's a big job."

"Yeah."

"Maybe if we go around it?" he suggested. "You stay put and I'll come around to where you are." She did and he handed her a pair of scissors. "Can you cut a straight line?"

"Of course," she said with confidence, but then she didn't. Her line was all zig-zaggy, veering off center. She pursed her lips together but he chuckled.

"That's okay," he said. "We'll tuck that part under." He picked up the tape and she folded over the uneven part, making a straight edge. Derrick pulled out a long piece of tape and leaned in while she held both parts of the wrapping paper together.

"Don't move," he cautioned. He stood so close she could breathe him in.

He looked up and met her eyes, and her legs trembled. Like they might actually give way or something. Even in these practical shoes. "I won't."

"Good." He fastened the tape and lifted his hands. "Ta-da! Phase One, done!" But the moment they released the wrapping paper, it slid to the ground, circling around the bottom portion of the cradle.

His eyebrows shot up. "That works."

Meredith giggled. "We can always add a new piece for the upper section."

"Excellent idea. We'll cover the top after that, then lay the cradle on its side and do the bottom."

"We might want to take the sheets and mattress out and wrap them separately in that case. So they don't jumble around."

"You're very good at organizing." His eyes twinkled. "Do you run a TV show or something?"

"Yeah, I've learned to think on my feet." She stared at her new shoes. "Thanks again for the shoes. They were definitely unexpected."

The air hung heavy as he gazed into her eyes. "So were you."

That sounded more than friendly to her. That sounded interested. And romantic.

And ohhh nooo… She worried, worried, worried that he was falling for her, too.

In the next instant, she hoped that he was. She couldn't help but wonder what might have happened if there'd been no Olivia in the picture. If it had only been him and her.

His cell *dinged*, shattering the moment, and he

pulled it from his pocket.

His face fell and she guessed it was bad news. "Uh-oh."

"Who is it?"

"Olivia," he said, looking up. "And boy, is she ticked."

"What?"

"She looked you up and found all the stories about our engagement, including the video clip the press took at my cabin."

Meredith gasped. "Oh no."

"Oh yeah."

"What are you going to do?"

He quickly texted Olivia back. "I'm saying I can explain everything and not to panic." He shook his head. "But five will get you ten, she will."

A rapid string of texts came back at him and he silenced his phone.

"Sounds like she's already there."

"Yeah." He sighed. "That's why I said I'll drop by later after lunch."

"After you deliver the cradle and not before?"

"William and Sofia are already expecting us at two and you and I have to eat sometime."

She knew he was right, but Meredith also suspected he was stalling. His phone kept buzzing in his pocket. Probably Olivia going ballistic. Maybe if Meredith was in his shoes instead of in the brand new ones he'd bought her, she'd be stalling a bit, too.

CHAPTER TWENTY-FOUR

An hour later, they shared a happy moment in Grandmother Margaret and Grandpa Chad's living room. Derrick delivered his cradle and Sofia and William's response was exactly what Meredith thought it would be. William even got a little misty-eyed.

"It's wonderful," Sofia said, holding the baby. "Julia still sleeps in our room, but we've been using the portable crib. This cradle's so much better."

Grandmother Margaret nodded. "It certainly looks like it's been made with love."

It was just the seven of them in the living room. Sofia, Julia, William, the grandparents, and Meredith and Derrick. Hope and Brent had gone into town to run errands, and Sally was out for a run. Titi Clarita had returned to the guesthouse for a rest after lunch. According to the others, Olivia was still there, too. She supposedly had a work knot to untangle that had prevented her from joining the rest of them for breakfast. She'd evidently still been "untangling" at lunch.

"I think I'll brew myself a pot of tea," Grandmother Margaret said. "Would anyone like some? We still have plenty of treats leftover from the shower yesterday."

"I'll take a spot," Grandpa Chad said.

"Me, too." Sofia smiled. "If you've got herbal."

"We have peppermint and chamomile in the

pantry," Margaret told her.

"Need any help?" Meredith motioned with her chin for Derrick to skedaddle. This was his perfect opportunity to slip away and have his one-on-one with Olivia.

He nodded, but honestly didn't look like he wanted to separate from the safety of the others. He shifted on his feet and Meredith sent him a second pointed look. It was now or never really, and Derrick knew what he needed to do.

"I think I'll go and check on Olivia," he said after a lull, "and that work knot of hers."

• • •

As Derrick walked out the back door, he bumped into Sally jogging up to the porch in athletic clothes, a ponytail, and a headband.

"Did I miss it?" she asked, before pouting. "*No. I wanted to see the big surprise.*"

"The cradle's in the living room by the piano if you want to take a peek."

"Can't wait. I'm sure it's gorgeous."

Sally had always been so supportive of him, even though they were very different. Derrick couldn't imagine going to law school any more than Sally could envision building a boat. She claimed she wasn't creative and couldn't even cook. Those party games had taken ingenuity, though, so his baby sis did have skills beyond practicing family law.

She put her hand up to her mouth and whispered. "I think something's up with Olivia."

"Like what?" he asked, wanting to know how much the rest of them had guessed.

"Nobody's sure." She rolled her eyes toward the guesthouse. "But we think it might have to do with Meredith." She leaned closer. "You two were looking awfully chummy after the diaper-changing game yesterday."

He'd hoped no one had noticed that little moment. "We were just happy we won."

"I know that," Sally said. "But does Olivia?"

She wouldn't now. Especially after what she'd found online.

Derrick strode toward the rose garden, his eye on the path beyond it.

You've got this, he told himself again and again—until his stomach felt uneasy.

What was the *deal* with him?

But he knew the answer before he'd finished asking the question.

Meredith.

He was glad she'd liked the sneakers he'd bought her. He'd found her reaction charming. Then she'd asked him to take her out on the water—just the two of them if the intention of her question was what he believed. He'd spent the drive to his grandparents' telling himself taking her out would be a nice thank-you for her matchmaking efforts on his behalf. Nothing more, nothing less. Even if he'd not been dead set on keeping up his end of their plan, she'd pretty much assured him that there'd never be anything more between them last night during their drive home. He'd been so disappointed, he'd headed straight to his room and tried to clear his mind with a little ESPN.

He'd ended up thinking about her instead.

Whatever had happened—or had almost happened—last summer was history now. He needed to man up and go in there and talk to Olivia now.

He reached the guesthouse and lightly knocked at the door, thinking Clarita was napping.

"Come in," she said brightly, proving she wasn't. He found her reading wildlife magazines on the sofa, which really didn't seem like her jam. "I needed a break from the ghost stories," she said, and for the first time Derrick noticed how Meredith slightly favored her.

It was something around the eyes and how they crinkled when she smiled. Meredith had a beautiful smile and he guessed it would look just as pretty when she was in her forties like her youngish aunt, and even older.

He tried to imagine Meredith at his grandmother's age, tending to a large brood who'd gathered for a holiday. She'd probably be a lot like Grandmother Margaret—bossy but loveable and completely dedicated to her family.

Clarita sent him a questioning look and he recalled why he was here.

"Olivia? Is she—?"

"Out in the gazebo," Clarita said. "Working."

• • •

"Olivia?"

She glanced over her shoulder seeming startled. "Derrick! Oh, hi."

She quickly shut her laptop but not before he saw what she'd been doing: shopping for nail polish.

Irritation spread through him. "You blew my family off to buy nail polish? We all thought you were working."

"It's not just nail polish." She raised her chin. "I'm getting other mani-pedi stuff, too."

"What does that have to do with the Park Service? I'm struggling to imagine you doing park ranger things with a full set of nails."

"Oh. Um." Olivia bit her lip. "Nothing. But, actually, quite a lot." She fussed with her hair. "Derrick, what are you doing here? I don't want to talk to you."

"Well, I'm sorry." He pulled out a chair and sat beside her. "We have things to discuss. I don't want this to be a repeat of yesteryear."

She wore a bikini top and a sarong skirt and had obviously been in the hot tub. There was an empty drink glass beside it sporting a colorful paper umbrella, and the lid was flipped open, hot water churning.

"If you must know," she said haughtily, "I was buying beauty products to soothe my jangled nerves."

"This is about the story, isn't it? The one about me and Meredith."

"You said that you were *friends*, Derrick. Not engaged to be *married*."

"I know. And—Olivia—you've got to believe me, because it's true. That whole story on the internet is a fabrication."

"Whose fabrication? Yours and Meredith's? Why?"

"No, not ours. Well, not mine. Not her fault, either, really."

"Somebody had to have started it."

"If you have to blame someone," he said, "blame Tanya from *Talk Time*."

"Tanya Gibbs?" Olivia's eyes widened. "OMG, I *love* her."

Why didn't that surprise him? "Join the club."

Olivia raised her eyebrows. "What does Tanya have to do with any of this?"

"She had Meredith on her show to interview her, and somehow the interview got out of hand and I came into it."

"Came into it how?"

"By…being mentioned as Mer's possible boyfriend?"

"See!" she said as if she'd known something was up all along. Olivia bristled. "And I wish you wouldn't call her 'Mer.' It reminds me of my uncle's horse farm in Kentucky. That's not an affiliation any woman would want to have. Trust me. It smells *awful* there."

Derrick dragged a hand down his cheek, wondering if this was worth it.

"So, you're *not*," she said carefully, "involved with Meredith for real then?"

"No. The media got hold of the rumor and then it spread like wildfire. In certain circles, anyway."

"So why didn't you put a stop to it?"

"It all exploded so quickly there wasn't time. Plus, she was up for this big promotion, a syndication deal for her show—and now streaming—"

"Streaming? Ooh. That sounds exciting."

"Yeah, and I didn't want to blow it for her by creating another media storm on top of the existing one."

Olivia thought on this. "So you were playing the gentleman?"

"*Yes*, that's it."

Olivia folded her arms in front of her and was quiet for a couple of minutes. Which was a thousand times better than the volume he'd been expecting.

After a beat, she finally said, "I can live with that. Assuming you end the charade soon."

"We intend to."

"When?"

"Just as soon as she gets word."

"When will that be?"

"By Wednesday at the latest, but Mer's thinking she'll hear by Monday now."

"Monday?" Her face brightened. "Oh! That's good."

Derrick was relieved she was being so understanding, and doubly glad she wasn't shouting at him.

"Derrick," she said, derailing his train of thought. "I've got something to tell you and it's shocking."

He stared at her and waited.

"I'm not really a park ranger."

What? She'd made that up, but why? "But what about Acadia?"

"I was living there with Paul."

"Who's Paul?"

"The park ranger guy I told you about. Remember? He's the one who got me my phone. We had a little relationship."

"How little?"

"Four years."

"Wow, Olivia." His head reeled. His instincts had been dead-on, apparently. Of course she wasn't a park ranger. Ordering mani-pedi stuff from the guest cottage. What else had she said that was a lie?

"Why are you grumbling?"

"I'm not"—he set his jaw—"grumbling." Maybe.

"Yes! You! Are!" she said, each word getting louder.

His heart ached with disappointment. "Please, let's not do this. Not here. Not now."

"Sorry." Her eyes watered, but she thankfully didn't cry. He didn't know if he could take that on top of the shouting.

"You should have told us about the park ranger thing." He shook his head. "Right from the start."

"I never said I was a park ranger," she protested. "You all did. Sofia didn't say anything about that when she called. Then, when I got here, that's all anybody was talking about, so I...you know." She raised a shoulder. "Did the gentlewomanly thing."

Derrick set his hands on his hips. "That is so not the same."

"Oh, yes it is. Very close."

"Nope."

"Uh-huh."

"Not true."

"Yeppers!"

He shook his head. "So, if you're not living in Acadia, where are you living?"

"I work at a day spa in Bar Harbor."

"Figures."

"That was rude. I have bigger plans."

"Oh yeah? Like what? Coming to Blue Hill to cozy up to your ex's family?"

"That's really unfair. Sofia wanted me here." The next instant, she looked hurt. "I thought you did, too."

He deserved that and he knew it. "I did. Do. Only, Olivia?"

"What?" She sounded about as irritated as he felt.

"When were you planning to tell me?"

"I just did!" She huffed. "When were you?"

He held up both hands. Derrick realized he was just as culpable as she was. He'd hidden things from her, too, and neither of their motives had been malicious. "You're right. I'm sorry."

She pulled a pout. "It's pretty sad that you're so judge-y. I don't get how you're so high and mighty with what you do for a living."

"What's wrong with what I do?"

"Nothing! That's exactly my point."

"You used to say I was wasting my life," he said with a bitter taste on his tongue.

"That's when I thought I was going to be a lawyer."

"Oh, I get it. It's a class thing. Now that you're not, I'm good enough for you?"

Her eyes flashed. "You're even worse than I remembered!"

Derrick raked both hands through his hair. "Ditto."

They stared at each other, breathing hard.

When they'd both calmed down, he asked her,

"How long have you lived in Bar Harbor, anyway?"

"About five months, two weeks, and four days."

"That's specific."

She studied her nails. "Ever since I moved out of Paul's."

"You lived with him in the park?"

"In the park, yeah, in his hut."

"So, what did you do all that time. Were you working?"

"Sure, I was. Looking after the animals."

"Which animals?"

She rolled her eyes. "He had a chinchilla and a llama, seven chickens, and a couple of goats—"

"Wait a minute, all in the park? Was he even supposed to do that?"

"*No*. But I never told anyone. I promised. Not even about the Boa—"

"Constrictor?"

"The worst part was feeding it. I had to keep my eyes closed."

Derrick felt all turned upside down, like he didn't know where to find the earth or the sun. This conversation had started out okay but it had taken a bad turn somewhere, and now it was in a downward spiral. On top of that, there'd been a whole lot of yelling.

He needed some space.

"You know what?" he said, standing. "I think I'd better go."

Her face fell. "You said we needed to talk."

"Yeah, but I'm feeling all talked out right now." His head was pounding, too.

Her eyes glimmered sadly. "I'm sorry, Derrick,

about the park ranger thing."

"It's fine. Really fine." He exhaled. "But I want you to tell my family," he said. "About your real job in Bar Harbor, and the park ranger thing." He heaved a breath. "There's a lot you don't know about what they went through last year. If you and I have any shot at going anywhere, you'll need to come clean with them."

His stomach clenched. Was that really what he wanted? To be going places with Olivia? His gut churned but then he steeled his nerves.

She didn't hesitate. "Consider it done."

He had tons to process here. Things to think through. He was fine with her job, of course. Olivia could do, or be, whatever she wanted.

Only, everything about this seemed wrong.

So incredibly wrong.

He almost felt sick to his stomach.

"Where are you going?" she asked as he left.

"To clear my head."

CHAPTER TWENTY-FIVE

Derrick met up with Meredith at the main house and called her into the kitchen from the den, where she'd been visiting with his family. His face was flushed and he seemed out of sorts.

"I need to head back to my cabin. Do you want to stay here, or come with me? If you stay, I'm sure someone else can bring you back later."

"No," she said, worried about him. Clearly his talk with Olivia hadn't gone well. "I'll go." She hated seeing his mood shift from upbeat to downcast. He'd been so happy presenting the cradle to William and Sofia just half an hour ago. Now he looked like he'd lost his best friend in the world.

They said their polite goodbyes to the others, then Derrick drove them back to his place without saying a word. They'd return to his grandparents' house tomorrow afternoon in time for drinks and dinner with his folks and Sofia's parents. At that point, the whole clan would be there. Meredith had figured on Derrick and Olivia being a couple by then.

But, given Derrick's current expression, that didn't seem likely.

"If you want to talk about it…" she said.

"No." He softened his tone. "Not right now."

She decided to let him open up when he was ready, because she intuited he ultimately would. So she waited and appreciated the pretty vistas along the way until he finally breached the silence, tightening his grasp on the steering wheel.

"She's not even a park ranger!" His jaw tensed. "Can you believe that?"

"Olivia?" Meredith knew Olivia had been hiding something. She just hadn't been sure what. "Did she tell you that?"

"Yeah, and also that she didn't pass the bar."

"Wow. That was a downer of a conversation—for her."

"She didn't tell me all at once," he said testily, though Meredith understood his anger wasn't targeted at her. He was peeved with Olivia. "She told me about the bar over frozen yogurt."

"She couldn't really help that, Derrick. Not if she studied, and I'm sure she did. The bar can be hard to pass. A lot of people—"

"Yeah, yeah. I know. But a lot of people don't go on to lie about their profession."

True, but embarrassment was a real thing, and was especially hard for someone like Olivia who seemed very focused on keeping up appearances. "What was her reason?"

"She said it was our fault. My family's for laying it on her. She works at a day spa in Bar Harbor."

"Ah," Meredith said. "That explains a lot." Like her eyebrows, and her nails, and her perfectly coiffed hair…

"Anyway," Derrick said. "She kind of blew me out of the water with that. Plus, she got shout-y."

"Oh no."

His shoulders drooped. "I'm afraid I got a bit shout-y, too."

"I'm sorry that things were rough. Did you talk about the fake fiancé thing at all?"

"Yeah." He frowned. "I told her."

"And?"

"Amazingly, she was okay with that." He shook his head. "It was some of those other things she said. Like she couldn't resist pushing old buttons."

"I'm really sorry," Meredith said, because she was. She hated that Derrick and Olivia had had some huge, knockdown, drag-out fight. "Maybe this big blow up is only temporary? Sometimes you have to get out everything that's bothering you to move forward."

"Yeah, I don't know," he said sourly. "Maybe."

They reached his property and pulled into the drive.

He turned off his ignition then sat there stewing.

She wished she could think of a way to help him. "Can I make you some coffee? Or fix you something to eat?" She glanced at his outbuilding. "Maybe you'd like to tool around in your workshop for a while?"

He followed her line of vision, then his gaze settled on the boats beside his workshop. "You know what always makes me feel better?" he asked. "Getting out on the water. It clears my head and helps me focus on the positives in life, you know?"

She liked the way he looked at her, like she was one of those positives.

"So, what do you say?" He grinned and her heart skipped a beat. "Want to go out with me and forget about our worries for a while?"

"I'd love that," she said, meaning it absolutely.

• • •

Meredith changed into shorts and a light wind-breaker because Derrick warned it might be chilly on the water with dark clouds rolling in. He led her to the overhang beside his workshop and two kayaks, one yellow and the other orange.

"Oh! We're going out in those?"

"What did you expect?" he teased. "The rowboat?"

Yes. She worked hard to mask her disappointment. "No, kayaking is good. Great! Only..." She set a hand on her hip and studied the craft. "I've never tried it before."

"Just follow my lead." He gave her a life jacket for her to strap on. "You'll do fine."

Yet, once they'd launched their kayaks from the dock, she wasn't doing "fine" at all.

"Dig in deeper with your paddle," Derrick instructed.

She did and her kayak turned in a circle. Argh.

He chuckled. "Equally on both sides."

She tried that and started going toward a bank at the far side of the cove. He caught up with her and grabbed onto the rear end of her kayak, pointing her in the direction of the bay. "Let's go that way."

She laughed. "I'll do my best."

But he kept racing ahead. "Hey, Derrick!" she called below the wind. "Wait up!"

He grinned over his shoulder. "Sorry about that. Not used to slowpokes."

She stuck her tongue out at him, happy to see him having fun and not thinking about Olivia anymore. Actually, she was ready to stop thinking about her, too. "I'd like to see you try fitting into my world."

He laid his paddle across the top of his kayak in front of him, waiting for her to catch up. "In television?"

"On set, yeah. In full makeup and everything."

"Oh, no you don't. No makeup for me."

"Only face powder so you won't be glossy."

"I'm afraid 'glossy' is my look. We call it sweaty up here."

"Oh yeah, I forgot. It's very hot in Blue Hill."

He leaned toward her with daring in his eyes. "The hottest."

A sharp breeze blew and she shivered. "Doesn't feel terribly hot now."

"That's because a storm's coming."

"When?"

"Not for a while." He studied the sky. "Probably after sunset." He nodded for her to keep paddling. "You'll warm up after a bit."

She was already exhausted and they'd probably only traveled fifty feet. "How far did you want to go?"

"I thought maybe a couple of hours."

The blood drained from her face. "*Hours*?"

He chuckled. "All right, Mer. Given that you're new to this, I'll cut you some slack. Want to say an hour and a half?"

"How about thirty minutes?"

"Sixty."

"Forty-five."

He stuck out his hand. "Deal!"

She reach over to shake it, and her kayak rocked sideways.

"Steady as she goes," he said, easing her craft upright.

"So this helps you?" she asked, her breathing growing heavy. "Getting out on the water?"

"Yep. Always has."

"Since when?"

"Since I was a kid and Grandpa Chad took me."

"Kayaking?"

He shook his head. "Sailing on his big boat and fishing in the rowboat sometimes. The fishing was my favorite part because it was always just the two of us."

"Your brothers didn't go? Or Sally?"

"They're squeamish." He made an exaggerated face and she laughed.

"But not you, huh?"

"I have a stomach made of steel."

Yeah, she'd attest to that because she'd seen him with his shirt off. Her heart got all fluttery just thinking about it, then she told herself to stop.

"That rig back in the cabin is the one that belonged to my grandfather. He doesn't use it anymore, so he gave it to me."

"The rowboat? Cool."

"I gave him a boat once, too: a canoe. It was one of the first things I built and not really that great, but he acted like it was the most amazing gift in the world."

"You do amazing work, Derrick. I know you

could tell how touched Sofia and William were by the cradle."

"That made me happy, yeah."

"You're an interesting man."

"What do you mean?"

"It makes you happy to make other people happy. I haven't met too many guys like you."

"Then you probably hang out at the wrong bars."

"Ha. I don't go to bars. Well, not a lot, anyway."

"What?" He held a teasing glimmer in his eye. "I thought that's what you hot Boston chicks did? Hang out in bars with your girlfriends torturing men with your good looks."

She chuckled at him calling her a hot Boston chick. "Ooh, who's being flirty-flirty now?"

"I'm not flirting, Mer. Just stating facts."

"Well, your facts about me and bars are wrong. I'm not really your bar-scene kind of girl."

"No? I would have figured you for a pool shark or something. Stepping all over the competition in those very high heels of yours?"

"Ha!" She glanced down at her feet, glad to be wearing the sneakers he'd given her.

She was so engaged in their conversation she hadn't realized they'd traveled nearly halfway across the bay and were approaching a small island.

"Is that where you met Jack?" he asked after a moment.

"In a bar? No." She didn't mind the question. Somehow her relationship with Jack felt ages ago right now. "It was after a football game. I asked for his autograph."

"Seriously?" He seemed to admire her nerve.

"Yeah, my friends and I went down on the field."

"Wow. Impressive." He set his jaw. "Guess it's going to be hard for most guys to live up to that."

"Who? Jack?"

"Well, yeah."

She took in his handsome profile and the way he glided so seamlessly across the water, while she chugged along, breaking a sweat. "Women look for lots of things in guys," she said. "They don't have to be pro ball players or famous." She cocked her chin. "Some say that even boatbuilders will do."

He belly laughed. "You're a good woman, Mer." His smile warmed her. "One day, the right man will come along for you."

"Thanks." That's what she wanted to believe, too, with all her heart. It was probably too much to hope that he'd be someone as wonderful as Derrick.

He stopped paddling as they approached the banks of an island.

"Sometimes I like to hop out here and walk around, but it will get those new shoes of yours muddy."

"I'm not opposed to a little mud."

His forehead rose and then he chuckled. "Oh right. I do remember that part."

"I'm not as fragile as you think, Der."

He smirked. "Fragile's not a word I'd use to describe you." He ran his kayak aground and hopped out and she did the same. Her feet hit the sticky bottom and sank in. She tried to hide her grimace but wasn't quick enough because Derrick chortled.

"I warned you."

"No problem!" she said, trudging forward with a *slosh, slosh, slosh…* "I've got this."

"You're a very good sport when you want to be," he said, when they reached the rocky bank.

She stared down at her legs, caked in mud splatter up to her thighs. "Told you I wasn't opposed."

He cocked an eyebrow. "Actually. It looks pretty good on you."

A sharp wind blew and she zipped up her jacket under her life vest.

"Cold?" he asked her.

"I'll be all right." She stared up at him and suddenly felt better than all right. She was swept away in his deep blue gaze.

He lifted a hand and gently pushed back a lock of her hair that had blown up against her cheek. Her pulse raced and she felt warm all over. "You certainly will be, won't you?" He smiled affectionately. "You're the sort who always lands on her feet."

"Derrick, I…"

"You're an incredible woman, Mer," he said. "Strong, fierce, invincible."

"I don't know about the invincible part," she said weakly, because she sensed her resolve crumbling. She hadn't been able to stop thinking about that moonlit moment on the dock, and now the memory washed over her again. Drenching every inch of her soul with what might have been. Her and Derrick together just like they were now.

He searched her eyes. "Last summer," he rasped.

Her heart beat harder. "I've been thinking about that, too."

He traced her cheek with his finger and her face heated. "I haven't been able to get it out of my head... Haven't been able to get *you* out of my head. Especially lately."

His eyes caught the glint of the water as waves splashed up against the bank, soaking their shoes and ankles, but she was no longer chilled. His stare made her skin tingle all over. Did he want to kiss her? Then he brought his arms around her and she was certain he did. He tightened his embrace and she clung to him, sheltered from the winds as his husky words raked over her.

"I missed my chance at the wedding," he said, "but I don't want to miss it now." He held her closer and her heart pounded. "Mer?" he asked. "May I kiss you?"

He dove into her eyes and her lips trembled, aching, yearning for his kiss.

"Please," she breathed.

He grinned sexily and nibbled at her bottom lip until she thought she'd go insane wanting him so badly. "Derrick…"

He cradled her face in his palms and gave her a longing look. "If only I'd done this then."

She nodded because she'd shared that fantasy.

Then his mouth claimed hers, gently at first until he increased his pressure, his growing hunger clear. His muscles flexed, rock solid, as he deepened his kisses again and again—and everything else fluttered away.

Her thoughts were like dandelion petals scattering before a storm and dancing above the waves of a choppy blue ocean.

Thunder boomed and he broke away.

"Oh, Mer. Man, I'm—"

"It's…all…right," she said, her breath ragged. "It was me, too."

He checked the sky with a worried glance. "We need to head back."

CHAPTER TWENTY-SIX

As they paddled back to his cabin, Derrick kept up the chitchat to distract himself from what had just happened. That kiss with Meredith had been…wow. Nothing he'd experienced before. She'd been warm and passionate and giving, sending electrical currents from his head all the way down to his toes. Then zipping right back up again. But, beneath all that heat, there'd been something more. Something tender and filled to the brim with emotion.

What had he been thinking, risking things with that kiss? Meredith wasn't interested in him in that way. Or was she? She'd said she hadn't been able to stop thinking about last summer, either. Maybe they hadn't missed their chance at Brent's wedding. Maybe there was still a way?

He peered over at her as they propelled their kayaks forward. She was doing better than before, but showed signs of tiring. He intentionally slowed his pace so she wouldn't lag behind. Yet he didn't want to slow down too much. A light rain began falling, pelting them from the sky, even though no rain had been predicted before nightfall. He blamed those fierce north winds that sometimes ushered in unpredictable weather.

"Bet this is an adventure you don't get in Boston."

"You're right about that. I spend most of my time indoors."

"What about exercise?"

She looked at him like he'd accused her of something.

"I mean, not that you look like you need it…" He stumbled over his words, not aiming to insult her. "Just for, you know, stress relief and staying fit?"

"I have a gym membership," she said.

"Oh yeah? That's great."

"Can't remember the last time I used it." She scrunched up her face. "Might be expired."

He chuckled. "I don't have much of a set routine, either."

"Yeah, but you work on your feet."

"You think on yours."

She blushed, and he wished he hadn't said that. Because, obviously, neither of them had had their wits about them on that island. Should he apologize? But he'd already done that and so had she. Would she ever bring it up again? Or would they both pretend it never happened? He didn't want that. He hoped she didn't want that, either. He also didn't want to overanalyze it now. This wasn't the time.

"Tell me about your family," he said, searching for another topic of conversation.

"What? Why?"

He shrugged. "I'm curious."

She set her chin, still powering ahead with her paddle. "Well, my parents like to stick their noses in my business." She giggled. "Obviously. But they both love me very much and I love them."

"I love your Titi Clarita. She's great and seems

to have your best interests at heart."

"She does, and has always been there for me. She's ten years younger than my mom, so sort of between Mom's generation and mine. It's been helpful having her advocacy."

"Oh yeah, like when?"

"Like, when my parents didn't want me to go to after-parties from the prom, because they feared it would lead to my downfall."

He chuckled. "Did it?"

"No." She smiled her pretty smile. "I got to stay out all night, but totally behaved myself. If my parents had had their way, I would have been home by eleven."

"Eleven's pretty early for prom night."

"That was my regular curfew." The rain picked up and they both leaned forward quickening their strokes. "What was yours?"

He laughed at the idea. "A curfew? Didn't have one."

She gaped at him. "You're kidding."

"Nope. My brothers didn't, either. But Sally had to be home by midnight."

"How unfair!"

"That's what she tells my folks. To this day."

"I can see why she'd be upset," Meredith said. "I didn't have brothers and sisters, so there was no one else to compare myself to. Although, it's often that way in our culture. The boys get more latitude than the girls."

"What do you think about that?"

"That it's sexist."

"I agree that the rules should be evenly enforced among boys and girls."

She smiled at him. "Yeah. Although I don't really blame my parents for being strict. When they married, they were older, and it was on account of me."

He took a moment to process this. "Ahh."

"Not that any of us regrets it."

"Let's hope not! If you hadn't been born, you wouldn't be *here*."

"I know."

"And that would be a shame," he said and her cheeks colored.

They paddled into the cove where his cabin was located, and she motioned ahead with her chin. "Look! Over there! Someone's on your deck."

He strained to see through the rain that was streaking down harder. His heart seized up. It was impossible to miss the frilly sun hat and her long red hair. She sat on a deck chair, fully exposed to the rain and on her lap she held a picnic basket. *Olivia.*

· · ·

Meredith couldn't believe her eyes. Olivia was sitting outside of Derrick's cabin getting drenched. They paddled up to the dock and Derrick got out of his kayak first, extending his hand to help her out of hers. The dock was slippery, but she and Derrick managed. He handed her the paddles to hold and hoisted the kayaks out of the water.

"I'll take these back to the shed," he told her. "Why don't you go on and get out of the rain?" He shot a glance at the cabin and Olivia, who waved. "Take Olivia inside with you." He shook his head. "I can't imagine what she's doing here."

Meredith had a pretty good idea. She was here to patch things up with Derrick from their earlier squabble. Disappointingly, she had mixed feelings about that, especially after that amazing kiss. Then she told herself not to jump to conclusions based on an isolated event.

"Right," she said, holding the paddles upright, so each one rested with one end on the dock. "Want me to carry these for you?"

"No. Leave them here." He lifted the kayak over his head in one swift movement, using it to partially shield himself from the pouring rain. "I'll come back for them." Before she turned away, he said, "Wait! Leave the life vest."

Meredith shrugged out of hers and hurried up to the deck where Olivia sat outside the sliding glass doors.

"Olivia, it's pouring!"

"I know." Olivia looked at her with sad eyes. "I didn't want to go in uninvited."

"Well, you're invited now." Meredith tugged at her arm, urging her to her feet. "Come on, let's get out of the rain."

They shook themselves off before stepping inside and Meredith went to grab some towels from the laundry room. "Here, you're soaking wet." She scrubbed a towel against her clothing as Olivia dabbed at her drenched sundress.

Olivia scanned Meredith's outfit. "You are, too."

"Olivia," Meredith asked, even though she suspected she knew. "What are you doing here?"

"I came to apologize." Olivia glanced at the picnic basket she'd left by the glass doors. "And bring a picnic. Before the rain came, I was going to suggest to Derrick that we go out on his rowboat. I thought that might be…you know." She lifted a shoulder. "Romantic."

Just like she had that morning. "Oh."

"I never dreamed it would start raining so hard. The weather app on my phone said the storm wasn't coming till later."

"I guess those things can be wrong."

"Yeah."

Meredith's cell buzzed on the kitchen counter and she went to check. "I'd better take a peek and see who that is. Might be my aunt about something." Yet it wasn't Clarita at all. It was a text from Beth.

Bummer news. So, so sorry but the streaming deal didn't go through. No syndication deal, either. It was a numbers thing. Nothing more. Cut-throat competitive business. Sadly, all about that bottom line. Better days ahead. Big hugs.

Meredith set down her cell, suddenly lightheaded.

"Is everything all right?" Olivia asked.

"Um, yeah." Meredith rubbed the side of her neck, realizing how damp her skin was and that her hair was a dripping mess. "That was just my assistant in Boston."

Olivia frowned. "Bad news?"

Meredith pulled herself up by her bootstraps. She'd been knocked down before and had picked herself back up. She'd come back from this.

She pressed her lips together to keep them from quaking when her eyes burned hot.

This is ridiculous. I am not going to cry in front of Olivia.

Olivia approached her. "I know you don't know me very well, but if there's anything I can do to help...?"

Meredith hated that Olivia was being nice to her, and then a small light turned on in her soul. When she looked at Olivia's sweet face, it beamed brighter, filling her whole insides with a warm glow. Meredith knew what she needed to do. Her time here in Blue Hill wouldn't be a total loss if she came away from it by accomplishing at least one of her goals.

She could still help Derrick and Olivia. And, because she'd begun caring for him so much, that's what she wanted for him. To make him happy. Yeah, they'd had their steamy kisses on that island. But that had been in the heat of the moment.

Derrick had loved Olivia for ten long years.

All Meredith had done with that kiss was confuse him. Now she owed it to him to help him see straight and finally have the future he wanted. It was so close now. Achievable.

Olivia's presence here proved that.

It was a rare feeling for Meredith, this sense of altruism. She took a moment to bask in it, deciding that it made her think differently about herself and the world in general. Derrick was always doing thoughtful things for other people, but that wasn't her typical MO.

While she'd clung to lofty ideals about bringing

fated couples together through her work, she'd mostly done it because the publicity had helped cement her career. She did things for others when there was an endgame in sight that would benefit her. Not this time, though.

It was time to think of Derrick and what his life might have been like if she hadn't interfered: lonely and full of regret over his divorce. The only way to make her interference palatable was to right that wrong by delivering Derrick the greatest gift of all: his long lost bride.

"Maybe we should get you out of those wet clothes," she said to Olivia. She sized her up, figuring she could find some of her own things that might fit, even with Olivia being taller and slimmer. The outfit she came up with might be baggy, but at least it would be nicely coordinated—and dry. "You'll catch your death. How long were you out there?"

"I'm not sure. Twenty minutes?"

"Oh no. Well, here…" Meredith ducked into the laundry room and then handed Olivia a fresh towel. "Maybe you should take a hot shower and change. I'll grab some of my clothes for you to wear."

"I'd hate to put you out," she said, but then her teeth chattered.

"See there?" Meredith said. "You're freezing. Go shower and I'll make us some coffee."

Olivia nodded and Meredith said, "I'll leave the clothes outside the bathroom door."

• • •

Meredith showered after Olivia, expecting Derrick back shortly. But, by the time she was done in the bathroom, he still hadn't returned.

"I saw him outside on the dock, tying up the rowboat with extra lines," Olivia offered. "And he was carrying deck furniture to the shed. We must be expecting really bad weather."

If she weren't so pretty, Olivia might look silly wearing Meredith's baggy yellow Capris, cinched tightly with a belt and her long-sleeved cotton top with daisies on it. But the fact was Olivia was still stunning, even with her makeup washed off and with un-styled wet hair.

Meredith poured them both coffee, worrying about Clarita and the others back at Derrick's grandparents' place. "I should probably check on my aunt in a bit."

"Good idea," Olivia said, likely thinking Meredith meant by phone or text.

They both sat at the table for a moment and said nothing. Winds howled outdoors and rain pounded the tin roof. The front door cracked open and Derrick entered the cabin, drenched.

"Hey, ladies. Glad to see that you got dry." He removed his shoes and headed for the bathroom. "Think I'll go next."

Meredith understood this was her chance to talk with Olivia. She also knew she should head out soon, if she was going to leave before more of the storm set in. She'd decided to go and stay with Clarita in order to provide Olivia and Derrick with some valuable couple time.

After the shower started up, Meredith addressed

Olivia. "I heard you and Derrick had a small spat back at the guesthouse."

"Yeah." She sniffed and wiped at the corner of one eye. "It was kind of like old times."

"Olivia?"

"Hmm."

"Do you care for Derrick?"

"Of course I do."

"No. I mean *care* care. As in, are you interested in being with him? Because you know…he's a really great guy."

"I know. That's why I felt so bad about all the shouting."

"I think he felt pretty bad about that, too."

"I did love Derrick once. A whole lot."

"I'm sure you did. I mean, you got married! Right?" Meredith forced herself to smile. Boy this was harder than she thought. "I'm sure he loved you, too."

"It's hard to know what time has changed, and what it hasn't," Olivia said. "You know?"

Meredith considered the picnic basket. "What did you bring for supper?"

"Just a couple of sandwiches. I also brought brownies. Grandmother Margaret made those. I'm not much of a cook," Olivia admitted shyly.

"I doubt the fact that you're not a gourmet matters to Derrick," Meredith told her. "That didn't seem to bother him the first time."

"No."

"Besides, there are bound to be lots of other things you're good at."

"Oh yeah? Like what?"

Meredith swallowed hard. "Uh. You tell me."

Olivia rolled her eyes toward the ceiling, thinking. "I've always been really great with animals."

"Yes! There you go."

"But it's not exactly a talent."

"Sure it is. Not everyone is like that. Some people consider it a gift."

Olivia appeared distant a moment. "A gift. Hmm. I like that."

"A lot of people use their gifts in their careers. Have you considered that?"

"You mean using my love of animals in a job? I thought of vet school once, but wasn't any good at biology." She frowned and Meredith felt sorry for her. "Turns out I wasn't so great at pursuing law, either."

"You'll find your way. What led you to Bar Harbor?"

"Harry. The guy I dated after Paul—"

"The park ranger?"

"Yeah, but I honestly liked Paul better. He had lots of animals at his place. Harry was allergic. That's why things only lasted two weeks."

"See," Meredith said, growing animated. "I sense a theme!"

"Yeah, that I move from man to man. I get that."

That wasn't exactly what Meredith meant. But she also wanted to make sure Olivia wasn't using Derrick as just another stepping stone. "What about doing something for yourself?"

"I do! I work at a salon. And it's…all right." She giggled. "But I'd much rather be a client than a manager to tell you the truth. Which is why, when

Sofia called, I—" She bit her bottom lip, clamming up.

Meredith leaned toward her. "You what?"

"I thought it would be good for me and Derrick to reconnect. I mean, the Albrights have so much going for them."

"Their money, you mean?" Meredith was aghast. *Olivia's a gold-digger?*

"Not only that. They're fun people, even if they get sort of carried away at times."

Meredith massaged her forehead, hoping she wasn't reading this right. If Olivia was only after Derrick's family's money, that would be terrible. She couldn't endorse that.

"You know Derrick's an instructor at the boat school," Meredith said. "And a very proud guy. I'm sure he supports himself and doesn't rely on his family's wealth."

"No, but there still are certain perks."

Meredith was about to convince herself she'd been wrong to try to help Olivia, but then Olivia said, "Like the way they all seem so fond of each other. There's a lot of love in that group. Anyone can see that. I'm sure that you have."

"Um, yeah. Of course."

"You couldn't fault a girl for wanting to be a part of it. Especially when..." Olivia's eyes glistened. "I want to do things better this time."

"Better?"

"Less angry. More loving. I'll even learn to cook!"

"Oh!"

"Derrick's so wonderful." Olivia sighed. "I can't

believe I ever let him go."

"So you *are* interested in giving things another try?"

"Only if he is."

The shower stopped running.

"Olivia," Meredith said, standing. "I want you to tell Derrick all of those things you just told me. Well, maybe not all of them. But about the love within his family, and how you want to do better." Meredith picked up one of the suitcases she'd packed while Olivia was in the shower. She'd already placed her other luggage in her car, including that shoe rack from Derrick. She'd had to bite back her tears seeing that. It would be a keepsake from her time here, she guessed. Something to remember him by, however sadly.

"Wait? Where are you going?"

"To stay with my Titi Clarita."

Olivia's worried gaze trailed to the window and the trees bending sideways in the wind. "Are you sure you should be driving in that?"

"I'll be okay, but I'd better get going before things get worse."

Olivia nodded from where she sat at the table. "Be careful. And, thanks!"

Meredith halted at the front door. "Just one more thing," she said before leaving. "Be good to him. No shouting, okay?"

CHAPTER TWENTY-SEVEN

Titi Clarita was surprised to see Meredith at the door, and even more startled by her luggage. She'd left her large suitcase in her trunk for now and only carried her tote and small rolling bag. "*Mija*," she said. "Oh no, what's going on? Are you all right?"

Meredith moved past her and into the guesthouse, setting her stuff down.

"You'll be proud of me. I did the right thing."

"The right thing how?"

"I think it's going to work," she said. "Derrick and Olivia getting back together."

Clarita's eyes registered worry. "I see."

"Do you mind if I stay here?"

"Of course you should stay, but what about Olivia?"

"The weather's pretty bad. I'm guessing she'll stay at the cabin tonight."

"And Derrick? He's fine with this?"

"I think so. I left when he was in the shower."

Clarita shook her head. "Olivia told me she was going out to talk to him. What did she say?"

"I wasn't a witness, but did get a preview. I've got a hunch it's going make an impact on him."

"You believe he still loves her?"

"I believe that he *wants to*." Meredith felt herself crumble. "Why does it feel so wrong? Doing what is right?" Heat prickled the backs of her eyes and Clarita pulled her into a hug.

"You've fallen for him yourself, haven't you?"

When Meredith didn't answer, Clarita hugged her harder. "It's okay, I can understand why, and I don't blame you."

"But I blame myself," Meredith blubbered. She was crying now, even though she tried to hold back her tears. "And it's all been for nothing, Titi Clarita. Nothing at all." She wept, sobbing harder. "I didn't even get the streaming deal!"

Clarita patted her back. "Well, there's always syndication—"

Meredith shook her head.

"No?" Clarita said softly. "Not that, either?"

Meredith stared at her teary-eyed. "I really am a wreck, aren't I?"

"Maybe so. But you're an accomplished one." She held Meredith's chin. "You're a great matchmaker, Meredith." More tears leaked from her eyes, because her aunt never called her by her stage name. "And your show will go on, do you hear me? Maybe you didn't get the wider distribution deal this week. But, in the future? Who knows? Never give up on your dreams."

"You're right." Meredith cleaned her face with the tissue Clarita handed her. Then she loudly blew her nose. "I have a lot to be thankful for. My job. Mom and Dad." She looked her sweet aunt in the eye. "You."

Clarita braced Meredith's shoulders. "We just have a couple more days to get through. Unless you want to leave sooner?"

"No. I wouldn't do that to William and Sofia. Grandmother Margaret and Grandpa Chad, either.

Not after the hospitality they've extended." She drew in a deep breath and released it. "Besides, I need to see this thing through with Derrick and Olivia. I promised him."

"That's my girl. Thinking of others." Meredith felt like an enormous phony, until Clarita added. "For once."

Meredith gasped but then she burst into laughter. Clarita was laughing, too. "You can't help it that you were a spoiled only child."

"Titi Clarita!"

"The important thing is that you're growing out of it now." Clarita winked. "Hmm?"

"Argh, but these growing pains hurt."

"Naturally, they do," Clarita said. "Would chocolate help?"

Meredith's spirits brightened. "You've got chocolate?"

"Margaret dropped by a nice big batch of brownies earlier. Chewy coconut walnut."

"Oh yum."

"Have you had dinner?"

"No."

"Then I'll make up a plate of cheese and crackers, too." She gave Meredith a motherly smile. "Why don't you change into pajamas, and we'll have a girls' night."

"Watch rom-coms?"

"Of course!" Clarita paused. "Milk with the snacks or wine?"

Meredith chuckled. "Let's say wine."

She felt so much better after talking to her aunt. Even though her heart was breaking inside, she could find a way to ignore that for the time being with delicious brownies and funny and romantic movies in the mix.

She carried her rolling bag downstairs, deciding to sleep on the pull-out sofa in the cozy den. She didn't want to stay in the room with the twin beds where Olivia had stayed, and her aunt occupied the master bedroom on the main floor.

She set her small suitcase on a chair and unzipped it, tugging out the football jersey…then stopped, looking down at the piece of clothing. She'd told Derrick she'd kept it because it reminded her of the hopefulness in that relationship. Was that really it, or had she unknowingly been nursing her wounds these past two years about Jack?

Part of her had been thinking she'd ditch it once she had a new man in her life, which was a pretty stupid excuse for hanging onto it anyway. She didn't need an old jersey to remind herself that she was special. Derrick had made her feel that by just looking into her eyes. This thought made her burst into tears again.

But enough! She had to stop! She didn't need to rely on a guy to make her feel good about herself. She could do that all on her own by being a caring and giving person.

She wiped the tears from her eyes, gathering her courage.

Forget about the past.

Forget about Jack.

And most critically, forget about Derrick.

She was done with the fantasy of imagining he might actually fall for her, when all along he'd wanted Olivia. And who wouldn't want Olivia, really? The woman was seriously about as perfect as any woman could get, even if she wasn't a park ranger.

She trudged up into the kitchen, where her aunt was preparing the food and pouring them glasses of wine.

"What are you doing?" Clarita asked, noting her determined gaze.

Meredith stepped on the pedal of the kitchen trashcan and flipped it open.

"Moving on," she said, dumping the jersey inside.

• • •

Derrick sat with Olivia in his kitchen, his gut all twisted up inside. Meredith had bolted out of here without so much as a word of goodbye. If she was going to go, she'd probably left at a good time. The storm had started in earnest. Fierce winds ripped across the bay, which was pummeled by torrents of rain.

Olivia fiddled with the picnic basket on the table. She'd said she'd come to talk and now it was just the two of them. He realized it was late and that he should probably fix them something to eat. This storm wasn't lifting for a while.

"Hungry?"

"Maybe a little."

He eyed the picnic basket. "What did you bring us?"

"Simple stuff. Sandwiches." She peered inside

the basket and pulled a face. "They're kind of wet now."

"I've got a frozen pizza in the freezer?"

Her pretty face lit up. Somehow it didn't hold the glow that Meredith's did, though. "Pizza sounds great."

Winds howled and they both glanced at the dock. "You should probably stay over," he said. "I don't think you should be driving anywhere tonight."

She blushed. "I can stay on the sleeper sofa."

He reached for the pizza in the freezer, thinking he wouldn't have it any other way. "Sure." He reached in the fridge for a beer. "Want one of these, or some wine maybe?"

She shrugged. "I'll take a beer." He set her bottle down in front of her and readied the pizza, popping it in the oven. Then he sat down at the table with her.

"Derrick," she said. "I'm sorry for all the shouting. I really am."

He frowned, embarrassed he'd lost his temper, too. "Yeah, same."

"I like us better when we're talking."

"Me, too." He chuckled and took a sip of his beer. Still, he felt anything but lighthearted. Having Olivia here was fine, and he appreciated that she wanted to apologize. But he couldn't help but feel like the wrong woman sat at his table.

Her forehead creased. "What's wrong?"

"It's nothing. It's just Meredith left kind of abruptly. Did she say anything?"

"Only that she wanted to check in with her aunt."

"I hope she got there safely."

"If she'd had any trouble, I'm sure we would have heard."

He nodded, knowing she was right.

"Olivia." He cleared his throat. "Seeing you again has been—"

"Great, right?" She grinned and his heart sank. He hated to disappoint her.

"I'm not so sure."

"Not so sure about what?"

"Not so sure about us." He shot her a questioning look. "Are you?"

She bit her lip. "Honestly? No. But Derrick, if there's a chance, don't you think we should try? I mean, I'm prepared to try harder. I've always loved your family. All of you. And you and I—back in the day—we had something, right?"

"We did." He swallowed hard. "But that was then and this is now."

"What's that mean?"

"Times have changed. *We've* changed."

She ducked her chin. "I'd like to think for the better."

His tensions eased. "Yeah, maybe so."

She stared at the table, thinking. "You know," she said, "we don't have to decide anything today, or even tomorrow. This is Julia's weekend, right? Maybe we should keep it that way."

Derrick nodded, appreciating her kindness. "I think that's wise."

"So then, here's what we'll do." Her green eyes sparkled. "Let's take the pressure off, and see what happens?"

That sounded super to him. "I'm up for that."

"We had something once," she said. "So maybe we will again. And, Derrick?" Her eyebrows arched. "It's really *okay* if what develops between us turns out to be just friends. It's been nice to get a little closure, you know?"

He felt like a two-hundred-pound weight had been lifted off his chest. "I'm so glad you said that."

She grinned then teased. "And I'm so glad that you've got pizza. It smells delicious."

He chuckled, feeling a million times better about everything.

"Yeah." He took a swig of his beer. "It does."

She clicked her beer bottle against hers in a toast. "So here's to the christening then."

He toasted back. "Here's to Julia." In his heart, he was thinking of his niece, he really was. But he was also thinking about Meredith.

• • •

Meredith and her aunt went up to the main house at a little after eleven the next morning. William and Sofia had taken the baby out for a stroll and Margaret was busy in the kitchen, with Chad at her side wearing an apron and helping her chop cooked ham for ham salad. He dipped his fingers into a pickle spear jar on the counter and munched on one. Margaret slapped his hand.

"Stop that! You'll eat them all."

"No, I won't," he said. "We've got a second jar." He winked at Clarita and Meredith as they passed through the room.

"Need any help?" Clarita asked.

"Just help yourselves to some coffee," Margaret said.

"Or to a Bloody Mary," Chad said. "There's a pitcher in the fridge."

"Ooh," Clarita said, then Meredith whispered to her. "Let's wait until the others do."

When they reached the den they found Hope and Brent, and Sally all holding Bloody Marys, with celery stalks poking out of their glasses. Derrick and Olivia were there, too, and also had cocktails. Meredith stifled a laugh at how quickly her aunt tried to scurry back to the kitchen.

Sally stopped her with a cheery hello. "Meredith! Clarita! Good morning."

They all exchanged pleasantries commenting on the wicked storm last night. Meredith saw that Olivia was still dressed in her too-loose borrowed clothing and seemed to be sitting extra close to Derrick on one of the sofas. Clarita spotted the couple's proximity at the same time and turned to Meredith.

"Ahh, maybe I should grab our drinks now?"

Meredith glanced at Derrick and he squirmed, like he'd been caught between a rock and a hard place. Maybe he was remembering their kiss and regretting it. "No. Let me."

She ducked into the hall leading to the foyer, clutching her belly when her stomach flip-flopped. The hall was shadowy with sunlight spilling in through the sidelights flanking the front door. In the dancing sunbeams, she saw sparkly stars. Or maybe she was growing dizzy.

She felt a hand on her shoulder and turned around.

"Mer? Are you all right?" Derrick looked more handsome than ever in his morning stubble, which he hadn't bothered to shave. Or maybe Olivia hadn't given him time. This last thought made her feel even sicker than before. "You look kind of pale?"

Meredith straightened her spine. "I'm fine. How are you?"

"Okay." He frowned. "You took off last night without any warning."

"I wanted to give you and Olivia some space."

"Space for?"

"Talking." She swallowed past the tender knot in her throat. "Patching things up."

"I see."

"And did you?" Her voice quaked. "Patch them up?"

"We talked, yeah." He shifted on his feet. "About a lot of things."

"Well good, that's good." Meredith licked her dry lips, which was the wrong move, because that only made her think of how he'd kissed them. How he'd devoured her mouth with his. Her cheeks burned hot under his stare.

"I wish you hadn't run off like that. You and I didn't get a chance to talk ourselves."

"It's all right," she said. "Accidents happen."

His forehead rose. "Accidents?"

"Yeah, look Derrick." She dropped her voice in a whisper. "We don't have to talk about it. Neither of us was thinking. We made a mistake."

"A mistake." He exhaled sharply and then his shoulders drooped. "Yeah. I guess so."

His eyes glimmered sadly and her heart ached. He probably felt terrible about letting her down, but she was big enough to take it. She wanted his happiness first.

"You really are a top-notch matchmaker," he said in a melancholy way. "No doubt about that."

She adjusted her hair, feeling unsettled. "I…try."

"Thanks for your help with Olivia. Getting her here, and all that."

Her heart ached painfully. "No problem."

He took a step back and so did she, increasing the distance between them.

"Have you heard anything about those contracts?"

"Not yet," she lied. What was the point of laying that bad news on him now? "But hopefully soon!"

He nodded. "I saw you packed your things."

"I uh, yeah. I figured maybe it's best for me to stay over here now. You know." She shrugged. "In case you and Olivia—"

"Me and Olivia." He set his chin. "Right."

Strange that he didn't look happy about it. What was worse, he appeared upset with her. She frowned. Maybe that kiss had been too much. They'd both gotten in over their heads and messed things up between them. Now their interactions would always be awkward until she left Blue Hill. Which was why she'd rearranged her schedule so she could leave here tomorrow, right after Julia's christening.

"Well, Mer," he said. "I hope things work out for you."

"Thanks, Derrick. You, too." She pursed her lips, holding herself together. "So, anyway. I guess we should—?"

"Get back to others. Sure."

He exited the hall and she held her hot cheeks in her hands.

She took a few deep breaths to center herself before entering the kitchen.

"Did someone say Bloody Marys in here?" she asked Chad and Margaret, forcing a grin.

"Yes, indeed," the older man said. "Help yourself."

CHAPTER TWENTY-EIGHT

By the time Derrick's parents arrived, everyone was in good spirits. Everyone except for him. His earlier conversation with Meredith had left him off-kilter. She'd called their kiss a mistake. And who knows? Maybe it was. If that's what she believed, she'd obviously not been experiencing the same vibe that he was. He'd been wrong about so many things, including Olivia. Why not be wrong about Meredith, too?

He glanced at Olivia sitting by his side, recalling their conversation last night. She was good to give him space—give both of them space, really. After being around Meredith, Derrick doubted he'd ever feel more than chummy about Olivia. Meredith had changed his view about a lot of things, including the qualities he wanted in a woman. But she had her TV show in Boston and his life was definitely here.

His dad, Parker, strode into the den wearing a grin. "Well, here's the happy brood!" He held out his arms and hugged them all one by one. Parker's dark hair was graying at the temples, and his eyes were blue like Derrick's, although he probably resembled Brent the most. Derrick's blond-haired, dark-eyed mom, Elsa, was not far behind him. She circulated the room, issuing hugs and heartfelt greetings before stopping to squeal with delight over baby Julia.

"Will you look at how big she's grown!"

She got to Meredith next. "Oh Meredith, what fun to see you! We're so happy that you're here," she said. Parker greeted Meredith, who introduced Titi Clarita. Derrick watched the swirl of activity and waited for his parents to notice Olivia.

"O-liv-ia," his mom said. "Aren't you a sight?" Weirdly, she didn't rush to hug her like she had the others and Derrick had a suspicion that he'd been right when he'd asked Sally about his mom's feelings. His mom had her reservations about Olivia, too. Was it for the same reason? Maybe so. Although Olivia had cleared up a lot of things yesterday and he did believe she valued him now, that still didn't mean they were right for each other. And it wasn't like they hadn't been trying.

"Hi Mrs. Albright." She smiled at his dad, too. "Mr. Albright. Great to see you both."

Sofia stepped in. "William and I learned Olivia was living close by, so we decided to invite her to the christening."

Elsa clasped her hangs together. "That's what we heard." She shot Derrick a curious look but he shook his head. If his folks were worried that he and Olivia had already gotten back together, they had no worries now. His mom almost sighed audibly at his silent signal.

"Oh! Well!" Elsa said. "This is just…super." She gave Olivia a hug. "So glad you could join us." Her gaze swept the room, including Meredith and her Titi Clarita. "So fun that all of you could join us."

"Hel-lo!" an upbeat male voice called from the hall. "Anybody home?"

"Of course they're home," a woman answered in

lilting tones. "You saw all the cars!"

"And that," Sofia said, "would be my parents."

Derrick's grandparents went with Sofia and William to greet Sofia's parents at the door. William carried Julia, who peered over his shoulder bright-eyed.

"Wow-wee!" Sofia's mom said. "Will you look at our big little girl!"

The baby gurgled in response, causing chuckles in the foyer.

Sofia led the group back into the den, where Parker and Elsa also welcomed them. Sofia's mom now held the baby, snuggling her close.

"This is my mom and dad," Sofia said, addressing the room. "Ginette and Amar Fuentes." The thin, dark-complected man with gray hair and a beard smiled around the room. "Hello, everyone."

His slim and pretty wife wore her hair in tight charcoal-colored ringlets. Her eyes crinkled when she smiled. "Good afternoon."

"You remember William's brothers Brent and Derrick from our wedding," Sofia said to her parents. "This is Brent's wife Hope and"—she shot a cursory glance at Olivia—"Derrick's ex-wife and um…our old friend, Olivia. And, you know Sally."

Sally waved hi.

Sofia nodded toward Meredith and her aunt. "These are our family friends, Meredith Galanes and Clarita Rincón."

Ginette grinned at the group. "So nice to see you all again, and to meet the rest of you."

Olivia seemed to suddenly become aware of her outfit. When they'd arrived, she hadn't wanted to disturb Meredith and her aunt in the guesthouse in case they were still sleeping or getting ready.

William had given Derrick the side-eye when he'd seen him and Olivia pulling into the driveway together, but Derrick hadn't told him a thing. Mostly because there wasn't much to tell. Nothing had happened with Olivia and it was looking less and less likely that it would.

"Eeep! I nearly forgot," she said. "I meant to go down to the guesthouse and change before lunch." She sent a questioning look at Margaret.

"There's plenty of time. You run on ahead."

• • •

Later that afternoon, the group played a croquet game on the back lawn by the water. Meredith had pretty much ignored Derrick through most of the lunch, but she'd done so in such a sly way that the others had failed to notice. Sofia's mom discovered common connections between some of her friends and Meredith's family in Miami, and they'd spent a lot of time talking about that.

Olivia tugged at his arm as he picked up the croquet wickets by plucking them out of the ground. "That was fun. A lot better than the baby shower games."

He frowned. "What was wrong with those?" His gaze traveled across the lawn to where Meredith slid croquet mallets back into the holder, working alongside Sally. Hope and Brent gathered croquet balls off the grass and put them away. They bantered back and forth among themselves, but

Derrick couldn't make out what they were saying. Then they all laughed and stared at him.

"We were just talking about the baby game!" Sally called. "And your buffing action!"

Derrick wryly twisted his lips. "That was my winning move. Ask Mer," he said, attempting to draw her into the conversation.

She grinned but her smile looked stilted as she gave a thumbs-up, and Derrick was discomfited by her reaction. Not forty-eight hours ago, they'd been close. Or, at the very least, on the same team. Then they'd experienced that moment on the island and he'd thought something deeper was developing between them.

Now, though, it seemed like they were at odds. That disturbed him, and it honestly shouldn't have. When they'd met last summer, they'd stayed "at odds" with each other the entire week. The way they'd left things in the hall had been uncomfortable, but he wasn't really sure what they had left to say. She'd made it very clear that her focus was still in getting him and Olivia back together, and that their kiss had been a mistake.

"I thought that diaper game was disgusting." Olivia wrinkled up her nose. "How did Sally think of that?"

"Come on," he said. "It wasn't that bad."

She noted his gaze on Meredith. "You and Meredith aren't talking much."

People were filtering back to the house for some downtime before the pizza supper. The Fuenteses had offered to bring in this casual dinner as their treat. They'd gone upstairs to settle in and unpack.

So had Derrick's parents. Grandpa Chad and Grandmother Margaret were resting, while Clarita had gone back to the guesthouse for a breather—which probably meant a soak in the hot tub she'd been enjoying so much.

"I guess things have been busy," Derrick said.

"I like Meredith. She's nice." Olivia gave a wistful smile. "She gives good advice, too."

"She's had a lot of practice."

Olivia giggled. "Yeah, but I wasn't talking about her matchmaking advice."

"Then what were you talking about?"

"I was talking about me, silly." She grinned. "My life! My goals!"

This threw him because Olivia hadn't bothered to broach those topics with him. "Oh. Um. You and Mer talked about those?"

"Yes, we did."

"Well?"

She rolled her eyes, appearing impish. "I'm still deciding."

"Ahh. So…that's great," he answered, having no clue what she was hinting at.

"Derrick," she asked, "what are your life goals?"

"Well, I'm already the director of the boat school, so that one's met."

"Anything else?" She leaned toward him in a flirty manner. "Marriage? Babies?"

He blanched and she swatted his arm. "I'm talking in the *future*, Derrick. Not anytime soon. And also—hey—not necessarily with me."

He swallowed hard as Meredith disappeared into the main house behind Sally. Suddenly, all he could think of was his and Meredith's goofy attempts to wrap the cradle. And then, the competitive gleam in her eye when she'd pinned all those baby things up on the clothesline. And the way she'd molded up against him when she'd kissed him on that island, setting his world on fire…

"Derrick?"

"Huh?"

"I was asking about the future. When we were younger, you said you were unsure about kids. Is that still how you feel? Because, over the long-term, you know." She shrugged. "I'd probably want them." Her eyes glimmered in the sunlight. "How about you?"

"What?" he asked, undeniably distracted by thoughts of Meredith cradling a small infant in her arms. Then she emerged from the house holding Julia and settled down in a rocker. Her voice drifted toward him over the lawn as she spoke with Hope, who sat beside her, but it was hard to make out what she'd said.

Olivia noted where he was looking and mistook his interest in Meredith for an interest in the baby. "It's kind of fun to imagine it, huh?" she said. "Having one of your own."

"Yeah," Derrick answered. But he wasn't imagining having a child of his own with Olivia. He was fantasizing about having one with Meredith.

CHAPTER TWENTY-NINE

"What were you doing up at the house all that time?" Clarita asked, coming back inside from the deck. She'd just climbed out of the hot tub and had a towel wrapped around her swimsuit.

"Watching Julia. Sofia and William looked like they really needed a rest, so I volunteered to keep an eye on her."

"That was nice of you."

"She's such a sweetie. It was no bother."

"I noticed you *not talking* to Derrick," Clarita said sagely. "All during the games today."

"Oh no. Was it that obvious?"

"Probably only to me."

"He thanked me, you know."

"No, when?"

"In the hall," Meredith said, "before lunch and before all the parents got here." She wasn't about to tell Clarita about that kiss. That would only add fuel to the fire about her speculations.

Clarita studied her a long while. "If your feelings for Derrick are that strong, maybe you should talk to him, *mija*."

She didn't even bother denying it. "What? Now? And ruin his chances with Olivia? No. I won't do that."

"How do you know it's Olivia he really wants and not you?"

"I'd say that's fairly obvious. They were pretty

much inseparable today."

"Maybe Derrick wanted someone to talk to, but the person he wanted wasn't available."

Meredith huffed. "Titi Clarita, please. Don't turn this around."

"Maybe he's confused, *mija*. Maybe if you talked to him—"

And confuse him further? No, she'd already messed with his mind enough. Messed with both their minds, and her heart was paying for it.

"No, Titi Clarita. I'm sorry, but you're the confused one. It's not me that Derrick wants. It's her."

"Thanks to you." She frowned sadly.

"Yeah." Meredith set her chin. "Thanks to me."

While her aunt changed out of her swimsuit upstairs, Meredith placed her newly folded clothing in her suitcase, then picked up the flat sneakers Derrick had given her to lay on top. They'd been muddy and wet from kayaking and the rain yesterday, so she'd had to run them through the guesthouse washer and dryer along with some towels to make them suitable for packing.

She stared at the canvas navy blue shoes, holding one in each hand. She'd never had a man give her sneakers before. In an odd way the gift had been almost romantic, because he'd thought of her and had wanted to make her happy. She could just imagine all the great and thoughtful things he'd be doing for Olivia, now that they were getting back together. Probably building her tons of fabulous furniture for their happy future together.

Her throat tightened, feeling tender and sore, and her eyes burned hot.

She kept telling herself over and over again that Derrick wasn't the guy for her.

He was Olivia's fated match. She imagined the two of them having their second wedding right here in Blue Hill, and her lips trembled. Then she blubbered out more tears when she envisioned Derrick saying, "I do" and taking Olivia in his arms. Olivia would be in a gorgeous wedding gown, wearing designer heels.

Her aunt appeared in the doorway, dressed and with towel-dried hair, looking all fresh and pretty. Everything that Meredith currently was not.

Meredith pressed the tennis shoes to her chest. "He gave me *these*," she said in a whimper.

Titi Clarita's eyes brimmed with sympathy. "Have you worn them?"

Meredith nodded through her tears. "One special time."

"They're very nice."

She met her aunt's gaze, feeling desperate and broken inside. "Do you think I'll ever meet anyone?" Her voice cracked. "Anyone as perfect as him?"

"Of course you will." Clarita scurried down the short flight of stairs to hug her. "You're a wonderful woman. Intelligent. Beautiful. Strong. You'll come through this. You'll see."

Meredith wept in her embrace, not bothering to hide it.

"All we have to do is get through tomorrow morning," Titi Clarita said. "And tonight."

Meredith groaned, then burst into more tears.

• • •

Meredith had less dealings with Derrick that evening than she'd expected, since he and Olivia pretty much kept to themselves. They appeared to be reminiscing a lot with William and Sofia, sitting in a group in the den and swapping jokes about the days when the four of them were friends and used to get together.

Julia dozed in her new cradle parked in front of the hearth, which was not in use during this time of year. Similar to lunch, the meal was informal, with most folks sitting around in the den and the living room on the far side of the library.

Hope finished visiting with Meredith, catching up with her about Jackie's new man, and with both of them agreeing they approved of the relationship. Hope left to go mingle with Brent, Clarita, and the "grown-ups" in the living room, and Sally came and sat beside her.

"How you holding up?" she asked quietly between munches of pizza.

"I'm sorry?"

Sally's gaze darted across the room to Derrick who sat by Olivia on one of the sofas. He'd finished eating and leaned back in a comfortable pose, as did she, the two of them nestled together like a pair of lovebirds.

"Okay, I guess." Meredith caught herself. "I mean, *really* okay. Great, even. It's awesome how everything's working out."

"Derrick and Olivia seem to be reconnecting,"

Sally said. Although she didn't exactly look grateful.

"I know you and Olivia have a past," Meredith whispered.

"It's nothing I can't put aside." Sally shrugged. "In light of Derrick's happiness." She turned to Meredith, pinning her with her dark gaze. "It's funny," she said. "I always had someone different in mind for my brother."

"Oh yeah?" She tried to sound casual about it, but Sally's hint was pretty obvious. "Who?"

"Someone who could keep him in line," she answered. "But in the right way, because she loves him."

"Their reunion is so new," Meredith said, trying to play the bigger person. "Eventually, love will come along."

"Hmm." Sally took another bite of pizza. "If you say so." She set down her plate and grinned. "After all, who am I to argue with you? You're the expert in matters of the heart."

Sure, I am. That's why mine is aching so badly.

Meredith decided to follow Hope's earlier lead and escape the den to "mingle." Sitting here watching the Olivia and Derrick show was doing her no good. "If you'll excuse me," she told Sally. "I think I'll go refill my drink and check on Clarita and the others in the living room."

After a bit, the evening wound down and people briefly discussed whether they should play another family game or watch a movie.

"Sofia and I will probably call it a night," William said. Sofia had slipped away to tuck Julia in upstairs, and he'd apparently encouraged her to stay there. "We'll probably just read for a bit before bed." Meredith could understand the new parents being tired. She also suspected that Sofia and William were a little more introverted than some of the others, so appreciated their alone time.

It occurred to Meredith that all of Olivia's things were still in the guesthouse. She wasn't sure whether Olivia intended to stay there tonight or move over to Derrick's. One thing was certain— Meredith wasn't going back to his cabin.

Brent and Hope decided to stay in the den and watch a little TV. Sally teased she'd give the newlyweds some privacy, disappearing to her bedroom on the third floor. Meredith stood in the foyer with her aunt and Derrick and Olivia at the bottom of the stairs talking to Sofia's parents.

Grandmother Margaret headed up the steps behind Chad. "Goodnight, all!" she said. "Nice day."

Chad waved. "See you young folks in the morning."

"Don't stay up too late," Parker warned. "We're leaving here at ten for the christening."

"I'll put some fresh muffins out in the morning," Elsa added. "Help yourselves!"

Margaret chastised her in a good-humored way. "Oh Elsa, you don't need to get up early and bake for us *again*."

"It's no problem," Elsa said. "Always happy to contribute."

When they'd gone, Clarita turned to the Fuenteses. "Thanks for treating us to pizza."

"It was our pleasure," Amar said.

"It's been so fun meeting you and Meredith

both. Amar and I are really pleased you could join us."

Amar checked his watch. "Well, Ginette. It's probably time we head upstairs ourselves."

Olivia glanced around and peeked up at Derrick, who shifted on his feet, his gaze darting from her to Meredith then back again. "I should probably go, too," she said.

"Yeah." Derrick nodded. "I'm going to get back to my cabin."

Clarita smiled. "That's my cue to say good night, too." She waved at Ginette and Amar, who'd nearly reached the second floor. "See you both in the morning!"

"Good night!" they called. Then Clarita opened the front door.

"Meredith," she said to her niece. "Are you coming with—"

"Just a sec." Derrick caught Meredith's eye. "If you have a moment?"

She felt her whole body flush. "Um, sure." She glanced uncertainly at Olivia, who stared at Derrick.

"I'll go with Clarita," Olivia said.

Was she planning to stay at the guesthouse or merely pack her things to take over to Derrick's?

She smiled at Derrick and answered Meredith's question. "Night, Derrick," she told him. "See you in the morning."

Meredith hadn't exactly planned on a slumber party with her aunt and Olivia. She hoped things wouldn't be too weird with the three of them staying there. Then again, Olivia had been there first, before her. It was only for one night anyway and

Olivia had her own room.

Derrick stared at his feet. "I can't believe that you're leaving tomorrow. It's only a few days early but still…" He looked up with his penetrating blue eyes. "I'd hoped you'd stay until Wednesday. The full ten days."

"Yeah well, I've got work to do." Sadness hummed through her. "We're taping on Tuesday."

"Tuesday? Wait." He studied her closely. "Did you get some news?"

Delaying telling him was pointless now, so she went on ahead. "Uh, yeah," she said. "About that…" She bit her lip. "The deals fell through."

"You're kidding me." His brow creased. "Both of them?"

She nodded. "I wish, but no. I heard from Beth yesterday—"

"Hang on? Yesterday? And you didn't tell me?" He looked crushed.

"I didn't want to spoil the moment—between you and Olivia."

"And this morning?"

"There never seemed to be the right time."

"*Any* time would have been the right time." He raked a hand through his hair. "I'm sorry, Mer. I know this was your dream."

"Other dreams will come along."

"Maybe so, but it would have been nice for you to have this one now."

"Yeah."

He blew out a breath. "So, what are you going to tell the paparazzi? What's the public message going to be?"

"Same as before," she told him. "That your ex came to Blue Hill for a family christening and, when you two reconnected, things sparked."

"Sparked, huh?" His face hung in a frown. "Funny that you'd say that."

"Funny?" she asked, not understanding.

"I just meant your choice of words," he said without explaining further.

Okay... "Anyway," she continued. "I still plan to use the same line about stepping aside for true love." Her heart pinged when she said it, because before it was just a cover story. Now, everything was painfully real. But Derrick could never know that.

He was finally getting his second chance with Olivia, and it would be selfish of her to ruin it for him by expressing her gushy feelings. What would that accomplish other than putting Derrick in an uncomfortable spot?

"So," he said after a pause. "I guess this is it then? After tomorrow I'll never see you again?"

"Not unless you invite me to your wedding." Her face burned hot. "I mean, some of my clients do, but I really wouldn't expect that this time."

"Slow down there, Mer. Nobody's announced any new engagements yet. In fact, Olivia and I are taking it slow. Extra slow." He chuckled and rubbed the back of his neck. "So slow I doubt it's going anywhere beyond us being friends."

This threw her for a loop. "What? But I thought—"

"It's pretty hard to focus on Olivia when my head is somewhere else." His gaze misted over and he set his chin.

Wait. Was he speaking about her? It was

probably too much to hope that her aunt was right. "Derrick," she asked. "What are you saying?"

"What I'm saying is…" His shoulders sank. "I'm going to miss you."

She waited for him to add something more but he didn't.

It was just like last summer.

"Yeah." Her lips trembled. "I'm going to miss you, too."

"Good night, Mer," he said, looking resigned somehow, and her heart broke in two.

Her throat swelled, but she managed to eke out, "Good night, Derrick."

Then she quickly turned away and walked briskly toward the guesthouse, ready to leave Blue Hill behind her—once and for all.

CHAPTER THIRTY

Meredith placed Clarita's luggage in the trunk of her rental car. She'd already loaded up hers, as they planned to get on the road right after the christening without stopping back here. They'd had minimal interactions with Olivia, who'd been polite and had pretty much kept to herself in her room. She'd left early this morning to ride with William and Sofia and help them with the baby.

Olivia would be staying an extra day so would have the guesthouse to herself tonight. Would she ask Derrick over for a drink in the gazebo? When he'd said that thing about them taking things slow and maybe not being anything more than friends because his mind had been somewhere else, Meredith's heart had given a hopeful surge. But then he hadn't exactly followed through by expressing his interest in her, either.

Well, she'd done her good deed in bringing Derrick and Olivia back together.

Now the rest of their future was up to them.

"Beautiful place." Clarita surveyed the property, the hemline of her lemon chiffon dress fluttering in the breeze. "I almost hate to leave it."

Meredith wore her flouncy floral skirt and white peasant blouse. The ensemble was maybe a bit date-like, but it was the most suitable outfit she had for church. When she'd arrived at Derrick's cabin, she'd brought mostly casual clothing.

"I know what you mean," Meredith said. "I'm going to miss being in Blue Hill."

"Keep telling yourself you're doing a good thing, because you are."

"Thanks, Titi Clarita." She shut Clarita's trunk with unexpected force. "I guess I'm just ready for all this benevolence to be over with."

Clarita frowned in sympathy. "It will be soon enough."

A short time later, Meredith walked down the sun-dappled sidewalk approaching the small white church with its tall steeple seemingly touching the clouds. The group was waiting on her and Clarita, who'd arrived there last. Sofia held Julia who was dressed in a darling white lace christening gown. Its matching baby cap was tied on with a silky ribbon knotted in a dainty bow.

Sofia's parents and William stood beside her and Olivia. Derrick was there, too, along with the rest of his family. He looked so handsome in a suit and tie that Meredith had to peel her eyes off of him as she and Clarita hurried up the steps.

"Morning everyone!" she said.

Clarita smiled. "What a nice-looking group!"

Grandpa Chad grinned. "You ladies look lovely yourselves."

Meredith turned her attention on Julia. "Aww, she's an angel."

"The christening gown belonged to my mother," Ginette explained. "It's been in the family for years."

"What a precious keepsake," Clarita said, admiring Julia.

Julia gurgled and Sofia jostled her against her shoulder. "Let's hope she stays quiet during the service."

Meredith guessed that she would. The baby had barely fussed the entire time she'd seen her.

Maybe that was because Julia had been saving up for a momentous occasion like today.

The first sputtering cry came right after the family settled into the pews. Sofia, William, their parents, and the grandparents sat on the front row with the others seated behind them. Clarita scooted down so Meredith could sit beside her on the end of the pew adjoining the aisle. Olivia and Derrick were on Clarita's other side.

Sofia and William had all sorts of toys in their diaper bag to keep Julia distracted. They tried inserting a pacifier into her pudgy mouth, but she kept spitting it out. By the time the baptism ceremony began, the infant was cranked up and ready to roar.

The minute the holy water hit her forehead, she wailed. William shifted on his feet looking embarrassed and Sofia pursed her lips, passing Julia to the minister, an older man with silvery white hair. Hope and Brent stood close by, as the infant's designated godparents, while everyone tried to pretend that Julia wasn't screaming at the top of her lungs.

Clarita chuckled and leaned toward Meredith. "You were that way at your baptism, too. Very noisy."

Meredith giggled behind her bulletin. "Let's hope for everyone's sake it's over soon."

And it was. The minister sped up the service and

only walked Julia halfway down the aisle before returning her into William's open arms and issuing a quick blessing. Ten minutes later, the service had ended and the Albrights and company escaped nervously out of the church, accepting well wishes from others in attendance as they passed by.

The only one who hadn't seemed to notice Julia's ruckus was Olivia. Each time Meredith had peeked her way, Olivia had had her eyes on Derrick and not the service. She was probably planning what she was going to say about them giving things another shot. Meredith was glad she wouldn't be around for that part. She sighed, trying not to wonder about the possibility of her being with Derrick instead of Olivia, because clearly that wasn't happening. She drew in a deep breath to calm herself, repeating the mantra her aunt had encouraged. *You're doing a good thing.*

At last, her time in Blue Hill had finally ended.

• • •

Clarita and Meredith hugged everyone goodbye in the parking lot beside the church, thanking the Albrights for their hospitality and Sofia and William for accepting them as party crashers.

"You can crash our parties anytime," Margaret said with a big hug.

Meredith's heart hurt when she realized she'd miss Derrick's grandma as much as the rest of them. There was even something about Olivia she'd miss. Strangely.

Olivia hugged her and whispered, "Thanks for

your tips! I plan to act on them today."

"Oh?" Meredith stared at her, not knowing what she meant and maybe not wanting to. Maybe Olivia was going to finally make her big play for Derrick by suggesting they start dating. So much for taking it slow. She was probably ready to step on the gas.

Meredith glanced at Derrick who was hanging back from the group, and then more family members pressed in for hugs from her Titi Clarita. The Albrights were a really huggy family. In that way, they reminded Meredith of her own.

Derrick was the last to approach her. Some of the others were still talking to her aunt.

"So." He shoved his hands into his slacks pockets. "I guess this is it then."

Unlike everyone else, he didn't hug her and maybe Meredith was glad. She didn't know how she'd take being in his arms again, even briefly. "Yeah, guess so."

His blue eyes glinted in the midday sun. "I'm sure you'll do great things in Boston."

"Thanks." She glanced at Olivia and her heart sank. "I'm sure you'll do great things here."

He nodded.

"Oh Derrick!" Grandmother Margaret said. "Would you be a dear and help your grandpa get his seat back? The controls are stuck on his car again and he wants to drive."

Derrick set his chin. "Sorry," he said to Meredith. "I'd better—"

"Sure, sure. Go."

He walked away and Meredith's heart thudded dully in her chest. His farewell had felt incomplete, though she wasn't sure what she'd expected.

Clarita hugged her the hardest. "Well, *mija*. This is it until we see each other again in Miami or Boston."

"Take care, Titi Clarita, and thanks again for everything. Give my love to Mom and Dad."

Clarita got in her rental car and the others headed toward their vehicles with waves.

Meredith climbed into her convertible and pushed a button to lower the roof. Given the dark clouds thundering in her soul, she could use all the sunshine she could get.

Once she got back to Boston, things would look brighter. She'd devise a plan for getting her career back on track, beginning with a big reveal show about her sad engagement breakup and the important way it had ended...with her stepping aside for true love.

She saw Derrick and Olivia standing together, chatting with Sofia, and tears prickled her eyes. She held them back and slid the key into her ignition.

When she looked up, Derrick was striding in her direction. Her heart leaped but then it fell when she saw the sad look in his eyes.

"You know," he said, "we didn't get a proper goodbye." He leaned toward her with a hug and she returned it, her battered heart aching. His embrace was tender and warm, but crushing in its finality.

"Goodbye, Derrick."

"Take care of yourself, Mer."

"Thanks. You, too." She bit her lip, ready to put this agonizing moment behind her. "Um, I'd better get going. I've got a long drive."

"Yeah." He thumped the side of her car and frowned. "Safe travels."

• • •

The drive back to his grandparents' place was gruelingly slow. Derrick felt like it took an hour to go those last fifteen minutes. In a way he hadn't expected, it had been really tough watching Meredith leave Blue Hill. He'd had this crazy idea about begging her not to go. He'd even thought about jumping into that car with her and heading down to Boston to begin a new life. But no. He'd never do that. His life was in Blue Hill and he loved his job at the boat school.

He also preferred the peaceful view of a moonlit cove over the glare of big-city lights, and the quiet rustle of the breeze through the pines to the wailing sound of late-night emergency vehicles. He got enough of that when he visited his grandparents in their ritzy brownstone in Boston. He didn't need concrete sidewalks when worn dirt roads did just as well for his morning runs. Boston Common was beautiful, but the enormous, planned park couldn't compete with the view of sailboats skimming across Blue Hill Bay in his mind.

Meredith had called their one passionate moment together a mistake. And maybe it had been, because now it was going to be twice as hard getting over her. No matter how much he wished things had ended differently, they hadn't. At least he was on better footing with Olivia.

Not romantically, though. He was more certain than ever that their chapter had closed. He just needed to find a way to tell her.

. . .

The rest of the afternoon was pleasant enough, with folks having cake and coffee on the back porch after lunch and enjoying the sunny weather. Derrick tried to keep abreast of the various conversations going on around him, but his mind kept drifting out to sea with the tide.

Olivia stayed beside him, chatting with his family, and it was easy to forget there had ever been rift between them. She really was a good person, and the two of them were getting along better than they had before.

But the vibe between them was definitely friendship. Nothing more.

Sofia's parents were the first to announce they needed to go.

"I have summer school classes tomorrow," Amar told them.

"Ahh, I remember those days," William said.

"Now he's lucky to get a break at all," Sofia added, but she was smiling.

"I don't mind the hard work." He lovingly gazed at his wife and the infant daughter in her arms. "It's been worth it."

"We're saving up for a bigger house," Sofia told the group.

"How exciting," Ginette said. "We didn't know."

She was already slipping on her cardigan and had gotten to her feet.

"We should probably hit the road, too," Parker said, standing. He nodded at Elsa as she carried some empty dishes into the house.

"All packed!" she answered. Her apologetic gaze swept the group. "It's been such a wonderful weekend. We really hate to go, but duty calls."

Derrick knew his mom's work as a magazine editor kept her busy, and his literary agent dad had an upcoming conference to prepare for.

"We need to push off, too," Brent said, nodding at his wife. "To catch our flight back to North Carolina out of Boston."

Hope smiled. "It's been so great seeing everyone."

"Am I the only one staying until tomorrow?" Sally complained.

"No," Grandmother Margaret said. "William, Sofia, and Julia will be here one more day."

"So will I," Olivia volunteered.

"No one needs to ask where Derrick's going to be," Grandpa Chad said with a chuckle.

"How much longer is your break?" his dad asked him.

"I've got one more week."

His mom turned to Olivia. "So then, will you be staying on?"

Olivia glanced uncertainly at Derrick. "We haven't actually discussed that."

"Oh well, you're welcome…" Derrick said, feeling suddenly on display. "Welcome to stay as long as you can, of course."

She dropped her voice in a whisper and said, "Maybe we'll discuss this later?"

After a brief lull, Grandpa Chad suggested they all take a stroll to the driveway to see the departing family members off. As the final vehicle disappeared from view, Grandmother Margaret spoke to the remaining group.

"We've got a ton of food left in the kitchen. I was thinking we might have leftovers for dinner?"

Sally wrapped an arm around her shoulders. "After that big lunch today, an informal dinner sounds great."

Everyone agreed that was a plan as they headed back into the house together.

Sofia grabbed the pram from the living room where she'd left it and spoke to William, who held Julia. He'd been burping her after her feeding and a cloth diaper covered his shoulder. "I thought I'd take her for a little stroll before it gets much cooler."

"You know what?" William shot a look at Derrick that he couldn't decipher. "I think I'll stay here."

"I'd love to come along!" Olivia said with a hopeful grin. "If you'd like company?"

Sofia took Julia from her husband and laid her down in the pram. "I'd love company," she said, smiling at Olivia. "Thanks."

After Sofia and Olivia left, Grandpa Chad turned to William. "I got a couple of new books in last week from my mailer book club. They're in the library if you'd like to take a peek."

"Sounds good, Grandpa." He placed his hand on

Derrick's shoulders. "But first, I'd like to talk with Derrick."

This sounded kind of ominous.

"How about a scotch?" William asked Derrick, pausing at the bar in the den.

"A scotch sounds good."

William fixed them both a drink and suggested they build a fire in the firepit on the patio. Temperatures were already dropping and it cast such a warm glow. Since the family enjoyed having traditional lobster boils and clam bakes out here, their grandparents had eschewed the idea of converting to gas, and none of the grandkids minded. Building fires together out in Blue Hill had become just another treasured Albright family tradition. Once Derrick and William had gotten the fire started, William settled into a chair with his drink. "Fun week here."

Derrick nodded sitting next to him. "Yeah. It's been great."

"Having family around's important."

"Especially when celebrating someone as special as Julia."

William laughed warmly. "Yeah, she's awesome."

"Sofia's awesome, too," Derrick said.

William sipped from his drink. "You and Olivia seem to be getting along."

"Who'd have thought?"

"That old tension's gone."

Derrick laughed. "I'm sure that's been a blessing for everyone."

"True." William chose his words carefully. "But something else is missing, too."

Derrick's chest constricted. There was a lot missing in his relationship with Olivia. He guessed he shouldn't be surprised that William noticed. Maybe it was obvious to everyone in his family. "Yeah."

Kindling crackled in the firepit and the smoldering logs above them caught fire. Flames leaped toward the sky, which hedged purple with night settling in. They heard a screen door open, indicating that the women had returned from their walk.

"No relationship is perfect," William said. "But sometimes that doesn't matter when you find the perfect woman for you."

Derrick stared at him, not understanding. He couldn't believe that Olivia—

William tilted his glass toward the house. "Something tells me that your perfect woman is not the one in there." He let those words linger in the air as the women gathered their things and came out to join them.

"Oooh, the fire's going!" Olivia said, arriving on the patio with a glass of wine. Sofia and Sally were not far behind her, and Sally held the baby.

William winked as the women drew closer, letting his brotherly advice sink in.

Their grandparents emerged from the house. Grandmother Margaret admired the sunset from the porch and Grandpa Chad took her hand. They looked so peaceful together, companionable, and still like they were very much in love.

And all these years later, wow.

Derrick's heart warmed.

Now that was the kind of relationship worth holding out for.

• • •

After dinner was done, Derrick approached Olivia. "Hey, do you have a sec?"

Her forehead creased. "Sure. Why?"

"I was hoping we could talk. In private."

"Oh, um. Okay."

She glanced around the crowded den as people ambled toward the French doors.

"Where?"

"There's nobody else staying at the guesthouse now. Maybe there?"

She nodded and shot him a curious look when he whispered to William they'd be back in a bit. Crickets filled the night air with their song as he led Olivia down the pebbled path. She followed silently along without questioning him further, and Derrick felt like the worst person on earth. She'd done nothing but try earnestly to repair things. But he couldn't keep up the charade of a friendship that might lead to something more, because he knew it never would.

"Can I fix you anything to drink?" he asked, as they entered the cottage.

"No, thanks."

He suggested they sit on the sectional sofa facing the water and she gave him a melancholy smile.

"Something tells me this is not a romantic talk. Otherwise, you might have taken me out to the gazebo."

Derrick felt even worse now. Had she imagined that he was going to declare his love for her, or suggest they start dating again?

"Derrick," she said softly. "It's okay." Olivia patted the sofa cushion beside her and he sat down, gathering his courage.

"Olivia—"

"No." She pressed a finger to his lips and met his eyes. "Me first."

This was a turn he hadn't expected, so he sat there waiting.

She folded her hands in her lap. "Hoo boy," she said with a shaky breath. "This is harder than I expected."

Derrick swallowed past the lump in his throat. "What is?"

She looked up, her green eyes misting. "Telling you how I feel."

"Maybe I should go first."

"Nuh-uh." She shook her head. "What I've got to say is important. And, after I do?" Her eyebrows arched. "Maybe what you have to say will be different."

"But, I—"

"Derrick," she said, giving him a stern look. "Stop being so pig-headed and listen to me. I'm trying to tell you that this is no good."

A tsunami of confusion swept over him. "What do you mean, no good?"

"You and me." She frowned. "Trying to make this work."

"But I thought…"

"I know you did, and I did, too. You weren't the only one, you know." She cocked her chin. "I've thought about you a lot these past ten years and always wondered what it would be like. Us getting back together. Only…it's not how I imagined. Do you know what I mean?"

"I think so."

"It's so nice *not* fighting." She laughed and rolled her eyes. "I really don't miss that part."

"But…?" he asked, leading.

"But," she said. "Not fighting's not enough. There has to be more. That's part of what I was talking to Sofia about. Getting her advice."

"On your walk?"

Olivia nodded. "Here's what I think. I think we make great friends." Her eyes sparkled tellingly. "I mean, friends and nothing more."

Derrick heaved a breath, releasing a load of anxiety. *Yes.*

"Derrick," she said sweetly. "Please don't take this the wrong way, but I don't want to be a boat-builder's wife. Not even a boatbuilder's girlfriend, really."

He chuckled at her choice of words. "*What?*"

"It's not that I don't admire what you do, or respect it. Because I do. It's just that…" She lifted a shoulder. "I'm tired of pinning my ambitions to guys. I have other goals in mind. Meredith helped me see that. Goals that will take me to places besides Blue Hill, because there are certain things I can't do here. At least, not as well."

She apparently read his lost look because she added, "Meredith asked me what I wanted to do with my life."

"And you've decided?"

"About a lot of things, yeah." She nodded.

"Including that I'm not really happy moving from man to man."

"Oh."

"It's not you!" she added hastily. "It's all about me and what I want for my future. And that future doesn't involve me moving here to be with you."

"Where then?"

"I don't have that part figured out yet. But I do know one thing—whatever I do with my life, I want animals in it. Lots and lots of animals. Which is why"—she gave an impish grin—"I'm thinking of starting an animal rescue."

"Olivia," Derrick said, meaning it. "I think that's spectacular."

"I know, right?" She bounced in her seat. "Think of all the good I can do."

"A *ton*."

"I need to do this, Derrick. Do something for me for once that really feels right." She frowned. "Do you get that?"

He nodded. "More than you know."

"I'm so relieved you understand," she said. "I didn't want to let you down. Not after all the trouble you went through. And Meredith, she took pains to get us back together, too."

"I'd like to believe some good has come from this," he said. "You and I have learned to get along."

"Yeah." She chuckled. "I think that's better for everyone."

"Agreed."

"And there's me and Sofia," she said. "I've missed her friendship so badly."

"I know she's really happy that you guys are

back in touch."

"So!" she said. "What were you about to tell me?"

He hesitated, not wanting to hurt her feelings but then decided the truth was best.

"Pretty much the same thing."

"That you want to start an animal rescue?"

"No, I think I'll leave that to you."

"Kidding!" she said, shoving him playfully.

He chortled out loud and hugged her. "You're funny. I didn't know that about you."

"Some girls are full of surprises," she said, hugging him back.

CHAPTER THIRTY-ONE

"I want you to go back through the story again," Jackie said. "And this time don't leave anything out."

Meredith sighed. She'd already been through the story in detail and wasn't sure she had the heart to repeat it. "I've already told you everything."

"How about Olivia?"

"When I left, the two of them were like peas in a pod." She could have said, *like Sweet Pea and Cuddly Bear*, but just the thought of voicing that out loud made her nauseated.

"Ugh. That's what I was afraid of." Jackie frowned above her paper cup and Meredith realized how much she'd missed her. Their friendship had fallen by the wayside over this past year, and Meredith wanted to improve things. "Brent always said Olivia had a way of getting her hooks into Derrick."

Jackie mentioning Brent made Meredith aware that this conversation might be sensitive for her. She'd been engaged to Brent, after all. "He was there, you know," she told Jackie. "With Hope."

"Yeah, Hope mentioned the christening and that they were going." Jackie smiled but her eyes looked sad. "You know what? I'm really happy for them, her and Brent. I reconciled with that a long time ago. They're a very good match, much better than he and I ever were. But I don't have to tell you that," she joked. "You're the matchmaker."

"Yeah." Meredith chuckled sadly. "I was right about them at least. Not so sure how things will develop between Derrick and Olivia, though."

Jackie shook her head and scowled. "Olivia. Right."

Meredith studied her a moment. "The Olivia I met is probably pretty different from the one you heard about."

"What do you mean?"

Meredith set down her cup on the small café table in the cute coffee shop. "She was actually okay, Jackie. Not mean-spirited or conniving, or anything. I really believe she loved Derrick once, and wants to love him again."

"Ahh. But she doesn't already?"

"Hard to say."

"What about him?"

"I believe they're both trying. I mean, Olivia's probably trying. Derrick, he…was a little unsure about things."

"Sometimes you can't fit a square peg in a round hole," Jackie commented. "From what I've heard, the two of them were like oil and water before."

"Well, maybe ten years have changed that? Things may have been a little awkward between them at first," Meredith conceded. "But as time went on, they got better." Whether that'd be enough remained to be seen.

Jackie thumped her fingers on the table, thinking, and for a moment she was indistinguishable from her sister apart from the haircut. Jackie had grown out the layers in her hair and now wore it pulled back in a ponytail.

After a beat, she met Meredith's eyes. "You really fell for him, huh?"

"I thought I…felt something." Meredith rolled back her shoulders. "But, apparently, I was wrong."

"Derrick does have his good qualities," Jackie said, "if you can overlook his big mouth."

Meredith laughed at the truth in her comment. "Yeah." Heat burned in her eyes and Jackie touched her arm.

"Hey," Jackie said. "You're going to come out of this okay. You'll see. When you go back on the air and tell your story, your viewers will go nuts with support for you."

Jackie leaned toward her. "Ironically, this disaster with Derrick could make your career. You'll be proving to the entire world that you're not just a matchmaker extraordinaire. You're one with compassion. With heart. A woman who puts true love first, while sacrificing her own happiness. You'll get plenty of media coverage then. After that, who knows? Maybe that exec will reconsider your streaming deal, and those other networks will come knocking?"

Meredith brightened at the possibility. "Do you really think so?"

Jackie grinned. "Things can only go up from here."

She certainly hoped so, because for the past twenty-four hours Meredith had felt like she was at rock bottom. And she'd sunk very low. She'd been crying her eyes out over losing a guy who had never been hers to begin with.

But she needed to get over it and do the big girl thing. Go on her television show and spill the whole can of beans about what had really happened. She wasn't going dish out the set-piece tale she'd come up with in the beginning. She planned to lay the whole truth bare and tell her viewers everything. About how she'd had no boyfriend in the picture when Tanya Gibbs had pressed her on it and had been embarrassed to admit that for fear of losing face.

About how she'd arrived in Blue Hill with a pot roast and a plan. The way she'd unexpectedly fallen head over heels for the man she was supposed to be setting up with somebody else, because he was honestly that amazing. And how she'd followed through with her mission to set him up with his ex, in spite of her breaking heart.

Yes. She needed to do it. Get everything out in the open and let the cards fall where they would. Maybe Jackie was right, and her coming clean about the situation would lead to her greatest success. But, even if it didn't, Meredith needed to be honest for her own sake.

And also, maybe, just maybe—way down deep in her soul—she hoped Derrick would catch wind of her confession and learn the truth about how she felt about him. Even if it was too late, he'd at least know how greatly Meredith had come to care for him.

"So?" Jackie questioned. "What do you intend to do?"

Meredith set her jaw in a determined fashion. "Tomorrow's Tuesday, so…I go on with the show."

They started to stand and Jackie peered under the table, her mouth dropping open.

"Cute canvas shoes." She stared Meredith in the eye. "I've never seen you in anything but heels. Where did you get them?"

. . .

Derrick stopped by his grandparents' place to say goodbye to Sally. He'd said goodbye to Olivia last night, since she'd planned to head out early. With Sofia and William leaving today, there wasn't much point in her staying on, not after the honest conversation she'd had with Derrick about their non-relationship.

When Derrick reached the main house, Sally had already loaded up her car and had her sunglasses perched on the top of her head. She wore shorts and a T-shirt, looking ready for a comfy drive back to Bangor. "I thought you weren't leaving until later?"

"I decided to get an earlier start." She shrugged. "I was just hanging around here waiting for you."

"That's sweet."

Sally laughed and slapped his back. "Yep. That's me all right. The super sweet baby sister."

They walked back toward the house. "Do you have time for a cup of coffee?"

"Sure."

Derrick passed his grandmother in the hall. She was headed outdoors wearing gardening gloves and holding her sheers. "Nice of you to come and see your sister off," she said. "Just brewed a fresh pot of coffee."

Grandpa Chad exited the kitchen, gingerly holding a full mug. "Derrick." He nodded at his grandson and kept walking toward the library. "Don't forget to come and get us before you go," he called back to Sally.

"Wouldn't dream of it, Grandpa," Sally said.

She and Derrick headed out onto the porch, each holding a mug of coffee. It was another gorgeous day with clouds dotting the azure sky. Sally sat on the porch swing, propelling herself backward periodically with a push of her running shoe clad toes.

Derrick was in his standard workshop fare. T-shirt and jeans. While the temps were warming up, he preferred working in long pants around power tools, and he wanted to get more work done on that pie safe today. Once his classes started up next week, he'd have less free time and he aimed to have it finished before his grandparents returned to Boston.

"All in all, it was a good time." Sally gave herself another shove in the swing. "Wouldn't you say?"

"Yeah, really good. The baby shower was a raging success."

"It was tons of fun. Everyone was such a good sport. Including you and Meredith."

She cast her gaze toward the flower garden where Grandmother Margaret worked and the path beyond it. "Saw Olivia's car leaving the guesthouse this morning."

"Did you?"

Sally's eyebrows arched. "She took off awfully early."

"Yeah." Derrick drew in a breath and released it. "We had a talk."

Sally frowned. "Oh no. What happened?"

"Nothing bad." He studied the waves rolling across the bay. "In many ways, it was the perfect ending."

"Wow. You guys had barely gotten started."

"We'd never gotten started, Sally." He met her eyes. "I mean, not again." He sipped from his coffee, feeling even more relieved about the situation today, because down deep it had never felt right. "Some things aren't meant to be."

"Right-o," she said. "But others are."

"What?"

"Come on, bro. Don't look so stunned. I'm talking about Meredith. Have you contacted her?"

"What? No. Why?"

"She'd probably want to know."

"That her stellar matchmaking failed? I doubt that very—"

"No," Sally said with a grin. "That you're single now."

"I've always been single," Derrick grumbled. "She knew that."

"You sure? Because I'm pretty sure she believed you were actually trying to get back together with Olivia."

He raked a hand through his hair, recalling their talk in the hall and then later when they'd said goodnight. He'd felt something between them, not just when they had kissed, but in all the time they'd spent together at his cabin and here at his grandparents' house. But she'd been so closed off, so determined that he and Olivia would work things out, that he'd believed she wasn't interested.

Had he misread everything?

"Derrick?" Grandmother Margaret called, striding toward the porch holding a hand-cut bouquet. "Would you mind getting the trash down at the guesthouse before you go and emptying the other bins upstairs? Our trash man comes tomorrow."

"No problem," he answered, mulling over Sally's assertions.

Sally finished her coffee and hopped down out of the porch swing. "I should probably get wheels on the road."

He stood to accompany his sister to her car. "Hey, about what you said—"

"It's just an instinct that I have." She tossed him a look over her shoulder. "Maybe you should try listening to your instincts, too."

• • •

Derrick walked down to the guesthouse, his hands wedged in his jeans pockets. The earlier sunshine had given way to an overcast sky, and a light drizzle fell. He didn't hurry along or mind getting wet. It reminded him of the time he and Meredith kayaked out to the island and had been caught in the rain on their way back. She'd been so pretty standing there covered in mud while the wild winds blew. He hadn't been able to resist kissing her.

He'd been even happier when she'd eagerly kissed him back.

Had Olivia not been waiting for him on his

deck, he and Meredith might have explored what he was sure had been building between them.

Instead, she'd bolted.

And then claimed it was a mistake.

Why?

Derrick entered the guesthouse, wondering if Sally could be right by some huge stretch. If there was even a *chance* Meredith was into him that would be a game changer.

He recalled her showing up at his cabin with a pot roast in hand and chuckled at the goofy way she'd traipsed through the mud to his workshop, and later tried to conceal her late-night ice cream chow down. Then there was her sunny smile as she'd helped him gift wrap the cradle, and her genuine belly laugh when she'd bested him at the baby shower clothespin game.

She'd told him about her family and her ambitions and he'd talked about his, too. Conversations with Meredith were so easy when they weren't purposely goading each other. And, even when they were, it was entertaining. Those dark brown eyes of hers were definitely sultry enough to stir a man's fire. His neck burned hot just at the thought of them. Then the rest of him burned hotter, recalling the feel of her in his arms. She was so soft and sexy, and yet strong underneath.

Exactly the kind of woman he needed to make him want to toe the line.

Derrick was great at his job, but he'd always aspired to having something more. A wife and, someday, a family. People he could care for and do for beyond himself. Seeing his brother so happy with Sofia and little Julia made him want that kind of life. But not just with anybody. And definitely not with Olivia. He'd clarified that now.

He reached for a spare trash bag under the sink and lifted the lid off the kitchen bin. He was about to haul the plastic bag out by its drawstring when he stopped short.

A piece of clothing had been plunged down inside it, partially buried in coffee grounds and discarded orange peels. Derrick carefully reached into the trash and picked it up by its sleeve, shaking the debris from the garment before holding it up.

"Well, what do you know," he mused to himself. "Mer's old football jersey."

She'd thrown it away, but why? Because she was tired of thinking of her ex? About those early glory days that made her feel special? Or because she was ready to move on?

He gazed at the shirt again, then he dropped it back in the bin, chastising himself for not seeing the situation for what it was sooner. William had been 100 percent right. Meredith was the perfect woman for him in every single way. And he wanted things with her, not just for now but forever. Including shared sunsets in their later years just like his grandparents enjoyed.

He just had to tell her, and hope with all his heart that she felt the same way.

Derrick stared out the window that overlooked the bay. He was going to do this.

Now, all he needed was a plan.

• • •

Meredith sat in the makeup trailer while April worked her magic. Her face was lightly dusted with powder and her lips outlined and painted in, while Joel wielded a wand, smoothing her curls with a flatiron.

The trailer door cracked open and her producer called inside. "Five minutes! We need you on set."

Meredith waved, her insides fluttering like she was suffering from beginner's stage fright. Sure, she'd done this a million times, but this was the first time she'd ever eaten crow on camera, and that notion made her slightly queasy.

Beth waited outside, wearing sunglasses and holding a clipboard, and the two of them crossed the studio lot together.

"This is going to go fab," Beth said. "I read through your script and it's fantastic."

Maybe so, but Meredith also intended to go a little off-script near the end. Only she hadn't told anyone that part. She needed to be sure she'd have the courage to do it, and she might not know if she had it until the last minute.

They entered the building with the set made to look like a Valentine's-themed living room. She scanned the coffee table, seeing someone had forgotten her coffee cup. *No. Not today.* She wanted real caffeine in it, not water.

She stepped onto the stage as the camera crew discussed details with each other, and April attached a microphone to her collar while running its barely visible wire down her back and clipping it to the belt of her shirtwaist dress. April leaned closer and whispered, "We're so sorry about what happened in Blue Hill. With Derrick."

Joel frowned. "And about that syndication deal." Meredith's seashell earrings clattered as she lowered her head and he spritzed her flyaways. "Those people upstairs never know what they're doing." He clucked his tongue. "Disgraceful."

"Thanks, guys." Meredith's lower lip trembled and she bit it. Then she realized she'd probably smudged her lipstick. *Nooo*. She needed to be on point today. She had important work to do. She took a seat on the sofa and raised her eyebrows at Beth. "Coffee?"

Beth stared at the coffee table. "Eep. Sorry." She spoke into her mic ordering someone else to bring it out pronto—and hot. She handed Meredith her script. "This one's been slightly updated."

"What?" Meredith was surprised. "Since when?"

"There've just been a few changes in the timing of commercial breaks. Pretty much everything else is the same."

She flipped through the script but barely had time to peruse it. "Oh. Um. Okay."

"Two minutes!" the lead cameraman called.

Meredith sent Beth a panicked glance. "How are my teeth?" She grinned really big. "Lipstick?"

"Yeah, hang on." Beth dug a clean tissue from her pocket and wiped what Meredith guessed was a crimson-colored smudge off of her pearly whites.

"Thanks!" Meredith watched the countdown clock and drew in a breath.

A second later, she beamed at the camera. "Hi, everybody! I'm Matchmaker Meredith and, wow, do I have a special episode in store for you today."

She leaned toward the camera conspiratorially. "And it's much more *personal* than you'd expect.

"Thanks in part to my good friend and early morning talk show host Tanya Gibbs, my life dramatically changed course lately. Some of you might have seen snippets on the news or read the rumors on social media.

"But you know what they say. You can't always believe everything you read—or hear. Sometimes it's best to get it straight from the horse's mouth. Or Mer's. Ha! That's me." She gave the camera a sad smile. "Just a little inside joke. I'll be sure to fill you in on the details when we get to *that* part of the story. And, trust me on this... They are heart-rending."

• • •

Derrick paced in an area they called the Green Room. He'd stayed at his grandparents' brownstone last night where he'd done some sleuthing and uncovered contact information for Meredith's assistant. When he'd contacted Beth, she was all over this plan, believing it fun and romantic. And also hoping it wouldn't cost her her job.

A flat-screen TV monitor was mounted on one wall and Beth came in wielding a remote and flicking it on. Then Meredith appeared in all her glory. She looked amazing on screen, like a really hot celebrity. She smiled at the camera, oozing confidence as she explained to her viewers that this episode would be unlike any other.

"It all started on *Talk Time* with Tanya," she

said. "Maybe you can relate to being put on the spot and not having the right thing to say? I know I'm a matchmaker and people expect me to be the best—including at managing my own love life. You know that expression; physician heal thyself? Sometimes doctors make the worst patients. We matchmakers, I'm afraid, are no better at helping ourselves."

Her pretty face hung in a frown and Derrick's heart went out to her.

"So, when Tanya asked me that question about who I was involved with, I'm afraid, dear viewers, I lied. Yes, I—Matchmaker Meredith—lied to you all by pretending to have a boyfriend, when the sad fact was I hadn't been on a date in Two. Whole. Years." Her eyes misted and she seeped sincerity. "And for that falsehood, I'm sorry. Though I'm not at all sorry about what came next."

Meredith shared that she was telling the story of her life. Her very sad and broken-down life, because she'd believed she'd found everything she'd wanted—only to have it snatched away. What had she wanted? And who'd done the snatching? She'd let everyone in on those secrets right after the next commercial break.

"Wow," Derrick said to Beth. "She's good. People must shout at their screens when a commercial comes on."

"Yeah. We tape things this way so everything dovetails well with commercials when we air. The pauses here won't be as long as real commercial breaks. Just a couple of minutes so the set crew can check her hair, etc. and she can glance at her notes, or whatever." She shrugged. "Don't have to worry about those viewing interruptions with streaming."

"She should have gotten that deal," he grumbled.

"Maybe it's not too late." Beth smiled at the pretty rose bouquet he'd set on the small couch beside him and opened the door. "For that and other things?" Before she left, she said, "I'll be back to grab you during the last ten minutes of the show. Be ready."

Derrick supposed he was as ready as he'd ever be. He'd talked it over with Brent by phone until one a.m. and Brent had assured him he was thinking clearly. When you find your perfect match, you go for her. He patted his jacket pocket, feeling for the ring box he'd tucked inside and chuckled with nerves and excitement. His grandparents were in on the secret—which meant the rest of his family soon would be, too—and Grandpa Chad had recommended a good local jeweler.

Derrick wasn't normally an impulsive guy. Of the three brothers, he was in many ways the most cautious. And yet, when he'd found that football jersey in the trash and processed what it meant, he knew nothing would stop him from getting to this moment. It was a sign that he shouldn't give up, not on someone as important as Meredith, and she would always be special in his eyes. He couldn't wait to tell her that.

He'd decided in that moment in the guesthouse that he didn't want to wait a second longer. Not when it was possible to grab so much happiness now. He didn't need to waste months and months dating Meredith when he had the possibility of becoming her loving husband as soon as possible. So what if she had her show in Boston and he had his life in Blue Hill? They'd make things work.

Meredith didn't tape her show every day, and much of her work could be done remotely. And, if she wasn't so keen on Blue Hill, Derrick was willing to consider living part-time in Boston. He could teach a few of his classes online. And anyway, at this point, a lot of his work was administrative.

All his priorities seemed to turn on their head when he realized that Meredith could actually be his bride. But she'd have to want him as badly as he wanted her, and there was a solid chance his rash actions would give her pause. She might want to take some time to think things through, and he'd be happy to let her. But he hoped she wouldn't torture him with the suspense for too long.

It was excruciating enough for him that he was actually going on camera, in front of God knows how many people, to lay his heart on the line. And yet, on a gut level he understood that when he did that Meredith would know that his motives were sincere.

Derrick hated the limelight, and calling attention to himself even more. But a bit of embarrassment would be worth it if it meant winning her heart.

It wasn't like they'd just met. They had, in fact, known each other since last summer. And when she'd shown up at his door with that pot roast, she'd been just as beautiful and infuriating and knock-his-socks-off desirable as she'd been before. Maybe even more.

The real difference between now and last summer was he hadn't been able to admit to himself how attracted he'd been to her then. And, when she'd first arrived at his cabin this year, he'd still been denying it.

Well, he was done denying things now, because he'd gotten to know the warm and wonderful woman that she was inside and out, and he was driven to understand her better. He wanted to be all-in with Meredith, and not just for the moment but for the long haul. Tomorrow and the next day. Then the day after that. He planned to say all that shortly.

In public.

He swallowed, hard, and returned his attention to the television. The show was back, and in front of the tens of thousands of people who watched the show, Meredith continued to open her heart. The segment moved things along with a media clip of the reporters at his cabin. He chuckled at the scene of the commotion with the press and the shocked look on his face when he'd opened his cabin door.

Then he remembered Meredith arriving with her Crock-Pot, looking dynamite in those heels.

The camera returned to Meredith in the studio. "And that was just the beginning of that incredibly wonderful week I spent in Blue Hill. It was frustrating and amazing, and really awesome, too, because I met this super special guy, Derrick Albright. Or really, I met him again, because we'd already met last summer at his brother's wedding.

"When Derrick and I first got to know each other, it wasn't insta-lust. It was more like insta-hate." She laughed. "But all of that recently changed, because"—she heaved a deep sigh—"I fell for the guy, I really did. The amazing thing is, he never knew it.

"Derrick is this ultra-talented boatbuilder, who can create just about anything with his hands, including sweet baby cradles. He made one for his brother's little baby, and that was just one of the first incredible things I learned about him that opened up my heart."

Derrick swallowed hard because he could tell this wasn't just TV talk.

She was speaking the truth.

"The more I got to know Derrick, the more I understood that he's not just witty and handsome. He's smart, tender, and caring..." She sighed. "Really, everything a girl could want. No wonder his ex, Olivia, wanted him back! And I could see why he wanted her, because, well...she's perfect.

"So. After the media thing got out of hand, Derrick and I cut a deal whereby he'd play along as my boyfriend to help me save face, and I'd help him win Olivia back, so he'd have something to gain." She gave a tearful chuckle. "I suppose you can guess who got the raw end of that deal? I never got the business contracts I'd hoped for, and Derrick got Olivia. But that, friends, is what fate had in store. I'll share more when we return."

Beth entered the Green Room, breaking Derrick's television trance. "It's time!"

"What?" He anxiously got to his feet. "Now?"

"It's now or never," she said with a grin.

Beth led him across the studio lot and to

another building. A short time later, Derrick stood off stage in a corner where Meredith couldn't see him. She was seated up ahead with her gaze on the camera. He drew in an unsteady breath. How official and amazing she looked. Also, a little intimidating if he was honest. She commanded the whole stage. This was her kingdom, her territory, and she was the reigning princess.

"So that's the way it happened, folks. The 'Unmatched Matchmaker' fell for the guy she was fixing up. Oh yeah." She grimaced. "Hook. Line. And sinker. Until Olivia understandably fell for him, too, and I knew I had to step aside. It was the right thing for me to do. In the face of true love."

She dabbed at the corners of her reddened eyes and it looked like she was really crying.

A cameraman sent her a signal and Meredith gave a barely perceptible nod.

"So, Derrick," she said, "wherever you are and if you're watching, I did this for you. Not because I wanted to, and not because it didn't break my heart. But because I wanted what's best for you, because that's the kind of person you are. You do kind things for others, and I wanted to be that way, too."

She gave the camera a shaky smile and he felt it in his soul. "You're a good man, Derrick. No, a *great* man. I didn't know that at first. But, little by little, you revealed yourself to me, and then suddenly it hit me." Her chin wobbled. "I'd fallen in love with you."

His mouth dropped open, but then happiness coursed through him. *She loves me, yes!*

Then a lightning bolt of terror, too. What was he

thinking—about to go on television? In front of cameras? Being recorded? What if he choked? Or worse, tripped? Now he knew why they called it stage fright. This was terrifying. But Meredith loved him and he loved her. So, so desperately. His heart pounded in his throat as Beth nudged him forward, into the lights and Meredith's view.

She jumped on the couch, startled. "Derrick?" she asked, growing pale.

"Keep rolling!" the producer shouted.

"What—" Meredith asked, dazed. "What are you doing here?"

Derrick froze in place, petrified by the blinding studio lights. His pulse thumped and his neck burned hot. Sweat broke out at his hairline. But he loved Meredith more. She was worth it. Worth anything. Worth everything.

He edged toward her, carrying his flowers and squinting against the bright lights. "I couldn't wait. Had to see you." He handed her the roses and she took them, gaping up at him.

"Meredith Galanes," he told her in front of her studio crew and however many viewers he was pointedly *not* thinking about, "I came here to tell you that your time in Blue Hill wasn't a mistake, and if it was a mistake then it's the best one you've ever made. Because when you showed up on my doorstep with that pot roast, I didn't know what hit me. Then I remembered how I felt every time I saw you last summer, and I realized this wasn't anything new. This deep attraction I feel for you."

Her eyebrows knitted together and those tears kept on coming. "But what—"

"Each time I saw you," he continued, "it was like this red-hot arrow pierced straight through my heart. Only, I didn't understand what was happening." He gave a hoarse laugh. "Hey, I'm a guy and only human.

"The truth of the matter is," he said, stepping closer, "I think I've always loved you, right from the very beginning when you berated me for crashing into your car, when it was really you who—"

She narrowed her watery eyes. "Oh no it wasn't."

"Oh yeah it was."

"No way," she said, but she was grinning.

Derrick plowed ahead, undaunted. "My point is, sweetheart," he said and she blushed, "I think you and I were precisely made for each other. I've never met any other woman like you. I wasted so many years believing my future might be in my past, but I'd really been waiting—*my heart* had been waiting—for the right woman to come along." He stared deeply into her eyes. "I was waiting for *you*. I want us to be together. Twenty-four-seven. And not as enemies or friends, or even just as lovers. I'm talking, as husband and wife."

"But, but…what about Olivia?"

"History."

"Oh no."

"Oh yeah." He grinned. "And it was her idea. Both of ours, truthfully. Because we talked it out and realized we were never meant to be together. Not the first time, or the second time, either. But you and me? I'm hoping…" He dropped down on one knee in front of where she sat on the sofa and the set crew gasped. "Meredith Galanes, I'm done with pretending to be engaged, and finished with acting like I don't care about you. Because I do care. I care more than you know.

"I'm crazy about you. You're warm and wonderful and funny and gorgeous." His voice grew husky. "Man, are you gorgeous—in every single way that I can think of." He swallowed hard. "What I'm trying to say is, I love you and don't want to live in Blue Hill without you."

He took the ring box from his pocket and her eyes went wide seeing the shimmering solitaire situated inside it. "I know your life is here and mine's in Maine, but I'm willing to work things out if you are. Because, my dear, sweet woman, there's no other person I want with me walking through life— whether it's down the country lanes of Blue Hill or the city sidewalks of Boston. As long as we're together, I'll be a happy man." He leaned toward her and whispered, "I'll even build you a cradle—or two."

"Oh, Derrick." She burst into joyful tears. "I'll probably need more shoe racks, too."

He grinned. "How many?"

She beamed up at him. "Maybe a dozen?"

He laughed out loud, his heart so light. "I'll build you any little thing you want."

He popped the ring out of the box and she grabbed it, shoving it onto her finger.

"Whoa. Eager, much?" He grinned in utter joy. "Does that mean yes?"

"Are you kidding?" She laughed, standing and pulling him to his feet. "You know it does!"

At that exact moment, he noticed her blue tennis shoes. "You're wearing them?"

She sweetly cocked her head. "They're my favorite pair."

"Oh yeah, why's that?"

She smiled through her tears. "Because I got them from you."

Her dark eyes sparkled and his heart floated up into the stage lights. This was the moment he'd waited for his entire life. A gazillion viewers be damned.

He took her in his arms and kissed her then with a deep and fiery passion.

And she gave as good as she got.

"That's a wrap!" a voice in the background said.

Then the room broke out in applause.

EPILOGUE

It was a gorgeous summer day in Blue Hill, Maine, with puffy white clouds hanging over the bay. A large wedding tent had been erected on the Albrights' back lawn facing the water. There was a prettily decorated wedding altar there, too, and the folding chairs were filled with family and friends dressed in their finest.

Meredith admired Derrick standing between the minister and Brent, who was serving as his best man. If she believed he'd looked dynamite in a tux two summers ago, that memory didn't hold a candle to his gorgeousness now.

They'd spent the past year navigating their engagement while working out the details of a two-career couple living in separate cities. Although they were never apart for very long. She arranged her taping schedule to maximize her short stays in Boston and Derrick joined her there as much as he could.

He'd adjusted his schedule so he'd be mostly handling admin stuff during her tapings, and he'd even taught a few classes online. On top of that, Derrick was writing a boatbuilding book and Meredith had gotten both her syndication and her streaming deals. Derrick's on-air proposal had gone viral, and *Matched Up*'s ratings shot through the roof.

Meredith smiled at the happy faces in the

crowd, so pleased that all of her and Derrick's loved ones had been able to make it. He'd been so great about everything, and had even flown down to Miami with her, soon after publicly popping the question, to formally ask her parents for her hand. That won him major points. Once he'd wore them down—and assured them he had only the very best intentions for their daughter—they'd fallen in love with him.

Meredith absorbed the stellar view, thinking there was truly no better place on earth to be married than here. When Derrick had gently floated the idea, she'd pounced on it. She and Derrick had chosen a classical Spanish guitarist to play during the ceremony, and the musician's joyful tunes filled the air. Beautiful flowers were everywhere, including in her stunning bouquet, which Grandmother Margaret had helped her select.

Meredith had asked her Titi Clarita to be her maid of honor. It was a little unconventional having her aunt fill the role, but the pretty bridesmaid shoes certainly fit her fun and flirty aunt, who'd recently begun a little romance of her own with one of Derrick's more mature boat school instructors.

Titi Clarita leaned toward her. "You're a beautiful bride."

"You really are," Jackie whispered from her other side. "I never thought I'd see the day." She sighed, appearing misty-eyed. "Me being back in Blue Hill." Jackie was still dating the same guy from last summer, and Sally had a new boyfriend, too. Love was breaking out all over it seemed, and

Meredith's heart felt happy and light.

She patted Jackie's arm. "Maybe it's time for everyone to lay old hurts to rest."

Jackie met her eyes and smiled. "Thank you for inviting me."

"We're all family now," Titi Clarita told her warmly.

The wedding coordinator, Eleanor Bell, tapped Clarita's shoulder. "Maid of honor," she said. "You're up next."

Apart from the honorary positions, Derrick and Meredith had decided to forgo having attendants. If little Julia had been a few years older, though, they might have wanted her as their flower girl.

The precious toddler sat on William's lap, who was seated next to Sofia. Olivia sat beside them, happy to be attending the wedding without a date. She'd started a state-wide animal rescue based in Belfast and had already helped so many needy animals find their forever homes.

The Albright family sat up front on one side of the aisle and Meredith's large extended crew sat on the other. While Titi Clarita didn't have children, Meredith's dad's four siblings did and many of the Puerto Rican cousins had arrived for the festivities. Meredith hoped the Albright clan would be up for a merengue or two. Knowing the Albrights, she suspected they'd be game.

"Meredith," Eleanor said. "It's your turn."

She grinned, because yeah, it finally was.

Derrick caught her eye and his blue gaze twinkled.

He was as ready as she was to get this done, and she couldn't wait.

So she walked down the aisle with a full heart to meet her perfect match.

Don't miss the new sweet rom-com about returning a sleepy beach town B&B to its former tourist-destination glory.

A Lot Like
LOVE

by Jennifer Snow

When Sarah Lewis inherits a run-down B&B from her late grandmother in coastal Blue Moon Bay, the logical thing to do is sell it and focus on her life in L.A. But when she learns that interested buyers will only tear it down in its current state, she feels a sense of obligation to her grandmother to get it back to the landmark tourist destination it once was...even if that means hiring the best contractor for the job, who happens to be her old high school crush.

Wes Sharrun's life has continued to unravel since the death of his wife three years before. Now with a struggling construction company and a nine-year-old daughter, he sees the B&B as an opportunity to get back on his feet. Unfortunately, despite trying to keep his distance, his daughter has taken a liking to Sarah, and his own feelings are tough to deny.

As they spend more time together painting, exploring a forgotten treasure trove of wine in a basement cellar, and arguing over balcony placement, the more the spark between them ignites. But will saving the B&B be enough to convince them both to take a second chance at love?

A brand-new small-town romance proving sometimes fake dates can turn into forever.

forever starts now

by Stefanie London

Single men are as scarce in Forever Falls as a vegetarian at a barbecue. That is, until Ethan Hammersmith moves in. After his fiancée gave him an ultimatum, he left Australia and never looked back. He isn't in America to find a new girlfriend, though. He's searching for the father he never knew. But now it's like he has a flashing sign above his head that says "available." Thankfully, the manager of the local diner is willing to give him cover—if only she weren't so distractingly adorable.

Monroe Roberts, town misanthrope and divorcée, knocked "forever" permanently off her wish list ever since the love of her life skipped town with the cliché yoga instructor. And good riddance. She's got this struggling diner to keep her busy, trying anything to boost sales…until a hot Australian strolls in and changes everything. Monroe's restaurant is packed full of women who aren't there to order food, unless Ethan is on the menu. This could sink her business faster than ever. So—light bulb—what if they pretend to be together?

It sounds like the perfect plan. Until they realize there is some very real chemistry in this fake relationship. But is it enough to heal two hearts that have been so deeply wounded?

Find out what happens when a woman shows up on his doorstep with a cowboy's baby all grown up…

Wishing for a Cowboy

by Victoria James

Janie Adams has been a single parent to her nephew since he was a baby. Fifteen years later, she's finally found out who his father might be, so the two of them travel across the country to find him. She'd do *anything* for this kid. But when they arrive in the small town of Wishing River, Montana, and Janie finally meets the ruggedly handsome cowboy she'd been told had abandoned his son, his shocked response changes everything.

Aiden Rivers can't dispute this is his kid when he sees his own features staring back at him, but he had no idea Janie's sister was pregnant when she left him. He didn't even know she had a sister—clearly they'd *all* been lied to. Now he has fifteen years of fatherhood to make up for and no idea how to be a dad. This was never in his plans.

Janie sticks around to help him ease into parenting, everything from showing him how to lure a sulky kid out of his bedroom to keeping up with the latest teen-speak. Together, they surprisingly make a good team, this city girl and country boy. But when the past catches up with them, Aiden and Janie must decide what's best for the boy who's connecting them, not only for each other…which could mean splitting them apart.

AMARA

an imprint of Entangled Publishing LLC